NEW YORK REVIEW BOOKS
CLASSICS

MOURNING A BREAST

XI XI (also known as Sai Sai; 1937–2022), the pseudonym of Cheung Yin, was born in Shanghai and immigrated with her family in 1950 to colonial Hong Kong. While working as a teacher, Xi Xi wrote poetry, essays, and fiction, publishing her critically acclaimed short story "Maria" in 1965, and her first book, the novella *East Side Story*, in 1966. Her novel *My City*, one of the earliest literary works to depict Hong Kong from the viewpoint of its ordinary residents, was first serialized in 1975 and published in full in 1979. She won Taiwan's prestigious *United Daily* fiction prize for her short story "A Woman Like Me" in 1983, earning her an enthusiastic readership in Taiwan and greater renown throughout the Chinese-speaking world. In the fall of 1989, Xi Xi was diagnosed with breast cancer, prompting her to record her reflections and experiences in *Mourning a Breast*, which was named one of the ten best books of 1992 by the *China Times* in Taiwan, in addition to receiving the Readers Best Book of the Year Award from *United Daily*. Nerve damage from the cancer treatment caused Xi Xi to lose full mobility in her right hand. As a form of physical therapy, she began sewing cloth dolls, puppets, and stuffed animals, resulting in the essay and photography collections *The Teddy Bear Chronicles* (2009) and *The Monkey Chronicles* (2011). Xi Xi's literary career was the subject of the 2015 documentary *My City*, and in 2019 she became the first writer from Hong Kong to win the Newman Prize for Chinese Literature. She published nearly forty books of fiction, poetry, and nonfiction, in addition to numerous newspaper and magazine columns and screenplays, and her work has become part of Hong Kong's official high-school curriculum in Chinese literature.

JENNIFER FEELEY is the translator of *Not Written Words: Selected Poetry of Xi Xi* and *Carnival of Animals: Xi Xi's Animal Poems*, as well as Chen Jiatong's White Fox series, Lau Yee-Wa's novel *Tongueless*, and Wong Yi's Cantonese chamber opera libretto *Women Like Us*. She is working on a new translation of Xi Xi's *My City*. Feeley is the recipient of the 2017 Lucien Stryk Asian Translation Prize and a 2019 National Endowment for the Arts Literature Translation Fellowship.

MOURNING A BREAST

XI XI

Translated from the Chinese and with an afterword by
JENNIFER FEELEY

NEW YORK REVIEW BOOKS

New York

THIS IS A NEW YORK REVIEW BOOK
PUBLISHED BY THE NEW YORK REVIEW OF BOOKS
207 East 32nd Street, New York, NY 10016
www.nyrb.com

This project was supported in part by the National Endowment for the Arts.

First published as a New York Review Books Classic in 2024.
Original Complex Chinese edition first published by Hung-Fan Bookstore,
Taiwan.

Earlier versions of several chapters first appeared in the following publications:
"Swimsuit" and "The Doctor Says" in *HEAT*; "The Bathroom" on the website
Our Xi Xi Our City; and "The Body's Language" in *Cha: An Asian Literary
Journal*.

Image credits: for page 297, Fernand Léger, *Three Women Against a Red
Background*, 1927 © ADAGP, Paris and DACS, London 2024; for page 298,
Henry Moore, *Reclining Figure* © The Henry Moore Foundation. All Rights
Reserved, DACS / www.henry-moore.org 2024.

Library of Congress Cataloging-in-Publication Data
Names: Xi, Xi, author. | Feeley, Jennifer, 1976– translator.
Title: Mourning a breast / by Xi Xi; translated by Jennifer Feeley.
Other titles: Ai dao ru fang. English
Description: New York: New York Review Books, 2024. | Series: New York
    Review Books classics
Identifiers: LCCN 2023029940 (print) | LCCN 2023029941 (ebook) |
    ISBN 9781681378220 (paperback) | ISBN 9781681378237 (ebook)
Subjects: LCSH: Xi, Xi—Fiction. | Breast—Cancer—Fiction. | LCGFT:
    Autobiographical fiction. | Novels.
Classification: LCC PL2862.I16 A7513 2024 (print) | LCC PL2862.I16 (ebook) |
    DDC 895.13/52--dc23/eng/20240220
LC record available at https://lccn.loc.gov/2023029940
LC ebook record available at https://lccn.loc.gov/2023029941

ISBN 978-1-68137-822-0
Available as an electronic book; ISBN 978-1-68137-823-7

Printed in the United States of America on acid-free paper.
10 9 8 7 6 5 4 3 2 1

CONTENTS

PREFACE

DEAR READER, when you open this book, are you standing in a bookstore? You've come to the bookstore today to have a look around and see if there are any books that pique your interest. You stumble upon *Mourning a Breast*—hey, what's this book about? There's no one around, so you casually pick it up. Out of all the books here, you just happen to flip through the one titled *Mourning a Breast*. Is it the word "breast" that grabs your attention, though you feign otherwise? At this very moment, when you think of breasts, what comes to mind?

This is a book about breasts. Breasts are the subject matter, though I suppose the content may be rather different from what you're envisioning. More than two and a half years ago, on a bright summer day, after this narrator had been swimming without a care in the world, she stood in the shower of the pool changing room and found a small lump in her breast, no bigger than a peanut. Soon after, it was confirmed to be breast cancer. This book tells the story of losing a breast. There are no melodramatic or sensationalist characters or plot twists. If this isn't the book you're looking for, carry on and good luck. However, I don't intend to lose you, reader, so come on, why not buy a copy of *Mourning a Breast* while you're at it, since on many levels, you and this book are actually quite closely connected? Are you a woman? May I ask how old you are? Please forgive me for being so presumptuous. Regardless of your age, the very fact that you can read these words is enough for you to be at risk for breast cancer. Let me put it this way: You're just like the narrator of this book, living freely and happily in the world. There's so much you've yet to do. The world is your oyster. Yet you're completely unaware that there's a tiny alien taking shape inside of you, scheming to supplant and devour you. That's the demon known as cancer.

The twentieth century is coming to an end. In this era of cutting-edge science and technology, cancer is growing more and more rampant. The number of people suffering from cancer is steadily increasing, while patients' ages are dropping to alarming lows. Are you a teenager in school? You say: I'm only sixteen—what do *I* have to worry about? Well, let me tell you, last year I came to know a breast cancer patient who was only twelve years old. Breast cancer is unpredictable. By the time you discover it, it's likely that a tumor has already formed, leaving you with no choice but to part with the breasts that we women hold dear, and from then on, there's no escaping death's shadow. However, breast cancer is still considered one of the most fortunate forms of cancer, as it exhibits clear signs, can be surgically removed, and is also preventable. Eating well works wonders, and thanks to the miracle of modern medicine, we can keep on living for a considerably long time. *Mourning a Breast* aims to discuss precisely these matters and was written to help you—not from an expert's viewpoint but from the perspective of a patient sharing her course of treatment, along with assorted reflections on her illness. A while back, a long-lost friend came across some selections from this book that had been published here and there. She started examining her own body, and lo and behold, she found that she also had breast cancer. Luckily, it was detected early; time is of the essence in treating this type of disease. If after reading this book, you begin taking better care of your health and paying attention to the various signals your body emits, then it won't have been written in vain.

Of course, I hope you won't get sick. Though birth, aging, illness, and death are inevitable for everyone, I don't want you ever to have to deal with cancer. Yet as the median age of the population increases, and the earth is desecrated day after day, we must psychologically prepare for the worst. Your elderly grandmother, mother, sister, friend, or colleague could get cancer. If such an unfortunate turn of events were to occur, what would you do? Sever ties with them because you're scared? Or lend a hand in the face of hardship? *Mourning a Breast* also touches upon these issues. Sick people don't need your pity, but your concern and assistance can give them emotional comfort and help support their fight against the disease.

From another angle, disclosing the disease is also a form of self-healing for patients. The Chinese have always been a people who are secretive about sickness and hesitant to seek medical treatment, concealing illness, especially of this kind, and considering it a taboo subject. As a result, not only the body but also the soul ends up sick. Psychiatrists treat illness by making patients aware of unconscious mental blocks, then confronting and resolving them. Your narrator openly details her illness but doesn't dare claim to smash any taboos, though this nevertheless can be considered self-help. The term "mourning" actually suggests that while we can't undo the past, we can focus on the future and hope for rebirth.

Or maybe, you there in the bookstore, you are a man. You may laugh and say: Breast cancer is something that only happens to women—what does it have to do with me? I'm sorry, but you're mistaken. Breast cancer is like the sun, shining on women and shining on men as well. Moreover, by the time it's detected in men, it tends to be more serious. No person is an island; you're a man, but you may have a mother, sister, and possibly a wife or a lover—if your other half gets breast cancer, what will you do? While your attitude reveals your personal feelings and standards, I suspect that our fear and avoidance of cancer are due mainly to ignorance. Clinging to ignorance is also an incurable disease.

When all is said and done, this is a book written using a range of literary techniques. Some friends regard it as a novel, and others as a collection of essays. Dear reader, you're welcome to categorize it however you'd like; this time, it's up to you. It's just that the life of the modern person is so hectic, and work is demanding. In your free time, take a walk in the country or by the sea, breathe the fresh air, swim, play ball, and look after your body. Perhaps it's not worth spending too much time reading this book—you're better off just flipping through a few chapters and choosing the ones that most interest you. If you're curious about cancer, skimming seven or eight paragraphs of "The Doctor Says" or "The Flying Guillotine" is more than enough. Where appropriate, I've inserted prompts throughout the book so as not to waste your precious time. If you're a self-preoccupied manly man, then scanning the section "Beards and Brows" should suffice. If you're a doctor, how about giving "Daifu Di" a try? If you don't like words and prefer looking at pictures, simply turn to the last few pages of the book—at first, there were only images, but I added some text, as I worried that staring solely at images might lead to a new kind of illiteracy. Are you someone who is hunched over a desk all day and enjoys sitting at home reading? "The Body's Language" was written just for you. We place too much emphasis on knowledge, at the expense of ignoring our bodies. Without a body, how would the soul have a place to rest? Are you about forty? Maybe "Math Time" is just what the doctor ordered—once you reach adulthood, you need to take responsibility for your own health. Is there a constant dull ache in your stomach? Have you packed on a few pounds? Are you chronically fatigued? Are you overworked? Please cherish your body and pay attention to your diet.

Maybe when you open this book, you're sitting at home. Are you one of my real-life friends? You've turned to this book not because you're in the mood for a story but because you're wondering how I've been doing these past couple of years. Dear friend, I'm grateful for your concern. I'm actually quite blessed. The past two years of my life have been like a magic-realist novel, a blurring of dream and reality, as though I'm under a spell, my entire being an ethereal fiction, whereas the city, streets, and friends within are all real. Yet am I not fortunate compared to someone who's paralyzed in bed, stuck in a vegetative state, or afflicted with AIDS? I can still enjoy walking down the street and taking in the scenery, read some books, write a few words, and on good days, I can even take short trips. I don't need to worry about putting food on the table, nor do I have to go to work. What more could I ask for? In these times, I've found I have far more friends than I realized, who treat me better than I ever could have imagined. I'm touched by the outpouring of care and support. Indeed, it's because of friends that I'm reluctant to leave this world. I'm but a very cowardly person, no braver than anyone else. Thank you, friends, for rebuilding my confidence. I'll live my life to the fullest.

June 1992

SWIMSUIT

I GENTLY rolled up the swimsuit, as though I could still hear the pitter-patter of falling water. I'd gotten a lot of use out of it this year. Since May, I'd gone to the pool a few times a week, often by myself. In the blink of an eye, it was suddenly September, the sun beating down so fiercely that the outline of my swimsuit was etched onto my body. All summer long, day or night, wherever I went, it was as if I were still wearing my swimsuit, the white shoulder straps and narrow leg openings swishing in sync with my skin.

One chilly March day, I was browsing in a department store, thinking I might take a look at the swimsuits, when I heard the rush of crashing waves blasting from the swimwear department. I hurried over to check things out—what were the new swimsuits like? Skintight, revealing, conservative, provocative? How hard it is to find a swimsuit that fits and is comfortable. It needs to cover you in all the right places, and when you put it on, it should allow for maximum freedom of movement. I picked out something colorful. Only a skilled swimmer would dare to wear plain colors, which vanish without a trace when submerged in water, like a black-clad figure adept at skulking around in the night. I was used to wearing flashy colors to attract the lifeguards' attention, to alert them to my presence at any given moment.

My swimming was poor, even terrible. In the pool, I stood around longer than I swam, and the moments I spent resting and gasping for air outnumbered those spent gliding forward. My friends liked to say: You need to come more frequently, take the plunge more often. Swimming with friends always buoyed my spirits. They gave me confidence and encouragement, as well as guidance. Last year, I stuck close to the edge of the pool like a penguin, panicking whenever water flowed into my mouth. Over the course of a year, things had improved tremendously. I could now swim from one end of the pool to the other, both the length and width, huffing and puffing my way across.

My friends weren't free every day. They had to go to work, so I went on my own. When I was alone, I didn't dare venture out to the deep end. Like a piece of drifting debris, I tended to stay near the side of the pool, gripping the edge when I ran out of oxygen. I always swam incredibly slowly. Other people paddled and kicked in seamless coordination, yet after one kick, I floated for a bit, then lifted my head to catch my breath. I swam as languidly as an angelfish in an aquarium. Even after swimming for several months, I still panted: I'm out of breath!

I often cried that I was out of breath. Perhaps this is why my family doctor told me: You need exercise, more exercise—do some cardio! Typically, I only took leisurely strolls, did some gentle flexibility exercises, dabbled in fitness dancing, and rode a stationary bike for a few minutes. While these activities stretched my muscles and bones, they didn't deliver much oxygen to my body. Meanwhile, playing squash and climbing mountains were too strenuous for me. I gave up jogging in the early morning because I loved sleeping in, and besides, there were no wooded areas with fresh air near my home. I decided to try swimming.

The strength of the sun in May was already extremely brutal, so I had to wait until early evening to head to the pool. The road leading to the pool was usually deserted, but as the sun began to set, pedestrians emerged in full force: in twos and threes, men and women, old and young, all bound for the pool. Some slung book bags and duffel bags over their shoulders, while others carried plastic bags. Everyone dressed casually in tank tops, T-shirts, and shorts, with either sneakers or flip-flops on their feet. Recently, two small snack stalls had sprung up at the pool entrance, one selling pig-blood curd stewed with daikon, the other fried chili peppers, tofu, and eggplant. Crowds flocked to them.

I was probably the only one who walked to the pool holding a nylon umbrella. The others all braved the harsh rays—I was an anomaly in that I loved swimming but feared the sun. After stepping off the bus, I had to walk a mile, without any awnings or balconies to shade me, the whole road scorched beneath the searing sun. Haven't scientific journals pointed out that too much sun exposure can cause skin cancer? Sunspots had been especially active recently. I was afraid of the sun, so I held an umbrella.

I liked to take along a nylon backpack when I went swimming. It was handy: I could hang it over my shoulders, and the bag was divided into two compartments. I placed a large towel, swimsuit, extra shirt, and change of underwear in the larger compartment, and soap, shampoo, and an eyeglass case in the smaller one. I usually wore a T-shirt, shorts, and casual shoes to the pool. Each visit, I spent as much time on the road as I did in the pool itself; my journey took about two hours roundtrip.

This year, the pool entrance fee rose by two dollars, but the increase was worth every cent, as the contents of the swimming pool had improved.[1] By contents, I mean the changing room. For a long time, the changing room had been managed by a few female attendants. Upon entering, there were individual changing stalls, and you handed over your clothing and other belongings to an attendant, who placed them in a metal basket. In turn, you were given a metal tag to hang around your neck, and they stored the metal basket on a huge shelf behind the counter. The counter separated the changing room into two unconnected parts, and you had to follow a certain sequence and procedure to pass from one area to the other.

The changing room had been remodeled. The counter, metal baskets, and huge metal shelf were gone, and the previously partitioned-off areas were transformed into one big room with an open floor plan. Where there used to be metal shelves, there were rows of brightly colored lockers. Everything was now self-service. There were no longer attendants shuffling around metal baskets. Swimmers locked their clothing and other personal items in a grid of lockers and took the key with them. The attendants' job was merely to discourage people from littering and running around soaking wet.

The shower curtains surprised me the most. Before, the room had never had any curtains in either the changing or shower areas. There had been a row of small stalls without any doors or coverings, everyone stark-naked, the girls blushing. A few friends would help out by unfurling a large towel and guarding the entrance to the stall, allowing the girl inside to shower without worry. One by one, they took turns, the hands that held up the towel aching.

I had often wondered who designed the pool changing room. A good structure is never as simple as an attractive exterior. What matters is the interior space, the feelings of those moving around inside: Are they safe, comfortable, at ease? The person who designed the changing room might not have considered these concerns. Perhaps the designer was a man who didn't realize that it wasn't optimal for women to meet each other in their birthday suits.

Water from the showerheads pitter-pattered down, women lathering their bodies with soap, making squelching sounds. Someone brought shampoo that permeated the room with the sweet scent of almonds. The young girls were bashful, the middle-aged women fearless. Here, pale backsides and small breasts were on display. In the sunlight, the contrast between dark and light skin was stark, flabby and fit bodies in full view. Women with perfect figures were a rare sight.

I often came by myself. With no one to hold up a towel for me, and no other way to hide myself, I had to turn my back on the world behind me and think of myself as an ostrich. Soon, however, I grew used to it—a naked body is nothing to be ashamed of, and the changing room was women-only. I'd take a quick shower, then come out wrapped in a large towel. A large towel helped me feel much more self-assured, allowing me to take my time getting dressed.

All the girls must have been over the moon when shower curtains appeared in the changing room of the pool whose price had risen. A basic plastic shower curtain hung from a horizontal metal rod at the entrance to each stall, the curtains adorned with lurid flowers in vivid and varied colors, every curtain a different shade and hue, as gaudy as could be, but the girls all oohed and aahed: Wow, shower curtains!

Hideous shower curtains have shielded the modest bodies of many a woman. Everyone happily stepped behind the curtains, water splashing everywhere, pounding against the hidden women's skin. Peals of laughter filled the room.

A hair dryer had also been mounted on the wall, a mirror affixed beside it, and everyone stood there primping and preening. When they came out of the pool, it was as if they hadn't been swimming at all, and had just stopped off at a café for afternoon tea. They were still impeccably dressed, not a hair out of place, glowing from head to toe, ready to attend a garden party.

The changing-room shower curtains only stayed up for two weeks before most of them had ripped, and the rest were torn down. And so, when they returned from swimming, the girls resumed their previous routine of trying to cover up and avoid being seen. Sometimes, several huddled in a group, holding up a large towel like they'd done before. It was as though their dignity had been stripped away all over again. Once more, people observed bodies in a range of skin tones without saying a single word. No one gasped in admiration or surprise, they only asked: What happened to the shower curtains?

I didn't know the current state of the changing-room shower curtains. Were they all torn down, or was there a new batch hanging? Had anyone complained? I hadn't been swimming in more than a month. If I were to walk around naked in the curtainless changing room today, would people be shocked when they saw me? Even if I could still step out of the shower wrapped in a large towel, would people notice something was wrong?

The pitter-patter of falling water echoed in my ears, and it was as though I could hear the squelching of soap on women's skin. Supple flesh, water, the sweet scent of soap. When could I go swimming again? I didn't know. I had no way of guessing, understanding, exploring, or predicting my fate. My mind swam with question marks, the answer to all of these questions the three words "I don't know."

I gently rolled up the swimsuit and tucked it in the drawer of my wardrobe. There were still two other new swimsuits inside the wardrobe—why had I bought so many last year? One was covered in a tropical forest pattern. Perhaps I liked not only the swimsuit itself but also the images on it, which made me think of Tahiti and a certain painter associated with Tahiti.

I had three swimsuits in total, but I didn't know when I could go swimming again. How much had changed in just one month. When I'd gone swimsuit shopping, how could I have imagined it? I stared blankly at the suits. My mother said: It's too cold to go swimming again. Yes, I agreed, it's too cold to go swimming again this year. My mother said: You'll swim again next year. I said, Mm-hmm, I'll swim again next year.

THE DOCTOR SAYS

CHATTING with the Family Doctor
Good afternoon, Dr. Lam.
Good afternoon. Oh, it's you. How have you been?
I'm doing well.
Great! Your older brother was here yesterday.
He's been in good health recently.
How about your mom? How's she?
The same—as chatty as ever.
That's how old people are.
We don't have the heart to tell her that you're emigrating.
Let's not bring it up for the time being.
You might come back?
We'll see. Here, let me take your blood pressure.
It's the Saturday-night flight, right?
Your blood pressure's normal: 130 over 75.
Do I need to take the medication as prescribed?
There's no need.
I only take it if it's over 90, right?
Let's have a look at your feet. Are they swollen?
No. What does it mean if they're swollen?
A potassium deficiency can cause swelling.
What should I do if I have a potassium deficiency?
Oranges are a good supplement.
But I want to travel. What if there aren't any oranges?
Where are you going this time?
I'm thinking of going to Mount Wutai.

You can eat watermelon.

Why did you tell me to eat oranges instead of watermelon?

Watermelon isn't available all year round.

Besides oranges and watermelon, what other fruits are high in potassium?

Bananas.

Why didn't you tell me to eat bananas?

If you eat too many, you'll get fat.

Conversation with a Female Doctor

How do you feel?

My whole body feels out of sorts.

Are you fatigued and aching all over?

I had a chest X-ray and an EKG two months ago.

Why'd you have an EKG?

I felt my heart beating wildly.

What did the report say?

There was nothing wrong.

Lie back on the table so I can examine you.

I often do a self-exam.

Does it hurt here?

Could it be heart disease?

Heart disease isn't like this.

What's it like?

It's also the wrong location.

I'm always out of breath.

That happens at your age.

And there are sudden hot flashes.

Sweating?

Uh-huh. Sometimes I'm dizzy, and my fingers go numb.

It's a symptom of your age.

My shoulders feel heavy. Is it rheumatism?

It's one of the symptoms.

Listening to What Another Doctor Says

How may I help you?

Oh, there's a lump in my breast. I found it three days ago.

Maybe it's hormones. It'll probably dissipate in a few days . . . All right
then, come back in two weeks. Two weeks won't make much of a
difference.

Listening to What the Same Doctor Says a Second Time

Um, it's been two weeks.

How do you feel?

The lump's still there.

Yes, it hasn't dissipated. How about I refer you to another doctor,
okay?

Answering a Surgeon's Questions

You found it how many days ago?

At first, three days. Now it's been seventeen.

Initially it was three days.

Uh-huh. The doctor told me to come back in two weeks.

You're sure it was three days?

I didn't find anything earlier.

Did you find it yourself?

Yes.

How'd you find it?

In the shower. I read a book that said to do self-exams.

It wasn't there before?

A couple of weeks ago, I saw a woman doctor. She did an exam.

For the time being, we can't determine what's going on.

So?

It's best to do a biopsy.

All right, let's do a biopsy.

Under general anesthesia would be best.

General?
The lump is small but deep.
All right, general anesthesia it is.

On Friday morning, I told my mother I was going to a friend's house. If it got too late, I'd spend the night and come back the following day. I also told her that my younger sister would hurry over after work and cook dinner for her. She didn't need to worry about a thing. I opened the nylon backpack that I usually took swimming. I swapped the large towel for a small one, removed my swimsuit and shampoo, and packed a can of milk and a roll of toilet paper. Additionally, I crammed in a portable music player, several cassette tapes, and four books. The four books were all *Madame Bovary* but in various translations, along with the French original.

I bought a boxed lunch from a fast-food restaurant and scarfed it down, filling up my stomach, and drank a large cup of hot water. I didn't eat any fruit. I didn't want the food to digest too quickly. Per the doctor's orders, starting at noon, I couldn't eat or drink anything. I usually have a slight stomachache and am frequently hungry. I didn't know if I could go for six hours without eating anything. I couldn't stand it but had no choice. Did I want to spew out all the food and water in my belly while I was in the operating room?

The trip from my home to the hospital wasn't far, but there was no direct bus, so I had to take a taxi. I always find taking a taxi to be too extravagant, especially when I'm not in a rush, but there was no other option. I was no stranger to the hospital. Six months ago, I accompanied my mother to the hospital to have a cataract removed. I was quite familiar with the second floor. There were nearly a hundred patients on the entire second floor, all having surgery.

I thought I'd brought everything, but it turned out one thing was missing: money. I took the letter the doctor had given me into the reception area and filled in the personal information. The clerk's first words were: A thousand dollars for the deposit. I'd forgotten about the deposit. I had to say: I forgot. The clerk straightforwardly continued: All right, when you're discharged, pay everything altogether. I'd registered my ID card. Were they still afraid I'd run off?

My luck wasn't too bad. I was assigned to the last room on the second floor, which had only four beds. The other three patients were quiet and didn't disturb one another, each person resting on her own. A female attendant filled the hot-water thermos for me, asking: Are you a teacher? I look like one, don't I? You do, she said. Yes, I used to teach, but now I'm retired, I said. I took out the toilet paper from my backpack and placed it on the small side table, then tucked the can of milk, my eyeglass case, pencils, and notepad inside a slim drawer. I hung the towel on the bar behind the side table.

The hospital must have been full. Even the admission procedures had spilled into the corridor. I went to the corridor to check in. Per hospital protocols, I was weighed, left a urine sample, and donned a wristband with my name. At first glance, it looked as though I was wearing two watches. The wristband didn't tell time, just my identity and medical history. It couldn't be given as a gift, nor could it be discarded. I told the nurse that my chest had been X-rayed a few months ago and was fine—there was no need to take another X-ray. She agreed. Perhaps I never needed any imaging in the first place and it had all been at my own suggestion.

I'd gone to the hospital alone, so I was the one who signed the consent form for the surgery. One's life is one's own responsibility. Was I the best master of my life, the only master? Once they're rolled into the operating room, many people leave their lives in the hands of others. Parents, children, and sisters all sign consent forms for patients, who often remain passive.

The nurse took me into a prep room to shave my armpit hair. I said there was no need for it, as people who swim regularly aren't hairy. She handed me a hospital gown, instructing me to change into it an hour and a half before surgery, and she also reminded me not to eat or drink anything. When I returned to my hospital room, it was only twelve-thirty. I still had six hours left until surgery. Stuck in the hospital for such a long stretch of time, what could I do? Read. One by one, I laid the copies of *Madame Bovary* on the bed and sat down in the rocking chair. I'd brought them with me because the wide bed allowed me to spread them out, because I had six hours of free time, and because I wanted to compare the differences between the original and the translations. I often compare translations—I'm someone who enjoys translating fiction in her spare time.

I'd brought four copies of Flaubert's novel to the hospital: the French original, the English translation, and two Chinese translations. What first caught my attention was the use of italicized words in the original. Flaubert was the father of the modern novel, a title he earned in part because of the emergence of innovative artistic forms in his fiction, especially *Madame Bovary*. For example, there are more than one hundred italicized words in the book.

A perfectly good novel can simply be narrated fluidly, the typeface completely uniform, so why add italics? Several of the italicizations are understandable, such as the titles of books and operas, Latin and other foreign languages, and nicknames—all cases in which it's fairly standard to use italics. Moreover, the book's subtitle is "Provincial Manners," and thus a lot of regional languages are italicized, and italics are also deliberately used to foreground clichés so that they can be distinguished from the original author's words. But the most profound function of Flaubert's use of italics is to stealthily shift the narrator's role without relying on punctuation to indicate explicitly a change in speaker.

From the first pages of the first chapter, you can discern the quality of the translation. In this chapter, fifteen-year-old Charles Bovary is going off to school. The italicized words include *nouveau, dans les grands, genre, Charbovari, Quos ego, ridiculus sum, dans la fabrique, faire valoir, jeune homme,* and *Anacharsis*. Here, *Charbovari* is a nickname, *Quos ego* and *ridiculus sum* are Latin, *Anacharsis* is the title of a travelogue, and the other italicized words are from regional languages.

The English translation is the strangest; it entirely disregards the italics, paying them no heed at all, and standardizes the typeface of the translated text. And so, when reading the English translation, one would have no idea there are italics in the French original, thereby erasing Flaubert's painstaking efforts. Well, there are a couple of exceptions. The book title *Travels of Anacharsis* is italicized, with "travels of" added as an explanation. *Quos ego* is likewise italicized, the translation specifying that these words originally were uttered by Neptune. *Charbovari* is exactly the same. The translator couldn't find a suitable English word for *curé* and thus also retains the French word in italics.

The first Chinese translation is slightly better than the English translation, adding quotation marks around the originally italicized words—for example, *nouveau* appears as "new student." But *genre*, *dans les grands*, *dans la fabrique*, and *faire valoir* are all ignored, and Neptune's phrase *Quos ego* isn't translated. Oddly enough, the translator adds quotation marks around words that originally aren't in quotation marks, such as "madame" and "monsieur."

The second Chinese translation is the best. All originally italicized words have punctuation marks added beneath the characters, to indicate italicization. Words originally in Latin are left in Latin and annotated. As for the accuracy of the text, that too is impressive. For the first chapter alone, there are a hundred and one explanatory notes containing detailed information and clarifying allusions, providing the reader with a wealth of supplementary knowledge.

In the first chapter, there are several lines of text that test the translator's skill, pertaining to how Charles Bovary's parents raise their son—his mother takes great pains, but his father harbors no illusions. There are two uses of italics in the original passage. One is *n'était pas la peine* (wasn't worth the trouble), and the other is *avec du toupet, un homme réussit toujours dans le monde* (with enough nerve, a man could always succeed in the world). "But to all this, Monsieur Bovary, having little regard for formal education, said it *wasn't worth the trouble!* Would they ever have the money to keep him in government schools, buy him a post, or set him up in business? Besides, *with enough nerve, a man could always succeed in the world.* Madame Bovary bit her lips, and the child drifted throughout the village."

This passage seems simple, but in fact it implies different narrators—in just a few short lines, the narrator changes five times. In the two instances where italics are used, Monsieur Bovary is speaking, and the latter phrase quotes a cliché. The other three sentences are the concealed narrator's words. This way of writing depicts the dialogue between characters in an indirect and free style. It abandons the customary line-to-line arrangement of dialogue that is indicated by opening and closing quotation marks.

The English translation follows the conventional practice and ignores all of this, merely adding an ellipsis after "in the world." This kind of translation poses no issue for modern readers, but it's somewhat unfaithful to the original work. The first Chinese translation doesn't translate "wasn't worth the trouble," and it adds quotation marks to the latter phrase to signify that it's a quotation. The second Chinese translation is the most conscientious, using quotation marks to accentuate both of the italicized phrases.

—Hey, are you still reading?

I quickly closed the books one by one and stacked them on the movable side table at the foot of the bed. The doctor had come in to check on me. There was still a peanut-sized lump in my chest. I'll operate on you in a bit, he said. He came quietly and left quietly. The doctor always wore a white shirt, charcoal-gray dress pants, and a tie emblazoned with a fire-breathing beast. I figured it was a school tie, perhaps from a medical school in the UK. I'd seen a fair number of doctors. Some looked like business people, some like butchers. This doctor wearing a British school tie looked very bookish, more like a university professor than a medical doctor.

I opened the four copies of *Madame Bovary* again. This time, I didn't look at the first chapter but flipped to the famous "agricultural show" in chapter eight. In the 1850s, Flaubert was already using the technique of alternating montages. On one side, there are lovers whispering sweet nothings, and on the other, the agricultural show is awarding prizes. Flaubert interweaves the dialogue without the explanatory "he said, she said," while still showing consideration for the reader's train of thought, using different punctuation marks to indicate who's speaking: « » for the voice of the chairman of the agricultural association, — for the lovers. This meticulously planned guidance fails in both the Chinese and English translations.

Hideous shower curtains have shielded the modest bodies of many a woman. Everyone happily stepped behind the curtains, water splashing everywhere, pounding against the hidden women's skin. Peals of laughter filled the room.

A hair dryer had also been mounted on the wall, a mirror affixed beside it, and everyone stood there primping and preening. When they came out of the pool, it was as if they hadn't been swimming at all, and had just stopped off at a café for afternoon tea. They were still impeccably dressed, not a hair out of place, glowing from head to toe, ready to attend a garden party.

The changing-room shower curtains only stayed up for two weeks before most of them had ripped, and the rest were torn down. And so, when they returned from swimming, the girls resumed their previous routine of trying to cover up and avoid being seen. Sometimes, several huddled in a group, holding up a large towel like they'd done before. It was as though their dignity had been stripped away all over again. Once more, people observed bodies in a range of skin tones without saying a single word. No one gasped in admiration or surprise, they only asked: What happened to the shower curtains?

I didn't know the current state of the changing-room shower curtains. Were they all torn down, or was there a new batch hanging? Had anyone complained? I hadn't been swimming in more than a month. If I were to walk around naked in the curtainless changing room today, would people be shocked when they saw me? Even if I could still step out of the shower wrapped in a large towel, would people notice something was wrong?

The pitter-patter of falling water echoed in my ears, and it was as though I could hear the squelching of soap on women's skin. Supple flesh, water, the sweet scent of soap. When could I go swimming again? I didn't know. I had no way of guessing, understanding, exploring, or predicting my fate. My mind swam with question marks, the answer to all of these questions the three words "I don't know."

I gently rolled up the swimsuit and tucked it in the drawer of my wardrobe. There were still two other new swimsuits inside the wardrobe—why had I bought so many last year? One was covered in a tropical forest pattern. Perhaps I liked not only the swimsuit itself but also the images on it, which made me think of Tahiti and a certain painter associated with Tahiti.

I had three swimsuits in total, but I didn't know when I could go swimming again. How much had changed in just one month. When I'd gone swimsuit shopping, how could I have imagined it? I stared blankly at the suits. My mother said: It's too cold to go swimming again. Yes, I agreed, it's too cold to go swimming again this year. My mother said: You'll swim again next year. I said, Mm-hmm, I'll swim again next year.

The large room with OPERATING ROOM written on the lintel above the door was not where the actual surgery took place but instead a lobby that led to the operating room. I arrived early. They parked my bed against the wall to wait. The clock on the wall pointed to six o'clock sharp. I heard the nurses chatting about who was buying dinner that evening. I heard the telephone ringing—a doctor from a clinic had called to book the operating room. The nurse replied, Oh dear, Saturdays are already fully booked.

They wheeled me into the operating room. I could only see the ceiling and the lintel we'd just passed. A cross hung on the lintel. A flying saucer–like mercury vapor lamp appeared in the middle of my head. I saw the doctor. He had on a cap that transformed his scholarly demeanor, giving him a slightly comical touch. A nurse untied the knot at the back of my gown, slipped my arms out of the sleeves, and stuck something on my legs. The anesthesiologist also came over and asked me my name, what procedure I was having, and who my doctor was. He said: I'm the anesthesiologist. I'm here to give you an injection. You'll sleep for a while. I said: Thank you.

I saw a bright pink curtain and heard a voice say: She's awake. I heard the doctor say: You're awake. You had a good rest. I stretched out my hands and feet—I could move them. The bright pink curtain. Of course! I was already back in my hospital room. Hadn't the anesthesiologist only just said, You'll sleep for a while? I pressed down on my chest. Some sort of gauze was stuck to it. Oh, the surgery was over. I had no idea. I had no impression of anything. It was a complete blank. I stretched out my left hand and opened the drawer of the small side table in front of the bed, feeling for my eyeglass case. My watch was inside. I checked the time: seven-fifteen. Perfectly precise. An hour of anesthesia, a blank hour of my life, without consciousness, without dreams.

My younger sister came to see me, bringing me dinner: my favorite chicken drumsticks. But I wasn't hungry at all, and in fact, I couldn't eat. A while later, my younger brother also dropped by, bringing me fruit, which I also couldn't eat. He asked me: How do you feel? I said, Fine, so he arranged for me to be discharged the following day, and went over the details of who'd pick me up, who to call, etc. Although it was a private hospital, visitors weren't welcome after nine o'clock. At nine o'clock, the lights in the ward would dim.

Six hours after the surgery, I'd be able to eat. My brother and sister said, Keep the drumsticks. At two in the morning, if you're hungry, you can get up and eat them. I didn't get up in the middle of the night. I went to bed just after nine and slept soundly until dawn. I felt great. I got up and washed my face, gargled, and brushed my teeth. I asked the nurse to open the can of milk for me and downed the whole thing, enough nutrition to last for three or four hours.

At eight o'clock, which was supposed to be when the female attendants changed the bedding, the head nurse gave an order to clean the ward, so all four of us patients went to sit in the long corridor, watching as a parade of hospital beds and movable side tables both big and small teetered out, the vases on the side tables clinking and clattering. I didn't care for the hospital gown, so I'd changed back into my own clothes and sat there holding my portable music player, listening to Spanish music. Manuel de Falla's *The Three-Cornered Hat* is quite animated, bursting with local color, the *click click click* of the castanets suitable for rattlesnake sound effects. Isn't that same sound also found in "Butantan," a movement from Ottorino Respighi's *Brazilian Impressions* that describes a house of reptiles?

When the Spanish National Ballet came to perform in Hong Kong, the standout was Maurice Ravel's *Boléro*, which they danced as a group. The set featured art nouveau mirrors, choreography that was richly varied, and folk costumes in vibrant hues. It was outstanding, a lively dance piece suddenly elevated to a higher level. However, the supposed highlight of the second half, *The Three-Cornered Hat*, was flat-out awful, the effect completely different from the recording, the fabulous solo missing, leaving only the background music. Even Picasso's set and costume design couldn't save the production, which culminated in a chaotic denouement.

The doctor showed up. Good morning, Doctor. He said: Hey, you're sitting in the corridor. He continued: Oh, you changed into your own clothes. Feeling rather chipper, I asked if I could be discharged. He said: All right, come to the clinic next week to have the stitches taken out. I phoned my sister in excitement and asked her to come help pay my medical bill. It turned out that the hospital accepted electronic payments—had I known earlier, I could've gone downstairs and settled my bill without bothering anyone.

When I returned home, my mother saw I was back and asked: Did you have a good time? My sister said, She didn't go to a friend's place, she went to the hospital to have surgery. She was afraid you'd worry. My mother said, What, you had surgery? What's going on? I'm scared. Heavens, I won't be able to sleep tonight.

Conversation with the Surgeon
I called you as soon as the report came back yesterday.
I got here as soon as I could.
The report confirmed it was a tumor.
A tumor.
A malignant tumor.
A malignant tumor.
Have any of your elder relatives had this kind of tumor?
My grandmother on my father's side had a uterine tumor.
The uterus is not the same as the breast. What about other relatives?
My younger sister.
She had one, too?
A benign fibroid, more than a decade ago.
In foreign countries, one in eighteen women have a malignant breast
    tumor.
Is it rare among Chinese people?
No, it's becoming more and more common.
What's the cause?
It's unclear. Genetics are a strong possibility.
I've never been married, and I'm of a certain age.
There's a good chance that has something to do with it.
So, what now?
I'm afraid it might spread or metastasize, so it must be removed.

When should the surgery be done?

The sooner the better, of course.

Let's do it immediately then.

Let me check when the operating room is available. Okay, tomorrow afternoon at three-thirty.

General anesthesia?

Of course, it has to be done under general anesthesia.

General anesthesia two times in one week?

No problem.

Then let's do it.

Be at the hospital tomorrow morning at nine.

If your family member or friend suddenly finds a lump in her breast, what should she do? Please tell her not to repeat the mistakes found in "Things That Are Foolish" on page 75.

THINGS THAT MAY

EXTERNAL environmental factors that may cause cancer:
black smoke billowing from chimneys
exhaust puffing from cars
river water polluted by industrial waste
fluoride, lead, cadmium, and beryllium in drinking water
cigarettes, secondhand smoke
fumes emitted from frying food in the kitchen
amaranth used to dye food red
brilliant blue FCF used to dye food blue
indigo carmine used to dye food black
sunset yellow FCF used to dye food yellow
nitrosamines used to cure meats
aflatoxins produced by moldy peanuts
pigs, cattle, and sheep injected with antibiotics
poultry injected with estrogen
artificial sweeteners, microwave ovens
glow-in-the-dark clocks, hair dye
air freshener, mosquito coils
insecticides, disinfectants
plastic wrap, scented cards
enamel, paint thinner
furniture made from particle board
carpet made from synthetic fibers
toxic gas generated by incinerating trash
ceramic bowls and plates with painted patterns
stonewashed jeans

pesticides on produce
waxy coating on fruit
milk cartons
low-sulfur coal
leaded petroleum
TVs, computers, ionizing radiation
excessive X-rays, ultraviolet light
alcohol

External factors that may cause breast cancer:
a high-fat diet
cooking oils rich in polyunsaturated fats
consumption of poultry containing excessive estrogen
drugs that contain estrogen
long-term use of hair dye

Internal factors that may cause breast cancer:
damage to the body's immune system

Genetic factors that may cause breast cancer:
a family history of breast cancer
a grandmother who has had breast cancer
a mother who has had breast cancer
a sister who has had breast cancer

Endocrine factors that may cause breast cancer:
having never been married
having been married but
having never birthed children
having birthed children but
having birthed the first after age forty

not breastfeeding after childbirth
miscarriage
hormone metabolism imbalance
taking birth control pills
menopausal changes
an apple-shaped body

Viral factors that may cause breast cancer:
unclear

Psychological factors that may cause breast cancer:
work stress
anxiety
anger
jealousy

If you're not a woman and would like to learn a
bit about breast cancer in men, please turn to
"Beards and Brows" on page 194.

THE FLYING GUILLOTINE

I WASN'T sure if the bottle suspended upside down beside my bed was filled with saline or glucose. A rubber tube hung down, dangling near my wrist. Because I was tangled in these bottles and tubes, I could only lie in bed. I couldn't get up and walk around, nor could I go to the bathroom. By afternoon the day after my surgery, the upside-down bottle was finally removed from my bedside. I heaved a sigh of relief, as I wasn't used to urinating while lying in bed, but most of all, because it had entailed inconveniencing others.

Oh, how liberating it was to be able to get out of bed freely and take a walk, so I peeled off the blanket and swung my leg off the bed. To my surprise, a solid object suddenly fell from my body. Because it was connected to a rubber tube, instead of plopping onto the floor, it dangled in front of the bed. I was genuinely taken aback: I had no idea what had happened. I quickly reached out, grabbed the object, and stuffed it back beneath the covers, then sat on the edge of the bed, not daring to move for a long time.

What on earth was it? Since I'd come out of the operating room, it'd been with me the whole time, sharing the same bedding while I slept for several hours, completely oblivious. Sitting on the bed, I pulled myself together and stealthily examined this object in the bedding. It turned out to be a soft plastic container, round in shape, with two or three accordion-like folds, allowing it to expand and collapse; it resembled a paper lantern from the Mid-Autumn Festival. I touched it. It was very warm, and when I moved it, it made a slosh-ing sound. There was liquid inside, red in color. There was a small tube at the top, the other end of which extended to my chest and abdomen, covered with adhesive tape.

In the operating room, I vaguely remembered hearing the doctor mention a "drip pan," which was probably what it was. There was a lot of bloody discharge in my wound, which had to be drained slowly. I peered at the "drip pan": one-fifth of the solution was bloody discharge that had flowed from my body. It wasn't blood, just *bloody discharge*, the solution neither thick nor dark. At five o'clock every morning, the nurse would come through the ward, taking our blood pressure. Many people were still asleep. In a dazed state, I heard the sound of her pouring liquid—she must have opened the lid of the "drip pan" and poured out the bloody discharge.

I nicknamed the "drip pan" the "flying guillotine" after the deadly weapon from martial arts films that looked like a bladed hat attached to a long chain. The first time I saw it, I was terrified. Gradually, I got used to it. When I moved my body or walked around, the bloody discharge sloshed inside it, reminiscent of a music box—if there was less fluid, it clinked and clanked; if there was more fluid, it trilled and rippled. However, the striking red of the bloody discharge seemed inappropriate for the public. And so, each time I got out of bed, I squeezed it flat, tucked it in the elastic waist of my pants, and concealed it with a large shirt. It became my secret.

When using the bathroom, of course I had to be careful and hold it in my hand. Once, I wasn't paying attention, and it dropped to the floor with a plop. Fortunately, it was made of plastic and didn't break. I carried a folding chair in with me when I showered. I could take off my clothes, but I couldn't take off the flying guillotine, so I set it on the chair. Whenever I moved, it clinked softly on the chair, accompanying the music of the water. As I showered, it danced with me. In the shower, I carefully traced its tubing; it was like a river, converging with countless streams, leading to my wound. The thinner tubes were hidden beneath thick layers of adhesive bandages and gauze. It was just like in the novel *The Dream of the Red Chamber*, where Jia Baoyu's braid is composed of numerous smaller braids woven into one.

The flying guillotine accompanied me for three full days and nights. I slept with it, and when I walked, I had to carry it carefully. It often reminded me of the fictional character Santiago Nasar from *Chronicle of a Death Foretold*, who, at the end of the story, holds a piece of intestine that has fallen out of his own belly. A woman was pacing in the corridor. She, too, carried a flying guillotine, but she cradled it in her hand, as though it were a moon cake. Another female staff member was constantly mopping the floor in the corridor. I didn't know who'd offended or angered her, but as she mopped, she muttered curses under her breath: May your guts be stripped and ripped and rotted, stripped and ripped and rotted! I listened with a pounding heart, as though I'd encountered an assassin from the reign of the Yongzheng Emperor in the Qing dynasty, wielding a "flying guillotine" that would decapitate someone, not knowing whose head it would sever.

Each morning, the ward bustled with various comings and goings. First, of course, were the nurses, who took patients' blood pressure and temperature, and emptied bloody discharge or urine from the drip pans and bags—all at five in the morning. Then the patients woke up, got out of bed, freshened up, and used the bathroom. The nurses distributed medication, and the patients ate breakfast. Following this flurry of activity, the female attendants came to change the sheets and pillowcases. During this time, those of us who enjoyed moving about would sit on the sofas in the long corridor. After sitting and sitting, we watched the doctors make their rounds.

As this was a private hospital, different patients had different doctors. Patient Number Five had three doctors in total. Sometimes they arrived one by one, and sometimes two showed up together. When a doctor came, the patient lay down on the bed, the nurse drawing the pink curtain around it, creating a space that seemed filled with secrecy. Some people stared wide-eyed, and some eavesdropped. Before long, the curtain opened, the doctor left, and the patient cheerfully proclaimed: I can go home!

Today, three patients were discharged. They went to call their relatives to come pick them up, then returned to clear out their drawers, preparing to leave the hospital. Their lab results had come back, all benign tumors—they were thrilled. Having spent about a week in the hospital, they'd come to know many of the women and had developed a rapport, so they exchanged phone numbers. Once their family members arrived and they settled their bills, they told each other "See you at the teahouse," then went off on their merry way. In hospitals, as in prisons, no one ever says, "See you again."

In the ward, there were ten patients in total. When the lab reports came back, confirming that their tumors were benign, they were understandably over the moon, but as for me, the tumor in my body was malignant. Sitting on the sofa in the long corridor, I saw the doctor head over with someone else, appearing very solemn. That person was a lab technician. The surgeon had never had much of a smile. I didn't know if it was his natural demeanor, or if it was because of my condition. Maybe it was an occupational disease—the more surgeries he performed, the less he smiled.

Did those ears outside the curtain hear what the doctor told me? He said they cut out four lymph nodes, one of which was slightly infected. Though he wasn't certain it was necessary, he recommended I undergo radiation. Who else heard these words, other than the nurse and me? Perhaps no one, as some people were busy packing up to leave the hospital, while several others were babbling on about lab reports, including Patient Number Six, who didn't have one. She'd already been in the hospital for a week.

While we were discussing lab reports, a nurse approached Patient Number Six and asked for her specimen. Everyone in the ward was dumbstruck—the specimen had gone missing. Patient Number Six explained that after her surgery, she was handed a plastic bag, which she placed on a small table. The thing they'd cut out was so unsightly, like a decayed tooth that had been pulled, that she'd thought it was useless to hold on to it, so her aunt tossed it in the wastebasket when she came to visit. Now, a week later, the nurse had come to collect it, but the garbage in the wastebasket had already been incinerated.

Without a specimen, how could they run a lab test? Without a lab test, how could they know what illness she had? The patient said: How was I supposed to know? No one told me to keep it. I've never been in the hospital before. I don't understand any of this.

I only saw the doctor and nurse come and go, not knowing how to handle the situation. In fact, I only heard Patient Number Six say, It's my fault—I didn't know. She blamed herself over and over. Since no one was investigating the matter further, it likely would remain unresolved.

The morning after my surgery, my specimen was also delivered. Inside a plastic bag, there was a floating mass that resembled a cluster of shredded cotton wadding: my breast. In one of the stories from *Strange Tales from the Liaozhai Studio*, a scholar meets a stunning beauty, enjoys a night of pleasure, only to discover the following day that he's been embracing a skeleton.[2] Truly, as the *Heart Sūtra* states, form is emptiness. A deranged perverted sex maniac used to live near my home. He was a taxi driver who would pick up lone female passengers, drive them to the middle of nowhere, chloroform them, and take them home. Then, he'd use a scalpel to cut off their breasts and genitals, which he soaked in alcohol. If he hadn't taken photos of these women's corpses and dropped the film off to be developed, it's unlikely he would have been found out. He'd already murdered and dismembered four people, his entire apartment filled with jar after jar of specimens. Were those breasts still intact? Or did they resemble clusters of shredded cotton wadding? Every time I pass his street, I feel a sense of foreboding.

The ward I stayed in was on the second floor, in the west wing of the hospital, the whole floor occupied by women waiting to undergo surgery. The operating room was at the end of the long corridor, with seven or eight wards on either side of the corridor. The larger wards could accommodate ten people, and the smaller ones, four. One of the wards was for elderly women who were cared for by dedicated nurses around the clock, hired jointly by the patients for 100 dollars a day. Most of these patients were here for cataract surgery. Six months earlier, my mother had been here for a day. The doctor's work was outstanding—a seventy-nine-year-old had both eyes operated on at the same time. The procedure was at six in the evening, and when the bandages were removed at nine the next morning, she could see clearly. She was discharged immediately. Advanced medicine is amazing!

The other patients in my ward suffered from abdominal issues. It was either the gallbladder or the stomach, the uterus or the intestines. The youngest girl was probably about fifteen and had suffered from appendicitis. She brought school textbooks so she could study and was discharged after two days without ever saying a word. Another woman in her thirties also had appendicitis, but she cried and wailed, constantly throwing tantrums and cursing up a storm at her mother, who had accompanied her. She rented a TV set from the hospital and placed it in front of the window. She watched TV alone till one in the morning, turning it off only when the nurse came to intervene.

Visible through the window was the east wing of the hospital across the way. That distant part of the hospital was home to the maternity ward. Surely it was a place brimming with happiness, filled with the joy of new life. Young first-time fathers, nervous yet excited, would bring elderly mothers and siblings to visit the new mothers. Was it a boy? Wonderful! A girl? Equally delightful! Over on our side, however, there were many long-faced people, moaning and complaining, and the grim faces of friends and family wandering throughout the ward. We were all pregnant—the women in the east wing were carrying little angels, while those of us over here were carrying demons.

My younger sister brought me food every day because the hospital didn't provide meals. Your only option was to ask the female attendants to go and buy some for you, but it'd be nothing more than ordinary restaurant fare, heavy on the meat and light on the vegetables. My family members all visited me, and everyone said: Get well soon. No one truly knew what was going on with my tumor. They could only offer hope and good wishes. Mom also came. She said: So, you're really in the hospital. I couldn't hide it from her this time. It was good to have family members visit, chatting and shooting the breeze. Time passed more quickly when my mind wasn't wandering aimlessly.

Of course, my friends also came to see me, some individually, some in groups, and they came many times. My little friend Sou-sou even brought me a cloth doll. During this period, they must have been running ragged, as they had to visit both me and Ah Tin. Like me, Ah Tin was sick and had a tumor. If she hadn't needed a physical exam when she applied for a new job, she wouldn't have known she had a tumor growing inside her body. After asking her seven questions, the doctor said she had a tumor on her uterus. Sure enough, they cut out a bowl-size tumor, with two smaller tumors attached to the larger one, which had blisters on it. Nevertheless, Ah Tin's prognosis was good—her tumor was benign, and she'd soon be discharged from the hospital and could return to work in a month. As for me, I too would be discharged soon, but there's no such thing as a complete cure for cancer. It can only be controlled, and the body gradually recovers, but it will never be completely cured. Once you have cancer, you'll be dealing with it for the rest of your life, harboring an unpredictable, misshapen monster that can strike at any time and swallow you up.

A group of friends went to visit Ah Tin and then came to see me. It was past nine o'clock, and visiting hours were over, the lights in the ward dimmed, so I sat chatting with them on the sofa in the corridor. How I wished this were our usual café where we could gab about everything under the sun. Read any good books lately? Have the new books we ordered arrived? However, with every passing minute and second, time flew by, and my friends had to leave. It was so hard to part with them. Nothing is more precious than friendship. Well, see you tomorrow. See you tomorrow at the café.

People would place vases of flowers outside the door in the corridor. My friends gave me a basket of flowers that was too big and would block traffic if I set it in the corridor. I put it under my bed so I wouldn't accidentally knock it over while sleeping. My friends left, and I wasn't sleepy at all, so I flipped through the latest magazines my sister had brought from home. One was a special issue in which

Hunan writers commemorated a friend who'd passed away from cancer. One of the articles detailed how the cancer cells had spread to his brain, requiring his brain to be opened up so the cancer could be cut out. The patient surprisingly asked a friend to film the process of opening his brain. The caption read: UNDER THE WHITE CLOTH, BLOOD GUSHED OUT LIKE A FOUNTAIN AS SOON AS THE KNIFE WENT IN. Reading that sent chills down my spine, and I couldn't continue any further.

The hospital didn't have a flower garden because it wasn't a convalescent hospital. When patients came here, it was mainly for surgery, and they were discharged within a week or several days. A garden wasn't what they needed; what they needed was an operating room. After having surgery, many patients were able get out of bed. I could already walk around by noon the following day. The wards were air-conditioned, an advantage of the private hospital. Of course, the higher fees reflected this. Resting in the air-conditioned ward was comfortable, but lying in bed all day wasn't a solution. Except for the period in the morning when patients sat on the sofa in the corridor and chatted while the bedding was changed, they mostly sat on their beds and rarely moved around.

Where could I go for a walk? I needed to stretch my muscles. The only option was the corridor. And so, I walked from one end of the corridor to the other and back again. The corridor wasn't long. At one end, there were two elevators facing the operating room. On either side of the corridor were the patient wards, with a spacious nurses' station in the middle. There was a clock on the wall that I always glanced at as I passed by. It took less than three minutes to go up and down the corridor, and it felt like time dragged on. And so, I walked slowly, carefully studying the nameplates outside the doorway of every ward. There were ten patients in each ward, and their names were posted in the slots next to the doors. Each name was preceded by a bed number and followed by the doctor's name. One doctor's name appeared three times. Ah, his business was booming.

My doctor had only me as his patient. Every day, he came to the hospital to see me. There was one doctor whose name I was familiar with because he performed my mother's cataract surgery. He had quite a few patients.

Apart from looking at names, when passing by the wards, I also peered at the flowers inside. Actually, there weren't many flower arrangements—instead, the bedside tables were covered with snacks and pieces of fruit, along with stacks of bottles and cans. At the end of the corridor, there was a smaller nurses' station, and then the restroom. Perpendicular to the corridor, there was a lobby connected to a passageway leading to the opposite-facing building. There were phones in the lobby, so often a few people gathered here to make calls. In one corner of the lobby, there was a larger-than-life statue of the Virgin Mary, surrounded by fresh flowers of varying heights. Even during the day, it was adorned with lights, as though it were eternally Christmas.

How exactly did Christmas come to be? Mary was unwed and had never been intimate with a man, and yet her belly gradually swelled up. If this had happened to any other woman, it would have been a tumor. However, Mary gave birth not to a demon but to a savior. In the novel *The Legend of the Swordsmen of the Mountains of Shu*, there is an unmarried woman who accidentally ingests a certain flower, leans against a rock to rest for a while, and mysteriously ends up pregnant.[3] After twenty-one years, she gives birth to a child, whom she names Born of Rock. But that's just the plot of a novel.

Some medical studies suggest that women aged forty to sixty are the most susceptible to breast cancer, especially those who have never been married. I am a prime example. I say "some," because there's always one study or another, but no definitive conclusions. Karl Popper tells us that no matter how many white swans we have seen, that doesn't prove that all swans are white. The truth is, there are various interpretations of the human body, and each of us harbors so many unknown elements within us. We have both reverence for and fear of mystical forces, which is the most enduring psychological commonality among humans, especially when these forces are attached to the human body. With the evolution of society, these forces have gradually become differentiated according to common practices: What one woman is pregnant with is a little angel, while what I was pregnant with was a dreadful little demon. The little angel leaves the mother's body after ten lunar months, is born, and grows day by day to become an independent and free individual; the little demon, on the other hand, refuses to leave the mother's body, never withering away, clinging to the insides, also growing day by day.[4] In ten months, or maybe ten years, it ultimately takes over, a presumptuous guest overpowering the host, who dies. It's a parasitic fungus, a creeping vine, that causes the host plant to wither away.

When Mary learned she was pregnant, she was terrified, but the angel Gabriel said to her: Mary, don't be afraid. There are countless frightening things in the world, but who will say not to be afraid? Over the phone, the doctor only said: It's a malignant tumor. Serious doctors don't add superfluous words. I felt like my head was filled to the gills with water, or frozen into a block of ice. Mary said: How can this be, since I've never been married? As for me, I didn't smoke, or drink, or eat barbecued or canned foods. Why did *I* have a tumor?

Where was my angel? Who would come and tell me not to be afraid? I finally met my own Gabriel, two weeks later, when I heard Ah Kin's voice on the phone. She didn't have wings or a halo above her head; she was just my fellow sister in illness. The first thing she said to me was: Don't be afraid.

There were ten patients in the large ward, the youngest of whom was the fifteen-year-old who had come in for an appendectomy. She was Patient Number Two. Patient Number Four was an unmarried woman with a benign thyroid tumor. She was often accompanied by her mother and her young fiancé. Patient Number Five was an unmarried woman. Every day she lost her temper and yelled at her mother. Besides me, the rest of the women were all married, and the majority were on the older side. Everyone Simone de Beauvoir had written about in *The Second Sex* was gathered here, except for children, that is.

What was going on in the mind of the fifteen-year-old girl? Was she haunted by the prospect of becoming pregnant and the fear of a difficult childbirth? According to Beauvoir, some young girls are so anxious about their bodies that they long for surgery, especially an appendectomy. In this way, young girls express their various misconceptions about rape, pregnancy, and childbirth. They sense some sort of ambiguous threat in their bodies, unknown, yet lurking inside, and hope that surgeons will rescue them from this danger.

When I gazed at the girl lying on the bed to my left, she appeared exceptionally serene. Did her five-foot frame embarrass her or cause her to suffer? Did her parents ever warn her to beware of men? Did they forbid her from going out at night or monitor her phone calls, letters, and friends? Did they try their best to raise her to be a "well-bred young woman"? None of this was visible on the surface. She was simply engrossed in reading, studying her textbooks. Probably she had an upcoming test or exam, and at this moment was pouring her heart into her studies.

Whenever I sat on the bed, spreading out my pile of books, I could hear murmurs from a neighboring bed. These were the intimate whispers between Patient Number Four and her fiancé. The words they spoke, I believed, were nothing more than a template, one which both parties were deeply immersed in. Marriage, says Beauvoir, is a destiny assigned to women by traditional society. Even during the twentieth century, a period of overpopulation, women were believed to have an inherent obligation to produce children for the benefit of society, and in order to do so, they were compelled to get married. To be unmarried was to be abnormal; if a woman was considered ugly or immoral, she was abandoned by the world of men. And so, a woman was either a parasite in her father's household or, like my mother, relegated to a humble corner of another family. She had to sever ties with the past and join the galaxy ruled by her husband, relinquishing the right to go out into the universe and shine on her own.

Were there no such problems nowadays? The lovers murmuring beside me—her future marriage surely would be devoid of calculation, disgust, or compromise. Such was the happiness of the modern woman. The couple would be getting married before long. In her mind, what did marriage involve? This man and this woman would engage in a highly intimate experience, under the guise of ceremony and flowers. Ah, how many brides run away on their wedding night, and how many brides are sent back to their parents' homes on the same night?

For the other patients, all of these things were history. Were they preoccupied with their husbands' promotions and children's education, as well as their current most pressing health concerns? Perhaps they'd gradually grown accustomed to becoming lifelong servants and long-term laborers for their families, believing life had to be this way. And so, they spent each day buying groceries, cooking meals, and doing laundry for their husbands and children, perpetually battling dust in a tiny living space.

Most of the women in the ward were either at or past the "dangerous age" to which Beauvoir refers. They welcomed the end of menstruation but were afraid of aging. They seemed to have lost their sex but to have become complete human beings; the moment they gained freedom was also the moment they couldn't utilize this freedom. What could women of a "dangerous age" do? With their husbands' financial stability, their children grown up and having flown the coop, and no more worries about pregnancy and childbirth, they could learn to play the piano, sing Chinese opera, travel, garden, and watch Western-style operas. It was truly a newfound, previously unknown freedom. However, disease now came at them from all directions at full speed.

Simone de Beauvoir never mentioned cancer. What if one of the women lying on either side of my bed had breast cancer? At fifteen years old, the likelihood of developing cancer was still far off, right? No. Recently there had been a case of breast cancer in which the patient was only twelve years old. What if the woman with thyroid trouble had breast cancer? Would her fiancé still marry her? People in love are fond of saying, "We'll grow old together, till death do us part." For love that's never encountered any hardships, such phrases are merely empty words. Illness, regardless of its magnitude, is a hardship.

Simone de Beauvoir never mentioned cancer. But Susan Sontag did, in *Illness as Metaphor*. The disease of the nineteenth century was tuberculosis, but in the twentieth century, it shifted to cancer; both diseases were enveloped in a veil of mystery. No one knew the cause of tuberculosis, and treatment methods didn't exist. Gradually, however, the cause was discovered, along with ways to combat it. Thus, by the turn of the twentieth century, tuberculosis was no longer a fearsome killer. However, it was during this time that cancer came along, insidious and of uncertain origin, whether genetic and/or environmental. Since that time, research has made significant progress, and in the twenty-first century, perhaps cancer and tuberculosis will be discussed similarly, the way people speak of the common cold or the flu. At the moment, AIDS is the foremost concern.

There are quite a few similarities between the onset and progression of tuberculosis and of cancer, yet there are also aspects that are nearly polar opposites. Tuberculosis is confined to the lungs. The patient exhibits various symptoms, such as coughing, wheezing, expectorating, and spitting up blood, symptoms that are clear and discernible; in X-rays, the body appears translucent. But cancer generally has no obvious signs; it's silent and well-concealed. When examined by ultrasound, the organs appear as dark, solid blotches. People with tuberculosis always travel, seeking cures for their illness. Sunshine and fresh air are beneficial to their health. That's why Keats and Shelley wandered from one place to another. Italy, the South Pacific, and the Mediterranean were all romanticized by writers with tuberculosis. But cancer? No environment can change the predicament of cancer. Even the brightest sunshine and freshest air are of no avail.

Illness in the nineteenth century truly was romanticized. Lyric poets and pianists were supposed to be delicate and thin, as well as impoverished, and steadfastly so. Nothing suited them better than the contraction of tuberculosis. For novelists, however, there was no harm in being chubby, like Balzac, convincing readers that if he didn't have all of France in his belly, he had Paris at least. However, look at artists like Chopin and Théophile Gautier, the tragic beauty of whose works seemed only enhanced by their sickly demeanor and Narcissus-like appearance. And while the novelists themselves may have been robust and sturdy, their characters often displayed the frailty of those with tuberculosis, weak to the point of heartbreak. Oh, Lady of the Camellias. Oh, Lin Daiyu. You can't imagine what it would be like for the Lady of the Camellias or Lin Daiyu to have breast cancer. That's a novel no one wants to read. There's much that can be written about a heroine who suffers from tuberculosis. She is always extremely beautiful, and the disease adds to her charm, a low-grade fever making it appear as though she's enhanced her pale complexion with rouge. The slightest breeze can blow her away—she's the very image of pity. But she can play musical instruments, is fond of flowers and the moon, often writes poetry, grieves the arrival of autumn and laments the passing of spring. She inevitably encounters a young man who loves her very much. Although he is poor, he is handsome. If he is rich, he is obediently filial toward his stubborn parents. However, none of this can save her, nor can the author, nor the reader. She is doomed to die in the arms of her lover. Such scenes have been made into movies or performed on the stage, bringing countless people to tears as they watch—the poor woman, the lingering love, the melancholic disease.

But there aren't any romantic films about cancer, unless we count romantic scenes before the onset of illness. A leading lady with cancer who writes poetry? Such a movie would have to be violent, because the appearance of cancer isn't ghostly or ethereal like tuberculosis—it's a thunderbolt, a sniper attack, a sudden strike. There's nothing romantic about it. Even as the twentieth century draws to a close, there has not been one profound novel written about cancer, other than Solzhenitsyn's *Cancer Ward*. Nor are there are any memorable films about cancer, except for Kurosawa's *Ikiru*.

The Dream of the Red Chamber is a story told by a stone.[5] This stone does not appear inside any of the characters' bodies. Among the numerous girls living in Prospect Garden, not a single one has breast cancer. Perhaps they don't have it because they are simply too young. Perhaps some do have it, but no one knows, since breast diseases are extremely private. Because it isn't suitable to let others look, nor is it easy to talk about, it remains unnoticed. It's like a disease that only has an implied meaning but lacks any explicit signifiers. Until the twentieth century, cancer was still hidden. In Japan, patients couldn't even be told the diagnosis. Everything was kept secret, because cancer was a word that was condemned as though it were a "crime."

If you have cancer, it's as if you're guilty of a crime. For instance, when there's a traffic jam, people call it a cancer of the road. When students aren't serious about their studies, or there's a lack of public support for teaching one's mother tongue in school, people call it a cancer of education. There are also cancers of society and the state— all these difficult problems, unsolvable issues, troubles, worries, sorrows, and predicaments are referred to as cancers, while those who actually have cancer quietly keep their secret to themselves in order to avoid condemnation.

When I had to return to the hospital for surgery, I considered again which books in translation to bring along. Perhaps Dostoyevsky's *Crime and Punishment*? But that was too heavy to hold. What about Donald Barthelme's *City Life*? But Barthelme had passed away from blood cancer; I didn't want to read him just now. Okay then, how about Li Li's translation of *Brave New World*? In the end, I decided against that one too, since Aldous Huxley's wife, Maria, had had breast cancer, and many years later, Huxley himself also suffered from cancer of the tongue, which recurred four times in three years and couldn't be cured.

In 1952, was breast cancer an incurable disease? Or, by the time Maria discovered the tumor, was it too late? Three years later, the cancer cells spread throughout her entire body, ultrasound therapy was ineffective, her liver began to deteriorate, and she was never able to see her husband's final novel, *Island*. What was Maria, who was suffering from breast cancer, thinking about before her death? She quietly introduced her husband to another woman. She arranged a successor wife for him, as though she were plotting a story full of extraordinary events.

I didn't take any of these books I had in mind to the hospital. Instead, I ended up bringing the even heavier *Lives of Gargantua and Pantagruel*.[6] I wanted to read something light in tone and cheerful. The giant Gargantua was born from an ear; actually, I've always thought that Mary conceived of Jesus through her ear. In those fifteenth-century Renaissance frescoes of the annunciation that I often looked at, didn't one of them depict an angel passing a message directly into Mary's ear? In the painting, a golden beam of light appears: the Holy Spirit.

At first, Gargantua studies for more than thirty years, but the more he studies, the dumber he becomes. As a result, he changes teachers, and Rabelais's ideal education for a French youth emerges. There are so many things for Gargantua to learn, and he studies a wide range of arts and skills. Literature, mathematics, astronomy, and music are all part of his curriculum, while in the afternoon he learns horseback riding, hunting, swimming, fencing, tightrope walking, and other physical activities. On rainy days, he stays at home to bundle hay, split firewood, saw timber, thresh sheaves of wheat in the barn, and study painting and sculpture. Additionally, he observes the crafts of metallurgy, cannon casting, weaving, printing, dyeing, minting coins, calibrating watches, making mirrors, refining gold and ore, and so on. His teacher also takes him to listen to lectures, public debates, lawyers practicing their oratory skills, recitations, court debates, and sermons. On rainy days, rather than collect plant specimens, they visit the shops of druggists, herbalists, and apothecaries, carefully inspecting various leaves, fruits, tree roots, plant roots, gums, seeds, and spices from foreign lands, and examining their refinement. They also go to watch jugglers, acrobats, magicians, and other performers, scrutinizing their movements, tricks, and somersaulting skills.

Is it not enviable to study like Gargantua? The scope is broad and interesting, and for three hours a day, a young page reads aloud to him. The strangest thing is that when he goes to the bathroom, instead of taking a book to read himself, he is accompanied by his teacher, who reviews the lessons he's read, explaining the difficult and obscure parts.

Reading *The Lives of Gargantua and Pantagruel* is such a pleasure. The two Chinese translations each have their own merits. Translation A is annotated in great detail. For example, it notes that black hellebore was a special remedy for diseases of the nervous system at the time, as mentioned in both Horace's *Ars Poetica* and Pliny the Elder's *Natural History*. Translation B, however, merely notes that ancient people believed this herb could cure madness, and translates it as "buttercup." The passage concerning buttercup mentions the name of Timotheus, with the annotation: A famous ancient Greek poet and musician. But Translation A's explanation elaborates further. In *Institutio Oratoria*, Quintilian says that the musician Timotheus charged double fees to students who had studied music elsewhere, because he had to put in more effort to correct their past mistakes. He even made these students swallow black hellebore.

I've often heard of music teachers facing this dilemma and of the tenacity of students' bad habits. The allusion to Timotheus refers to events that happened more than two thousand years ago. Why did Gargantua have to eat black hellebore? It's because he had studied with a lousy teacher, and the more he studied, the more ignorant he became. His new teacher had to purge all the diseased ways of thinking from his mind and overhaul his previous bad habits.

It's fascinating to see different translation methods when one compares translations. For instance, one version translates an after-meal sweet treat as "candied papaya," and one as "papaya jam." People don't usually eat jam after a meal, so it should be "candied papaya." As for musical instruments, one translation reads, "He learned to play the lute, harmonium, harp, nine-hole German flute, cello, and suona." The other rendition reads, "Gargantua studied the guqin, harpsichord, harp, German nine-hole flute, seven-stringed zither, and horn." The descriptions of singing also differ. One version reads,

"Singing four or five sections of music, or an entire set of lyrics," while the other reads, "Singing together a four- or five-part chorus, or simply singing songs as they pleased." These translations, which originate from the same text, have turned out so differently from each other.

There are 217 games Gargantua plays. Rabelais lists the names of various indoor and outdoor games, such as cards, chess, riddles, contests of skill, and wrestling. Translation A dispenses with the details, noting: "Here, the author lists 217 kinds of games, which roughly can be divided into four categories: cards, chess, contests of wits, and riddles, as well as several outdoor games; some of these games involve gambling, and some aren't clear enough in meaning, so they have been deleted."

Reading this passage, I could only sigh out loud, waking the woman in the bed next to me. Gargantua's games are, of course, the games of French youth during the Renaissance period. Aren't some of these—footbag kicking, musical chairs, chess, stilt walking, dice throwing, flicking shells, and cards—games that we still play now? Some also appear one by one in Bruegel's painting before our very eyes.[7]

If you're only interested in breast cancer treatment, then don't waste time—skip to page 104 and read "Tamoxifen."

AH KIN

First Phone Conversation with Ah Kin

Hello, is this Ah Kin?

Yes, this is Ah Kin. I was just chatting with Tin about you.

She told me to contact you directly.

How are things?

I just got out of the hospital.

You had surgery, right?

Yes.

That's good. Don't be afraid. Try to keep an open mind. Look at me.

The same thing happened to you?

Yes.

How'd you find out?

In the shower, I found a lump as big as a loquat.

And it didn't hurt?

Not at all. Just a little itchy.

Did you have it removed?

I had it removed immediately. That's the only way to be thorough.

What about your lymph nodes?

Two were infected. You?

One's showing signs.

Don't worry, with early detection and immediate medical treatment,
     it can be controlled.

How do you feel now?

It's been under control for five years.

Five years.

At the time, I was only thirty-five.

So young.

Yes. I had a hard time getting used to it.

You were only in your thirties.

My oldest child was five. My younger daughter was only a year and a half.

Such young ages.

At the time, I didn't know what I was going to do, but somehow, I'm still here.

Five years.

So, don't worry too much. Let things go, and look on the bright side.

Thank you. It's very kind of you to reassure me.

In fact, our case is the least serious. And science is so advanced.

It's the least serious?

I have some friends in the same boat as us. They're all still here.

You've put my mind at ease.

Feel free to call me anytime. We can chat about anything you'd like to know.

Thank you, Ah Kin.

Second Phone Conversation with Ah Kin

Ah Kin?

Hello, this is Ah Kin. How've you been?

I just had my stitches removed.

Your muscles are like sponges, right?

I don't feel anything at all.

It's like it's not even your own skin.

How long will it last?

A few months. Don't worry—it's like this at first.

It'll get better later?

Uh-huh. Are you taking any medication?

Every day. You?

I did at first, but I stopped.

Why?

You know, this kind of medication is supposed to induce menopause, but I hadn't gone through that yet.

What happened when you stopped taking it?

It turned out that the treatment for my ovaries threw me into menopause anyway, so I couldn't have more kids.

You were only in your thirties.

I have two kids. That's enough.

Two kids. You don't need any more.

Do you need radiation?

The doctor says it's up to me.

You should do it.

I think so too.

Do it. It's like buying insurance. I have some friends …

What about them?

Things turned out well for those who received it, and not so well for those who didn't.

Then I'll do it.

May I ask what line of work you're in?

I used to teach. Now I'm retired.

That's good. You don't have to work. You can focus on resting.

I just care for my mom at home.

Radiation will take up a lot of your time.

How much?

Around two hours a session.

How many sessions?

My course of treatment was six weeks.

Did you go every day?

First, I saw the doctor, had an exam, had simulation markings drawn, and then I scheduled my appointments.

Was the wait long?

The more people, the longer the wait. Plan on three months.

Three months altogether.

You don't have to go to work—that's good.

Do you work?

I used to work in a clinic, but of course I quit after.

Are you mainly resting now?

No. Every day I go grocery shopping, cook meals, take care of the
kids, and supervise their homework.

When do you have downtime?

I'm free in the afternoon, when the kids are at school.

I want to ask, what should I eat?

Eat more fruits and vegetables. Drink plenty of soup. Avoid foods
that are pan-fried, stir-fried, smoked, or deep-fried.

Okay.

Carrots are the best. My body isn't great—I can't stomach them raw.

Must carrots be eaten raw?

It's best to eat them raw. You can also juice them. Even drinking the
juice upsets my stomach.

What should I do then?

Make soup. Drink carrot soup regularly. Adding carrots to fish soup
also works.

I can drink carrot juice. I tried it recently.

That's good. Never eat goose, duck, shrimp, or crab.

Oh, okay.

Don't eat chicken either. Some people say it's all right, but I still
avoid it.

Don't eat chicken.

I haven't eaten chicken or eggs in three years. Don't eat raw fish.

Don't eat raw fish.

The older generation thinks it's good, but it's not.

Doesn't it help to keep the wound closed?

If the stitches are too tight, the flesh will become puckered and cra-
tered.

No raw fish.

Also, stay away from raw medicinal herbs for now.

Thank you, thank you.

Third Phone Conversation with Ah Kin
Ah Kin, it's me again.

You're welcome to call anytime. How've you been?

I'm going to the specialty unit.

You've made an appointment with the doctor, right?

Yes. What should I expect?

For now, just an exam and some sketching.

And then radiation.

Yes. After determining the treatment site, they'll mark the area on your body.

On my body.

Uh-huh. Red and blue like a map. Don't wash it off when you get home.

Don't wash it off.

Don't bathe after radiation either.

Don't bathe.

It was awful for me. It was the height of summer—July, August.

Now the weather's cooler.

My younger sister made the mistake of washing it. The treatment site developed small blisters.

Oh dear.

It looked like she'd been scalded by boiling water. She ended up being treated for a week.

Your sister's sick too?

Same as you and me.

Many people seem to have this kind of illness.

More and more, just like Western women.

What a disaster.

Ah, sometimes they apply color up to your neck. It's hideous.

Other people can see it.

Exactly, so I wore shirts with high collars.

You had to go out and buy special clothes, right?

It's better in cooler weather. You can wear turtleneck sweaters.

Or a scarf.

Bring a thermos of water to drink. After radiation, your throat will be dry, and you'll be exhausted.

Is it terrible?

You won't want to eat at all. Someone lost twenty pounds.

What about you?

I lost ten pounds. Also, my arm became less flexible.

How long did it take you to recover?

Two full years. I had a lot of complications.

It's good you were able to recover.

My older sister was super energetic. She went back to work after only
two months.

Your *older* sister?

Yes, she's the same age as you.

She also got sick?

The same illness as us.

And your younger sister?

My younger sister also.

Three of you?

Yes, and all of us the same illness.

*What if your family member or friend also gets
breast cancer, but doesn't know a woman like
Ah Kin? Please turn to page 230 and read
"Things That Are Known."*

THE BATHROOM

I HADN'T properly bathed in two weeks. Fortunately, it was September, and the weather was cooling off. Instead of bathing as usual, I could only take partial baths, dabbing my upper body with a damp washcloth.

A week after coming home from the hospital post-op, I went to the clinic to have the surgeon remove my stitches. I didn't know why he hadn't stitched up my wound with a fishing-line-like thread that wouldn't have needed to be removed and could have remained in the wound, gradually dissolving over time. For patients, so many things are unclear, and no one gives us a choice; we're like helpless little lambs. For all I knew, the surgeon could have used sheep intestines, thick and black, reminiscent of beef tendon. Lying back on the exam table, I felt the doctor tear open the large bandage on my chest and remove the stitches with scissors, the sound crystal-clear, a clean and neat *snip*, *snip*.

How many stitches? I asked.

Twenty-five, he replied.

Twenty-five stitches—that's a long centipede. I remember falling and injuring my head in school when I was a child. The school doctor immediately stopped the bleeding and stitched up the wound. By the time my mother arrived, my head was all bandaged up so that I looked like a Sikh person in a turban. Back then, after the blood had streamed down my face, I rested at home for a month before returning to school, and I had only had *three* stitches in the back of my head. Now I had *twenty-five* stitches. I couldn't bring myself to think about it.

The incision was long, and the stitches had to be removed over the course of two sittings. The first time, every other stitch was snipped with scissors, the short pieces of thread like severed parts of an earthworm. In fact, the wound had already closed, and tissue connected skin to skin; even if the stitches had been removed all at once, the wound wouldn't have split open. But the doctor was cautious, which made me feel more at ease.

A few days later, I went back to the clinic a second time, and the large bandage on my chest was torn open again, and the remaining stitches snipped one after the other, as though I were a shoe and the doctor a shoemaker. All of the stitches were removed. This time, the doctor did not apply a large, wide bandage over the incision; instead, he crisscrossed the wound with strip after strip of narrow bandages, resembling a double-gated door sealed shut with strips of paper, a practice employed in imperial China when the occupants of the house had offended someone in the government. During this visit, the doctor informed me that I could shower when I got home. The water would naturally loosen the small seals on the wound, so they wouldn't need to be ripped off.

Finally, I could shower! I could stand my entire body beneath the showerhead and let the water flow over me. The most relaxing part was washing my hair—I no longer had to bend over and bury my head in the sink. In fact, I couldn't easily lift my right hand above my head, so I hadn't been able to give myself a haircut. After I got home, I took several showers, but the small bandages didn't loosen. I left them on until a few days later, when one by one they fell like yellow leaves from a tree, and the shackles of my wound were lifted completely.

I loved the bathroom in my family's home. It had been our favorite place. We paid for it in installments—because we weren't rich, we could only choose a small unit, comprised of one large room, a kitchen, and a bathroom. The bathroom was like an elevator car, with only a toilet and tiny sink inside. We'd cleanse ourselves using the handheld shower head that hung on the wall. I worried every time I used it. There was nowhere to place my dry clothes, and I even had to hide the toilet paper. Of course, it was cold water that sprayed out. After showering, the toilet, sink, walls, and door panel would all be wet, and the water on the floor, unable to drain quickly enough, would flow out the door. Taking a shower, followed by the grueling cleanup of wiping the walls, wiping the door, wiping the toilet lid, and mopping the floor, was hard work. We bathed in order to clean ourselves, but the labor afterward left us covered in stinky sweat from head to toe. When it was cold, we had to boil water in order to bathe, but there was no place to set down the water pot. Who could sing in such a bathroom?

Your home doesn't have a bathtub either? she asked.

My home doesn't have a bathtub either, I said.

I was on the phone with my friend who loves cats, chatting about everything under the sun. We began discussing bathtubs. Nobody had one. I could only sigh—I certainly had a fair number of poor friends. Half a year later, she called to tell me she now had a bathtub. Necessity is the mother of invention. Be inventive. Just move the wall between the bathroom and the kitchen, and voilà, problem solved. I understood at once.

My kitchen was exactly twice the size of the bathroom and could accommodate a refrigerator and tabletop sewing machine. The truth was, I didn't need such a spacious kitchen. And so, I pulled out a ruler, measured from left to right, spent a week drafting blueprints, then hired a mason to come do renovations. A wall torn down; a wall built; a drain, electrical wiring, and plumbing installed; dust and debris flying everywhere—at long last, the bathroom was constructed. The small kitchen seemed even better than before, as it was outfitted with tidy cabinets that stored all of the clutter. Only kitchen appliances such as an electric rice cooker, a propane cooktop, and an electric kettle remained on the counter. Of course, the refrigerator was moved to the dining room, and the old sewing machine was so outdated that I simply gave it to my neighbor.

I didn't expect the remodeled bathroom to be so satisfying. A three-piece ivory-colored bathroom set, exceptionally pleasing to the eye, the floor inlaid with tea-brown fireproof bricks in a running-bond pattern, the walls covered in square white tiles with subtle designs that stretched from the floor to the ceiling. The bathtub was low and wide, equipped with an electric water heater—bathing was now truly a treat.

It was just a week of dust and banging, just two days of having to use the neighbor's bathroom, and then all the disruptions and racket were over. The bathroom had space for not only a washing machine but also a portable radio. Towels hung on the tiled wall, and a huge mirror was affixed above the sink. There was a louvered door, two large windows, and a built-in cupboard with medicine bottles, makeup, shampoo, and soap hidden inside. When friends dropped by to see it, they all oohed and aahed in surprise. *What a lovely bathroom!* It was lovely because the proportions didn't match the rest of the unit, just like a shabby hut in the countryside that seemed like it should've been fitted with a latrine. However, shouldn't a person's most essential, most comfortable living space be the bathroom?

I phoned my friend who loves cats and *Peanuts* comics and told her: I have a bathtub at home too. We both felt incomparably happy. She came to my place to have a look—in fact, I'd also gone to her home to check things out. Who'd have thought we'd end up fussing over such frivolous things? Strangely enough, though the bathroom had doubled in size, the kitchen didn't look small. Even with three or more people inside, it didn't feel cramped. And so, we stood there with wide smiles on our faces.

I loved the bathroom so much that I often brought in a small stool and read books while listening to classical music on Radio 4. Suddenly, on a whim, I'd fill the tub with sweet-smelling bubbles and soak in it—indeed, this was the golden age of stretching out and cleansing my body. Lying back in the bathtub was so comfortable, Mozart's piano concertos flowing like pearls, seahorse bath salts smelling like waves, an old book telling a faded and far-off story.

Now, all the joy in the bathroom had gone. I was so repulsed by it that I no longer took bubble baths, nor did I linger inside reading books or listening to music. Each time I showered, I just quickly rinsed myself beneath the showerhead, then dried off and got dressed.

The bathroom had become my battlefield, and I distanced myself from it like a deserter. I struggled to escape my body as though I were escaping a terrifying ghost.

At last, I had to confront reality. The small bandages that acted as seals had loosened and fallen off, revealing my wound in its entirety. Looking down, I saw a long scar on my chest, calling to mind a railroad zigzagging through the countryside. I held out my hand to compare; it was precisely the length of my palm. I suddenly remembered that back when I used to sew clothing, I had added a zipper of this exact length to a skirt.

A man who'd had a breast tumor was interviewed on the TV news. He was in his fifties. Perhaps because he was a manly man, when he bared his chest to the camera lens, I only saw a horizontal incision across his chest. Nothing else was different. It was the equivalent of seeing other people's scars from an appendectomy or C-section—it didn't shock me at all. The man didn't have bulging breasts. He reminded me of a wounded soldier who'd been on the battlefield.

I thought I was in the same situation as the man on TV, only I had a zipper-length incision, but no, that wasn't the case. The scar on my body was oblique, sloping at a 45-degree angle from the side of my ribs up to my chest, spanning several ribs. The entire breast was missing. The entire breast, including the nipple, areola, mammary gland, and large amounts of fat and connective tissue.

The structural unit of the middle gland of the breast has been compared to a peach tree in March. The cystic lobules formed by glandular tissue and the mammary lobules are like clusters of blooming peach blossoms, and the glandular cells where milk is produced are like petals. Milk flows from the peach-blossom-like glandular tissue into the branch-like mammary ducts and is then funneled into the trunk-like lactiferous ducts. Each breast has fifteen to twenty cystic lobules and a corresponding number of lactiferous ducts arranged in a radial pattern in the center of the nipple.

The peach-tree-like glandular tissue is, of course, the main structure of the breast, but it's only a small percentage of the overall volume of the breast. The contour of the breast is mainly composed of fat and connective tissue, including the Cooper's ligaments. The peach tree that had been on my body, along with the soil around it, was missing. If my right breast was once a hill, it was now a sunken valley. If it was once a pale and delicate bun on a plate, now all that was left was an empty plate. I quickly got dressed then rushed out of the bathroom.

How did the eighteenth-century Frenchman Georges-Louis Leclerc, comte de Buffon, put it? There are three types of monsters who can be distinguished from humans: The first type is a monster formed by an excess of organs; the second type is a monster formed by a lack of organs; the third type is a monster formed by an inversion or misplacement of organs.

There are so many monsters in the world: nine-headed birds, two-headed snakes, the three-eyed deity Huaguang, the thousand-armed Buddha—all of them are monsters. If you flip through the pages of *The Classic of Mountains and Seas*, *Investiture of the Gods*, and *Journey to the West*, they're full of all sorts of monsters.[8]

"Heavenly Questions" from the *Songs of Chu* asks: "Where does the mighty nine-headed snake slither to and fro?" The snake in question was a large, venomous snake with nine heads. This was a monster formed by an excess of organs.

Discourses Weighed in the Balance reads: "There is a three-legged raven in the sun." When the legendary archer Hou Yi shot at the suns, he shot down nine of them, and thus nine three-legged ravens died. This mythical bird in the sun had three legs. This was a monster formed by an excess of organs.

"Classic of Western Regions Beyond the Seas" from *The Classic of Mountains and Seas* reads: "The Land of the One-Armed People is located north of the Land of the Three-Bodied People. There they have one arm, one eye, and one nostril." The people in this country only had one arm, one eye, and one nostril. They were monsters formed by a lack of organs.

Chapter six of *A Garden of Anomalies* reads: "During the Yuanjia reign of the Liu Song dynasty, a one-legged ghost suddenly appeared to Song Ji of Yingchuan in the daylight. It was about three feet tall." As there are one-legged people, certainly there are one-legged ghosts. A one-legged ghost is a monster formed by a lack of organs.

"Basic Annals of the Three Sovereigns," the supplement to the *Records of the Grand Historian*, reads: "One with a snake's body and a human head has the virtue of a sage." Fuxi was said to be the son of the God of Thunder. Studying how spiders wove webs, he built a ladder to scale the heavens. With a human head and snake's body, Fuxi was of course a monster formed by an inversion or misplacement of organs.

"Classic of Western Regions Beyond the Seas" from *The Classic of Mountains and Seas* reads: "The deity Xingtian came here and fought with the Supreme God to see who had greater spiritual powers. The Supreme God cut off his head and buried it on Mount Changyang. Thereupon, Xingtian used his nipples as eyes, his navel as a mouth, and grasping his shield and battle-axe, he danced." The headless Xingtian was a monster formed by both a lack of organs and an inversion or misplacement of organs.

Eunuchs in the Forbidden City were monsters formed by a lack of organs. Sima Qian was a monster who wrote the *Records of the Grand Historian*. I was a monster. I'd lost a breast—I too was a monster formed by a lack of organs.

Falling out of love with the bathroom was one thing, wondering whether I was a monster was another, but regardless, I still had to go into the bathroom every day, and I had to bathe. Sitting in the tub, initially I worried that the wound would break open. In fact, my concerns were unfounded. The wound was stitched perfectly, granulation tissue growing over it. I'd never seen such a tight and seamless zipper. Who was the first surgeon? Whose idea was it to cut open someone's skin and then stitch it back up? It's like sewing clothing.

Sewing the skin on a person's body looks similar to sewing clothes, but it's actually not the same. Only primitive people sewed clothing as if stitching up skin. Primitive people's clothing was made from leaves and animal hides. The leaves didn't have to be stitched—they could protect the body by being draped around it and hanging down, discarded a couple of days later after they had withered. Animal hides were real clothing and marked the advent of sewing. Two animal hides, perforated at the edges, were joined together with sinew. Although the two skins were joined together, there was a gap in between, resembling how we lace up sneakers today.

The jade garments stitched with gold thread in ancient times and the iron armor for soldiers during the Qin dynasty followed the same method used to sew animal hides, the key difference being that the four corners were linked together, then wrapped and fastened with gold thread. But you can't sew clothes this way. Clothes can't have gaps everywhere. You have to sew them tightly so that they're as strong as a city wall, a seamless heavenly robe. The fabric used nowadays is different from animal hide, much softer, but even animal hides can still be seamless. Fabric can be folded, leaving an edge on the back side. After it's sewn, the fabric can be flipped over to the front side and ironed smooth and neat. Jade, iron, and hard leather can't be folded. You have to pierce holes, pull thread through the holes, and close up the seams. It's the same with skin.

Skin isn't fabric. It can't be sewn inside out. Fortunately, the way God created the human body is extraordinary. Stitched-up skin has blood vessels and nerves, epidermis and dermis, hair follicles and sweat glands, yet it can regulate its own growth, skin connecting with skin, reuniting in no time. The human body is a true heavenly robe without any seams. The body that undergoes surgery is left with only a scar, totally leakproof. Life is so amazing: half an earthworm can be reborn, a starfish can be perpetually regenerated, chickens can be fitted with duck wings, a pig kidney can be transplanted into a human body.

My friend who loves cats and *Peanuts* comics and Truffaut films also loves her bathroom. What does she think about when she sits in the bathtub? Stitching things together? Ah, that's a possibility. The stitching she has in mind certainly has nothing to do with clothing or skin but instead, film, where stitching becomes splicing. She might think about *Jules and Jim*, *The 400 Blows*, *Close Encounters of the Third Kind*, *The Wild Child*, and so on. In fact, a film is a flowing jade garment stitched with gold thread, bits and pieces linked together.

A couple of decades ago, I and my friend who loves cats and *Peanuts* comics and Truffaut films and Mozart's music became obsessed with film splicing. Back then, we used to go to Studio One several times a week as though we were taking classes, watching works by Antonioni, Luchino Visconti, Fellini, Godard, Truffaut, Louis Malle, Kurosawa, Mizoguchi Kenji, Kobayashi Masaki, and many other directors then unfamiliar to us. After watching and watching, we wanted to make our own experimental films.

This involved scrimping and saving, buying a Super 8 camera, buying film, writing a script, and scouting the streets and alleys in search of the right scenery. The effect of using a handheld camera was that the footage was jerky, constantly shaking, which could only be described as extremely realistic. My friends all shot films, ten to twenty minutes in length. Pleased, they put on an experimental film exhibition. I didn't go out and shoot a film. In my mind, I compiled a series of dissolving shots—pendulum / cradle / wooden horse / swing—swaying back and forth, but I couldn't lift the camera. It was too heavy. My dream of editing, directing, and shooting a film vanished.

I may not have shot an experimental film, but that didn't mean I didn't conceive of one. A series of shots would appear in my head. The Odessa Steps sequence in Eisenstein's *Battleship Potemkin* is truly a classic montage; arranging the three lions in a different order would have an entirely different meaning. I pondered such questions as: Should a film opt for Renoir's single-shot mise-en-scène, or Eisenstein's style of montage editing?

I saved up some money and bought a 16-mm projector and a small splicer. This type of home splicing machine was really small, like a hole puncher, no bigger than a point-and-shoot camera. You could pick up the film and splice it yourself. If you didn't want a certain section, *chop*! The little machine was sharp and precise, just like Justice Bao Zheng's guillotine that chopped the head off of the heartless and unfaithful Chen Shimei, swiftly cutting the film into two sections in one clean cut. Destroying something was the easiest thing; constructing something was the hard part. You had to join two frames of film, but it was a struggle for the little splicing machine. Special glue was applied to the edges of the frames, then they were stacked so they overlapped. Next they were glued together and pressed firmly. The film would seem secure, but during the projection, suddenly it would break again. This method of stitching was neither how primitive people sewed animal hides nor how modern people sewed clothing—there were no needles, no perforations, no seams, no threads, only adhesive, close encounters of the third kind indeed. The "work" I submitted to the experimental film exhibition was entirely comprised of discarded footage that I'd spliced together, dozens of pieces in total. When projected, after a while, the film would break, then it would be joined back together, and before long, it would break again. Fortunately, those who attended the film exhibition understood the situation; they were patient and didn't complain, unlike the midnight moviegoers who sliced up their seats.

My friend who loves cats and *Peanuts* comics and Truffaut films and Mozart's music doesn't necessarily think about movies while lying in the bath. How were the cosmic creatures and humans spliced together in *Close Encounters of the Third Kind*? Music. There was no need for strings, threads, bones, needles, or glue, and written words didn't work either. Modern and ancient people could splice together written symbols, while space creatures relied on acoustic symbols.

Marble is a cat who belongs to my friend who loves cats. Marble is sesame-colored and marbled all over and loves eating plastic bags. My friend always has to take care to hide the plastic bags at home, or they'll become a delicacy if they come into contact with Marble. All that chewing—I don't understand the taste and appeal of plastic bags, eating them to the point of indigestion, then troubling one's owner to pull them out the tail end. Marble is as naughty as a toddler, and my friend treats Marble like her own child.

According to expert research, any part of the human body, with the exception of hair and nails, can grow a tumor. In the realm of living things, both plants and animals can develop cancer. Cattle, sheep, dogs, cats, fish, shrimp, insects, turtles—there's no exception. I don't know what kind of cancer cats get. Do male cats get intestinal, stomach, liver, or nasopharyngeal cancer? Do female cats get uterine or breast cancer? When a cat develops a malignant tumor, there must be no way to save it. Who will perform surgery on a cat to remove it? Are there hospitals for cats to receive radiation therapy?

If Marble were to get cancer, my friend who loves cats would be at a loss for what to do. I think she'd probably be the first person to advocate for radiation therapy for cats, or she might join forces with a friend named Mai who also loves cats, and Mai's friend Yeung, who may love cats, and a bird-loving friend named Wai who often drinks tieguanyin tea with them, and they'd rally a group of people, and together organize an animal cancer prevention society.

I hope that Marble and my friend who loves cats are happy and healthy, sitting comfortably in a chair and listening to Mozart. Ah, Mozart! The Cultural Centre has opened, and the building's outward appearance seems to have been poorly received. People have voiced various criticisms: It faces the sea but doesn't have windows, which is a waste of a perfectly good sea view; it's oddly shaped, and nowhere near grand enough; it lacks Eastern flavor, and there's no artistic feeling; the color is too pale. My friend who loves cats shared her opinion over the phone. *It's terrible—it looks just like a bathroom*. At different times, in different places, we have different feelings about the bathroom.

THE SWING

JUST PAST six in the morning, there were hardly any pedestrians on the road that led to the swimming pool by the sea. Who'd go swimming so early? Though it would be scorching by the afternoon, it was gradually getting cooler now. I got into a taxi and told the driver to take me to Tai Wan Shan Swimming Pool. Going swimming so early? the driver asked. No, I said, I'm just going to do some exercises in the athletic field next to the swimming pool. The taxi traveled down a desolate road, newly constructed factory buildings on either side, a deserted scene of dust and debris devoid of human activity. The road hadn't been paved yet, and its muddy edges were overrun with weeds and wildflowers. It was a road I knew all too well. Just two months ago, I'd walked it two or three times a week, carrying a backpack with a swimsuit inside. But now I was empty-handed, without a bag, only a wallet and keys stuffed in my pockets.

I hadn't been swimming since September. I kept thinking about the steps leading down into the pool and the lifeguard's large umbrella, but now I couldn't swim—I even had to be careful while taking a shower. I had left the hospital with my chest still bandaged, the back part of my side swollen like a giant gummy candy. After the surgery, the doctor instructed me to move my arm. Even lying in bed, I swung my arm back and forth like a pendulum; I had asked the nurse for an extra pillow, propping it under my arm to elevate it.

The man in "Guan Guan Cry the Ospreys," the first poem of *Book of Songs*, pines for his ideal mate, a virtuous fair maiden, and is unable to sleep at night, tossing and turning, a fate that must have been very painful.[9] But I think he was much more comfortable than I was.

Being able to toss and turn is a blessing—at least the whole body is free to roll around. After my surgery, I couldn't toss and turn. My body could only lie flat. What if I wanted to turn? I could only turn slightly to the left, and I couldn't turn at all to the right. That side was completely numb and swollen, as though the doctor had tied a piece of pork to my back. Patient Number Seven took a pill for her gallbladder. The doctor instructed her to lie in bed for two hours without turning. This was truly torture. After lying there for an hour, she started complaining. Oh, how she envied those who could toss and turn.

The athletic field next to the pool was bustling with people doing exercises early in the morning. They'd arrived by way of a clean asphalt road lined with row after row of beautiful high-rises. There weren't many trees in the field, but because it was by the sea, the air was especially fresh, and the area was spacious. In addition to a large soccer field and two basketball courts, there was also an area to rest, with stone benches and tables. By the sea was a long promenade where people walked and did their morning exercises. This athletic field was a little different from others because it was by the sea, so there was a group of strong swimmers who came here regardless of the season. Entry to the pool cost 10 dollars, but to go everywhere else was free, and behind the athletic field's grandstand, there were changing rooms and restrooms, with fresh water for rinsing off. Moreover, swimming in the sea was certainly more open and freer than in a pool, and seawater didn't have the chemical smell of pool water. Of course, to swim here, you had to have strong swimming skills.

By the shore I often watched people out at sea, watched them swim to far-off places, climb onto a reef, or rest on the steps of a small pier that extended out into the water. I watched some of them run to the changing rooms to fetch fresh water, carrying buckets across the soccer field to the beach to rinse their bodies. They always said it wasn't cold, but those of us watching found the morning wind cool. Men, of course, didn't wear swimsuits. They wore swimming trunks. If a man with breast cancer had undergone surgery and had a long scar on his chest, would he wear a full-body swimsuit from the 1920s?

Maybe it would set off a new trend of nostalgic fashion. Among the strong swimmers, there was a woman who wore a tight-fitting swimsuit; she looked agile and healthy, which I greatly envied. The body beneath that swimsuit must have been in perfect condition, without any flaws or scars. Perhaps she took such happiness for granted. The woman's swimsuit was patterned with a dense cluster of flowers, a combination of many colors. After rinsing her body with fresh water, she merely wiped her wet limbs with a towel, put on some sports clothes, and left with an empty bucket. When she got home, naturally she'd take off her swimsuit and change into other clothing. As for me? I now wore a strange new type of costume that I never needed to take off. It was in the style of pop art, probably designed by a painter like Dalí, and the tailor was, of course, a surgeon.

Since I'd left the hospital, I was constantly in good spirits, as though I had never undergone surgery. Other people had said that their surgical wounds were painful and prevented them from sleeping at night, but I had no such symptoms at all. From the time I was admitted to the hospital until I was discharged, I didn't have a moment of pain. Initially, I thought I was going to suffer, but that turned out not to be the case. The greatest physical pain I'd ever experienced in the course of my life was as a teenager when I had a misaligned tooth extracted, and the few times when I'd eaten something bad and gotten diarrhea. I was extremely fortunate to have undergone surgery without any suffering. There was no pain after surgery, only some inconveniences—for example, being unable to bend my right hand behind my back when showering, or not being able to turn onto the affected side when I slept. In all other aspects, nothing had changed. I could still go shopping, take walks, read books, and eat. My mental state, however, was inevitably different. After all, I was a cancer patient. I looked healthy on the surface, but who could say what problems might be lurking? Such thoughts were truly depressing, and having to face radiation, which scared many people out of their minds, was also rather daunting.

When I left the hospital, it felt as though I'd picked up my own body from the hospital bed and brought it home. Now, it was left to me to take care of it. Before this, I never really knew I had a body. The books I'd read had focused on caring for the soul. As a result, the body was completely set aside, and while my soul had seemingly made no progress, my body had secretly deteriorated. The body is very strange: If it doesn't cause problems, doesn't give you a bit of pain, doesn't give you some stimulation, then you don't pay any attention to it. Ah, I had a body—what on earth had happened to it? Why did a tumor grow? There are many causes of cancer. Some are caused by environmental pollution, some by genetic factors, some by toxins in food. I couldn't control the environment; it depended on the collective efforts of everyone in society. Genetic factors were also beyond my control. If my parents and ancestors had such genes, then I could only accept my fate. In fact, neither my mother nor either grandmother had ever had any history of breast cancer. My paternal grandmother died of a uterine tumor. Might it have been cancer? This happened several decades ago, and it was now impossible to investigate. None of my female cousins had cancer, so the impact of genetic factors probably wasn't significant.

Well, then it had to have been food. Yes, I was sure that food had caused my cancer. Of course, I knew that diet affected health, that fatty foods can lead to heart disease and hypertension, and that drinking coffee stimulates the mind—this is all very basic common sense. And so I didn't drink alcohol, coffee, or soda, and I didn't smoke. I also avoided fried foods of any kind. Given all of this, how did I end up with a tumor? One reason occurred to me: I had a sweet tooth. I loved eating desserts. When celebrating Lunar New Year at home, I ate copious amounts of chocolates, candied lotus seeds, and eight-treasure rice. Regardless of whose birthday it was, I was the one who ended up in charge of the birthday cake. When dining out at buffets, I ate little else, mainly enjoying a mountain of cake. The desserts I ate on a regular basis were even greater in number. In recent years, I hadn't been going to work, so in my spare time at home, I ate red bean porridge, glutinous rice cakes, sesame paste, and tofu pudding. All of this eating made me chubby. My friends knew I had a sweet tooth. At every gathering, they left me double portions of tong sui dessert soup. A friend from Taiwan invited me to tea, and knowing I had a sweet tooth, insisted that I have cake. Alas, you are what you eat. I'd eaten so many sweets, and all those deadly sugars and fats had accumulated and formed a tumor.

Of course, the world is full of people with a sweet tooth. Every year, every month, Germans and Americans consume great amounts of chocolate and ice cream, but not everyone ends up with breast cancer. It also has to do with one's age and life history. I had just reached the age at which the disease was most prevalent, plus I'd never been married or given birth to children or breastfed a baby, and my hormones were at an unbalanced stage. Add to these factors all of those sweets—would it not make the cancer cells ecstatic? As Goethe supposedly put it: By forty, you have the face you deserve. By forty, one must of course also take responsibility for one's own health. After leaving the hospital, the first thing I resolved to do was give up sweets.

My friends advised me to take up tai chi, since I was temporarily unable to swim, and daily walks didn't count as aerobic exercise. I inquired at the Urban Council Leisure and Sports Department, but the tai chi classes in the parks near my home all started in August, which didn't work for me. However, the new class at the seaside athletic field just happened to start on October 1, and the tuition was cheap, only 40 dollars for three months. But the real cost was much more, because the journey from my home was quite far and circuitous. I could take a bus, then walk for fifteen minutes, or I could travel ten minutes there by taxi. The instructor was middle-aged, perhaps in his fifties. He taught the Wu style, which was relatively easy to learn, and the horse stance, one of the fundamental postures, didn't have to be too strenuous. The tai chi classes run by the Urban Council generally preferred the Wu style, maybe because the instructors all obtained their teaching licenses from the same tai chi association, or maybe because many of the people learning tai chi were older.

Wu-style tai chi suited me perfectly. The small-frame routine, with its emphasis on subtle, compact movements, was just the type of nonstrenuous aerobic exercise that I needed. The instructor also taught slowly, introducing one or two moves at a time, with most of the class devoted to practice. There were more than twenty students in total, practicing together, which was nice; the atmosphere was altogether very pleasant. It was supposed to start at seven. At seven, there were often only three or four early birds there, then people arrived one by one, some even half an hour late. Perhaps it was because when the weather was chilly, they were reluctant to get out of bed. Most people wore workout gear, but some wore dress shirts, suit pants, and leather shoes, because they went to work after tai chi. The instructor took attendance every day, and there were always a few absences. Some people missed too many classes and couldn't keep up, so they simply stopped coming.

The class took place three times a week, an hour each session. I never missed class, because I had to prioritize my health. In the beginning, I relied on an alarm clock to wake me. Initially, I didn't want to get out of bed, but gradually, I woke on my own without needing an alarm. At daybreak, I heard the birds chirping. These birds were the best clocks—their chirping was in sync with the seasons and the sunlight, chirping earlier in the summer and later in winter. If I didn't hear the birds, I gathered it was raining. After each class, our instructor went home right away because he also had to go to work. Later, we learned he had a job at the post office. Some classmates saw him when they went to buy stamps. Among my classmates, there were several housewives who didn't go to work. They got up early in the morning with their children, and when their children went to school, they came to learn tai chi. After the instructor left, they hung around the athletic field, discussing their children's homework and their own health. Some of the housewives studied tai chi for health reasons. If they weren't suffering from backaches, then their bodies were generally frail. They often saw many doctors, and chatted about various illnesses. One very overweight classmate studied tai chi in the hopes of losing weight, but you can't lose weight by doing tai chi. Perhaps she ended up disappointed. I, however, felt great. Regularly practicing tai chi in the athletic field was very relaxing. Lingering by the sea among the trees and flowers, taking in the fresh air, was the best part of my morning routine. Sometimes when it rained, I couldn't practice tai chi, and I felt as though something was missing, as if a day without tai chi was like a day without eating.

In the middle of the rest area and the seaside promenade, there was a small playground with bouncy horses, a jungle gym, and swings. This early, the children hadn't yet come to play by the sea, so the swings became the adults' cradles. These were sturdy swings, capable of supporting an adult's weight. They didn't swing high but swayed low to the ground. I sat on one, watching the sea gently ripple, watching the distant ferries, cargo ships, and buildings on the other shore in the hazy dawn light gradually becoming clear and bright. The sun was ever so golden, floating among the buildings, not yet radiating daggers of light.

The TV show I had watched last night featured another character dying of cancer, which is the easiest way to make a character disappear. There's no need to act out the illness or describe it in detail—simply mention that cancer has been diagnosed, and before long, the character is gone. This time, the sick character was the female protagonist's mother. The show wanted to leave the heroine all alone, beset by tragedy, so they had her mother succumb to cancer. In fact, it wasn't so bad, because the woman was a good and honest, kindhearted elder. In many TV series, the characters who get cancer are big drug lords or heinous villains, and it seems like some sort of cosmic retribution. Illness is linked with things like feng shui and karma. It's unfortunate enough to get sick, but having to deal with such societal discrimination on top of it is both absurd and lamentable.

I used to love swinging. On the swings, I'd think about all the happy scenes from my childhood, as if they were part of a Schumann suite. But now, sitting on the swing, what came to mind was Kurosawa's *Ikiru*. I thought of the old man with terminal stomach cancer, sitting on a swing in a children's park, singing:

> Life is fleeting
> Fall in love, maidens
> While your crimson lips haven't yet faded

> While you can still love—
> For there is no tomorrow

There is a stinking cesspool of mosquito-infested, stagnant water in the neighborhood of Kuroe. Children who drink water from it develop rashes, and people have to endure the cesspool's stench. Some women went to the Public Affairs Department to file a complaint, hoping the cesspool could be turned into a children's park and athletic field. There is a notice on the information counter at the Public Affairs Department that reads: THIS COUNTER IS SET UP FOR YOU. YOU CAN CONTACT CITY HALL THROUGH THIS COUNTER. INQUIRIES AND COMPLAINTS ARE ALL WELCOME. This is, of course, just bureaucratic language. The public affairs staff member directs the women to the Public Works Department.

When they arrive at the office of the Public Works Department, the staff member says that this matter falls under the jurisdiction of the Parks Department.

The Parks Department says it seems to be related to hygiene.

The Health Department instructs them to go to the Environmental Sanitation Department.

The Environmental Sanitation Department tells the women they need to go to the Department of Prevention.

As soon as the person at the Department of Prevention hears the word "mosquito," the women are sent to the Department of Infectious Diseases.

The Department of Infectious Diseases staff member swats a fly, directing them to the Sewage Department.

The Sewage Department says that at present, there's a road passing though there, so they need the approval of the Roads Department.

The Roads Department states that the policy of the City Planning Department is still to be determined.

The City Planning Department says that the Fire Department wants to reclaim the area due to an inadequate water supply.

The Fire Department says this is entirely nonsense—they don't need dirty water.

So they go to the Education Department in search of a child welfare officer, who says to go find a city council member.

The city council member personally introduces them to the deputy mayor.

The deputy mayor says he is delighted that citizens are so enthusiastic about making complaints, and the Public Affairs Department has been established precisely for this purpose. Thus, he tells them to go to the Public Affairs Department.

The old section chief afflicted with stomach cancer is like a player in a game of bureaucratic soccer, where for more than twenty years, tasks have been kicked around and dropped. Every day seems busy, but in fact, nothing is accomplished at all. To apply for a new wastebasket, the number of pages of the application you would have to write would be enough to fill said wastebasket. Doing nothing is the rule of survival in this bureaucratic structure. Facing death, the cancer-afflicted section chief can break the rules, and he runs around, trying to get things done; in the end, the stinking cesspool in Kuroe becomes a children's park. On the night he dies, he sits on a swing in the park, singing. The film's original title is *Ikiru: To Live*. The local Hong Kong translation is *Ode to Leaving Behind a Good Name*. The original title is better. Living in the world should entail doing something good for the community, no matter how small. What does it matter whether one leaves behind a good name?

Issues between people, and issues within ourselves, likewise often display a sort of passing-the-ball attitude. When cancer arrives, various departments within society pass the buck, as do the organs in our body—there isn't a single entity willing to question themselves, to take responsibility. What's the payoff for taking on the responsibility? Sitting on the swing, I contemplated these things, contemplated what I should do. Could I still donate blood to others? Were my corneas and kidneys suitable for transplantation to people in need? Probably no one would even want them. There have been cases where doctors have transplanted kidneys from deceased individuals to patients, and though the deceased had cancer cells in their bodies, they had never developed the disease. However, after transplantation, these cancer cells unexpectedly became active and proliferated in the recipients' bodies. What should those of us with cancer do for the world? I think the first thing we should do is to live life to the fullest. Since October 1989, I've become a file that contains my medical records and treatment process in the oncology unit of the Sha Tin Public Hospital. This file can serve as research material: How long can a patient with breast cancer live? What are the effects of radiation therapy? When is the cancer likely to recur? Or perhaps it'll never recur at all, no metastasis, only good health, effective medication, and so on. Such a file, along with those of other patients, can be used to calculate the incidence rate, treatment efficacy, and survival rate of breast cancer in Hong Kong, China, and East Asia, serving as research material for the World Cancer Society. People with cancer should strive to live life to the fullest. Any taboos should be broken through; any illnesses should be treated. Cooperation between patients and doctors can inspire the medical community, and also bring hope to others living with cancer.

THINGS THAT ARE FOOLISH

WHEN I found the lump, I mistook it for hives, which I periodically developed here and there. And so, following an old remedy, I cleaned the area with soap and hot water and dabbed on some peppermint oil. In fact, if you have a growth elsewhere on your body, you can use a hot compress and apply a medicinal oil, but for breast lumps, it's best not to disturb them, and by all means do not squeeze them hard. If it's a benign tumor, that's fine, but if it's malignant, doing so could provoke changes.

I developed a lump in my breast. I was remiss not to pay close attention to its appearance and characteristics. Hives usually itch and tend to be on the surface of the skin, whereas tumors are neither itchy nor painful, buried deep beneath the surface of the skin, adhering to internal tissues. If you encounter this kind of lump, you should see a doctor at once, or even consult two or more doctors.

Having developed a lump, I drank mung bean soup, thinking it could help detoxify my body. Didn't the renowned sixteenth-century pharmacologist Li Shizhen claim that mung bean soup could eliminate heat and toxins? How reckless to mischaracterize Li Shizhen this way! What Li Shizhen actually said about mung bean soup was that it could remove toxins in the body that have accumulated from eating toxic foods, not toxins from tumors. Moreover, for this kind of detoxification, there are other medicinal formulations, depending on the clinical symptoms. Drinking mung bean soup for two weeks had absolutely zero effect on me. Mung bean soup can neither induce abortions in naive girls nor dissolve tumors in ignorant women.

Because of the lump, I went to see a surgeon, who said he wanted to cut it out and test it. I immediately nodded in agreement. In fact, we should think thrice before doing anything major that requires surgery or excising part of the body—why place so much trust in a single doctor? Plus, I didn't know this doctor at all. I didn't know a single thing about his medical skills and ethics. Nowadays, doctors who are raking in the big bucks are everywhere. Surgery is no joke. If you have a lump in your breast, you should get examined by multiple doctors, keep calm, and find a qualified surgeon to do the procedure.

I didn't expect a public hospital to have an excellent oncology unit for diagnosis and treatment. Generally the wait time isn't long for tumors, and surgery can be done soon. Of course, some people may be biased against public hospitals, assuming that the surgery may be performed by interns, and so they go to private hospitals. Medical expenses in private hospitals are fifty times higher than those in public hospitals. A patient who had a tumor excised at a public hospital and stayed there for ten days paid less than 300 dollars. I spent a week in a private hospital and paid more than 10,000 dollars, and dropped another 1,000 dollars on tamoxifen.

Ah Kin said she lost five pounds after her tumor was removed. As soon as I heard this, I scrambled to eat more meals and pack on some weight before my surgery. As a result, everyone else who had had surgery had lost weight, and I was the only one who had gained. I was smug, thinking I was so clever. Little did I know that, in fact, I was overweight, with slightly elevated blood pressure, and shouldn't have gained weight. Surgery should have been an opportunity to lose a few pounds. Moreover, the food I was stuffing my face with before surgery, such as chicken drumsticks, contained a lot of fat, which wasn't good for my body.

For my first meal at home after surgery, I went to the kitchen to get clean chopsticks so I could serve myself food from the shared dishes. My family members glared at me and scolded me. Cancer isn't contagious, like tuberculosis—there's no need for special serving chopsticks. And so, I ended up using my own chopsticks as before.

Upon learning that I had a malignant tumor, I assumed I needed to prepare for my funeral. This was due to my own ignorance about cancer. With prompt treatment, the survival rate for early-stage cancers is as high as 90 percent. Several friends told me that their mother or aunt had been diagnosed with breast cancer when they were in their fifties, and they were still alive and healthy well into their seventies. Because of my illness, I threw away a lot of things, as though they also were tumors. The most regrettable items were books. I must have tossed half of them. Nowadays, when I browse bookstores, I can't find replacements for most of the discarded titles. How foolish I was, but it's too late for regrets.

Don't have the time and interest to read large chunks of long-winded text, and wondering if there are other short chapters like this one? Please turn to "Non-Stories" on page 101.

BUTCHER DING

I HAD NEVER thought about taking up the sword; the word "sword" always made me think of unconventional individuals with extraordinary abilities. The swordsmen and swordswomen in literary chronicles are not only proficient in swordsmanship but also capable of incredible feats, such as leaping across rooftops and scaling walls. Some of them are even skilled in sorcery and can use poison to melt bones. Swordsmen and swordswomen are respected because they uplift the weak and overthrow the strong, but in fact, most of them are merely assassins, ancient "terminators" (like in the science-fiction film), loyal only to their masters.

I finally took up the sword because of my instructor. After I underwent surgery, my friends urged me to learn tai chi, so three times a week, I went to a seaside athletic field relatively far from home to study with a tai chi practitioner. It was a class with more than ten students, including young people in their twenties and even elderly people in their seventies—surprisingly, women made up half the class. The instructor arrived early. While others were reluctant to leave dreamland, he'd already been demonstrating his sword and knife skills on the field. The early arrivals could witness his martial prowess. His knife techniques were swift and fierce, stirring up the air with swishing sounds; when he wielded the sword, however, it seemed to carry a blend of strength and softness, a unique gracefulness. If the sword were gendered, as French words are, it probably would have originated as masculine and gradually turned feminine, in contrast to the knife.

Some of my classmates wanted to learn other, additional martial arts after studying one set of tai chi forms for half a year—every class simply involved repeated practice. The instructor was pleased and willing to teach us after class. Anyone who had time to stay could learn at no extra charge. The majority of those wanting to learn the sword and knife were women. The instructor said women were particularly well-suited to learn the sword for two reasons: One, it was elegant, and two, it wasn't overly intense. And so, I started learning the sword, move by move. Tai chi boxing and tai chi sword were originally the twin sisters of Chinese martial arts. If I didn't perform well, it became a gentle exercise, but done beautifully, it was a dance.

I never expected that tai chi sword would become a special type of physical therapy for me. After my surgery, my arm and ribs would swell, which could only be alleviated through constant movement. After studying tai chi for half a year, I could move my arm freely, but sometimes it still swelled up. Surprisingly, practicing with the sword helped heal the swelling. A few times when it rained and I couldn't practice, my arm gradually swelled up again. From then on, I didn't dare to neglect it and was diligent in my practice, and feeling great.

When the Tang poet Du Fu was five years old, he watched Lady Gongsun perform a sword dance in the Jiangnan region. Fifty years later, he saw her apprentice, Twelfth Lady Li, perform in Sichuan. "Sword dance" is the name of a type of martial dance. Did they hold swords in their hands? It seems like there are swords, and double-edged swords at that, casting intertwined and intermittent glimmers of light in Du Fu's poem:

> Flashing like a thousand suns shot down by Archer Yi
> Lofty like a group of gods soaring with dragon teams
> Advancing like a thunderbolt rumbling with rage
> Halting like the streams and seas freezing into a clear gleam[10]

Du Fu truly wields the pen like a sword, then uses the sword to elicit the feelings of the individual and even of the country. As the scholar Wang Sishi says: "Seeing the sword dance recalls past wounds—'bringing up matters evokes deep feelings.'" However, Wang Sishi then concludes: "Otherwise, it's just a dancing girl, hardly worth shaking his pen over."[11] There are always such interpretations full of bias.

There seem to be no images of sword dances in ancient Chinese paintings. However, there is a North Korean woodblock print where, upon closer examination, what the woman holds in her hand appears to be not a sword but a knife, single-edged, kept close to the body; conversely, the sword is double-edged and must be wielded away from the body—otherwise, you could easily cut yourself. The Qing dynasty artist Jiang Rong did paint a noblewoman performing a sword dance, but unfortunately, the long sword hangs from her waist and isn't held in her hand at all. In fiction, there is a woman named Zhao from the Wei and Jin dynasties who is skilled at wielding the sword. The text doesn't specify what type of sword she uses, but even with a bamboo stalk she is able to showcase her exceptional abilities. Swordsmen and swordswomen in modern novels often use flying swords, which can even give off light—gold, silver, blue, and yellow. The depth of the swordsmanship can be discerned by the color of the light. Swordsmen and swordswomen can also fly with their swords, which would make a great scene in a science-fiction film. In the park at night, I often see a man demonstrating the sword, flashing silver in the moonlight. On the evening of the Mid-Autumn Festival, the park is at its liveliest, with many children brandishing battery-powered lightsabers and reenacting *The Empire Strikes Back*, the last sword dance of the twentieth century.

Of the sword dances I've seen, the one I admire the most is from a video recording of the opera *Farewell My Concubine*, in which Mei Lanfang dances with a pair of swords that flit like butterflies. The two swords are adorned with long silk tassels, which makes it more difficult, because if the dance isn't performed well, the silk tassels can become entangled, locking the swords in place. I didn't have a precious sword—all I had was a series of rusty iron pieces that could be extended or shortened at will. The advantage was that my sword was easy to carry, just like a retractable umbrella. Carrying a long sword on the street is an extremely conspicuous affair. A modern-day General Han

Xin might face fewer humiliations from thugs, but might also be stopped by the police and asked for identification, accused of carrying a dangerous weapon.

Every Tuesday, Thursday, and Saturday I went to the distant athletic field by the sea to practice the sword with my instructor. The other days, I practiced on my own in the park near my building. No matter how early I got up, there was always someone doing morning exercises in the park, always someone who had arrived earlier than me. If there were military roles to be assigned, I certainly wouldn't have played the part of the famed strategist Zhang Liang.[12] When did these early birds arrive? Four or five in the morning? Sometimes a group of teenagers hung around the park, huddled together and leaning against tree trunks, with their soda cans and plastic water bottles strewn all over the ground. They weren't early birds but rather nightingales who hadn't returned to their nests the previous evening, having spent all night in the park.

Early mornings in the park, there were very few young people and not a single child. The majority were elderly people, several doing gentle exercises together, seven or eight practicing a simple form of boxing. There were also those who jogged at a leisurely pace, faces glistening with sweat and panting, which made me concerned for their well-being. Of course, exercise is beneficial, but strenuous exercise may be harmful to the body, especially for those over the age of forty. Most people in the park were around sixty, their hair white. Some walked, and some did deep-breathing exercises, making me feel peaceful and serene.

In addition to the elderly, there were quite a few sick people in the park as well. Every day, an elderly woman in a wheelchair was brought to the park by her son and daughter-in-law. Because they came every day, they were familiar with many people. The group of women who did gentle exercises often chatted among themselves: What a dutiful son—she must have accumulated good karma over many lifetimes. Another added: It's rare to have such a virtuous daughter-in-law. Then they shared stories about their own family affairs—children, daughters-in-law, and the like. The wheelchair would enter through the park gate, be rolled toward the other end of the flower-lined path of the athletic field, and stop. The elderly woman, supported by her daughter-in-law, would get out of the chair and take careful steps.

It was evident that the person in the wheelchair was ill, but illness isn't always as clear as day. That person who holds the "golden rooster standing on one leg" stance for a full five minutes might have kidney problems. This overweight middle-aged person, bending over with their protruding belly, might have heart disease. Take me, for example: Who could tell I was a cancer patient? People are like this, neglecting their health in their daily lives, but once they fall ill, they panic and focus on exercising.

There were also people practicing tai chi in the park. With just one move such as "cloud hands," you could probably determine which school of tai chi they belonged to. No matter the school, I always watched for a while. This person's movements were jerky, like the stop-motion dance of a wooden puppet. This person flowed smoothly and seamlessly, reminiscent of a graceful ballet dancer. I was a beginner. I knew my own performance wasn't up to par, but where else could I practice, if not in the park? I had to hide in a secluded corner to practice. It was hard to escape the public eye, but I didn't mind. It occurred to me that Lady Gongsun was also a folk dancer, performing on the streets and in the squares. With such impressive skills, of course she attracted a crowd of onlookers, some seated, some standing, and thus in the eyes of young Du Fu "the spectators were like mountains." A set of tai chi, if performed quickly, took twenty minutes; if slowly, half an hour. I always performed it slowly: I had no choice but to go slow, because if I were to do it any faster, I'd easily lose my breath.

After I finished, I'd take a break for a bit, then practice the sword. Since I started learning tai chi, every time I went to the park, I carried more and more things. At first, I went empty-handed, then I carried a small cloth bag with a light jacket inside, and gradually I added an umbrella, then later a thermos of water, and finally, a sword. Not to mention the towel and wallet in my pockets. Each time I arrived at the park, I found a suitable spot, then hung my small cloth bag on the chain-link fence.

After I finished exercising, I was in no hurry to go home. It was so early, what would I do at home—go back to bed? No, taking a stroll in the park was much better. The azaleas were in full bloom, a swath of purple, pink, and white along the fence, singing of the brilliant spring day. Bit by bit, the sky would become brighter and whiter, the sun would emerge, and soon light would shine on the treetops, marking another clear day. At this time of day, the air was the freshest, the flowers and grass emitting sweet smells. I took a walk along the small path between the bushes, letting my lungs soak it all in.

Across the road at the back of the park, there were two sets of buildings with completely different appearances. The one on the right was more than ten stories tall. It wasn't a residential building, but instead consisted of two huge gas drums, black cylindrical structures, with steel ladders positioned beside them that curved and spiraled upward, much like a maze in a picture. All day long, the drums emitted a heavy mechanical noise, groaning like a wounded beast even into the night. Once it was dark, the ladder paths were lit by rows of vertical and horizontal white neon tubes, casting a ghastly pale light.

To the left of the gas drums, there was a row of silent low-rise buildings, just two or three stories high, grayish-yellow in color. This presence was accompanied by an odor, a murky, foul stench that persisted over the years, as though the smell were a tangible, transparent object. Nearby residents lived with this odor. The row of low-rise buildings that occupied half of the long street was the government slaughterhouse. The gas drums and slaughterhouse were tall and short neighbors, seemingly unrelated, but they subtly echoed each other. Standing on the park's lush green grass and gazing into the distance, the drums reminded me of the gas chambers of the Nazi concentration camps during World War II. People deemed "inferior" and "impure" were marched into the gas chambers one by one, and transformed into wisps of smoke; such slaughter was nearly devoid of any trace of blood.

I don't know how cattle are slaughtered in the slaughterhouse. Nepalese Gurkha soldiers slaughter cows during New Year celebrations, beheading them with curved daggers, an occasion to flaunt their heroic prowess. I believe there are no such warriors in the slaughterhouse. The slaughterhouse kills numerous cattle on a daily basis. It is said that they use guns to shoot the cattle in the head, then hang them on moving hooks for bloodletting and butchering. The internal organs are displayed beside the hanging cattle carcass from which it came, for the health inspectors to check. Those that aren't diseased will be taken to the market to be sold. I heard about a new machine that strips the entire layer of skin from the cow that's placed inside it, spitting out bloody beef. I dare not imagine what the beef looks like. At street corners and the ends of alleys, there are snake shops, and in the markets, frogs, partridges, and softshell turtles, stripped of their skin and still wriggling ceaselessly. There are always people from the older generation who make up strange stories, saying a butcher was mistakenly rolled into a machine, skinned alive, and spat out.

Likewise, I have no idea how to slaughter a pig. I only know the traditional method, where a pig is tied to a wooden stool, and the butcher strikes with a knife, splitting open the pig from its throat all the way to its belly. Naturally, there are also rumors about the butcher who accidentally cuts open his own intestines. It's all a misfortune of life. Standing in the park, separated from the buildings by the roaring traffic on the road, I never heard gunshots ring out from the slaughterhouse, nor the howls of pigs and cattle. Did residents who lived near the slaughterhouse hear these things? Presumably not, as it appeared there were no complaints from readers in the letters to the editor of the paper or on the TV program *Citizen Voices*. So then, slaughtering thousands of animals in broad daylight was a quiet business. My friend who loves cats wrote that the most tragic film, to her mind, is Robert Bresson's *Au Hasard Balthazar*, inspired by Dostoyevsky. In the end, after the donkey is shot, it shudders and walks into the midst of a flock of sheep, sitting there quietly, with the sky above and the earth below; it silently awaits its final moment. She watched the film twice, always wanting to cry out loud, but was unable to do so. Whenever she thought about it, the ending still pained her. The towering gas drums were black, while the side of the slaughterhouse facing the park had eroded to a dirt-yellow color over the years. Every day it was washed, water gushing out, all the slaughter seeming to spread continuously from the darkness in every direction.

Standing in the park one morning, I saw an unusual sight: a cow and calf taking a stroll on the grassy slope outside the iron fence of the slaughterhouse. The cow stood there dazed, while the calf wagged its tail, bowing its head to graze. What a heartwarming pastoral image of mother and child. Who would know that on the other side of the iron fence was a slaughterhouse? Life and death were separated by a mere fence. The cow was probably brought to the slaughterhouse already pregnant and was permitted to give birth, resulting in the calf, but would this change their future fates?

There is a saying that cows cry when facing their executioners. It seems that such incidents have also happened in the slaughterhouse. A cow being led to slaughter charged out of the narrow road and ran into the courtyard. No matter how much it was tugged and pulled, it refused to budge, and suddenly the cow knelt down and shed tears. The slaughterhouse staff all said: Just spare this one. But the boss didn't agree. This was a slaughterhouse, not a pasture; they continued leading the cow up the sloping narrow path, and it wasn't long before the cow was suspended on the hoist, slowly gliding down. There's more to the story: Things didn't go so well in the end for the boss. Of course, some cows are lucky. A while ago, there was another crying cow, but it was pardoned and sent to a Daoist temple to live out its remaining years, and it even became an attraction for visitors. The writer Qian Zhongshu once joked that doctors are also a kind of butcher, but in my opinion, sometimes butchers are also doctors.

Spanish bullfighting is really and truly bulls fighting. It's bulls resisting the curse of their fate, the struggle of life. The bulls cannot vanquish the spears, swords, and various opponents who take turns wearing them down, and they die having exhausted their strength. Ordinary cows have no room for a final battle and can only await their inevitable demise. Do the cows destined for slaughter possess a sixth sense? No one cares about the cows' feelings. If the world were divided only into two categories, those who slaughter and those who are slaughtered, I'd still choose to be slaughtered.

In Zhuangzi's writing, the cow is almost invisible. What we see is Butcher Ding.[13] Zhuangzi says that after he perfects his skills, he doesn't need to use his eyes to see the cow. He understands it intuitively, relying on the principals of nature, following its inherent way, slaughtering a complicated cow with ease, like a cellist playing a concert with closed eyes. It's strange—while I was lying in the operating room, seeing the surgeon donning a white robe and green cap, I suddenly thought he was Butcher Ding. I also finally grasped the second half of Du Fu's line "the spectators were like mountains, their color sapped away." Was he an ordinary butcher who replaced his knife every month, or a skilled butcher who only replaced his knife once a year? In his mind, was I a person, or was I just a tumor?

Waiting in the hospital bed for nearly fifteen minutes, all I could think about was butchering a cow. The doctors and nurses all showed up early, but the anesthesiologist was missing. There must have been a traffic jam—he charged in fifteen minutes late. This time, I saw the anesthesiologist's appearance: He was short and stout, like the actor Cantinflas in the film *Around the World in 80 Days*. Ah, Passepartout was present—we could start the show.

Beforehand, the nurse had applied adhesive tape to my legs and helped me slide out of the sleeves. I heard the doctor request a "drip pan," using the English words. I didn't know what that was. Once the anesthesiologist arrived, the surgery began soon after. I wasn't the least bit afraid. I only heard the anesthesiologist say: I'm going to give you anesthesia, and you'll sleep for a while. I said, Okay. He injected the needle with the IV into my wrist and placed an oxygen mask on me. I took a few breaths, still aware of everything. Someone drew a map on my chest. Something was icy cold—possibly the medicine. Oh no! They were going to cut open my chest, but I was still conscious! I wanted to speak, but I couldn't make a sound. I tried gesturing with my hands and feet, but my hands and feet didn't get the memo and wouldn't move. Everything failed. And so, I tried blinking my eyes to indicate that *no, no*, I was still conscious. Whew, they hadn't started operating at that moment. When I blinked again, I was already lying in my hospital bed. It was four hours later. The surgery had taken two hours.

Who invented anesthesia? It's nothing short of a lifesaver for patients. Think about the immense courage and endurance it takes for Guan Yu to endure bone-scraping treatment in the historical novel the *Romance of the Three Kingdoms*, or for Cao Cao to have his head opened and brain operated on, but this of course is all in the realm of fiction. However, the real-life Hua Tuo invented the powdered anesthetic mafeisan more than seventeen hundred years ago. He had his patients ingest it with alcohol and fall into a deep sleep before performing surgery on them. How remarkable. When the anesthesia took effect, I didn't feel anything at all. Was this what death is like? Well then, perhaps death is an extremely comfortable thing. If a person can depart in such a way, what's wrong with it? Some time ago, there was the unfortunate case of a patient who died during surgery due to the incorrect use of an oxygen tank. I think that if I were in that situation, I wouldn't feel regret; having no feeling would be much better than feeling anything, because once you start to feel something, it's mostly pain.

In the operating room, for several hours, I had no awareness at all. During this time, the doctors and nurses must have been busy: sterilizing the skin, making an irregular fusiform incision around the breast, first cutting the epidermis and then cutting the dermis, separating the skin flap, clamping the subcutaneous tissue with hemostatic forceps, covering and protecting the skin flap with moist gauze pads, cutting and ligating at the same time, dealing with veins, arteries, and nerves, cutting off the pectoral muscle, dissecting the axillary vein and removing the axillary lymph nodes, cutting the breast tissue, removing the surgical specimen, stopping the wound from bleeding, thoroughly irrigating the wound, inserting a drainage tube, connecting a negative pressure suction tube, then suturing the skin. Ah yes, the patient's condition was very good—no need for a blood transfusion or skin grafting.

In the operating room, was the doctor cutting and slicing with his scalpel in silence, focusing on the task at hand, or was he talking and laughing, in an almost dance-like rhythm? My hunch is he was talking and laughing. Amputating a breast is not major surgery. There aren't a lot of intestines involved. My younger sister also had a small tumor. It was benign, and as it was only a minor procedure, she didn't need anesthesia. She kept her eyes open and watched the doctor perform the surgery, witnessing the blood, needle, and thread through the mirror, how the doctor sewed stitch by stitch, tied a knot, sewed again, then tied another knot. My sister is gutsy—I'm sure I wouldn't have dared to look.

My friend told me that when he was a child, while goofing off playing soccer, he fell and split open his lip. He went to the doctor and received five or six stitches, without any anesthetic, simply observing the doctor and nurse chatting about weekend programs while stitching him up, a single thread, pierced downward, pulled out, drawn across, bent down, making a stitch, tugged taut. My friend became a leather shoe. He believes that if a surgeon were ever to lose their job, they could easily change careers and become a cobbler.

Our family doctor, who'd emigrated and wouldn't return for half a year, might be surprised to see my condition. He'd treated me before he left. Other than slightly high blood pressure, I'd still been in fairly good health. In medical school, our family doctor studied both internal medicine and surgery, but he rarely performed surgical procedures, almost never, because he was left-handed and found it inconvenient. He enjoyed playing the piano in his free time, going to the horse track on weekends. When he performed surgeries, what went through his mind—which horse would cross the finish line first, or the steady rhythm of baroque music?

Many doctors are fond of music and can play an instrument or two. Recently, a group of music-loving doctors formed an orchestral group. Because they didn't have a flute player, they only formed a string ensemble, actively practicing "Greensleeves" to raise money for patients in Nam Long Hospital. Hearing the name Nam Long Hospital is alarming for cancer patients, as it's a convalescent hospital for patients with terminal cancer. Although it's referred to as a place for convalescence, in reality, it serves as a gateway to another journey: the afterlife. For terminal cancer patients, doctors often have nothing left to say, so they pay tribute with music, raising funds for the hospital, making patients' journeys a little more comfortable. This also provides additional funding for the research center to help save those who are sick and those who may become sick.

Did the doctor who operated on me also love music? We were such strangers to each other—he didn't know me, and I didn't know him, yet my life was in his hands, and I had to trust him. What went through his mind while he was performing my surgery? In his eyes, was I a whole cow, or just some cow bones, tendons, and flesh? The anesthesia was truly marvelous. When things turned gory, I was suddenly absent. For me, surgery was just like Zhuangzi's tale "Essentials of Nourishing Life," about Butcher Ding cutting up a cow—I saw only Butcher Ding but not the cow. Before I had a chance to see or feel the blade, the doctor had wiped it clean and safely stored it away. After writing about Butcher Ding, Zhuangzi went on to write fifty words about the one-footed Commander of the Right. I used to think that this was a disjointed style of writing. What was the connection between butchering a cow and a limping foot? Reading it now, I feel I have a deeper understanding than others might. Wholeness or deficiencies of the physical body, regardless of whether innate or human-made, indeed do not matter.

Was the cow that Butcher Ding cut up a living cow, its four feet bound, unable to move? Was it conscious? At that time, of course, there was no anesthesia. Did the cow cry out? Zhuangzi didn't address these details. In the writings of this philosopher who saw unity with all things, the cow is inevitably an objectified alien being. As for the bull in the bullfighting arena, it certainly suffers. The mountain-like spectators can see the bull's struggles. The cruelty of bullfighting lies not in the bull's fated death but in the prolonged process of suffering. Where are the voices of the Society for the Prevention of Cruelty to Animals?

Sunlight shone down on the grass. It was another clear spring day. Hallelujah, I was still alive. I carried the small cloth bag home, the iron sword clanging inside. Might the sword of decisive battles and the sword used to pierce bulls someday become part of a national sword dance?

CRABS

EVERY autumn, my friends and I get together to hike in the country, admire the lanterns of the Mid-Autumn Festival, go mountain climbing during the Double Ninth Festival, and so on. There are also two special activities we always do: eating snake and eating crab. The former is relatively simple—we find and join an organized snake banquet. Our group occupies one of the dozens of tables that fill the floor of the restaurant holding the banquet. Two bottles of medicinal wine are placed on the table, and a large dish of snake soup is always served first. Everyone has two bowls of it, and before we know it, our bellies are half full, our faces flushed with warmth. In truth, we don't really care about eating; we just want to come together and talk, so we find reasons like these to gather. We meet face-to-face twice a month. Eating is secondary; the main focus is our conversations. Most of us live in different neighborhoods and have to go to work every day, so just a few of us meet up regularly for coffee or beer. Only the snake banquet draws the whole group together. When we're all there, it's certainly lively, everyone gathered around the dining table, with black goat, softshell turtle, stir-fried snake slivers, and sticky rice, plus wild game—sometimes there's even muntjac venison. Cantonese people truly are barbarians when it comes to eating. What can't we stomach? While eating snake is a festive affair, the banquet is, after all, in a public place, which doesn't compare to the comfort of being at a friend's home. Thus, all things considered, we're more enthusiastic about eating crab.

Come autumn, my friends and I always indulge in a few crab feasts. Abiding by the old saying "females in the ninth month, males in the tenth month," in September, we eat female crabs, and male crabs in October.[14] We also follow the tradition of incorporating a few chrysanthemum flowers, just like others do. The crab banquet is, of course, another large gathering of more than ten people. We first coordinate over the phone to set a date, choosing a weekend or holiday. We head out at dusk, in groups on various routes, to gather our provisions. Some of us select and buy the crabs, purchasing four or five kilos of them, along with perilla leaves; others buy wine—one rice, one a high-grade huadiao; still others buy dried tofu, brown sugar, ginger, scallions, and other ingredients.

Each home offers a unique charm, depending on which friend is hosting our feast. Some friends' apartments are spacious, with a dining table that can be extended so more than ten people can squeeze around it; some only have a small round table, so they open up another folding table, place them side by side, and cover them with a tablecloth to make one large table. We have no shortage of culinary experts, who naturally assume the role of head chef, showcasing their prowess in the kitchen, filling the air with fragrant steam. Most of my friends savor each bite, as they meticulously dissect the crab bit by bit, inch by inch; they are truly outstanding deconstructionists. There are also some friends who eat very quickly, barely touching the crab legs and claws, casting them aside, *whoosh*. While you're still crushing the legs with a cracker, they've already devoured the contents of five shells. Some people wolf down food without savoring it, their teeth even crushing the shells into bits, all while complaining about the inconvenience. But the atmosphere is everything—drinking wine, engaging in lively discussions, rinsing our hands with tea, sipping ginger tea sweetened with brown sugar, all while lauding crab as the best delicacy in the world, yet lamenting its increasingly high price.

Indeed, as this delicacy becomes more and more expensive, if we see fresh crab that has just arrived by air and is priced low, we place an order at once. Through a friend who works at the airport, we ordered a basket of crabs that had been flown in and distributed them on the spot. I brought home a dozen or so, and invited a few friends over to enjoy them with me. I hadn't anticipated having any difficulties beforehand. It was only when I returned home that I realized that these distinguished guests who'd just arrived by plane were different from those sold in the shops. Each crab was free and unrestrained, without any bands around its claws. As soon as the lid of the basket was opened, all six legs moved in unison, crawling rapidly, each giant claw stretched high. They were impossible to handle. However, one friend volunteered, claiming he was a crab-catching pro. Having been a mischievous child, he had abundant experience catching shrimp and crab along the coast in the rural New Territories. As he stepped forward to show off his skills, everyone was skeptical, wondering how this scholar who was as frail as a feather would conquer these gutless gentlemen. Sure enough, he lived up to expectations, as he caught each crab with his hand, pressed his index finger on its back, and with his thumb and middle finger lifted the edges of the shell, holding the whole crab hostage as his right hand picked up some straw twine, and with the help of his teeth, wrapped it round and round, managing to tie up each crab one by one.

We were tipsy with wine and the crabs had just finished cooking, when someone suddenly asked why crab was so delicious and thus was eaten by people. If crabs were rats, their lives would be spared. Furthermore, in our zest for crabs, we should beware the karmic wheel—one day, the crabs would return to exact their revenge. This was truly prophetic, as I myself was pinched by a crab. The English word "cancer," derived from Latin, means "crab," because crabs are hard, tyrannical, and take a sideways approach, running rampant and unbridled. The Chinese character for cancer, 癌, has no special meaning, but it is a terrifying pictograph. The second character in the Chinese word for leprosy, 痲瘋, contains the word *wind*, 風, as one of its components, and *wind* is connected to another skin malady, as it is also the first character in 風疹塊, which means "to break out in hives." Meanwhile, the second character in the Chinese word for tuberculosis, 肺癆, includes the character for labor, 勞, as one of its components, suggesting this condition is a malady of overwork and malnutrition. But the character that signifies cancer, 癌, instills fear in people. The heart of the character consists of the symbols meaning "products," 品 on top of the one representing "mountain," 山. When traveling to the countryside, you'll often find sacrificial offerings arranged in such a shape on wild mountainous terrain. Demons in fiction possess formidable martial arts skills, and they practice with skeletons and bones, stacking skulls in a 山 shape. From a pictographic viewpoint, the Chinese character for cancer literally evokes the spine-chilling image of white bones piled on mountains and hills.

The first time I met an actual cancer patient was thirty years ago. I had just graduated from the College of Education and was teaching in a primary school. For the first two years, I was an intern. The school was full of experienced teachers, among them a male teacher in his early thirties who was suffering from nasopharyngeal cancer. Of course, I knew that there was such a disease as cancer in the world, but I'd only seen it in movies or read about it in books—it seemed like a distant rumor. Moreover, this cancer always occurred in foreign countries, and the patients were complete strangers to me; it was as if I were reading about the Black Death. Whether it was in Boccaccio's *The Decameron*, Defoe's *A Journal of the Plague Year*, Flaubert's *Sentimental Education*, or Camus's *The Stranger*, I always felt the Black Death was just fiction, a part of the backdrop. It was irrelevant to us.

However, here was a cancer patient in our midst, a living, breathing individual who worked with us in the staff room and crossed paths with us in the corridors every day. The entire teaching staff felt sorry for him, and an underlying sense of grief and fear permeated the school. He was a strong, robust man whose major had been physical education. Normally, male physical education instructors mostly taught the higher grades, but that year, due to his illness, he was assigned to teach first and second grade. The children, who were as small as crabs, were surprisingly attentive as they listened to him.

How was his disease discovered? everyone kept asking in hushed whispers. He went to the dentist because of a toothache, and much to his surprise, after a filling and a tooth extraction, they found he had cancer. He continued working at school while undergoing treatment. Nasopharyngeal cancer didn't involve surgery, only radiation therapy. I noticed that the area around his eyes and nose was getting darker and darker. I saw him in the corridor as he silently led a group of first-grade students in a neat line from the classroom entrance, each student closely following the next, their hands behind their backs, hugging the wall, heading to the playground in an orderly fashion. He always walked in front, with the class monitor at the rear, turning off the lights and closing the door along the way. His young pupils were as quiet as church mice—physical education was their favorite subject, and if they were noisy, they had to stay behind in the classroom.

But his physical strength gradually declined. Radiation made him tired and weak. Several times, I passed by the lower-grade classrooms, noticing that the classroom lights were off but his students hadn't gone to the playground. They sat there quietly, resting their heads on their desks. He sat at the desk in the front of the room, with two naughty children crawling beneath his desk, chasing each other. Seeing this situation, everyone felt sad, unsure of how to help. Should we substitute-teach for him? In that case, would he come to school and just bide his time from the start to the end of the school day? How would he pass the long hours?

He carried a small mirror with him at all times, and every now and then, he'd look into it, like a girl who loved getting all dolled up, but he wasn't primping or applying makeup; he had lost sensation in his cheeks, and tears would fall without his knowing, so he would check the mirror frequently, and if he saw any tears, he would wipe them dry with a handkerchief.

After a few weeks, he stopped coming to school. Obviously, his condition had worsened. Small groups of colleagues visited him at home, but he didn't want to see anyone. News trickled in day by day. He had lost weight, a 150-pound person wasting away to less than 100 pounds. He no longer spoke, nor did he see anyone. Finally, the dreadful news arrived. Such a promising young individual, without any prior signs of illness, who had only discovered the disease when he went to the dentist to see about some bleeding after a tooth extraction. Perhaps the cancer was already at an advanced stage. He left behind a young wife and a daughter who was just over a year old. He himself once said that had he known he was sick, he never would have brought his daughter into this world.

When we bumped into each other in the corridor, we would brush past each other, smiling and nodding. After he fell ill, I became quite wary of him, always trying to find a way to avoid him, taking detours as though he had leprosy. I thought that even the tears and snot on his face were infected, and it seemed as though I might also become infected passing by him. He became a pariah. How ignorant we were about cancer in those days.

The death of the physical education teacher cast a shadow on my young heart, but the emotional burden wasn't too heavy. All I knew was that the man who suffered from nasopharyngeal cancer might have brought it on himself due to his smoking and love for salted fish and pickled vegetables. Maybe it was his own fault. Amid everyone's sighs were admonitions not to smoke or eat foods like salty fish. How fragile life is.

It was thirty years later that I learned that women also suffer from nasopharyngeal cancer and that the number of people with cancer was on the rise. When I happily set off to teach primary school at the age of twenty-two, who would have thought that thirty years later, I myself would also become a cancer patient?

A decade later, the impressions of that physical education teacher and the horrors of his cancer had gradually faded from my memory. I transferred from the school where I'd been teaching to another primary school. I was assigned to teach Class C of the sixth grade, the worst-performing class. Since I was a new instructor, naturally I was given this class. The students in sixth grade had to sit for exams, for which they required extra tutoring during the holidays and early-morning instruction on school days. The workload was heavier for me than for other teachers. If it had been Class A, it would have been worthwhile, because my hard work would have yielded a harvest, but for Class C, it was rather like planting flowers on a sandy beach.

Nine years of compulsory free education, in which children from all walks of life are given the opportunity to attend school, is a benevolent policy; however, it may have been driven by political considerations, in order to counter foreign criticism of local child labor. Flaws were unavoidable. While children were forced to attend school for nine years, for economic reasons they weren't allowed to repeat grades. As a result, no matter if they learned anything or not, they were still promoted to the next grade. Some children graduated from primary school without even knowing their ABCs. If their academic performance was poor, they naturally lost interest in class, leading to a breakdown of order. What could I do with such a class? I could only resort to desperate measures, attempting to breathe life into a dead horse.

I became the head teacher for Class 6C, and the vice principal took charge of the Chinese-language classes. The vice principal was about fifty years old, tall and thin, and walked at a snail's pace. I couldn't help but notice his dark complexion and gloomy demeanor, his ghostly movements. We didn't converse much on a daily basis, but when I waited outside the classroom for him to finish class, or when we crossed paths, we'd nod politely at each other.

I had just started teaching at this school, and I didn't know it or my colleagues or my students very well, but there was no difference between this school and my old one, in terms of administration, curriculum, and the like. Government schools were much the same, and most of my colleagues were also from the College of Education and shared the same teaching methods. However, the vice principal's teaching method truly took me by surprise. Whenever I entered the classroom at the end of his class, the chalkboard would be densely filled with Chinese characters, and the students would all have their heads bowed, solely focused on copying the characters. After a week of this, I felt a sudden fire ignite within me. Although Class 6C had the poorest academic performance, how could he not explain the texts in class and instead only have them copy down notes?

Those of us who came from the College of Education were familiar with the five-step teaching method: preparation, presentation, association, generalization, and application. A teacher in the classroom should face the students, engaging in dialogue and interacting with them. How was it possible to have one's back turned to the students for the entire class, just writing on the chalkboard? I asked the class monitor what they did during class, and the answer was: Copy from the board. Every day? Every class was like this. In fact, with our current technology, there was no need to take notes manually. They could be photocopied and distributed, or written on stencil paper and printed. Such precious class time simply shouldn't have been wasted.

I had an extremely negative impression of the vice principal. As I had just arrived in this new environment, I wasn't sure whether I should immediately file a complaint. I thought these sly old foxes, having secured their positions, were simply going through the motions, hampering students' progress. The only good thing was that his calligraphy was very beautiful; the class was basically a calligraphy exhibition. What was strange though was that the disorderly Class 6C was extraordinarily quiet during his lessons, truly as silent as the grave. I thought the students were all well-versed in the ways of the world. Given the vice principal's high position and authority, they dared not act out.

One day, I was casually chatting with some students, and I brought up the subject of the Chinese-language class. Only then did a student tell me: The teacher can't speak or make a sound, so that's why we copy down notes. Were there teachers in the world who didn't speak? They weren't dictionaries. The student said: He's sick. Sure enough, I finally found out the full reason in the staff room. My colleagues were wondering who would replace the vice principal, who would soon be unable to return to school because he had cancer.

He was the second cancer patient I had known personally. He also suffered from nasopharyngeal cancer, yet continued to come to school every day, undoubtedly aiming to endure work for as long as possible so that he could continue to receive a monthly salary and earn more money for his family. The school also specially arranged for him to teach classes that were less demanding—teaching Chinese to Class 6C seemed to be the most suitable. I didn't have many interactions with the vice principal at the new school. A month later, he stopped coming to school and then passed away.

Cancer was no longer an illusion but an occurrence right beside me. I felt deeply guilty—all this time, I'd been unjustly maligning a good teacher. Despite his illness, he kept on teaching, but because he couldn't speak, he just wrote on the chalkboard. The children were also understanding and exceptionally well-behaved, never causing any disruptions. Wasn't this a form of education as well? They didn't make much progress in their studies, but they silently experienced the sorrow of life. They also learned to be compassionate and considerate. These are difficult things to teach from textbooks. This was the teacher's final lesson.

The vice principal and I taught the same class; often he would teach one period, and I would follow immediately after. I couldn't help but be disconcerted, because although he didn't carry around a mirror, he frequently covered his mouth and nose with a handkerchief, which meant that his hands had likely come into contact with fluids, and of course, his hands touched many things in the classroom—he'd move chairs, pick up chalk, place his books on the desk, turn on the fan, close windows, flick the light switch. Every time I entered the 6C classroom, my whole body felt uneasy. Should I touch the desk, open the drawers? As a result, I set all the books that should have been on the main desk on the students' desks instead. When using chalk, I selected a brand-new piece, never touching a used one, or I brought one from another classroom, or wrapped it in a handkerchief. I dared not rest my hands on the desk, and I hurried off as soon as class was over.

I was also worried about the students. Would those sitting in the front row become infected? Some teachers' saliva sprayed everywhere, as though it were raining. Fortunately, this person didn't talk and always faced the chalkboard. Initially, when I saw him covering his nose and mouth with a handkerchief, I thought he was afraid of the flying chalk dust. I'd been worried the whole time. Thankfully, a month later, the vice principal no longer came to school. My ignorance had made me a person who took pleasure in someone else's suffering.

For decades, I knew nothing about cancer, but my family members and friends were more knowledgeable. They knew that cancer is simply an abnormal division of one's own cells, not a virus, nor a bacterium, and not contagious. This was indeed a blessing in the midst of misfortune. I was able to go about my normal life at home, just as before, though at first, I had worried whether I should separate my dishes and chopsticks and isolate myself from my family.

My friends were all wonderful. With them, too, I was concerned, wondering whether I should accept invitations to their homes. What would I do when it came to food? Should I bring my own utensils? Or should we use paper cups and plates and plastic cutlery? But my friends acted just as they always did, all of us eating together using the same tableware and cutlery. When I felt tired, they even let me lie down on their beds to rest. Reflecting on how I'd needlessly worried back in the 6C classroom, I was truly ashamed. Since autumn began, no one had mentioned eating crabs again. Indeed, many things had happened this year, a heavy feeling weighing on our hearts like a stone. A friend living in Gaomi Township in Shandong Province wrote to inform me that he'd been appointed president of a rural cancer prevention association. The locals had sculpted a stone statue, depicting a woman wielding a sword and stepping on a crab, symbolizing the conquest of this terrible disease. Now that I wielded a sword every day, could this vicious "crab" be conquered?

NON-STORIES

A WOMAN in the United States had a family history of breast cancer that affected both her mother and younger sister. When would
it be her turn? She worried about it so much that she came up with
a way to exorcize the eternal shadow by going to the hospital and
having both breasts removed. Would she get breast cancer in the
future? Who could answer this question? Many years later, people
who have undergone surgery have had a recurrence in the same place,
regardless of whether there are still breasts there. Breast cancer is an
adenocarcinoma and is related to the gonads—removing the breasts
is no guarantee against uterine cancer in the future.

The Pacific yew is the most precious tree in American forests. It can
be refined into medication to treat ovarian cancer, but the traditional
logging practice of clear-cutting entails cutting down the trees without
first stripping the bark, leading to 75 percent of the bark being burned
as waste in slash-disposal fires. The Forest Service's solution has been
to enact legislation that prohibits the burning of yew bark. The 850,000
pounds of yew bark now collected in the United States each year is
enough to treat 13,000 cancer patients. It takes sixty pounds of bark,
or three mature yew trees, to treat one cancer patient. As people have
come to learn that the trees are valuable and profitable, however, the
felling of these trees has increased. Sourcing yew bark also poses
another problem, as the yew turns out to be the habitat of the endan-
gered spotted owl. It's become a dilemma about saving humans or
saving the owls.

A diet book on the market contains a strange and sensational recipe. The ingredients include ten crab shells with claws, as well as several kinds of medicinal herbs, two of which are frankincense and myrrh. In treating illnesses, doctors often use poison to fight poison. Since cancer is a kind of "crab," using crab shells as a cure is like asking the troublemaker to undo the trouble they've caused. Frankincense and myrrh call to mind the precious gifts that the three wise men from the East brought to Jesus. It would seem that these two medicinal herbs might have also been useful for Mary—who knows whether she might have had breast cancer. Before the Common Era, there was no radiation or chemotherapy. Even if a tumor could have been removed surgically, mafeisan, the oral herbal anesthetic, didn't exist yet either.

I came across an extremely bizarre piece of news, and it wasn't April Fools' Day. It was reported that five female Soviet astronauts had returned from outer space, all pregnant. Before launching into space, certainly they had undergone physical examinations and hadn't been pregnant then. Four of them were unwilling to give birth, and only one had her baby. What kind of "creature" was that? Since there weren't any male astronauts, and they'd been in space for several years, was it parthenogenesis? Or a space tumor?

A doctor misdiagnosed a woman with breast cancer and performed surgery. The woman went to court for compensation. In such a case, the legal proceedings aren't the main focus, nor is it how the woman discovered she'd had a misdiagnosis. Anyone suffering from breast cancer would probably hope to be in her shoes. Compensation isn't important, as long as the doctor says: It was a misdiagnosis, and the surgery was a mistake—it's not cancer at all.

With the increase of breast cancer patients, some private medical clinics have also set up mammography machines. Of course, the fees are astronomical. Perhaps this is why business isn't good. It's not profitable. Breast cancer prevention hasn't become widespread beyond self-examination. A journalist interviewed a medical center about whether they would buy additional testing machines. The answer was no because there weren't many customers, and moreover, most people suffering from breast cancer were old women or ignorant women who wouldn't go in for testing even if they had an opportunity.

No one likes dealing with cancer except doctors and research scientists. Nor does anyone like things associated with the word "cancer." In recent years, however, there have been exceptions. There's a kind of frog in Argentina that's not green but brown. Its name was originally Budgett, which is the name of a cancer cell. If you examine the frog closely, it resembles cancer cells under a microscope, so it was called "cancer cell frog." The name is weird, but the frog itself looks fascinating and cute. It's flat and round, like a red bean paste pancake. Quite a few children raise them. The frog is worth a lot of money. At first, it cost 5,000 dollars, but after being artificially bred, it was mass-produced and sold for 300 or 400 dollars. The "cancer cell frog" is one of the ten most popular pets in the United States today. Sooner or later, people will discover that "cancer" is a multifaceted thing.

Are there other snippets like this? Please check out "Things That Are Known" on page 230.

TAMOXIFEN

THE SURGEON started me on a medication called tamoxifen. I took one tablet every day, twenty milligrams. For the first three days after my surgery, a nurse came to the ward four times a day dispensing medications. It was standard practice to send them in tiny paper cups, giving the false impression that they contained small cakes or chocolates. Was that too much to hope for, that there could be a garden party or birthday party in the hospital? Alas, there were only pills inside the cups. Some people got seven or eight. I got one. It was the sort of thing depicted in a Magritte painting: one side gray, one side red—I was too lazy to imagine that one half was water, the other fire, or that one half was a fish, the other a cigar. I'd seen many such pills before. Aside from the color combination, this pill wasn't very remarkable. I guessed it was simply an anti-inflammatory and analgesic little fellow.

There was nothing special about tamoxifen, either. The color was white, the shape oblate, just like the chocolate beans kids love to eat. The fourth day after my surgery, the doctor told me from that day on, I would take this medication daily for at least two years. Taking medication for two years isn't really all that long—my mother has been taking medication to control her high blood pressure for twenty years. The day I left the hospital, the doctor gave me only three pills; I had to go downstairs to get the rest. When I got to the pharmacy, I noticed a long, serpentine line of people and decided to forget about getting the medicine there—I'd buy it at the market instead. Who would have thought this medication would be so expensive: 10 dollars a pop, whereas cabbage only costs 3 dollars a catty. My mind immediately began to add, subtract, multiply, and divide—the medication alone would cost 300 dollars a month. But what could I do? I had to take it long-term. I could skip meals, but the medication was a necessity. All I could do was clench my teeth and buy a hundred pills to start with, which, according to my calculations, would only last three months.

My friends brought me the latest medical reports and many books on tumors. I skimmed them in my free time. This tamoxifen wasn't actually a real anticancer drug, just something that maintained the body's hormonal balance. According to Western medicine, one of the main causes of breast cancer is female hormonal imbalance, a condition caused by high estrogen levels; if the hormones can be controlled, the incidence of tumors can be reduced. It's not a real anticancer drug, but it controls the hormones. Because this medication has been researched, approved, and prescribed by doctors after numerous clinical trials, there's probably some benefit to it. It's a solution for when there's no other solution.

Now I understand why women with breast cancer shouldn't eat chicken. Chicken is an excellent food source that is rich in protein, with much less fat than pork or beef. If a sick person eats chicken, they can regain their physical strength faster. However, over time, chickens have become poisonous. Factory farms are to blame. Nowadays, the businesspeople who raise poultry put who knows what in the feed in order to make the chickens grow quickly, and they also inject them with who knows how many hormones. We buy chickens at the market. They are plump, white, and beautiful. Who knows if they are filled with excessive hormones? Perhaps eating such chicken could cause breast cancer.

The day I was given tamoxifen, the doctor also told me the test results: No cancer cells were detected in the tissue around the breast. There was a slight metastasis in one of the four lymphatic nuclei. It wasn't dire—it was an early sign of a tumor. In this case, the doctor didn't think radiation was necessary, but he let me choose. To be on the safe side, however, I elected to undergo radiation.

Western medicine generally adopts a three-pronged approach to treat breast cancer:

1. Mastectomy
2. Radiation therapy, also known as radiotherapy
3. Pharmacotherapy, also known as drug therapy

This is the breast cancer treatment trilogy. Since I'd already taken the first step, I thought it was best to complete the entire course. Moreover, though the tumor had been removed, cancer cells are different from viruses. They roam freely—who knew where they were currently playing in my body, or whether there might still be some lingering in my chest area, singing?

People in Hong Kong refer to radiation therapy as electrotherapy. Of course, I have no idea what electrotherapy is. It sounds difficult to deal with—the prefix "electro" is especially terrifying. It reminds me of the torture of an electric chair, or the electric perm I had when I was young, smelling the stench of something scorched, feeling the roots of my hair burning hot. Or maybe electrotherapy is similar to having a tooth extracted, sitting in a chair and trembling from head to toe. Fortunately, my guardian angel appeared once again. Ah Kin assured me there was nothing to worry about. There was no pain at all. It was just like having an X-ray, only for a longer period of time.

Ah Kin thought I should get radiation because some patients who didn't ended up in trouble again. She also chose the hospital for me. Rumor had it that a patient at a certain hospital had vomited blood after receiving radiation. It was the cancer cells that were supposed to be killed, but the person was also almost killed instead. Which hospital was the best? Private hospitals were extremely expensive. Of course, I could go to a public hospital. There were three hospitals in Hong Kong equipped with radiation therapy facilities. Sha Tin Public Hospital was ideal for breast cancer patients because there was a new oncology unit dedicated exclusively to breast cancer, and thus there was no need to wait with other cancer patients. What was even more reassuring was that the doctors, nurses, and even the staff there were kind and attentive.

I obtained a referral letter and my medical records from the surgeon, then went to the hospital to register. I was overjoyed when they accepted me. Although it was a long journey, two or three hours round trip, the bus went from terminus to terminus. As soon as I got on the bus, I closed my eyes and rested. I didn't feel tired. Sometimes I looked at the river and mountains as though I were taking a trip. It had been a while since I'd traveled somewhere faraway. When would I be able to do so again? Truthfully, I wasn't sure. Sha Tin was the farthest place I could travel at that time.

Registration was supposed to be at nine o'clock, but in fact, just after eight, there was already a long line at the cashier. When seeing a doctor at a public hospital, it's essential to familiarize oneself with the location of each department and the queuing order. At this early hour, the doctors hadn't yet arrived in the consultation rooms. Perhaps they had just finished breakfast and were tending patients in the upstairs ward, clutching their stethoscopes, with the nurses at their heels. People who wanted to see the doctor lined up at the cashier and paid a consultation fee of more than 20 dollars. After being handed a receipt, they headed to their respective departments: obstetrics and gynecology, otolaryngology, dermatology, oncology—each had its own location.

Oncology was on the second floor, with corridors extending in all directions. The first time I came, it was as though I'd entered a maze, running around in circles until I finally stumbled upon the right unit. It was just a little after nine o'clock, but the waiting area was full of people. I scanned the sea of dark heads; there must have been a hundred or so people. So many people suffered from breast cancer! I was surprised—this disease was really a formidable threat. A row of five consultation rooms faced the lobby of the oncology unit. The first one with the open door was the registration room. I got in line. Inside, the nurse took our weight and blood pressure. This was my first visit, so they also measured my height and handed me a cup to provide a urine sample.

We all waited in the lobby. At about ten o'clock, the doctors must have finished seeing their patients in the ward. The doors of the four consultation rooms opened every now and then, and nurses called in patients. I hadn't brought any books to read or my portable music player so I could listen to music. I surveyed the people around me. Some were in small groups, discussing the curative effects of food, while others were silent and solemn. There were young women and adult men in the crowd, presumably accompanying their family members for a consult. Therefore, there weren't as many patients as I'd thought. But when one person falls ill, especially with this kind of disease, her friends and family members seem to be stricken too. Though they hadn't had to register, they were also waiting.

Many patients were elderly and white-haired. They were supported by their family members and had trouble walking; there were husbands accompanying their wives, and there were daughters accompanying their mothers. Middle-aged patients accounted for about half of us, ranging from overweight to thin. From their outer appearances, you couldn't tell these women had cancer. It was only when their names were called and they entered the consultation rooms that they were revealed to be patients.

A nurse walked out of the registration area and asked those of us who were new patients to raise our hands. There were three raised hands, including mine. Seeing that I raised my hand straight and high above my head, the nurse complimented me: Wow, you're holding your hand up so high. I replied: I exercise every day. She said: Yes, it's essential to exercise regularly, especially for your arm after surgery—otherwise, you'll have to do physical therapy. The hand next to me sighed and said: Alas, mine's too swollen to move. Only then did I notice that the woman's entire arm resembled a thick lotus root.

The nurse handed each of the three of us a piece of paper, with a notice that read:

To whom it may concern: Your cancer is confirmed to be non-contagious, but the family prevalence rate is higher than that of the general population. The department is very concerned about this issue and has received requests for physical examinations. Therefore, the department has set aside every Tuesday at

2:00 p.m. for scheduled examinations for your daughters or sisters aged forty and above. All personal information will be kept confidential.

I continued to sit in the lobby and wait. Some of the patients who'd arrived after me had already been admitted to a consultation room, while I was still waiting. In fact, the two people sitting next to me who'd raised their hands were also waiting. It dawned on me that this was our first consult. Others had come for follow-up visits. They came every other month or two, while the consult for those of us who were here for the first time would take longer, and so we were pushed to the end. Sitting in the lobby, I read the notice over and over. Who says that public hospitals aren't any good? They not only take care of the patients themselves but also consider their family members. Cancer is not an infectious disease. Examining our sisters and daughters is a compassionate policy.

I kept coming back to this sentence: *All personal information will be kept confidential.* Was cancer something to be hidden from ordinary people? Did having cancer mean this person was unclean, poisonous, bacteria-ridden, deformed, or harboring a dirty little secret? In the late 1980s, did cancer patients still have to be treated like lepers during the Middle Ages? Back then, leprosy was a taboo in Western society, and patients were discriminated against, ostracized, and expelled, forced to hide in remote mountain areas or migrate to islands, or put on rickety old ships to drift aimlessly at sea. In *Madness and Civilization*, Foucault quotes from the ritual of the Church of Vienne: "My friend, it pleases Our Lord that you have been infected with this disease, and you have the greatest honor of the grace of Our Lord, who wants you to be punished for your sins in the world."

When I was in the College of Education, my classmates and I took a field trip to Hei Ling Chau, a famous small island that had been designated as a leper colony. The whole island was inhabited by lepers so they could be isolated from the outside world. Some of my classmates said: Don't get infected. Some said: Be careful if you have a cut on your body, because leprosy can lie dormant for twenty years. In the end, everyone still went on the trip. The patients were not to be feared. Although some people had swollen fingers, they were in fact in recovery. Today, leprosy has been eradicated. The small island is no longer a forbidden place, and the leper colony is history. So what about cancer? Why keep it a secret? It's not something unclean, nor does it spread germs. The truth is, it is safer to be around cancer patients than people who have a cold or the flu.

By the seventeenth century, leprosy had disappeared from Europe, not because of the effectiveness of medical treatment but because of isolation measures, as well as the disruption of Eastern sources of infection after the Crusades. Yet the pattern of isolating others hasn't changed; it is eerily similar how vagabonds, criminals, the mentally disturbed, and the consumptive have filled the role of the leper. By some standards, times have changed—so is there more sympathy and understanding for cancer patients nowadays? The notice I held in my hand was a tactful acknowledgment that we might feel a sense of guilt, complicity with our own imperfections. Lowering its voice to a whisper, the notice was intended to comfort: *How embarrassing this must be for you, but rest assured, we won't tell anyone else.*

I waited in the lobby until eleven o'clock, when the nurse finally called me. Instead of entering the consultation rooms that faced the lobby, we passed through the registration area and turned down a corridor, behind which there was another row of rooms. Why were there so many doctors? As soon as I entered, I saw five or six of them in white robes. A female doctor invited me to sit down and asked me a series of questions: How had I detected the tumor? How had the surgery gone? How did my body feel now? She wrote down my replies, taking notes as though she were a journalist conducting an interview.

I lay back on the table so she could examine me. The procedures and movements had become familiar to me. Every time I saw the doctor, they pressed down on my neck, ribs, abdomen, and chest. I got a better look at the doctors in the room. There were five of them, one woman and four men, all rather young. After the female doctor finished the examination, the male doctors came over and asked whether they could take a look and palpate my body. I immediately said, no problem. Such polite doctors, so respectful, so young, so sincere—suddenly, it clicked.

—You're medical students?

They laughed.

—Doing your internship?

They nodded their heads.

Surely there were patients who refused to accept their participation, who didn't want students involved, thinking that hospitals treat patients as guinea pigs. But I welcomed them with open arms—they should be exposed to real patients. I was reminded of when I was at the College of Education, studying theory and pedagogy while interning at a proper school. Twice a year, we visited different schools to teach real students. The teachers came to observe us while we taught, sitting in the classroom and evaluating us. Thus, when we became teachers, we weren't strangers to the classroom.

I told them, You're welcome to examine and treat me. You're medical students—do more practice, do more research, quickly, so you can save us in the future. They just smiled, both solemn and shy. When I emerged from the room, I returned to the waiting area. The scene just now had been a practical lesson for medical students; I still hadn't seen the actual doctor. I didn't feel like I'd wasted my time, though; in fact, I was rather pleased. It turned out that disease could also be an opportunity to learn, a mechanism for creation. It was as though I had another body, as though I were detached, having become an observer of myself. I'd also come to practice getting to know myself.

Finally, it was my turn. Inside the tiny consultation room, there was a writing desk, chairs, and an exam table. The doctor was sitting down, while the nurse stood, leaving an empty chair for the patient. Hey, here were the five medical students I'd just seen, coming to class again! They sat against the wall in a curved line. In the presence of their teacher, they appeared more rigorous, sitting rail-straight. I smiled at them. The doctor flipped through my medical records, read the letter from the surgeon, asked me the usual questions, and examined me. A blood test was required for the first visit. The doctor himself drew my blood, modeling the procedure to the students at the same time. As he tied a rubber tube around my left arm, he spoke to the students in English. Of course, medical schools teach in English. He mentioned some technical terms that I didn't understand, while the students listened attentively.

—Can I get my teeth checked?

—Umm...we don't check teeth here.

Ha! The doctor had misunderstood me, thinking I wanted *him* to examine my teeth—I simply wanted to ask whether I could go to the dentist to have a cavity filled, because with some cancers, you can't have any dental work for a year. I was terrible at expressing myself.

The doctor's hands and mouth worked nonstop during the consult. As he spoke, he picked up a pen and filled out three stiff cards, instructing me to make appointments with various departments for chest imaging, pelvic imaging, and a full-body bone scan. I reached for the cards, inadvertently covering my left arm where blood was still being drawn, possibly blocking the students' line of vision. I wanted the students to have a clear view of the doctor's demonstration, so I shifted my body slightly. Little did I know that this movement would affect the doctor's work. He quickly removed the needle and drew blood from my right arm instead. What a fool I was! During a blood draw, moving around could complicate things if the needle broke.

The doctor didn't waste a single second. As he drew my blood, he asked me a series of questions:

—Are you on any medication?

—Yes, tamoxifen. One pill a day, twenty milligrams.

—Did the doctor give it to you?

—No, I bought it myself from the pharmacy.

—How much for each pill?

—Ten dollars.

—Wow, ten dollars!

The doctor gasped in surprise, then said to the students in English:

That's exorbitant! These companies really know how to make money—it's too expensive. The students didn't say a word, but only nodded to show their understanding. Suddenly forgetting that the doctor hadn't been directing his comments at me, I answered in English, Yes, it's too expensive. As soon as I uttered the words, I realized I was talking too much, and rushed to cover my mouth with my hand. The doctor maintained his composure and asked me:

—How many did you buy?

—One hundred pills.

—One hundred isn't enough. You need to take them for at least half a year.

—I'll buy more when the time comes.

—From now on, the hospital will give you the medicine. Let us know after you've finished the hundred you bought.

I quickly thanked him. When I got home, I prattled excitedly: I can save three hundred bucks a month. What's so bad about public hospitals? Paying taxes for so many years has paid off—now I can enjoy some of the benefits. My younger sister said: I'd rather pay taxes all my life and never ask for anything in return, particularly free medicine from the hospital, and especially free tamoxifen. Confused, my mother asked: Which Ah Fen is that? Are you talking about Auntie's eldest daughter?

THE THIRD KIND OF EYE

GOD SAID: Let there be light. And there was light.

With light, there was day and night on Earth; with light, plants could carry out photosynthesis and produce food; with plants, herbivores had sustenance for survival; and thus, humans proliferated on Earth. With light, people could see things. When the sun went down, people sought out various light sources: darting fireflies, glowing phosphorous, and burning oil. Gradually, there were electric lights. Light allows us to see. We are always looking, observing everything around us, looking at things near and far. But there are so many things in the world—big, small, far away, concealed, deeply hidden, and ubiquitous—that we can't see with our naked eyes, so we create telescopes, microscopes, cameras, scanners, and other eyes: humanity's third kind of eye. In hospitals, people use a variety of technological eyes to observe the cosmos below the skin.

I arrived at the radiology department of the hospital, a place where this family of light congregates. Coming out of the second-floor oncology consultation room, I held three stiff cards in my hand, much like those people with vouchers to exchange for a dozen cakes. However, the cards in my hand weren't festively adorned with big red and gold letters but were dull and depressing, filled with the doctor's handwriting. Each one had to be handed to a different small department, all of which were part of the family of light.

The first card was for a chest X-ray, which could be done on the same day and didn't require a separate appointment. A chest X-ray is a simple task. Who hasn't had one? In a public hospital, however, the time it takes to get a chest X-ray is much longer than at other places because you have to wait, wait some more, keep on waiting, and patiently endure all this waiting, which is good training to become a calm and patient fisherman. Waiting is a characteristic of hospitals, especially public hospitals. In such a place, wouldn't you get to know, understand, and experience the conditions of the general public seeking medical care? People were lined up at every corner, the benches filled with people. Did the opening of the center for boat people in Pak Tin increase the burden on the Sha Tin Public Hospital?[15] The hospital was responsible for the health of 800,000 New Territories residents. The influx of boat people was said to have prevented many local expectant mothers from being able to secure a spot in the delivery room. Were there any cancer patients among the boat people? If so, the lines for diagnosis and treatment would have been even longer.

I had to wait in line three times in order to complete a single chest X-ray. First, I waited for my name to be called, and then I went and changed into a white gown with ties that knotted at the back. The natural light made the corridor so bright. It was an especially sunny day. The sunlight shone on the gray walls of the building, creating contrasting lines of light and shadow; the sunlight shone on the broad leaves of the evergreen plants, revealing colorful and variegated layers; the sun traveled at full speed through the air, like a golden ship sailing through specks of dust. Hey—what is light exactly? Oh, it's an electromagnetic wave that can elicit visual perception. If it passes through a prism, you would see the colors of the rainbow. I didn't see a rainbow though, nor could my eyes see infrared and ultraviolet light.

The actual chest X-ray didn't take more than a minute. A large eye stood behind me. I could even hear it breathe. When it breathed, I couldn't breathe; I had to hold my breath and fill my lungs with air. If you were to send an X-ray photo to a friend, they'd certainly think you'd lost your mind. People only want to see your face, your eyes, your mouth to recognize you. Of course, for some people, if you're a woman, what they'd love to see is your breasts, the part covered by clothing. Is there anyone interested in getting to know your lungs, your heart? Probably only the doctor. The person who claims to love you wouldn't want to see your heart in an X-ray. *The Magic Mountain* by Thomas Mann contains a surprising exception. The protagonist falls in love with a woman and keeps an X-ray of her in his pocket. Every time he pulls it out to look at it, all he sees are delicate bones and the black-and-white interplay of light and shadows. Is it that love has penetrated the bones?

I had to wait again in the waiting room, wait to see whether I'd moved my body, whether the image was clear, whether it needed to be retaken. Well, this was an interior room without windows, so there wasn't any natural light. There were fluorescent lights everywhere on the ceiling, illuminating the area as though it were daylight. Obviously, it *was* daytime, but they had to use light to replicate the effect of daylight. Light has no feet, but it can soar and dance. It flickered on my hair, shoulders, and arms, darting from afar and bouncing back again. Newton said that light is composed of elastic particles emitted by luminous bodies, so the propagation of light can be direct, reflected, or refracted. In earlier times, scientists believed that light was a wave, with both long and short wavelengths. Einstein, on the other hand, stated that light exhibits wave-particle duality, possessing both wave-like and particle-like characteristics.

I still had two more cards in my hand, both of which required special appointments, as the examination of bones and the pelvic area was not as simple as taking a one-minute chest X-ray. The third eye needed to observe slowly, to look carefully, and moreover, the entire human body is composed of bones from head to toe, as opposed to being entirely made of lungs. Since things had taken a long time, there were even more people waiting in line. I went from department to department, handing over cards, weaving through the winding corridor. This was room 11, that was room 26. So many rooms! The corridor twisted and turned, and there were doors on both sides. Some opened at a knock, revealing people bustling inside; some were tightly closed, shrouded in mystery. The corridor was filled with people sitting as usual—aside from those perched on long benches like dazed birds, there were also hospital beds being brought in from the wards, clinking bottles suspended above them. Additionally, there were patients in wheelchairs, wearing the hospital's thick quilted gray coats, their medical records resting on their laps. In the corridor, there were also small carts with glass covers in which newborn babies slept; at such a young age, they were already subjected to the torment of illness. Why? They couldn't talk. All they could do was cry. The adults didn't cry. The ones in pain moaned, and those who'd been waiting a long time glanced at their watches and yawned.

This was my second visit to Sha Tin Public Hospital. The first had been two weeks earlier. At that time, I brought the letter from the surgeon to the registration counter to apply for a consult and schedule an appointment. Only today did I finally meet with a specialist in the oncology unit. In the future, how many more times would I have to come here—ten, twenty, fifty? I didn't know. I went to the retired civil servants pension department to request medical documents. They gave me four pages of medical records. I said, It's not enough. I need radiation therapy. Give me twenty. Perhaps in the future, I'd have to come here every day like I used to go to school or work. If only I really were going to school or work. I genuinely missed those days of school—how wonderful it was, sitting in the classroom listening to the physics teacher talk about light, how romantic it was, watching a prism transform daylight into a rainbow. How many times had I written "time flies like an arrow" on the pages of my composition notebook? Time really does fly like an arrow, and its speed is similar, even faster; its form is similar, with comblike parallel beams of light. How comfortable it would be to walk in the sunlight for a while. Some light emanates in a cone shape, the rays tapping my skin like a cone, relieving stiff muscles and crystallized joints. Light is nature's finest acupuncturist. The study of light led indirectly to the transformation of the European art world, giving rise to Monet, Pissarro, and others . . .

The radiology department was filled with third eyes, both small and large. Once again, I found myself there, standing at the door to room 13. Peering inside, I saw a gigantic basin-like eye. This time, my bones would be examined by a process officially known as "radionuclide imaging." Before the day of the appointment, the registration department sent me a sheet of paper listing several key points to follow, two of which weren't difficult at all. The first was that the examination might take the entire day; the second was that I should bring one liter of water. What I found rather challenging was having to abstain from eating or drinking for twelve hours before the examination. What could I do if I wasn't allowed to eat anything? My stomach wasn't very good—I needed to eat something every three or four hours, or I'd get a stomachache. I couldn't eat for six hours before my surgery, and in the end, I got through it, but this was twelve hours. However, having counted the hours, I filled up on food before midnight, slept, and powered through until I arrived at the hospital at eleven-thirty. There weren't many people having their bones scanned. I was the first to arrive, and only one person was after me. One machine, it turned out, could serve only two or three people a day—no wonder it was necessary to schedule an appointment.

A doctor in room 13 gave me an injection in my arm and told me to come back at two. Oh, so it took a few hours for the injection to take effect. In the meantime, what should I do? The doctor said: Go eat, and remember to drink water—drink as much as you can, and try to finish one liter. And so, I took my backpack and went to the hospital cafeteria. My backpack was heavy because there was a liter of water inside, clanging as I walked. The cafeteria was on the first floor of the main building, quite spacious and teeming with people. People who were sick, not sick, visiting the sick, and working for the sick all ate here. The dishes were listed one by one on seven or eight signs at the entrance, people huddled around to make their choices. Doctors also came, along with nurses and other health-care workers, white robes fluttering, blue uniforms moving about, more than a hundred people in my line of vision.

I saw the oncologist who diagnosed me and later designed my simulation markings. Let's see, what was he eating for lunch? Was it a rice dish? Did he choose beef or a chicken drumstick? Neither—he only bought a sandwich and walked away carrying a paper bag. He probably went back to the dormitory to eat. I ordered a rice dish and found a corner to sit down and eat. This meal had no vegetables, only protein and starch. That's how it was dining in the cafeteria. I didn't order tea. I took a cup, drinking water while I ate, placing the entire plastic bottle of water on the table. After I finished eating, I continued to pour and drink the water, cup after cup. Within an hour and a half, I had to finish all the water. No one looked at me. They must have seen a lot of people drinking water nonstop like this. Good, no one paid me any attention. I finished the bottle. I glanced at a watch on someone else's wrist. It was only one o'clock. I still had an hour to go. I had a book in my backpack, but I didn't feel like reading after eating, so I decided to go for a stroll instead.

My knowledge of the hospital was limited to the wards, operating room, nurses' stations, bathing areas, bathrooms, pharmacy, cashier's office, and registration counter. These were the places I'd been to. In reality, there are so many departments in a hospital that ordinary people simply didn't know about. A hospital of such enormous scale was especially mazelike. Those who came there only saw one aspect, or just a partial outline of it. Some people went to the morgue to identify a corpse, some were admitted to the intensive care unit for lifesaving treatment, some gave birth in the emergency room, some visited friends and family members in the nurses' quarters, some dined in the cafeteria, some pushed the wheelchairs of their loved ones into the garden so they could bask in the sun. Hospitals are like the huge villas found in novels, filled with hundreds of rooms, each with different contents. Custodial rooms, disposal rooms, supply rooms, various staff members' offices . . . Who really knows the structure of the entire hospital? Perhaps the hospital director, but even that person's knowledge may be limited to the administrative departments. The ones who truly know the hospital's every pavilion garden, every room, every staircase, every corner are probably the ones who designed it.

Behind the cafeteria were the administrative departments. I wandered back and forth along the long corridor. On one side, there was a row of rooms, including the hospital director's office, the assistant administrative director's office, the general secretariat, and so on. Here was the general affairs department, the payment department, the medical records department, the complaints department, and the like. These seemed to be related to me in some way, yet they also appeared to have no connection to me at all. Over there was an electronic banking counter and the hospital gift shop, which were unexpectedly deserted. I left the building and went outside. The October weather was unusually warm, the sun shining brightly. Down a flight of stone steps, there was a pleasant little garden, where some people sat eating from lunch boxes, some read the newspaper, some had nodded off, and some slept on stone benches. Here there were pavilions and corridors of greenery. Such comfortable sunlight! I placed my backpack under my head, draped my jacket over my body, and lay down on a bench for a late-morning nap, managing to drift off into a hazy sleep.

I gradually woke up because my stomach was full of water. The doctor had said that I needed to expel the entire liter of water I had drunk. For the next hour, I rushed to the bathroom every ten minutes. Assuming I'd drained myself of all the water, I punctually returned to room 13. Just then, a gurney pushed past me and entered the room first. I waited half an hour, and then went to the bathroom several times more. What part of the body did the person lying on the gurney need to have imaged? He couldn't get out of bed and was quite elderly. Was it an issue with his thyroid, liver, gallbladder, kidneys, or maybe lungs? I was going to have my bones imaged to see whether the cancer cells had spread there.

For bone imaging, I didn't have to change. I could wear my own clothes. As soon as I lay back on the table, the nurse asked: Have you gone to the restroom? I said I'd gone many times, and I'd just come back. And so, I lay down on the bed, but as soon as the machine's large eye started scanning, the nurse said, No, it won't work—your stomach is full of water. How strange that in just a short time, my belly was full of water again. I had no choice but to get up and walk through two winding corridors to go to the restroom, a trip that took me about five or six minutes. Fortunately, this time we could proceed.

The imaging was performed by a huge machine that looked like a giant-eyed dinosaur. I lay on the platform of its abdomen. Its gigantic disk-shaped eye started moving from the top of my head all the way down to my feet, then circled beneath the platform, returning from the tips of my toes back to the top of my head, capturing images of the bones in both the front and back of my body. All I could hear was a mechanical hum. Opening my eyes, I watched this strange large machine moving slowly. Ah, the dinosaur was singing. At the time, it was as though I were onstage participating in a magic show, performing tricks like a beautiful woman being sawed in half or levitating under hypnosis. If I closed my eyes, would the scanning table rise into the air with me on it? If a buzz saw came roaring over, what should I do to complete the magic trick?

The imaging process took a full half hour. The nurses in the room sat at their work desks and weren't idle, even when the machine was running. They had the results of the imaging for the patient before me, so they called the responsible doctor over the loudspeaker to come view them. The patient was still waiting outside the door and hadn't left. Just like chest imaging, bone imaging required waiting outside the room for a while to see whether the obtained images were clear. If they were blurry, another image needed to be taken. As I lay on the scanning table listening to the singing of the giant-eyed machine, I remembered when the doctor in the oncology unit had asked me whether I had bone pain throughout my entire body. The question was simple, but I had no idea what bone pain felt like. Pain is often hard to describe. A toothache is the most acute, probably because it's nerve pain; those pains that course throughout the body, suddenly aching in the back, then in the lower back, then completely disappearing after a few days, are probably muscle pain. Stomach pain has many patterns, sometimes feeling like someone is digging and chiseling, sometimes burning near the rib cage, sometimes like a needle prick, sometimes like an inflated balloon blocking the area. You say it's painful but isn't too severe, you say it's okay yet you feel uncomfortable, you go see the doctor, you go for an electrocardiogram, but no obvious symptoms can be found.

Perhaps the first image wasn't very clear. They needed to do a bit more, perform another scan of the abdominal cavity. This time, instead of lying on the scanning table, I stood on the floor while the large-eyed machine lowered its head in front of my stomach to take the scan. Such a huge machine could move left and right, up and down—it was very flexible. You wouldn't know how far medical technology has come if you haven't seen the medical equipment with your own eyes. Of course, developed countries have many such machines, but how many does Hong Kong have? Do they need to be repaired frequently? Are there enough to use? Oh, I could go home. I'd arrived at the hospital at precisely eleven. Now it was after four. I would still need to buy groceries and cook dinner once I got home.

THE DREAM FACTORY

WHAT DO I have compared to others in this world? Wealth, good looks, knowledge, health? I have none of those, but I do have friends. In this regard, I'm truly more blessed than most. I have a circle of close friends, all of whom are wonderful to me. Some care about me but don't necessarily show it on the surface; they're more introverted, hiding their feelings inside, but I can feel their concern in many small ways, which is very moving. Some brim with enthusiasm both inwardly and outwardly; their personalities are more extroverted—if they see I'm having trouble, they rush to help. One such friend is Ah Zan. When I had my surgery in the private hospital, Ah Zan and a group of friends came to visit. After my other friends left, she insisted on staying. She was afraid that during the night, I might be lonely, sleepless, or in pain, so she rented a rollaway bed next to mine. It must have been miserable lying in that kind of bed in such a strange environment, staying awake all night to look after me, whereas I sawed logs until dawn. At five o'clock, the staff came to collect the beds, waking up any accompanying friends or family members. Fortunately, I didn't need to eat, drink, or use the bathroom during the night, nor was I in any pain, so I didn't end up causing Ah Zan any trouble.

How lovely it is for friends to gather. In the past, we often traveled in groups of five or ten to places such as Ürümqi and Turpan in Xinjiang, Harbin and Jilin in the northeast, Suzhou and Hangzhou south of the Yangtze River, the ancient city of Xi'an, and even other countries, including Turkey, Egypt, Greece, Spain, and Portugal. Ah Zan was part of this group. Sometimes we met at someone's home, or went on a camping holiday, drinking red wine and eating, chatting about everything under the sun until dawn. Those were such blissful days. But now we gathered in the hospital, silent the whole night. Having Ah Zan with me there was truly a huge help. After my surgery, I didn't eat, drink, or use the bathroom until noon the following day, when I suddenly needed to pee. However, I couldn't get out of bed because of the bottles hanging above me, the plastic tubing still connected to my arm. I had to ask Ah Zan to find me a bedpan. To my surprise, just five minutes later, I needed to pee some more, so once again she went to fetch the bedpan. Five more minutes passed, and what on earth—how did I *still* need to pee? These disturbances continued for a full hour. Finally, I simply left the bedpan on the bed, afraid to remove it. It was extremely embarrassing to ask my friend to retrieve and empty the bedpan constantly on my behalf.

Ah Zan had the day off from work, so she volunteered to accompany me to Sha Tin Public Hospital. Early in the morning on the day of my appointment, she brought over a bowl of bird's nest soup she'd especially stewed for me to drink before we set out. This time, I was going to the hospital for simulation. It was as though I were attending an art class where I could unleash my creative genius and imagination. Ah Kin had filled me in ahead of time on what the simulation process entailed. Symbols would be drawn on my body to facilitate radiation treatment. And so I didn't panic, knowing that the process wouldn't be painful, just time-consuming because it involved waiting in line and visiting various small units.

The hospital's simulation unit was located in the basement of the specialty building. We arrived on time to find the corridor already swarming with people. Wow, so many people were undergoing radiation therapy, and they were new cancer patients. Was cancer becoming more and more prevalent? Of course, I always subtracted a few people when tallying up the number of patients, since most were accompanied by one or two family members. Along both sides of the corridor there were doors every few steps, and from time to time, a nurse would pop out, calling a name. The doctor who examined me turned out to be the same one who'd first diagnosed me in the oncology unit nine days earlier. He even drew my blood. This time, I didn't see any medical students, only doctors and nurses. The doctor was studying some X-rays, the walls adorned with radiographic skeletal images.

I lay on the bed so the doctor could examine me, and then the nurse sketched some symbols on my skin with a pen. After she finished drawing, she snapped an instant color Polaroid and showed it to me. It was truly the most extraordinary photo I'd ever seen. There was only a partial body in the picture, specifically the upper half: the right side of my torso and the front chest area. Because it was in color, I could see the red and blue lines crisscrossing my skin, and among these lines, there were grayish-brown surgical scars resembling railroad tracks. I was reminded of works of art known for their abstract lines, such as paintings by Mondrian, Klee, and even Miró. If the photo were a painting, it would have been a colorful feast for the eyes. I said to the nurse: This is really interesting. I think I caught her off guard, because she told me: You're the only one who's ever said that. The nurse was gentle and kind. She told me that after completing radiation therapy, everything would be fine.

What the nurse had drawn was only a rough sketch. I lay on the bed, the door to the room opening and closing every now and then. When it opened, a doctor would come in, or sometimes a nurse. Ah Zan sat on a bench in the corridor outside the room. When the door opened, did she see me lying on the bed? Did the other people sitting on the benches also see me? Did they see my naked body? Maybe they did, maybe they didn't, because although the bed faced the door, it was right against the wall, and the line of sight of those seated outside wasn't high. The doctors and nurses streaming in and out naturally paid me no heed, as they were used to seeing such sights day after day.

One of my secondary-school textbooks included the Ming dynasty prose piece "The Peach-Stone Boat," which contains the phrase "bare chest and exposed breasts." The teacher glossed over this line, no doubt because everyone understood what it meant, but an even like-lier reason was because it touched upon something taboo, causing the teacher's voice to suddenly become muffled when reading the word "breasts." The students covered their mouths and snickered. We were a bunch of girls, unruly-haired young things in our early teens, and the more taboo something was, the more sensitive and curious we became. Of course, now I was no longer young, but breasts were still a very private part of the body; however, in a hospital, is there any privacy to speak of? I had to repeat the same cycle over and over: unbutton, undress, and bare my body; get dressed, button up. Moreover, I had to do this in front of total strangers. In some rooms, I undressed as soon as I went in. In others, I first changed into a white gown, but since I had to open the front flap, there wasn't much difference, except that when I walked around, I was dressed decently enough so as not to catch a cold. But eventually, I got used to it. An old moral code teaches us that the body is immoral and shameful, and to value the physical body is akin to spiritual degradation. As a result, the majority of people tend to overcorrect, feeling ashamed even to face their own bodies; when it comes to looking at other people's bodies, they think it is obscene. When did our literature and art, and even our philosophy, begin to separate the soul from the body, placing content and form in opposition to each other? Did it begin when Adam and Eve were expelled from the Garden of Eden?

Once the rough sketch was finished, the actual drawing took place in the drawing room across from the consultation room. Of course, upon entering, I once again undressed and lay down. Two nurses carefully drew heavy lines on my chest with blue and red pens, assessing and measuring as though they were drawing a precisely detailed map, the horizontal lines delineating level lines and contour lines, the vertical lines representing mountain chains and rivers. This map had to be as accurate as possible—otherwise, the radiation beam might zero in on the wrong target, harming my body or not effectively killing the cancer cells. They had a hard time drawing in my armpit region, as the surgical incision was long, sloping inward toward my concave armpit, but it was nevertheless a crucial site because the lymph nodes had been removed.

Coming out of the drawing room, I returned to the simulation room so that the doctor could check whether the positioning was mapped out correctly. I heard the person who drew it say, Oops, this part is too high. I also heard the doctor say, This part is a little bit low. Maybe it wasn't easy to be precise, or maybe it was that my situation was more challenging. Regardless, in the end, the drawing was well-done. Before I left, the nurse handed me a stiff brown card to take to the registration desk to schedule my radiation therapy appointment. A small note was attached to the card stating clearly that the designed graphics shouldn't be washed off; if the colors faded, I could come back to the simulation unit at a specified time for a touch-up.

Coming out of the simulation room, there was yet another room I needed to visit, so I chatted with Ah Zan on the bench in the corridor. Whenever I came out of a room, I described to her what had just occurred. This happened four or five times. We both remarked how busy it was here, how the doctors and nurses seemed never to have a spare moment. But the nurses were extremely kind, just like the ones in the second-floor oncology unit. They never shouted at patients, and if there was something a patient needed to know, they carefully explained it over and over. Ah Zan sat in the corridor for a long time. On the wall opposite the bench there was a wooden rack with several pamphlets stuck inside. We pulled out a few to read. One was called RADIATION THERAPY, and one was DRUG THERAPY. Both were useful, so I kept them. There were two advertisements for nutritional milk powder. I was familiar with this kind of powder because I always bought it for my mother. There was also a pamphlet for END OF LIFE CARE, which I didn't take because it was too depressing to look at. Another was for a CANCER HOTLINE which patients and family members could call with questions; it was a service organized by recovered cancer patients themselves. I took one. I didn't think I'd need to call them because I already knew Ah Kin. Ah Zan had always been interested in medical matters, so she swiped a few pamphlets as well. She even planned to buy the nutritional milk powder for her mother.

The next room I went into was the mold-making workshop. The floor was blanketed with dust, much like a pottery studio. I changed into a white gown and lay down. A woman placed a piece of cloth over my chest, then smeared a white paste onto it. I only felt a warm sensation. Before long, the paste on my chest swelled up into a thick layer that turned out to be a plaster cast of my torso. I didn't realize that a cast could be made so quickly, and the process was so fascinating. In just a few minutes, a plaster cast of my body shape had been molded. The mold-making workshop was actually one giant room. There was a small curtained-off corner with a bed, while the rest was a spacious workshop where people worked amid piles of plaster. The mold makers would also lift up the curtain and come over to retrieve the plaster casts. They must have been used to seeing naked people; as for me, I'd also grown used to exposing my naked body in front of strangers.

The woman who made my cast gave me a tissue to wipe the gypsum powder off my body before I changed. I wiped and wiped but couldn't clean it all off. I didn't dare rub too forcefully, as I had a large wound on my chest, with markings drawn around it—it would cause a lot of trouble if I erased them. When I arrived home, I carefully dabbed the area with a towel, but the powder still wouldn't come off. As I couldn't take a bath or shower, I was truly at a loss. Fortunately, it was mid-October, and it wasn't too hot, so I didn't sweat much. Ah Kin told me that her plaster cast and design graphics had been done in the sweltering August heat. To keep from sweating, she mostly stayed indoors with air-conditioning and rarely ventured outside.

The gypsum powder and colored markings accompanied me for so many days that gradually I felt I'd turned into Mad Monk Ji Gong—just by casually wiping my body, I could produce a shiny black mud pellet.[16] If only it really were a magic cure-all! I was relieved that the colored markings were confined to my chest. The uppermost line only reached my collarbone, rather than climbing up my neck to my chin, so I didn't need to wear high-collared clothing to hide the lines. Ah Kin said her case was different. The lines extended from her chest and crawled up her neck, creating minor inconveniences in her daily life. For instance, if she wore an open-collared shirt, the lines on her neck would be exposed. Walking down the street or taking public transportation, she always attracted curious glances. Those who didn't understand would assume she had tattoos; those who did understand would know it was cancer. Whether it was tattoos or cancer, many people would find it frightening. In order to avoid arousing suspicion, she would cover up the lines. It was summer then, and Ah Kin had to wear turtlenecks to conceal her neck. Luckily for me, I had no colored lines on my neck. If my collar was open, you could see the colors on my collarbone, but as long as I fastened the buttons to the top, everything would be covered. In the early morning when I went to the athletic field to practice tai chi, I wore a baggy T-shirt and tied a silk scarf around my neck. It was only October, and I looked as though I were dressed for a chilly winter, but I was simply covering up a secret.

Many years ago, a friend who lived in the dormitory of a movie studio often invited me to come hang out on set. She knew the directors and crew, so we'd stroll through the studio, watching as they filmed. Sometimes, while simultaneously watching various productions, it was like flipping through different books and glimpsing the authors' writing processes beyond the pages. It always left me uncertain of whether what I saw was real or an illusion. The movie studio was just like the so-called dream factory of old Hollywood, a place where all kinds of daydreams were manufactured for the world. The actors dressed in costumes from various eras, repeatedly performing life's joys and sorrows, reunions and partings. The courtyard corridor with which we'd just become familiar was suddenly dismantled before our very eyes, transformed into a winding alley. But the crew members behind the spotlights were very real, each facing their own realities.

The simulation unit in the hospital basement gave me the same feeling as the dream factory, reminding me of when I used to wander around the movie studio. In those days, another friend created sets for the studio's design department—painting portraits of actors playing chivalrous heroes, painting clouds on curtains, staging snow scenes using Styrofoam. Once the shoot was over, the designs were discarded, vanishing without a trace. If only the hospital's simulation unit was the same, and the lines drawn on people's bodies were just temporary tattoos for shooting a story about tattoos. After shooting ended, the colored lines would all be washed away, the actors resuming their original identities.

The plaster-mold room in the basement was just like the prop factory for a movie studio. It was the most wonderful place to shoot a science-fiction film, perfect for manufacturing freaks and monsters, and the effects were realistic, with dust floating about and sludge everywhere. The hospital and the movie studio were practically interchangeable. At first glance, the people shuttling back and forth in the corridor of the design room—some donning hats, some draped in long gowns—might have been mistaken for directors and actors. Was the large machine on this side of the drawing room a crane camera? And in the room where X-rays were scrutinized atop light, could it be that a director was working against the clock in the editing room? Wandering around the movie studio, I'd been an outsider. Presently, in the basement of the hospital, I understood that I'd awakened from a dream. This wasn't make-believe. I placed my hand on my chest— I had indeed taken part in a performance, and I'd lost a breast.

During this period, I only occasionally flipped through books, watching more movies instead. No, I didn't go to the cinema, but stayed at home watching videotapes. In recent years, I had enjoyed watching a lot of science-fiction and supernatural films. I still like watching anything that can fly: Peter Pan, Dumbo, flying carpets, flying saucers... It so happened that a series of science-fiction films were broadcast on TV in the middle of the night. My friend recorded them for me, and I became immersed in the world of fantasy. As for horrifying supernatural films, the one that has consistently captivated me is probably *Nosferatu*. My friend who loves cats and films translated *Dracula* and *Frankenstein* years ago. The latter was originally written by Mary Shelley, the wife of the poet Percy Bysshe Shelley. The earliest *Dracula* film perhaps dates back to Murnau. I watched it in Studio One. Back in my younger years, Studio One was a classroom for us film enthusiasts. We went there three or four times a week, as though attending classes; German expressionism, French New Wave, Italian neorealism, and Japanese Bushido, as well as various Swedish and Polish masterpieces—we didn't miss a single one. Murnau's *Nosferatu* is a classic, with a chilling, eerie atmosphere that sends shivers down your spine. The Count embarks on a long journey in search of the female protagonist, traveling by coach and by ship. Wherever he goes, however, he must always bring his own coffin. It is the source of the fulfillment of his desire. This is the past rejecting its own past, haunting the present. Our young people travel to the countryside, happily carrying bags on their backs; his burden, however, is like an odorous bag of bones he can't get rid of. If this is also a form of "post-existence," would you be interested? Later, Werner Herzog further developed the same theme, but it was obviously much more superficial; still, there are some notable parts, such as one scene, in the middle of the night, when the vampire runs around the square, his robe gently fluttering, like something out of a nightmare. When he first sees the female protagonist, Count Dracula says: "What a lovely throat." Rewatching the Herzog version videotaped from a Hong Kong TV broadcast, the Chinese subtitles translated this line as: "What a lovely photo." "Throat" was mistranslated as "photo." Women have been the objects of the male gaze since ancient times, but one thing can be viewed in different ways. Most people look at a woman's face; some, her breasts; some, her throat.

Murnau's and Herzog's female protagonists, driven by love, are willing to sacrifice themselves in order to eliminate Dracula. However, vampires are already dead. Their elimination in Murnau's film is the dissolution of the physical body, which vanishes in an instant. *Nosferatu* is intriguing, as is Roman Polanski's *The Fearless Vampire Killers*. The most interesting scene is the final one. The master and apprentice, who are determined to uphold truth and justice and eliminate vampires, end up turning into vampires themselves, bringing vampires out of the castle and into the human world. Do vampires advancing toward the human world symbolize a kind of blood cancer, metastasizing, spreading?

Although vampires can't fly, they resemble bats. The one who is adept at flying is Superman. These characters have superhuman abilities, though one is righteous, and one is wicked. Superman comes from the planet Krypton, but even he can lose his powers at times. Vampires must suck blood, hiding during the day and emerging at night. Daytime vampires are the equivalent of a powerless Superman. Superman's power lies not in boundless strength—mending fissures in the Earth's crust, or lifting a frozen lake up to the sky and transforming it into rainwater—but in transcending space and even time. He flies faster than the speed of light. When his girlfriend dies in an accident, and he can't save her in time, he flies around the Earth in reverse, turning back time to retrieve the past. In this way, he's able to prevent the disaster from happening in advance. If only this method could be used to cure cancer. Most cancer patients are unable to predict the latency and activity of tumors, and by the time they find out, it's often too late.

Another film with impressive special effects is *Who Framed Roger Rabbit*. It features a cartoon rabbit. What attracts me to this film is how humans act alongside the cartoons, a breakthrough in cinematic technique and animation. Can novels also do this? I'm not sure what method would be used to express it. In *Who Framed Roger Rabbit*, aside from Bugs Bunny, almost all the Disney cartoon characters return to their alma mater like old schoolmates: Mickey Mouse, Donald Duck, Peter Pan, the Three Little Pigs, and so on. Cartoons tend to end on a comedic note. In animation, no living beings die. Every life-form makes a strong comeback. Even if they fall from a high cliff into a deep valley, or are flattened into a thin sheet by a steamroller, soon they'll stretch their limbs, move their eyeballs, and start running everywhere. There's no old age, illness, or death in the cartoon world. Cartoon characters are like angels.

Alien is a film rich with feminist implications. It used to be that most of the strong characters in films were men, but gradually women have filled these roles as well. The female protagonist in *Alien* not only has a strong physique, resilient willpower, and the courage to shoulder responsibility, but she also has a maternal side. She's tall and clean, her words and actions are those of the modern woman. This is a female heroine created by the dream factory. The alien creatures in

THE DREAM FACTORY · 133

the film, metamorphosed from cocoons, growing and bursting inside human bodies—are they not symbols of rampant cancer cells? The aliens are also quite maternal, with many legs and a hard exoskeleton on their backs, mysteriously appearing and disappearing; they have a silent incubation period and are incredibly secretive. Once they spread, they proliferate to other corners, capable of both shrinking and expanding, making them nearly impossible to eliminate. To deal with cancer, patients need to be like the strong heroine.

Carrots are said to help fight cancer, as if they were garlic or the peachwood swords used to subdue vampires. During this time, while I watched videotapes of science-fiction films, I drank a lot of carrot juice. At first, a friend gave me a juicer, then supplied me regularly with copious amounts of carrots, practically turning my home into a carrot warehouse. There are also many varieties of carrots. The ones sold in the market are muddy, fat, and difficult to swallow after chewing. They're perfect for juicing—three of them can yield 250 milliliters of juice. The juicer squeals like a butchered pig when it's powered on, as though it's murdering some living creature. Does juicing count as an act of killing? A living carrot, shorter by a section in the blink of an eye, and in another blink, the dry dregs fly in all directions, a bloody river flowing out. Every time I eat carrots, I feel like Roger Rabbit, but when I drink carrot juice, I feel as though I've turned into a vampire.

The philosopher Susanne Langer cites R.E. Jones to point out that moving pictures break free not only from spatial restrictions but also from temporal restrictions; moreover, they possess the uncanny ability to move forward and backward in time and space. Whether it be Superman, Roger Rabbit, or the astronaut heroine in *Alien*, upon closer examination, the character inevitably appears superficial and unable to withstand scrutiny. However, they represent a collective subconscious aspiration in ordinary people toward a dreamlike transcendence of this finite life.

There was a period of time when my friends often talked to me about Laozi and Zhuangzi, mentioning Laozi's breadth of mind:

All things arise without rejection
Bearing without possessing
Acting without expectations
Achieving without claiming credit

Then we naturally transitioned to discussing Zhuangzi. Zhuangzi's "Wandering Free and Far" elucidates the concept of freely wandering in the infinite.[17] Isn't it about transcendence from the constraints of the various objective conditions of worldly life, freely wandering through limitless time and space without relying or depending on anything? Zhuangzi wrote about the giant Peng bird waiting for a strong wind in order to embark on a journey to the South Seas, showing that the giant Peng bird was restricted by time; meanwhile, the smaller birds could take flight whenever they pleased, but they could only fly as high as the weeds and the elm and sandalwood trees, falling after just a few meters, revealing they were restricted by space. The former could wander "far but not freely," whereas the latter could wander "freely but not far." Zhuangzi starts with birds, then extends to plants, and then to human beings, explaining that all beings, whether large or small, have their own limitations and dependencies, inevitably constrained in one way or another. Among them, human beings have the most constraints. Time and space are obvious constraints, but our self-imposed shackles are even more numerous, such as the opposition between the self and other, the pursuit of fame and fortune, and the like. Of course, we couldn't help but ask, was this realm of wandering free and far concrete and attainable? Zhuangzi's answer is: "It's a land where nothing really exists." In other words, an ideal spiritual realm, a longing for and pursuit of freedom. Zhuangzi was the greatest dreamer.

Having simulation markings drawn on my body didn't mean that the work was done—I still had to undergo a computer scan. A few days later, I returned to the radiology department. At eight o'clock on a Saturday morning, an hour before the official opening time, the staff in the scanning room was already on duty. Despite the early hour, I was still third in line. However, being first in line didn't mean being examined first, as another bed from the ward upstairs was wheeled in, creaking and clanking. It was an emergency. Bottles hung on racks above the bed, swaying along the long corridor like lanterns in the wind. There was a frail old man with a pale, ashen face lying on the bed. He was rushed into the scanning room at once. Everyone else had to wait outside the door for an extra hour.

I was third in line, with two men ahead of me. Fourth in line was a woman who was hard of hearing and wasn't originally from Hong Kong. Every time the nurse came out and said something, she couldn't hear it clearly, and would ask me: What was that? I'd say, There's an emergency case that went in first, or, They said, sorry we have to wait, but it can't be helped. Sitting at the entrance to the scanning room, I unexpectedly ended up serving as a loud-voiced interpreter for half the morning. I'd brought along a book to read, just one, *Legend of the Tattooed Woman*, a Spanish literature annotated reader containing twelve short stories from Mexico, Central America, and the Caribbean, with the Spanish and Chinese on facing pages. I focused on "It's Because We're So Poor" by the Mexican author Juan Rulfo, carefully reading the Spanish text and studying the Chinese word by word. The text was accompanied by notes on the Spanish words, which made it as useful as a textbook. I paid particular attention to this piece, as it was a story I'd translated several years ago, based on an English translation. Now, reading the original text, I could see the original sentence structures. Back then, why had I been so concerned with faithfully translating sentence by sentence? I was merely translating the writing style of the English translator. I have to agree that secondhand translation is by no means ideal, and as a translator, one can't place complete trust in it. When translating this story, I was always perplexed by one character, a twelve-year-old girl named Tacha—was she the narrator's elder or younger sister? In both English and Spanish, the term for sister does not distinguish between elder sister and younger sister, unlike in Chinese, where the clear differentiation of kinship titles reflects our feudal traditions. The art historian

E. H. Gombrich was correct when he stated that one benefit of learning to translate another language is that it teaches us that beyond certain superficial common understandings among humans, there are deeper aspects that cannot be translated, reflecting the communication of cultural traditions that stem from different roots. I had pondered over this character for a long time, translating her as the elder sister. Now, upon rereading, I realized she was actually the younger sister. Alas, I'd mistranslated a crucial relationship between the characters.

The number of people waiting in line grew, until more than ten people were sitting on the long benches. As nine o'clock approached, the little rooms along the corridor began to open up one by one as the staff trickled in. A woman unlocked a door, retrieved a teacup, washed it clean, then brought it back. The doctors' names and department designation were clearly written on the doors. The names of foreign doctors were listed in both Chinese and English, side by side, their names translated in a lively and joyful manner, like model characters in government announcements reminding people when to renew their ID cards, bestowed with names such as Brilliant Brocade or Youth Evermore ... Many people walked past us, including an elderly white-haired foreign gentleman holding a leather bag, wearing charcoal-gray tweed slacks, a thick cotton shirt with dark red stripes, and brown suede shoes—I mistook him for an artist. As he passed slowly through the corridor, he nodded at us and greeted us good morning in Chinese. He opened a door and went into his room to work. The door didn't shut all the way, leaving it ajar. I could see the lights were on, and I glimpsed him sitting in a swivel chair with his back to us, examining X-rays. I didn't know whose medical condition appeared in the images. I envied the doctor for being so old yet so healthy, and for being able to put his knowledge to good use.

An elderly lady also came down the corridor, her stride brisk and her back straight, her spirits high, all by herself. She must have come for a scan too. It was hard to tell what ailed her, as she didn't look one bit sick. Many elderly women her age walked with a faltering gait, always supported by a family member on either side, their faces filled with worry. Next came a younger girl and a middle-aged woman. Since it was Saturday, the young ones didn't have to go to school or work, so they tended to accompany their mothers. Whether they arrived early or late, everyone had to wait an hour or two.

I was third in line. After the hospital bed was pushed out of the scanning room, to my surprise, some men were next to undergo the scan. First, of course, were the ones who were first and second in line, and then, unexpectedly, the ones who were fifth and sixth in line. They all went in ahead. Perhaps they were separating men and women, or maybe sorting by case type. Finally, the nurse called out a string of names and told us to go and change our clothes. Fourth in line again asked: What's going on? I said, We're going to change our clothes. There were two changing rooms. Fourth in line and I went to change first. When I came out, I was slightly taken aback to find that it was the young woman who'd gone into the changing room, not her mother. She emerged with the ribbons of her gown tied behind her. I said, You have the gown on backward. But she said, No, it's supposed to be worn this way. I didn't know what illness she had. Maybe there were different ways to wear the gown, depending upon the illness.

Three white-gowned angels. Later, I came to hear their names every day. Fourth in line was Lee Ping, the elderly lady was Wu Man-kuen, and the young woman was Zong Suk-man. Fourth in line took a while to come out of the changing room. She said to me: Ah, next time, I'll remember to bring a big plastic bag—look, now I have to carry around this pile of clothes I've changed out of. The computer scan didn't take long; it was probably just capturing images of the part where the design had been drawn. The doctor who first examined me in the oncology unit also came to take a look at the results of the computer scan. I supposed each patient's case was handled by a dedicated doctor. I used to think that doctors simply sat in the consultation rooms seeing patients and made their rounds in the wards, but it turned out that their workload wasn't light at all. For example, this doctor saw patients in the oncology unit's consultation room, designed markings in the simulation unit, and also monitored the progress of the imaging and scanning rooms. He could only be described as hardworking and high-achieving.

If this is too much mumbo jumbo, and you want to read about breast cancer treatment, please turn to "Magic Bullet" on page 162.

ARCADES

A PAGE from an 1852 Paris guidebook reads: "These arcades are a new invention of industrial luxury. Their ceilings are inlaid with glass, and the ground is paved with marble, forming passageways to connect blocks of buildings. They are the product of the shopkeepers' collective efforts. Both sides of these passageways are lined with elegant and luxurious shops, illuminated by lights hanging overhead. Thus, the arcades can be likened to a miniature city, or even a miniature world." For more than a century, arcades have proliferated like vines, becoming a feature of the modern urban landscape.

As the city has flourished, the arcades have spread too, rising along with the buildings, arches interlocking with arches, converging into other arcades, arcades stacked atop arcades, forming multitiered vertical streets. The arcades extend in all directions, their corridors connecting buildings, turning into elevated streets—there's no longer any need to live on the surface of the Earth's crust. Starting out from this point on one of the city's second-level streets, you'll zigzag through an air-conditioned building lobby, cross a mile-long bridge, step onto an electric staircase, and return to the bustling ground level. If you're a hiking aficionado, here you'll find ferries that will take you to the outlying islands, where you can enjoy the bright sunshine and fresh air. Continuing from here, you'll pass through more air-conditioned buildings, entering and exiting, suddenly cold then hot, quiet then noisy. Adopting the mind-set of a tourist, you can leisurely observe the view: On the mountain-shaded road, you see the flow of traffic beneath your feet, the park beside you, the postmodern buildings in the distance.

This building is, of course, a high-tech product. Its name is the HSBC Building. It's exactly the same color as an airplane, because some of its building materials are indeed the same as those used for airplanes and space shuttles—such expensive materials! But it's light-weight; can you feel its lightness? Its body seems to have the wings of a seagull, stretching out as it soars. Perhaps the feeling of flight isn't that prominent, but you can sense its brightness, its delightful transparency, which is due to the light-control system operated by electronic instruments, able to quickly and effectively adjust the brightness indoors, thereby also conserving electricity.

You can just keep heading east on the elevated street, walking on and on. With each step, the bank gradually moves before your very eyes. The silhouette of the bank is particularly interesting. At this moment, it really looks like a robot. Aha, another strange building appears in front of you. Is it also a bank, a modern Tower of Babel? The small windows in the glass curtain wall are wide open in a V-shape. The bank hasn't been completed yet. Come back and see it in the future. By then, however, all the windows will be tightly shut.

Just continue forward. Up ahead is the Lippo Centre, two build-ings whose bodies, seemingly studded with Juliet balconies, sometimes twist and turn like windmills. Do you need to apply for an "entry permit" to travel to Taiwan? Duck inside and go through the for-malities; the administrator will be happy to give you directions. No, you're just passing through, so move on. The Admiralty corridor is up ahead—cross the footbridge, and you'll reach Pacific Place. All the beautiful and ugly characters in the city have gone there, the yuppies have found their new Garden of Eden: the Seibu Department Store.

I didn't walk through either of these east-west corridors. Today, I came over from Kowloon Peninsula, crossing Victoria Harbour by ferry. Where was I going? I had no particular place in mind. I'd become a flaneuse, simply roaming about. Once, while I was taking the MTR in Sha Tin, a woman slipped into the car before the doors closed.

—Is this the train to Kowloon?

—I'm not sure.

—Not sure? Then where are you going?

—It doesn't matter. Anywhere will do.

She didn't understand, of course, that I had plenty of time, that I had gone out for a leisurely stroll with no specific destination in mind. The direction of the train made no difference to me. I couldn't lie in bed at home all day saying that I was sick. Roaming about kept my feet moving, increasing my lung capacity for breathing, allowing me to take in the sights around me. I chose the ferry because, except for the parks and countryside, the air in the harbor was the freshest. On the ferry, I felt carefree, gazing at the undulating rhythms of the waves that called to mind a piano sonata.

Coming out of the Star Ferry Pier, you can climb up to the elevated street. The few rickshaws parked at the bottom of the stairs are leftover colonial cultural relics that have traveled from the distant history of transportation development. Different streets have given birth to different modes of transportation. Elevated streets, electric conveyor belts, and vertical ladders stretch out before us—streets without vehicles are the best walkways. I walk slowly, seeing others of my kind, people who are similarly idle, with nothing to do. They don't beg but merely drift about; their homes are in the passageways where crowds shuttle back and forth. Stacked cardboard boxes form the walls of their homes, and their beds are mats and newspapers, bridging the gap between the outdoors and indoors. Comparatively, the urban drifters here lead frugal lives, because under the footbridge near my apartment, several vagabonds also reside, and they have not only iron beds but also a table and chairs. On the table are sealed glass jars full of olives, as well as metal cans. They keep two cats who catch mice for them. They also have a dog who often sprawls in the middle of the road, projecting an air of indifference to poverty, causing pedestrians to take a detour.

The graffiti artist Tsang Tsou-choi—the self-proclaimed "King of Kowloon"—clearly hasn't visited here, because wherever he goes, he leaves his calligraphy behind. Someone once said: "The meaning of life is to leave a mark." He's left brush-written notices all over Kowloon: TSANG TSOU-CHOI IS THE EMPEROR, AND THIS IS HIS LAND. These words have appeared on granite columns and plastered walls, even on a flagpole in Tsim Sha Tsui.[18] Over the years, we've come across his name here and there. Some of his work has been erased, some washed away by the rain, and some taken down and relocated. Our city is under constant renovation. But he always manages to leave traces of his name, and he always finds places to write it. He's been more prolific lately, inscribing the names, places of origin, and addresses of his brothers, father, and other family members, insisting that this is his territory. After practicing calligraphy for so many years, it's strange that his penmanship hasn't improved. Is it because he only cares about himself? His whereabouts are unpredictable; no one knows where he'll show up next. However, if you don't deliberately seek him out, he'll appear before you when you least expect it, brush and ink in hand, writing earnestly, an elderly man holding a wooden cane, who doesn't get around very easily. I recently discovered that he's updated his methods, writing calligraphy on paper and making mass photocopies that he then posts everywhere. It makes an impression: Tsang Tsou-choi is omnipresent, having entered the age of mechanical reproduction.

Women wanderers are comparatively fewer. However, Moll Flanders and Tsang Tsou-choi are equally famous in Hong Kong. I call her Moll Flanders because that's the name of the female protagonist in Defoe's novel, a precursor of the woman wanderer in European literary history. Tsang Tsou-choi is a symbol in our lives. We read his name and understand its meaning, but we rarely meet him in person. But as for Moll Flanders, you can see her almost every day. She's outside the entrance to the eyewear shop in the Landmark, the most glorious place in the city. She uses her attire to inscribe her name here. Her actual residence seems to be elsewhere, as there are no beds or even walls here, but she positions herself by the entrance every day, working day in and day out, a veritable figure of the Central District. If you come often, you can't help but acknowledge the absolute harmony between her and this flourishing, beautiful space, as she often holds personal fashion exhibitions. She has many clothes, the colors bright, the materials exquisite, the styles fashionable—it's only because they've been worn for a long time without being dry-cleaned that they've gradually faded. Most likely, affluent women of all ages have donated their castoffs to her, turning her into a fashion model for passersby to stop and admire. What attracts people to her, however, isn't so much her clothing as her personal taste. The clothing alone isn't what makes a person stand out—it's how it's put together. Every day, she comes up with new combinations, such as a bright yellow-and-black polka-dot knee-length wool skirt paired with harem pants of the same fabric and colors, accessorized with a jade-green scarf. She matches red with green and blue with yellow, precisely the palette of the impressionists. She never neglects accessories: a simple scarf wrapped around her neck today, tied around her waist the day before, tied around her forehead the day after . . . She finds her own joy, truly standing out among the realm of idlers. Who knows—perhaps she's a lyric poet of the era of advanced capitalism.

Aside from the wanderers who sleep out in the open, there is another category of flaneurs who also roam the city. Unlike the vagabonds beneath the footbridges, they have families, loved ones, and places to return to each night to watch TV and eat dinner, but they have no steady employment. It's not that they lack talent—in fact, maybe they're *too* talented—it's simply that they have no interest in working at a fixed time and place. They might engage in various short-term odd jobs, such as planning film festivals or art events, organizing exhibitions, or pursuing freelance work. They don't like working on a regular schedule, and so they have more leisure time to roam the city. You occasionally encounter them during off-peak hours. Some appear disheveled and unkempt, looking just like vagabonds; some, however, are dressed to the nines, perhaps decked out in the latest styles. They're all intriguing individuals who often gather in sophisticated coffee shops, Luk Yu Tea House, and French-style outdoor cafés.

Today, I don't run into any of these vagabonds. I pass by the General Post Office and enter the Landmark commercial complex. This is the heart of the arcades. If you look up, you see a transparent ceiling, and the surrounding buildings all have glass curtain walls. Sunlight scatters a pattern of rays, a resplendent display of gold, jade, silver, and emerald, making you feel as though you're in a crystal canyon. What are your thoughts on modern or postmodern architecture? Yes, yes, form isn't important; what's important is social life. We place too much emphasis on functionality. Yes, yes, designing individual buildings may be interesting, each one more interesting than the last. But architects should have a broader vision, not just focusing on individual buildings. A building should be connected with other buildings; the buildings should be connected with the streets, and the streets should be connected with the squares. Whose words are these? Oh, I. M. Pei's.

Hong Kong was gradually built along the harbor, with streets running parallel to the water from east to west, so there are no sprawling squares, no squares filled with pigeons, no squares with bronze statues of heroes, no squares with soaring city gates. Would we regret the absence of squares? As a result, people moved the squares inside the buildings—just as there are arcade streets, there are also arcade squares. The shopping arcades all have magnificent names for themselves. What did you say? Oh, if we move the Tamar—the site of the Central Government offices—we can open up a Piazza San Marco like in Venice.

You're here, and you're here too. You're all here. The arcades are a small crossroads, an indoor public square. You're here waiting for friends because it's convenient and centrally located, the destination clear. You, on the other hand, are merely passing by, entering from Des Voeux Road Central and exiting onto Queen's Road Central, enjoying a few minutes of air-conditioning, temporarily escaping the outdoor clamor and exhaust. You're here to eat lunch. The restaurants downstairs and on the second floor are nice, but they tend to fill up. Sitting here, don't you feel like all eyes are on you? You've come to have a look at the new fall clothing lines. You're here on a quest, or perhaps to go hunting, like a hound sniffing a wild deer's tracks.

Those who regard the arcade as a footbridge have passed by. If you're a tourist, you should head to Upper Lascar Row to search for antiques; if you love excitement and novelty, you can check out Lan Kwai Fong. Oh, you should visit Lan Kwai Fong at night. The people

eating lunch begin cutting the food on their plates, while those waiting for friends stand by the fountain. The fountain isn't operational
today—there are no jets of water, no lights. Today, the square is so
quiet, with no car exhibitions or afternoon music, only a few people
slowly strolling past the shop display windows. Glass is truly human-
kind's greatest invention. With glass, people can communicate with
the world outside the walls, keeping connected while maintaining
an appropriate distance. People always desire both contact and self-
preservation. With glass, there are glass display windows. With glass
display windows, the arcades become even more enchanting. Each
display window is an Aladdin's magic lamp, constantly producing
things that astonish and excite you.

You move slowly in front of the display windows, often pausing
to study them closely. As you walk, there's something magnetic pull-
ing you in. How do the objects inside the display windows captivate
you? You stand there quietly, eventually becoming motionless, a
hushed conversation unfolding between you and the display windows.
I can't hear it—there must be a secret code between you. Aha, you're
entranced, the display windows in the arcade have you in their thrall,
submissive, longing, waiting, hesitating, anxious, attached, and fren-
zied.

This shop displays the fall clothing line from Milan. What do you
know about Milan? Leonardo da Vinci's *The Last Supper* hanging in
a church, the World Cup, La Scala opera house, fashion houses? I'm
not sure whether you've heard of any of these names: Pietro Zamuner,
Franco Mella, Renzo Milanese, and Adelio Lambertoni? If not,
forget it. It doesn't matter—they're common names. These names
have piqued your curiosity. Would you like me to tell you? Okay,
they're priests from Milan. They're Italian, of course, but having lived
in Hong Kong for more than ten, even twenty years, they can speak
English and, even more so, Cantonese. I've seen these priests. No no,
I'm not Catholic! I didn't see them in church but on the street. I saw
them wearing twill pants, jeans, vertically striped or checkered
button-down shirts, horizontally striped and solid-colored sweatshirts,
sandals on their feet. They're probably on the street more than they

are in a church. They eat beef chow fun at food stalls, live on wooden boats in the typhoon shelter, and are also fond of motorbikes. Of course, they like watching soccer. I've seen them a few times: once singing their wandering song in Cantonese, and another time petitioning at the entrance of the Xinhua News Agency.

Oh, you're not interested in petitions and such. You leave me and go into the Milan fashion boutique. You're so young and elegantly dressed, you must be a yuppie. Just now at the tram station, I saw two yuppies in loose-fitting trousers, short-sleeved striped shirts, and pristine white canvas shoes, appearing pleased as punch with their footwear, wearing Schubert-style flat oval glasses. Single aristocrats pass by holy wanderers, and yuppies brush shoulders with yuppies. Nowadays, you're all wearing suspenders, a traditional garment that used to be concealed by a vest, but now it's the age of bringing inner beauty to the forefront. You likewise have a vagabond spirit, subverting the order of interior and exterior space. You're truly a fortunate generation, in a prosperous society, with affluent family backgrounds, and opportunities to pursue higher education—you've become the modern-day aristocracy.

You come out of the shop, carrying a small pale gray paper bag. With such a tiny bag after such a short time, I'm guessing you bought a tie or silk scarf. You are constantly consuming, constantly possessing, just like a great white shark. That's quite a nice suit you've got on. Such clothing perfectly matches the design of the HSBC Building, exuding a light and bright aura. If it's pure linen, that's good, as those synthetic fabrics are nothing more than polyester and acrylic, made from petroleum products, polluting the water and the air. How many highly toxic chemicals are used to make clothing, in washing, dyeing, and breaking down wood pulp? How much destruction lies behind a beautiful piece of clothing?

You came to the arcade together. Have you eaten lunch? Do you have to go to work? It's still early, let's admire the scenery here. This row of shopwindows is now adorned with fall colors, only displaying one outfit: a thick cotton floral shirt paired with a long twill skirt, a hand-knit sweater draped over the shoulders. Do you like this outfit?

Such a long skirt may not be suitable for work but would be perfect for sitting on a swing hanging from a tree branch in a lush green meadow. The tiny flowers on the shirt are brick-red, reminiscent of autumn leaves, giving you a warm feeling. But you really like that sweater, don't you? Because you point to it and whisper to her: I can't knit such a pattern. The entire sweater is full of stars, moons, flowers, trees, small brick houses, and flying birds. She says to you, Even if you could knit it, you wouldn't be able to find that type of wool. You can't reproduce the effect of the wool sweater because it has the faded color of bygone years—even if it's a new garment, it has an old-fashioned feel when worn.

In this display window, in addition to the outfit, there are also many deliberately showcased items: hardcover books with gilt edges, rotating globes, and exquisite little photo frames with sepia-toned photographs of people from the early twentieth century, glass-shaded lamps, and so on. These objects send signals to you, evoking your associations. Do you truly like this outfit? Or is it the image that the clothes represent? Just stand in front of the display window, letting the wings of the clothing carry you away, transporting you to the nineteenth-century English countryside, immersing you in the glory and romance of the colonial era, as though you have become, or already are, Daisy in F. Scott Fitzgerald's *The Great Gatsby*, existing in a world that's outwardly magnificent but internally decayed and corrupt. The symbolism of the outfit hints at notions of noble lineage. Ah, no, you say you only want to buy a pretty sweater, that's all? In my view, what you want to buy is nothing more than ideas and names.

You say that cotton products are nice, comfortable to wear, allowing you to breathe; cotton fabrics are renewable, easily decomposing after being discarded, without harming the natural environment. Thinking this way proves that you care about the planet we live on, and nothing is more urgent than self-preservation. But if the consumption of cotton is high, farmers will grow too much of it, depleting the land, and aren't pesticides also polluting fields, water, and the air? If you really want to protect nature, it's better to reduce clothing consumption, and choose durable and long-lasting garments.

You are ultimately drawn into the shop by the magnetism of the display window—in the arcade, who can break away from this irresistible magnetic field? I also feel a distant call, like the song of sirens on an island in the sea, constantly luring me in. On the ground floor of the arcade, there's a record store. How can I escape from Horowitz's performances of Chopin from the 1950s? Is the bestseller in the bookstore this week a book about food called *Healthy for Life*, or is it Stephen Hawking's *A Brief History of Time*? I wonder how Hawking is doing lately. The transformation of humans into stone in the novel *The Legend of the Swordsmen of the Mountains of Shu* is a reality for him. He is facing such a death, starting from his feet and progressing upward. His situation is even more frightening than Socrates's, as poisons act fast but diseases are slow. Compared to what Hawking is going through, cancer's nothing.

Oh, this shop catches my attention—it sells lingerie. In the display window, there are sheer silk undergarments draped over luminous mannequins, revealing white and pink hues that make the clothing appear diaphanous. The lace, texture of the fabric, smoothness of the skin—all of it is crystal clear. Such delicate, small pieces of lingerie suggest that someone's mistress is indulging in a warm scented bath behind a folding screen. If, at this moment, she absent-mindedly stroked her own breast and found a lump, what would she think? *I'll never be able to wear these beautiful pieces of lingerie again*. Is there a lingerie shop that sells bras for only one breast? How many women worldwide are diagnosed with breast cancer each year? The number is increasing, with the age of diagnosis decreasing. There must be savvy businesses targeting them.

Specialty lingerie shops for women with breast cancer wouldn't be located in the arcades. They can only be found in hidden upperlevel shops, known through word of mouth among a select few who discreetly go upstairs to make their purchases, like those pawnshops people always sneak into and out of. After my surgery, I tried to but couldn't wear my previous bras anymore. Could I use those padded bras stuffed with sponges? I didn't try. My friend and I frowned when we saw one. We often said: It's too scary—if it falls on the ground, it'll make a thud. There are really a lot of people wearing these bras. You can see them bustling about on the streets, armored like tanks. I haven't worn a bra since September. My underarm area is swollen; anything tight feels uncomfortable, and my incision can't tolerate the friction of the fabric. I only wear loose-fitting shirts, and I feel good. On the streets, I blend in with the crowd. In the arcade, I become a drop of water in a river.

Are you still in the shop, poring over that hand-knit sweater with clay-colored suede trim? I have to go, continuing my journey as an idler, taking the escalator from the third floor all the way to the ground floor. The bookstore and record store? I won't visit them today. Once you enter these shops, it's not easy to leave. Instead, keep strolling along the arcade. I pass the alluring display windows, exit the building, and cross the narrow road, arriving at the HSBC Building. You can walk freely through the ground floor of the bank, which feels refreshing. In northern China, there's a type of tower called a crossing street tower, built on a thoroughfare or a major street, with an arch-shaped tunnel underneath for pedestrians and vehicles to pass through. Yes, God isn't perched high above but resides in the heart of the buzzing city streets, considerate of busy virtuous women and devout men. Simply passing beneath the tower is tantamount to chanting sutras in a temple. The HSBC Building is also like this; it can be called a crossing street bank. The most worshipped god in Hong Kong is money—the crossing street tower is built in the heart of the streets, giving people more opportunities to contact the gods; of course, a crossing street bank needs to have many customers so that its business will thrive. So that its business will thrive, this building that is currently the most expensive in the world, a crystallization of cutting-edge Western technology, interestingly must also comply with the principles of feng shui. When submitting the preliminary plan, the architect, Norman Foster, had to first consult with a feng shui master. Hence, the architectural blueprint includes a feng shui sketch. The layout of the building's ground floor, the positioning of the escalators and two bronze lions, and the arrangement of the furniture in the offices were all determined by a feng shui master to attract good fortune, avert misfortune, and ensure a steady flow of wealth. The ground here is wave-shaped, perfect for teenagers who love skating; looking up at the ceiling above, it's also wave-shaped, like folded slate. Looking farther up from the first ceiling, there's another ceiling above it, everything transparent, the highest point consisting of fragmented beams of light. The ceiling above that is too far away—I can't see it. With so many glass ceilings, I'm afraid there are a lot of barriers to break.

Standing in the center of the ground floor of the bank, when you look up, you see soft light that's pleasing to the eyes. The most attractive feature of this building is the light—natural light. Above the glass ceiling is a light-filled central atrium. On the dome, there is a row of mirrors reflecting the sunlight collected by the outer mirrors, making the whole building bright and cheerful. The bank also gives the impression of being composed of stacked blocks, as though all of the lead plates and steel columns could be freely combined and moved at any time. In fact, this is precisely the architect's concept: In order to break fixed boundaries, the office partitions can be quickly altered. Would you like to look around upstairs? First, step onto this strange, transparent reptilian escalator. You're busy today and don't have time—okay, then just check out the escalator. The electric staircase, where you can see the moving contents—continuous steps, interlocking conveyor belts—turning somersaults in an endless loop. If the human body were also this transparent, would it be terrifying or lovely? All of our organs would be clearly visible, and we would all see one another's hearts. Red blood and blue blood, coursing through tubes; a chocolate candy comes in, soon becoming a gooey paste, flowing into the stomach. It's better to let the skin keep it all under wraps. However, as disconcerting as a transparent body might be, perhaps there wouldn't be the need to see the doctor as frequently. Lowering your head, oh, the blood vessels are clogged with thick fat, or the gallbladder is accumulating stones, as though it wants to transform itself into a pearl-producing oyster. There wouldn't be a need to take X-rays anymore.

Cross the street and walk up the spiral staircase next to the Hilton

Hotel, and you'll reach the footbridge. This is the most beautiful spot in the Central District. Don't go, don't go—stand here and carefully take it all in. From this angle, you can see all sorts of towering buildings, from different eras, of different shapes. The Legislative Council Complex is a low, two-story structure with both a domed roof and Romanesque columns, as well as stone-carved balustrades with intricate designs, embodying classical architectural elements. On the lintel above the main entrance, a blindfolded goddess still holds the scales of justice; it's best to weigh all laws on it first. City hall, the Prince's Building, and Furama Hotel are all iconic modern buildings, like Mondrian's paintings. Sadly, they lack Mondrian's vibrant colors.

Standing at this spot on the footbridge, there are three beautiful postmodern buildings right in front of you: the Lippo Centre to the east, the HSBC Building to the west, and the Bank of China Tower to the south. Ah, you say, the Bank of China Tower isn't postmodern architecture—I.M. Pei believes that modernism isn't yet finished. You don't care for the Lippo Centre. It looks a bit like the head of a person on the body of a fish, and the waterfall at the main entrance isn't easy to see. Those Juliet balconies are deceptive, as they're enclosed in glass—Juliet has no way to throw down a flower, and Romeo can't climb up. Plus, glass is a modernist thing. Looking at the HSBC Building from the side, it appears even more playful. Isn't it just a gigantic robot standing there? The crane on the top moves slowly, as if the robot is about to take flight. From this angle, you can see more arm-shaped support columns, postmodern architecture bringing the columns and embellishments of Gothic cathedrals outdoors.

Of all the buildings in the entire city, only the Bank of China Tower leaves you in awe. When you gaze upward, you marvel at its immensity. Not all buildings evoke this feeling in you. Only two others, you say—once, when standing at the base of the Cologne Cathedral in Germany and, another time, amid the numerous columns of the Luxor and Karnak Temples in Egypt. You can't just make a trip to Egypt or Germany every two or three days. For you, it may be a once-in-a-lifetime opportunity. However, surprisingly you can obtain this awe-inspiring feeling quite easily in the city where you live.

You've long felt that this vertical skyscraper isn't like a sharp knife, as people say, but an obelisk. Or perhaps this is just another interpretation among many. You've been to Egypt, as has the building's architect, who recently built a glass pyramid in Paris. The base of the obelisk is square, its tip pointed, inlaid with thin gold. When the sun hits it, it gleams, displaying the glory of the god Amun. The entire glass obelisk is shiny, with a rectangular composition made up of squares, the squares consisting of triangles, the triangles concealing countless more squares that are sometimes flat, sometimes folded, filled with a sense of dynamism. The glass pyramid in front of the Louvre and this glass obelisk are both part of I.M. Pei's Egyptian series. Ah, Egypt, ah, the pyramids, ah, the obelisk, all overlapping. What does it mean when such a towering monument appears now in the heart of Hong Kong?

COUNTERATTACK

YEARS ago, influenced by germ theory, people believed that the malignant transformation of cells started from one single cell that gradually proliferated and formed a tumor. This is the theory of unifocal origin. In recent years, the medical community has found that the origin of breast cancer is often multifocal, which has led to the concept of field cancerization. Although some people may only find tumors on one side of the mammary gland, breast cancer actually encompasses the entire mammary gland. It can appear in different places on one side of the mammary gland, or in various places on both sides as multiple independent cancer foci. Under different conditions, these cancer foci can develop into carcinoma in situ.

Cancer foci that develop and form in their original location are called carcinoma in situ. Some carcinomas in situ can remain dormant for decades. As for cancers that spread elsewhere, they are metastatic cancers and diffuse cancers. Cancer cells are colonizers of the body—in addition to incessantly proliferating, they also invade and conquer distant territories, migrating in large numbers, forcibly occupying the original organ tissue, causing the original cell communities to lose their independent sovereignty and to fall completely under their rule.

Some cancer cells spread directly, invading the surrounding glandular tissue and even the ribs of the chest wall, intercostal muscles, and the like; some cancer cells spread along lymphatic pathways, first forming metastatic foci in the lymph nodes, then penetrating the lymph node membranes, and extending beyond the nodes, forming long chains that roam freely throughout the body. Generally speaking, the lymph nodes swell when invaded by cancer, and small, dark-red firm nodules may also form on the surface of the skin, but sometimes this manifestation is hidden, with no visible swelling or granules, which is especially insidious; some cancer cells spread through the bloodstream. There are many interconnected networks between the lymphatic and venous vessels. Cancer cells can enter the bloodstream without a hitch through the gaps in these networks, traveling far and wide via this extensive network of rivers, invading the lungs, liver, and bones. Some patients refuse to undergo tumor removal surgery because the procedure sometimes damages blood vessels, disturbing the cancer cells which then easily infiltrate the bloodstream through the tears in the blood vessels, leading to an artificial spread of the cancer cells. Rather than risk damage from surgery, they prefer to let the tumor remain in the body. The portion removed during surgery is also wider than the scope of the tumor.

Radiation therapy has been used to treat breast cancer since as early as the 1920s. This defense force from high above is akin to sending bomber planes on a mission to destroy enemy-occupied camps; unfortunately, innocent civilians are inevitably harmed in the process. Initially, radiation therapy used radium and deep X-rays, but due to the low dosage and long course of treatment, the effects were insignificant. In the early 1950s, cobalt 60 was adopted, which evolved to the use of cesium 137, and later the linear accelerator was employed. Electrons, once accelerated, directly emit beta rays, also known as electron beams. When high-energy electrons rapidly penetrate the human body, at first the dose is uniformly distributed, but once a certain depth is reached, the dose quickly decreases. This is a characteristic of their physical dose distribution. This advantage of radiation is best suited for superficial treatments, such as breast cancer. Breast cancer tumors are mostly on the surface of the skin, unlike the lungs, stomach, and intestines, which are buried deep inside the body. Postoperative irradiation for breast cancer targets the chest wall, internal mammary region, and the supraclavicular region. If electron beams are used, the diseased tissue can be encompassed within the high-dose irradiation range, significantly reducing the dosage received in the deep layers of the lungs; therefore, the lung tissue is less susceptible to damage and is protected. Cobalt 60 rays have strong penetration capabilities, making them preferable for deep-seated treatments. In fact, some patients who receive cobalt 60 irradiation in the internal mammary region may later develop pulmonary fibrosis near the sternum or on the inner side of the lung apex. It's rumored that some patients have coughed up blood from the irradiation, probably due to the aftereffects of early cobalt 60 radiation. Today's radiation therapy no longer has such severe consequences. Aside from electron beams, other forms currently under development include photon beams, proton beams, negative pion beams, and high-energy heavy particle beams, among others. The future of these aerial combat forces is limitless.

Malignant tumors are an accumulation of various types of cancer cells. Some are rich in oxygen, and some are hypoxic. From a military strategic perspective, they pose thorny challenges to the medical task force. Oxygen-rich cells are sensitive to radiation and die upon initial exposure; hypoxic cells, however, are highly resistant to radiation, and despite repeated attempts to destroy them, they don't just die off. They are sluggish and slow-moving, and the farther they are from the capillaries, the more hypoxic they become, so radiation therapy must make a concerted effort to target these cells. First, the oxygen-rich cells are eliminated. One must wait for the remaining hypoxic cells, find ways to reoxygenate them, and increase their level of oxygenation and sensitivity to radiation. Once they turn into oxygen-rich cells, then they are destroyed. As such, radiation therapy can only kill one batch at a time, then patiently wait to attack the next batch, one after another, repeating the process until they are completely eradicated. Neutron beams, negative pion beams, and high-energy particle beams, which are currently under research and development, produce high ionization densities in the body, possessing significant destructive power against hypoxic cells, making them the most promising rays for treating malignant tumors.

As early as the nineteenth century, the medical community discovered that the growth of breast cancer is related to the menstrual cycle.

With the removal of the ovaries, the metastases in some patients has been controlled. This method of treating breast cancer by removing the endocrine glands is known as hormone elimination therapy, which falls under the category of endocrine therapy. The normal glandular organs in the human body contain special receptors that interact with hormones, and the receptor sites can initiate mutual interactions between hormones and cells. After a cell becomes malignant, all or some of its receptors may be retained. In these cases, its growth and function are still related to hormones, and endocrine therapy has an inhibitory effect on such types of cancer cells. This type of tumor is called a hormone-dependent tumor. If a cell loses its receptors during a malignant transformation, it won't be controlled by hormones, becoming an autonomous, hormone-independent tumor that does whatever it wants. In such cases, endocrine therapy isn't effective. Breast cancer tumors are partly hormone-dependent and partly hormone-independent, so even if the endocrine navy is mobilized, it can only control a portion of the cells. Originally, endocrine control therapy required the removal of the ovaries and other gonads, but now antiestrogens developed through research can be used to replace surgery, reducing harm to the patient.

What are hormones? They are a type of chemical substance found in glands in the body that can stimulate specific organs to perform specific activities. As early as the nineteenth century, scientists discovered there was something in the adrenal glands that could cause arterial constriction and an increase in blood pressure. Based on sound, "hormone" can be transliterated into Mandarin as *he'ermeng* and into Cantonese as *hoyimung*; there's also another rendering based on meaning instead of sound, which literally translates to "stimulating element." The hormone secreted by the adrenal glands is called adrenaline. Since the concept of "hormone dependency" was introduced, the medical community has been able to employ both "ablative hormone therapy" and "additive hormone therapy." The latter approach, which uses estrogen, androgen, progesterone, and glucocorticoid to treat breast cancer, has a forty- to fifty-year history. Among these is the use of antiestrogens, which are synthetic nonsteroidal compounds that can reduce the specific absorption of estrogen by various tissues both inside and outside the body. The earliest used was clomiphene, followed by nafoxidine, and then tamoxifen. All three are derivatives of triphenylethylene, similar to diethylstilbestrol in structure. Tamoxifen is effective against soft tissue metastases, but evidently powerless against distant metastases. Moreover, it's more effective in patients who've been menopausal for many years compared to those who've recently become menopausal. As for reactions, some people may experience mild decreases in white blood cells and plate-lets, as well as irregular uterine bleeding. If antiestrogens are effective in treating postmenopausal women, they can be used continuously for two to five years. Because endocrine therapy doesn't severely dam-age normal tissue, it's preferable to radiation therapy and chemo-therapy. However, it is generally less effective when used alone, and can only be used as an adjuvant therapy.

Each of us inherits half of our chromosomes from our mother and half from our father, so we possess certain traits from both parents. Our parents also have their own parents, and their parents each have their own parents as well. Thus, each of the forty-six chromosomes contained in human cells is made up of thousands of genetic traits. Every chromosome is composed of hundreds of smaller units, each of which controls a particular trait. Biologists refer to these smaller units as "genes." Chromosomes are made up of proteins and nucleic acids, and nucleic acid molecules are made up of units of nucleotides; mean-while, proteins are made up of units of amino acids. Three adjacent nucleotides form a group, corresponding to a specific amino acid. This corresponding relationship is called the "genetic code." Both genes and the genetic code have a close relationship with cancer.

The reproduction of human cells occurs through mitosis. The period from the end of one cell division to the next is considered one cycle. Chromosomes undergo replication during the interphase, and the process of evenly distributing the duplicated chromosomes into two daughter cells is called the mitotic phase. Cancer cells are originally normal cells. Although they are diseased, they still proliferate through mitosis. Therefore, to prevent cancer cells from proliferating through mitosis, the main task is to interfere with their replication process, which is the basis of chemotherapy. If the hormones used in endocrine therapy are a naval fleet, then chemotherapy's troops would be akin to a corps of marines. For breast cancer, chemotherapy is generally effective because it can destroy cancer cells without destroying normal breast tissue. However, it can still damage other organs, including bone marrow.

The effect of chemical drugs on cancer follows first-order kinetics, resulting in logarithmic killing. A proportionate dosage of the medication is required to kill a corresponding number of cancer cells. For example, if the number of cancer cells is (1×10^0), that's manageable; (1×10^1), (1×10^2), and (1×10^3) aren't difficult either; (1×10^4) can be cured with three courses of chemotherapy and (1×10^6) can be cured with four courses. However, once the amount reaches (1×10^7), it can't be treated with chemotherapy. On the one hand, the increasing number of cancer cells is certainly a factor. More important, however, is that as the mass of the tumor expands, the growth rate of the tumor slows down accordingly, and many cells become hypoxic.

Cancer cells grow more rapidly than normal cells. After mitosis, normal cells have a longer resting period, while cancer cells have a shorter resting period. If the diameter of a cancer cell is between ten to twenty-six micrometers, its weight would be around 0.01 micrograms. After multiplying twenty times, the cell count can reach 10^6, with a diameter of one millimeter and a weight of one milligram. After multiplying thirty times, the number of cells can reach 10^9, with a diameter of one centimeter and a weight of one gram. Generally, primary breast cancer that can be detected with the touch of a hand, or discovered by X-rays, is more than one centimeter in diameter. At this point, the number of cancer cells in the tumor can be as high as 10^9, having already undergone thirty rounds of multiplying. When the tumor load reaches 10^9, anticancer drugs are essentially ineffective. As such, for even a seemingly small tumor merely one centimeter in diameter, surgical removal is the only option. As for cancer cells that have undergone forty rounds of multiplying, the quantity can be as high as 10^{12}, with a diameter of ten centimeters in diameter and a weight of one kilogram. This stage is already the advanced phase of the disease.

At present, breast cancer treatment uses comprehensive methods, akin to deploying all three branches of the military: land, sea, and air. After surgery, some patients undergo radiation therapy or chemotherapy as adjuvant treatments. Each method has its pros and cons. A combination of surgery and radiation therapy is effective for most cases of early-stage breast cancer, as surgery isn't limited by tumor size and is effective unless the cancer has spread. Radiation therapy cannot reach cancer cells that have spread throughout the entire body, because it only irradiates specific localized areas such as the chest wall, internal mammary region, and supraclavicular region. Dealing with cancer cells present in the liver, lungs, and bones is challenging, as they truly are remote, far-off places that are hard to reach, just as how the authority of the emperor didn't extend into the distant mountains. The advantage of chemotherapy is that it can treat the whole body and is not limited by the spread of the tumor but instead by the tumor load. Regardless of whether radiation therapy or chemotherapy is used, surgical removal of the tumor is still beneficial. Without a large tumor load, radiation therapy can more easily eradicate the remaining residual cancer cells. However, those that have metastasized tend to grow faster, entering a rapid proliferation cycle, becoming oxygen-rich cells that are more susceptible to logarithmic killing by anticancer drugs.

Some people who develop malignant tumors don't undergo surgery or radiation therapy, or their treatment is incomplete, and yet they survive for a long time. Why? The human body has its own immune system. For example, lymph nodes are the imperial guards of the human body. This army includes numerous cells that combat enemies, the most famous of course being the T lymphocytes. Upon encountering cancer cells, they can secrete lysosome-like substances to dissolve the membranes of cancer cells, rendering them necrotic. The macrophages in white blood cells are even more renowned, acting like missiles that can track the selected cells and devour them in a display of zero-order kinetic killing. Additionally, there are NK cells, which, similar to macrophages, also possess the ability to recognize certain markers on the surface of cancer cells, identifying them as enemies. B lymphocytes, however, can only claim partial credit in combating the enemy because their vision isn't sharp enough, and they completely fail to see the true face of the colonial invaders. Deceived, they treat cancer cells as friends, unable to distinguish between friend and foe, and do not attack. Sometimes, these cells even defect from their native population and throw themselves into the embrace of cancer cells, transforming into cancer cells themselves.

Cancer cells are truly tenacious enemies, constantly proliferating, invading, and plundering, absorbing nutrients in the human body for their own use, and they also form self-protection mechanisms. Cancer cells attach themselves to the so-called blocking factors in serum in the blood, creating a strong fortress that renders T lymphocytes and macrophages powerless. Using the body's immune system to destroy cancer cells is known as immunotherapy. An advantage is that it only kills cancer cells without harming normal cells, and it impacts the entire body, rather than being localized. In this regard, the medical community has studied the use of BCG, interferons, lymphokines, and other methods to strengthen the patient's immunity. However, immunotherapy is only effective against residual cancer cells with a minimal load—recurrent tumors and tumors with heavy loads are beyond the capacity of the body's lymphatic forces. Generally, when a person develops cancer, it's actually due to a breakdown of the body's immune system. In ancient China, the emperor had six armies. To combat cancer, all six forces should be deployed: surgery, endocrine therapy, radiation therapy, chemotherapy, immunotherapy—what's the sixth one? Could it be traditional Chinese medicine? Some hospitals in mainland China have in fact incorporated traditional

Chinese medicine as part of treatment. After surgery, patients are divided into two groups. One group continues to receive radiation therapy, chemotherapy, or endocrine therapy, while the other receives traditional Chinese medicine, beginning one week after surgery, with a daily dose for three years. After three years, the frequency of medication is reduced as appropriate, and maintained for five or six years. There are more than ten kinds of herbal medicines used, and the results have been promising. Perhaps traditional Chinese medicine may be one of the hopes for future treatment. Prevention is better than having to seek a cure, but once the disease is present, there's no choice but to fight. This is a long-lasting and arduous counterattack that must be fought to the very end.

MAGIC BULLET

IN ADDITION to sculpting, Henry Moore also produced many drawings. These include depictions of people in caves, miners in tunnels, and refugees in air-raid shelters. The people in the caves stand like ghosts. The miners in the tunnels walk bent over. The refugees in the air-raid shelters lie on the ground along the walls, men and women, the old and the young; their bodies tightly wrapped in cloth resemble mummies. The first time I entered the radiation therapy unit, those images came to mind. The long corridor was filled with despondent-looking people on either side, just like the people in the air-raid shelters, suffering from the ravages of war. Their enemies were external, while ours lurked within.

Like the simulation unit, the radiation therapy unit was also located in the basement of the hospital: an underground space. The first section of the *Zuo Tradition*, titled "Lord Yin," narrates a falling-out between Lord Zhuang of Zheng and his mother.[19] His mother had helped his younger brother to sow rebellion, and after Lord Zhuang quelled the upheaval, he banished his mother to an outlying place called Chengying, and swore to her: Not until the Yellow Springs of the underworld shall we meet again. Afterward, he regretted this oath. All he could do was follow one of his minister's schemes and dig a tunnel. When he saw the springs of the underworld, he was finally able to reunite with his mother. The meeting at the Yellow Springs was the turning point of his rebirth. Lord Zhuang's minister advises him to deal with his mother as soon as possible, the way one would with a virus: It is best to take action early, and not let it spread; once it spreads, it is difficult to control. At that time, land was plentiful and people were few;

most lived aboveground, except for some primitive cave dwellers. As the population gradually increased, buildings began to reach for the sky, and also to extend deep underground. In the modern age, banks were built with underground vaults to store gold, cities dug underground railways, and the lower floors of shopping malls were transformed into food courts; the basements of ancient castles became dungeons, and some even expanded into private prisons. Many years ago, in order to evade the atomic bomb, numerous large cities built vast, sprawling shelters underground. I've been to these places. Is it an ancestral instinct to believe that being closer to the earth makes us safer? But being too close, and connected to the underworld, is another taboo.

The radiation therapy unit was located in the basement of the hospital and was by no means a playground; rather, it had the air of a dungeon, striking terror into people's hearts. The basement on this side of the hospital was actually the main hub for cancer treatment. It was divided into the oncology unit, the simulation unit, and the radiation therapy unit. After a reorganization, the breast cancer unit had been moved to the second floor, but other cancer patients were still diagnosed and treated in the basement. I followed the corridor from the simulation unit and turned left toward the radiation therapy unit. At first, I thought the plaster-mold room was at the end of the corridor, but it turned out that the entire radiation therapy unit was farther inside. At the intersection of the corridor, there were two tables with a hot water thermos and paper cups for those undergoing radiation. Clearly, radiation therapy was not a trivial matter.

In the radiation therapy unit, there were three large rooms along one side of the wall, each with its own inner room, divided into three groups. Each of the large rooms contained a large machine. There were no doors to the rooms, but there was a small corridor leading inside that was barred with a gate to prevent unauthorized individuals from passing through, like one might see in a parking lot. Only radiation therapists and patients could enter and exit the large rooms, and each time they did, the barrier gate needed to be opened and closed. Each large room faced the corridor and had an inner control room, similar to an observation or guard station one might find by a building. Half of the space inside the large room was equipped with a machine that contained, among other features, a closed-circuit television to record what went on in the room. There were three radiation therapists in each room, one woman and two men, working simultaneously. The first and second rooms were identical, while the third had a different kind of machine.

I was assigned to machine two, which was in the second room. The week after my computer scan, I received a call from the hospital notifying me of my radiation therapy schedule. By late October, I was a radiation therapy patient who had to go to the hospital every day. One machine could treat about three to four people each hour. In the course of a morning or an afternoon, it could accommodate around ten patients, which meant that with two machines operating, about fifty people could be treated in a day. Only three public hospitals in Hong Kong had radiation therapy equipment, and thus each day, the hospitals could provide radiation therapy services to 150 people, as long as these big-eyed machines were in good health themselves.

The nursing staff was very kind. People often complain about the poor attitude of nurses in public hospitals. The entire oncology unit, however, including the simulation and radiation therapy units, was an exception. The doctors and nursing staff were all amiable and approachable, greeting each patient warmly, carefully explaining what needed to be done; if a patient didn't understand, they didn't mind taking the trouble to clarify things over and over, as though they were all volunteers. Were the people working in the oncology unit given special instructions when they were assigned to this unit? Or were they particularly sympathetic to cancer patients? Regardless, they gave patients a lot of comfort.

Public hospitals can cultivate one's patience. I was a first-time patient, so my initial radiation therapy session took half an hour, but I underwent treatment for only a fraction of that time. The radiation directly irradiated my body for no more than a minute to half a minute each session. The rest of the time was spent measuring the precise location for treatment and adjusting the angle of the machine. The radiation therapy treatment room was as big as a classroom, with a G-shaped machine in the center, the curved part arced like a tele-phone receiver, the horizontal line indicating the table on which the patient lies. Against the wall was a row of tables stacked with plaster and fiberglass molds. As I lay on the table, the nurse retrieved the mold that belonged to me. The plaster mold was merely a prototype, used to create another bridge-like frame that resembled a fiberglass penholder inscribed with numbers. Ten days had passed, and the markings on my body surprisingly hadn't faded. They placed the bridge-like frame over my chest, turned off the lights, and measured the location. In the darkness, I saw the machine emit a red glow. After the location was adjusted correctly, the lights in the room came back on. This machine was a dinosaur with big, glowing red eyes.

The rays were radiation, and excessive exposure is harmful to the body. Therefore, when the actual radiation treatment was adminis-tered, the staff left the room, operating the machine from the control room. They monitored the situation inside the treatment room through a closed-circuit television, most importantly to ensure that the patient didn't move. Once the staff left, I heard them walk down the small corridor, and then the barrier gate clicked closed. Radiation therapy began. There was a beep, and the machine began humming. In the brightly lit room, the radiation itself was invisible. Only the chanting of the machine told me that the rays were penetrating my skin. Once, I timed it on my watch: one minute. In fact, one minute can be quite long. It's not easy to speak for one minute when taking a foreign language conversation exam. A chest X-ray, on the other hand, is a quick snapshot, lasting only a second.

In 1910, the medical community began to use pharmaceuticals to treat illnesses. People referred to the pills as magic bullets. Radiation is an even more powerful weapon, like machine-gun fire. After a minute, I heard the machine shut off, followed by the sound of the barrier gate in the corridor. The staff came in. Each radiation therapy session is divided into three different positions: front, side, and arm bend. The arm bend is relatively challenging because it's concave and requires lifting the arm up to the ear. It would be tough for someone who can't lift and straighten their arm. I underwent radiation therapy once a day, in each of the three areas. However, once a week, there was an additional treatment for the back; as such, one session usually took fifteen minutes, sometimes twenty.

Radiation therapy isn't at all scary—why do people pale at the mere mention of it? At first, I thought it would be like sitting in an electric chair, or like undergoing an electrocardiogram, with wires connected to my body. I was probably influenced by an image I saw on TV from a foreign medical report that showed a young boy receiving some sort of brain treatment. He sat in a chair wearing a ring that resembled a laurel wreath on his head; within the ring, gamma rays circulated, and took turns targeting the center of his brain. In reality, radiation therapy is similar to an X-ray, the only difference being that you need to lie down, and it takes a bit longer. Neither one is painful or itchy. Of course, I had no fear of radiation therapy beforehand, as Ah Kin had already told me what to expect; whereas for her, it had been a brand-new experience, one she had worried about and feared, thinking it would be torture. When I left the large room, the radiation therapist handed me two pieces of paper. One thick card served as my ID for daily treatment, while the other thin white sheet contained information about things to know and pay attention to during the treatment period. In fact, I was already aware of these things, as I had read the radiation therapy pamphlets from the rack on the wall.

1. RADIATION THERAPY

The principle of radiation therapy is to use high-energy radiation to inhibit the division and growth of cancer cells. This is usually carried out in one of two ways: one, using an external device to emit radiation outside the body; two, placing radioactive substances inside the body. These high-energy radioactive rays can eradicate cells within their range. Since cancer cells are extremely sensitive to radiation, they are destroyed before normal cells.

I had breast cancer. After the tumor was surgically removed, I underwent radiation therapy, as no surgeon dares to claim to have completely removed all of the cancer cells through surgery; the truth is, these cells are not visible to the naked eye. Moreover, the surgery might awaken some dormant cancer cells, causing them to become active. As a result, they may escape through the lymph nodes or blood vessels, spreading from the original site. Radiation therapy for breast cancer is conducted externally, whereas other types of cancer may require the placement of radioactive substances inside the body. Radiation can be both beneficial and harmful to the human body. While it can certainly destroy cancer cells, there are instances in which radiation may cause healthy cells to deteriorate; consequently, these previously healthy cells might abnormally develop into cancer cells. It comes down to the fate of the individual.

2. PREPARING FOR TREATMENT

Before one undergoes radiation therapy, a specialist will conduct a detailed examination of the patient to determine the distribution of the cancer and establish the scope of the radiation therapy map. The doctor may draw or tattoo lines and marks on the patient's body to specify the areas that are to receive radiation therapy. These marks should not be washed off until the entire treatment process is complete.

I had breast cancer, so lines and marks were drawn on my body, and a plaster mold was made, creating a penholder-like device that could be placed on my body to measure angles. For those patients with nasopharyngeal cancer who needed radiation in the head area, wouldn't such lines look like the tattoos of criminals in ancient times? Patients often continue to work every day, and they can't go around with their faces marked like they belonged to some indigenous tribe. The mold technician makes them a transparent plastic mold to fit over their head and face, and the marks and lines are drawn on the mold instead. In the radiation therapy department, I often saw staff wheeling a two-tiered wooden cart piled with plaster and fiberglass head molds, mask stacked upon mask, as though this place were a workshop for art students.

3. THINGS TO PAY ATTENTION TO WHEN UNDERGOING TREATMENT

The number of radiation therapy sessions depends on the type of cancer, its location, and the required radiation dose. Each treatment session only takes a few minutes and is typically administered two to five times a week, with the entire course of treatment usually completed within several days or up to two months. During radiation therapy, it is essential not to move so as to ensure that the radiation precisely hits the intended target each time. Radiation therapy doesn't cause pain or other discomfort. It's crucial to complete the entire course of treatment in order to ensure its effectiveness.

When the radiation therapist handed me the card, it indicated that my treatment period would be three weeks. I felt reassured, as Ah Kin's treatment period had been six weeks, and so I figured that my condition might be less severe than hers. Each radiation therapy session was very short, with each of the three areas taking a minute, adding up to three minutes in total. However, the commute to and from the hospital and the waiting time took up half a day. The reason that it had to be spread out over several weeks was simply because the body cannot tolerate receiving too much radiation at once, which would be fatal. I've heard that some patients, because of the inconvenience or the fear of side effects, refuse to continue treatment after a few sessions, which is a waste of all the previous efforts.

4. REACTIONS TO RADIATION THERAPY

After undergoing radiation therapy, patients might feel unusually fatigued or experience a loss of appetite, so they should schedule their activities accordingly, focusing on getting rest and proper nutrition. The skin in the areas that have received radiation may become red, darken, or start peeling, similar to the effects of sun exposure. These are normal reactions and will go away after the completion of the treatment. Take care to protect the skin in these areas, avoiding direct exposure to sunlight. Don't allow soap, makeup, perfumes, ointments, intense light, or hot water bottles to come into contact with these areas until they've fully healed.

My first reaction to undergoing radiation therapy was fatigue, which also may have been due to the daily commute to the hospital and the physical toll of travel. And so I tried to rest as much as possible. Other than practicing tai chi in the mornings and eating two meals a day, I slept the remainder of the time. At first, nothing happened in the areas where I'd received treatment. The skin wasn't itchy or painful, but later it gradually turned red and darkened. It also took a long time for the discoloration to disappear. Naturally, bathing once again became a challenge for me. I couldn't get soap or water anywhere on my chest area. I was afraid of injuring my skin and of erasing the marked lines. Because my chest area was covered by clothing, it could be shielded from direct sunlight, but patients with nasopharyngeal cancer might need to use an umbrella for protection. Of course, it's unsuitable for them to use cosmetics. Ah Kin told me her younger sister applied some ointment because her skin was itchy, which resulted in an adverse reaction that required medical treatment and caused her a lot of unnecessary trouble.

5. DIET

Patients undergoing radiation therapy should pay attention to their dietary nutrition to replenish their physical strength and repair damaged cells. Recommended foods include:
- Protein-rich chicken, fish, eggs, and dairy products
- High-calorie foods, such as glucose, honey, jam, and desserts
- Fruits and vegetables
- Plenty of liquids

For a poor appetite, the following methods can be tried:
- Eating when slightly hungry
- Eating frequent small meals
- Trying different recipes
- Dining with family and friends
- Listening to music or the radio, or watching TV while eating

On the first day of radiation therapy, the radiation therapist also gave me a prescription and instructed me to pick up the medications from the pharmacy. Of course, I knew what I'd be getting, as Ah Kin had informed me already. Actually, they weren't medications. One was a packet of vitamin C, one a packet of vitamin B, and the other a large packet containing a kilogram of nutritional milk powder, equivalent to the amount of milk in a large can. After radiation therapy, fortunately, I didn't lose my appetite, and I had no problem swallowing, probably because the area around my neck didn't undergo treatment. Ah Kin said her treatment area extended to her chin, which may have affected her esophagus and made eating difficult at times. I had stomach issues, and generally preferred eating small, frequent meals, and dining with my family so I didn't feel lonely. When it came to food, I was delighted by dessert, but I was afraid that eating too much might cause weight gain and impact my blood pressure, so I didn't dare eat it often, opting to eat more fruit instead.

6. OTHER REMINDERS

Before each treatment session, you may have to wait in the waiting area. It's a good idea to bring books or newspapers to pass the time. Avoid wearing too many layers—clothing that can be easily removed is best.

Since I'd started going to the hospital, I'd gotten used to lugging around books, but on those days when I had radiation therapy, I felt a little tired and would bring along instead a portable music player so I could listen to the radio and cassette tapes. Piano sonatas were the best, especially those by Mozart. The melodies were graceful and serene, cheerful yet with a touch of melancholy. As for clothing, although it was November and the weather was still warm, the basement was air-conditioned and particularly cold, so I always had to wear a shirt with a windbreaker, which I could use to cover the area below my waist on the radiation therapy table to keep warm. While I was undergoing radiation therapy, my post-op wound suddenly began to reject all kinds of clothing. Even just wearing a cotton undershirt didn't work; the friction bothered my wound, as though it were being lightly brushed. A shirt alone didn't work, either, and of course, wearing only a bra was out of the question. As a result, I came up with a makeshift solution: wearing a silk half slip on my upper body, positioning the elastic band under my armpits, which surprisingly worked. And so, every day I wore this bottom slip on my upper body. When I arrived at the hospital, I'd go into the restroom to change, sliding it down my waist. After the radiation therapy session finished, I'd pull it back up. Fortunately, after a while, the wound stopped rejecting all fabrics—otherwise, I would have had to get a specially tailored silk vest to wear as an undershirt.

I went to the hospital for radiation therapy every day. Because I saw the same people day after day, we gradually got to know each other. At first, it was just nodding our heads and saying good morning. Later on, we would sit together and chat. I saw Lee Ping, whom I'd first encountered outside of the computer scanning room, when she had asked me to translate loudly for her. The first sentence of these conversations was almost always the same: How did you discover it? It turned out that just like me, Lee Ping had discovered a lump the size of a small citrus fruit while casually touching her body in the shower. She also went to a private hospital to have it surgically removed and then to a public hospital for radiation therapy. It cost more than 10,000 dollars, plus a bag of blood, she said. Lee Ping was a little older than me, but she was lively. She always showed up alone, wearing an open-collared shirt that revealed the red and blue design lines on her neck, not covered by a scarf. In addition to radiation therapy on the second machine, Lee Ping also had to undergo treatment on the third machine, the same as Ah Kin. I felt fortunate that I didn't need to undergo this additional treatment. What kind of machine was it? There was no way of knowing. I only chatted with Lee Ping three times; because the mornings became too crowded, I was transferred to the afternoon. This allowed me to make my mother's lunch every day and wash the dishes before I set out. My mother always quietly grumbled: I'm old and in poor health. Why don't you spend more time at home keeping me company instead of going out every day?

When I arrived at the radiation therapy department in the afternoon, I saw Wu Man-kuen and Zong Suk-man. We'd also crossed paths before outside the computer scanning room. Zong Suk-man didn't talk to me; she always brought a book to read. I was consistently stunned by her beauty, as each time she appeared, she was dressed to the nines, sometimes in a long floral skirt, sometimes in a crisp pair of dress pants, always in a pleasing and harmonious color scheme, her curly long hair cascading down. The radiation therapy unit was air-conditioned, so she draped a sweater over her shoulders. Everyone else who came here had a downcast air, dressed in drab and even somewhat ragged clothing. Only Zong Suk-man brightened up the entire unit. She seemed to have come not to undergo radiation therapy but to attend a dance party instead. She looked very young, perhaps only around twenty years old, a sight for sore eyes. What was wrong with her? But I admired her very much. It was as though she wasn't ill at all.

Wu Man-kuen and I were in the same group, both assigned to the second machine. Sometimes, we were scheduled back-to-back. On several occasions, after she'd gone into the radiation therapy treatment room and it was time for the third part of her treatment, the radiation therapist called my name and asked me to wait outside the door. Once, I entered the treatment room as she was just getting up from the table and heading behind the screen to get dressed. Although she was draped in a hospital gown, I noticed thick gauze stuck to one side of her chest. Had the post-surgery dressing not been removed yet? If that was the case, she shouldn't have been receiving radiation therapy so soon. Wu Man-kuen always came and left alone, walking briskly and nimbly, her back straight. She didn't seem ill at all either.

After seeing Wu Man-kuen every day, we finally started sitting together and chatting. Still the same opening question: How did you discover it? She said she found the tumor in her chest and went to the doctor; after getting it checked, it was found to be malignant. That was nine years ago, when she was already in her sixties. Because of her advanced age, she decided not to have surgery and kept putting off treatment. Nine years later, the tumor had ulcerated and began to leak fluid, leaving her no choice but to return to the doctor and undergo radiation therapy. Several times after receiving radiation therapy, she needed the nurse to change the dressing for her. It's strange that some people find a tumor, undergo surgery and radiation therapy, and still pass away from the disease a year or two later, while others neglect their tumors and manage to live for many more years. Wu Man-kuen must have been a stubborn person. She was over seventy and came to the hospital every day. Her doctor recommended that she be hospitalized, but she refused, saying that beds were precious, and she didn't want to occupy one. Treatment only took one or two hours a day, and she preferred coming in on a daily basis. She lived in Sha Tin, and in addition to taking the bus, she still had to walk a stretch of the way. This was another woman I admired.

I also met a patient named Wong Fong. After inquiring, I learned she'd been suffering from cancer for fourteen years. She'd also developed a lump in her chest. After having it surgically removed, the doctor said that radiation might not be necessary, so she decided against it, and indeed, she was fine. After fourteen years, however, her surgical scar became itchy, and her cancer recurred, so she had to return to the doctor and undergo a fifteen-day course of treatment. The day I chatted with Wong Fong happened to be her fifteenth day of treatment. We were all happy for her, but when she went to see the doctor afterward, she was told she needed an additional week of supplemental treatment, which was disheartening. We felt vaguely under threat too. I didn't see her after that because she was transferred to the morning treatment sessions.

I always arrived at the radiation therapy department at two-thirty and usually left by four. Sometimes, however, the wait could be quite long. Once, I had to wait until five o'clock to begin my treatment, which also delayed the radiation therapist. Zong Suk-man and I were the only two people left that day in the entire radiation therapy unit. She was assigned to machine number one, so it was unclear who would finish first. As it turned out, her machine was slightly faster. I sat on a long bench outside the control room, lifting my head and glancing sideways to see the TV monitor. It showed a man lying in the radiation therapy treatment room with a fiberglass mask over his head, his appearance reminding me of the Egyptian pharaoh Tutankhamun. If I had gotten up and walked over to the control room for machine number one, I also could have seen Zong Suk-man in the radiation room on the TV monitor. Was she suffering from breast cancer? Or maybe a uterine tumor, or something else? I decided not to look. It felt unethical.

I didn't know whether it was merely my perception or actually the case, but the radiation therapists in the control room all seemed to be pale-complexioned, especially the woman at machine number two, whose face was practically ashen. Had working with radiation long-term affected her health? I heard that in this line of work, people needed to take breaks or rotate units every few months, but these specialized radiation therapists were absolutely crucial for the well-being of cancer patients. Their attitude was always excellent, and they were concerned about us. Sometimes they asked me if I was afraid of being alone in the big room, and if I wanted someone to keep me company. Sometimes, if the radiation therapist were male, he'd ask if I preferred to have a female radiation therapist present. On the wall in the lobby of the unit, there was a bulletin board filled with Christmas cards. They were all letters of appreciation from patients expressing well-deserved thanks to the doctors, nurses, and radiation therapists.

The radiation therapists cared for us patients like children. While I lay on the table so they could measure the position of the radiation, we also made small talk, such as:

Will the prince come here when he visits Hong Kong?
What would he come here for?
This hospital is named after him.
He's Prince Charles.
Also known as the Prince of Wales. [20]

The Prince of Wales did not come to Sha Tin Public Hospital. It was true, there wasn't much to see in this hospital. It wasn't newly built and in need of a ribbon-cutting ceremony, nor was the building architecturally remarkable. The prince enjoyed studying architecture, and instead went to the countryside to look at ancient Chinese houses. As for the Cultural Centre that looked like a giant bathhouse—I wondered what he might say when presiding over the opening ceremony.

The identity of the modern-day prince is actually quite awkward. They have no fiery dragons to slay, no princesses to save, and no thrones to contend for, giving the impression that their lives are dull and boring. Instead, their marital status becomes the focal point for the media. Prince Charles, with his penchant for architecture and a fascination with the ghosts of old castles, seems like a member of Ghostbusters. Is he unconsciously seeking that elusive fiery dragon, a symbol of what he's lost? The story of Lord Zhuang of Zheng, on the other hand, might well be seen as a variation of the numerous fairy tales of princes in foreign lands, even though this Chinese version is more complex and worldlier. Lord Zhuang of Zheng, because of the difficult circumstances of his birth, was disliked by his mother, who tried to reverse his status as heir apparent and replace him with his younger brother. He finally overcame the obstacles and ascended to the throne, punishing his mother and brother along the way. His younger brother, of course, was a metaphorical fiery dragon, a roadblock on his path to a happy ending. He ingeniously arranged for his younger brother to reveal his dragon's tail before decisively eliminating him. As for his princess? She became a repentant mother who lived apart from him (whether or not he had an Oedipus complex would need to be proven by literary critics more deeply versed in Freud). Many years later, what I mostly remembered about him was his magnanimity and flexibility, adhering to the promise he made as a ruler while also fulfilling his filial duties: He dug a tunnel to bring his mother back. Foreign princes climbed ancient castles, while he descended into the underground. How many associations might this underground tunnel that led to his mother stir in the minds of psychoanalytic critics? Once he had secured his position on the throne, as the saying goes, "They lived happily ever after." Having fulfilled both challenges, he became a ruler in both name and reality.

Prince Charles didn't descend upon the hospital named after him. He probably forgot there was such a place, plus, it wasn't haunted by ghosts. (This was a good hospital—there were no vengeful spirts, right?) It was actually a good thing that the prince didn't come, because whenever high-ranking officials would visit government institutions, the entire staff would grow anxious. There would be costly and time-consuming preparations and renovations to be done, which might not necessarily benefit the general public. There may have been another reason that the prince didn't visit the hospital: The medical staff was on strike, the walls covered with slogans. The nursing staff was working strictly by the book, on the verge of a partial strike. At first, I couldn't help but worry that if the radiation therapists were in a bad mood and working carelessly, wouldn't our lives be in jeopardy? In fact, there was no reason to worry. They didn't neglect their duties one bit.

The prince didn't come. However, an entire team of people arrived at the radiation therapy department. They turned out to be a group of newly graduated nurses, led by their supervisor and the department staff. They walked down the long basement corridor, the supervisor explaining things along the way. They even came into the radiation therapy treatment room to observe the procedure. At the time, I was supposed to be lying on the table inside the room, but it just so happened that on this day, the radiation therapist first arranged to see nasopharyngeal cancer patients, then women with breast cancer, so I was delayed. Otherwise, there would have been twenty or thirty people watching as I lay with my upper body exposed in the radiation therapy room. Instead, I sat on the long bench in the corridor, watching them: both men and women, the majority vivacious young women. How much did they know about breast tumors? The place they passed through, chatting and laughing, was the spiritual purgatory of which we were so afraid.

GALLANTLY DELIVERING THROUGH THICK AND THIN

A WEEK after I had begun undergoing radiation therapy treatment in the mornings, I was reassigned to the afternoon group. However, this morning, I had come to the hospital for an ultrasound examination of my abdominal and pelvic cavities. It had been scheduled after my bone scan, exactly half a month later. Of course, there were too many people on the waiting list. Since I was going to be at the hospital in the morning, the day before, I had talked to the radiation therapy team about changing that day's treatment to the morning as well. After the ultrasound, I would head to the basement. Otherwise, I'd have to make the trek to the hospital in the morning and afternoon, which was too much and too tiring. Who would cook for my mother?

Bone scans and ultrasound examinations are almost like jokes played on patients: One requires the patient to drink a lot of water in order to cleanse the intestines and stomach, then to expel the water to the very last drop; the other also entails drinking a lot of water, but the water must be held to make the belly swell, and not one drop can be released. The latter is certainly more difficult. Drinking a lot of water without being allowed to urinate is challenging. If you couldn't hold it in, wouldn't it be embarrassing? Before undergoing the ultrasound, I was sent a page of instructions:

> Twelve hours before the examination, refrain from consuming fatty foods (including milk).
> On the day of the examination, you can have a breakfast of nonfat clear liquids, such as plain congee.
> Before the examination, you can drink plenty of clear tea or

water to keep your bladder full, which is especially necessary for pelvic examinations.

Two additional points were mentioned: that pediatric patients should be accompanied by a family member, although it wasn't mandatory; and that if you needed to change or cancel the appointment, call to notify them as soon as possible. I didn't need to concern myself with these things. Usually, I had milk for breakfast, but since that wasn't allowed, early in the morning I went out to buy a bowl of plain congee. The thin, watery congee wasn't even remotely filling. When I set off for the hospital, I bought another bowl and took it on the bus. By the time I was almost at the hospital, I'd drunk half of it on the bus, finishing the rest at the hospital entrance. This way, I thought, I wouldn't faint from hunger. Since I didn't do well with being hungry, and my stomach gave me trouble, having something in it might help.

I also brought a liter of water. Each time I undertook the long journey to the hospital, I brought all sorts of things, as though I were embarking on an expedition. The ultrasound examination rooms were in the radiology unit, right down the corridor from the main lobby where chest X-rays were done; having previously undergone bone imaging and computer scans, I was already quite familiar with this place. I changed clothes especially fast, then sat on a bench and waited. An ultrasound is actually very quick, but because not every patient has the right amount of water in their stomach, some are asked to go out and drink more water, and it's often a half an hour before they finish the ultrasound, so there's always a wait. When my turn came, it was already eleven o'clock. When the nurse called out my name, I quickly downed the water. I hadn't dared drink it earlier, afraid I'd drink too much and need to go to the bathroom. And so, within a ten-minute period, I drank a full liter of water, and my stomach swelled so much I couldn't bear it.

The ultrasound examination room was not big, but it accommodated an exam table and a small TV set connected to the table. The conditions inside the patient's abdomen would be displayed on the screen in the form of light waves. Once again, I found myself interacting with light: the flash of the chest X-ray, the invisible beams of the scan, the red rays of radiation therapy, and now this fluorescence. Naturally, I had to expose myself again; light itself inherently implied exposure. The person in charge arrived with two others in tow, possibly new interns again. The nurse first smeared a slippery white ointment squeezed like toothpaste from a tube onto my abdomen and waist. The person in charge held a device resembling a microphone and pressed it against my abdomen. The diagnosis of the pelvic cavity went smoothly, and I heard him tell the other two people: This is exactly what I'm looking for. He spoke in English. I presumed he was referring to the water. I had consumed the right amount and had timed it well, thanks to Ah Kin's guidance. Next was the examination of the liver, which proved problematic. After trying for a long time, they couldn't capture an image of it. The person in charge seemed impatient. Why wasn't it working? He had me turn left and right, and even asked me to stand up. I looked at the screen, only seeing a fanlike pattern flickering and moving, but couldn't make sense of it. All I could read was my name and the doctor's surname on the screen.

The doctor started firing off a series of questions:

Have you ever had liver disease?
Do you drink alcohol?
Have you ever undergone liver surgery?
Have you experienced generalized itching?
Have you taken any anticancer drugs?
When did you undergo the surgery?
Is your urine yellow?

I'd never had liver disease, never had liver surgery, and didn't drink alcohol. The surgery to remove the tumor in my breast was on September 1. I took one tablet of tamoxifen every day. I hadn't paid special attention to whether my urine was yellow. As for generalized itching, I had sensitive skin, often breaking out in rashes, and exposure to pollen, dust, paint, and dirty water always made me itch.

When I went swimming, if the saltwater was dirty, my legs turned red and swollen afterward. As I answered these questions, I felt worried, because this was unexpected. Everything else was as Ah Kin had told me it would be.

The ultrasound technician prattled on and on, speaking to the other two people in English, at one point remarking that this woman was really strange, and another time, that the case was quite challenging. After a while, he grew irritated, questioning why I'd come so late, especially since I was already at this stage of radiation therapy. These words sent me into even more of a panic. Was it too late? I had had surgery in September, and underwent the ultrasound on November 3—was it too late? Should I have done the ultrasound before receiving radiation therapy? What did he mean when he said I was already at this stage of radiation therapy? Something had to be wrong with my liver, otherwise why would he keep asking me questions about it? Some of the questions struck me as strange. If I had had liver surgery, wouldn't I have a scar on my abdomen?

I told them that after the ultrasound exam, I still had to go to the basement for radiation therapy. I'd already scheduled the time, but it was almost noon, and the radiation therapist didn't know I was still upstairs. As such, the nurse phoned the radiation therapy unit and told them I couldn't make it on time. It was truly an instance of man proposes but God disposes. My radiation therapy appointment was changed back to the afternoon.

They wanted me to keep drinking water. The nurse gave me three paper cups filled with water, and I drank them all. It turned out my stomach could hold more water. And so, I lay down for another scan. Maybe they got the images they needed, because the doctor clapped and left. I wanted to ask questions, but there was no time. The screen was invisible again. The nurse handed me a piece of paper, instructing me to wipe the gel off my body, then to get dressed. A piece of paper couldn't possibly wipe away that much gel. Naturally, it all stuck to my clothes. The people sitting outside the door had to wait longer than usual, and by the time I came out, it was already twelve o'clock.

I couldn't make it home and back in two hours. I had to eat lunch in the hospital cafeteria and call home, asking my mother to take care of lunch on her own. We'd talk about it when I got home. We had plenty of staple foods at home, so I believed she could manage. I hadn't yet eaten much of anything that day. I couldn't stop thinking about what might be happening with my liver. I had no appetite, but I had to eat, otherwise, my stomach might ache, or I might faint. Since the morning, I'd only had two bowls of watery congee and bucketloads of water, resulting in several trips to the restroom, one after another. I bought a sandwich in the cafeteria and went out to the garden. It was still warm in November. The sun beating down on my body felt wonderful. People undergoing radiation therapy shouldn't be exposed to sunlight, and though I was protected by my clothing, it might not be good for me, so I sat in the pavilion, eating my sandwich and observing the people around me. A nurse was reading a book, and several doctors walked toward the dormitory. The garden was quiet, clean, neat, and spacious. There weren't many flowers, but everything was a lush green, calling to mind joyous days from many years ago feeding cherries to sparrows in the park. Now, however, I sat here in sorrow. I looked up at the hospital building, a place that people both love and hate. I was afraid of going to the hospital, but I had no choice. I propped my backpack as a pillow behind my head, and closed my eyes and rested for a while, but my mind remained alert.

I was in a good mood that day. The night before, as I flipped through books, I came across H.C. Chuang's *Reflections from the Diaspora*. One of the essays, "Literature and Film," mentions the Soviet director Sergei Eisenstein, who was probably the first person (in 1929) to point out cinematic techniques that Flaubert employs to captivating effect in chapter eight of the second part of *Madame Bovary*. Chuang's essay cites the classic agricultural show scene, where the words of high officials and nobles and the hushed whispers of the lovers on the sidelines are interlaced and occur simultaneously, his translation of this passage crystal clear, the punctuation marks fully in accordance with the original work, conveying Flaubert's intentions. This book inexplicably delighted me. Why hadn't those actual literary translators captured this layer of meaning? I supposed it was because they hadn't considered it from the perspective of cinematic technique.

Outside the ultrasound examination room, I had also read some intriguing excerpts of an essay titled "Rejection Letters Received by Famous Foreign Writers." A rejection letter to the British author Rudyard Kipling reads: "I'm sorry, Mr. Kipling, but you just don't know how to use the English language." The rejection for the American writer Herman Melville's *Moby-Dick* is: "We regret to say that our united opinion is entirely against the book as we do not think it would be at all suitable for the Juvenile Market. It is very long, rather old-fashioned, and in our opinion not deserving of the reputation which it seems to enjoy." His compatriot John Dos Passos received the following rejection for *The Great Days*: "I am rather offended by what seems to me quite gratuitous passages dealing with sex acts and natural functions." A rejection letter for the German writer Günter Grass's *The Tin Drum* states: "It can never be translated." Might hospitals also issue such rejections to patients? I'm sorry, but your liver cannot be translated into legible ultrasound images.

At two o'clock, I saw nurses dressed in white, blue, and red, walking in twos and threes from the dormitory back to work. I'd also begun heading to the basement lobby when I happened to spot the doctor who had designed my simulation markings. Suddenly, I called out to him. He stopped walking, and I asked: May I have a moment with you? After hesitating, he glanced at his watch and said, I have something this afternoon. I didn't say anything more. I'd been coming to the hospital for a while and had come to understand some aspects of a doctor's job. They seemed to work nonstop all day long. For example, this doctor not only did consults in the oncology unit but also worked in the simulation unit, designing treatment markings for patients undergoing radiation therapy. Whenever there was a bone exam or a computer scan, he was present too. Perhaps he also had meetings, and at this time, he was still on the clock.

Passing through the corridor of the simulation unit, I took a flyer from the rack outside the door to the plaster-mold room, a flyer I'd always been reluctant to touch. The words END OF LIFE CARE in large letters caught my eye. It was meant for the families of patients, informing them how to care for patients in their final stages, how to help them leave this world peacefully and calmly. I began reading, and the more I read, the sadder I became. Late-stage cancer patients, of course, didn't come here but were transferred to another hospital, which was also one of the cancer research centers. A while back, there had been some news involving that hospital. Patients from two different families had passed away, but the bodies were accidentally switched, and they were buried in the wrong graves. Others may have found this to be amusing, but what caught my attention was the line: Nam Lang Hospital, the deceased was over fifty and had suffered from breast cancer. A friend comforted me, saying that the cancer was already in its final stages when it was discovered, too late to be treated.

I underwent my routine radiation therapy treatment. I arrived early, thinking I could leave early, but to my surprise, the radiation therapist informed me it was my turn to see the doctor that day. That's when I learned that people undergoing treatment were supposed to see the doctor once a week so the doctor could monitor the progress of the radiation therapy, check for any adverse reactions, and ensure there were no errors. If there was a problem, treatment was suspended for a period. Patients could also request to see the doctor if they wished. There were two doctors on duty in the consultation rooms of the radiation therapy unit every day. Wu Man-kuen went to see the doctor because her tumor kept festering and bleeding, requiring her dressing to be changed. Only then did it dawn on me why the doctor had refused to see me just now. His shift started at two o'clock, and since the radiation therapy unit had doctors on duty every day, I could see a doctor then.

Holding the folder with my medical records, I sat outside the consultation room waiting. Before long, I saw the doctor. He turned out to be the doctor with the limp whom we often saw walking by us. What illness did he have? Polio? Doctors are also human, and of course they can get sick too. The doctor asked me how I was doing. I said fine, no adverse reactions, just fatigue. He said this was normal.

I told him I had an ultrasound that morning, and it seemed there might be an issue with my liver, but I wasn't sure about the report. He said the exam results wouldn't be available so quickly. Then, I voiced my primary concern: If it spreads to the liver, will it be problematic? He said, Yes, however, there are injections that can be given. The doctor was very good and tried his best to reassure me, but I knew that if something was wrong with my liver, I'd be in trouble.

When I went home that day, I wasn't sure whether it was psychological or something else, but I felt a faint pain in my lower back, so I went to the hospital early on Monday. The radiation therapist said, Oh, why'd you come so early? I said, I'm not feeling well. I want to see the doctor. And so, I took my medical records and lined up again. The doctor asked me what was wrong. I said my lower back was uncomfortable. He asked whether it hurt when I slept. I said no. He said it was nothing to worry about. I said I was worried about my liver. He drew a vial of blood for testing.

Still uneasy, I went to the surgeon for a follow-up visit and told him about the ultrasound. He said that ultrasounds aren't always accurate and that the person in charge must have excellent technical skills in order for the results to be reliable. He knew a lot of doctors. I mentioned my doctor's name, and he said he was a former classmate. As for the person in charge of the ultrasound, he was his former assistant. The doctor examined me and told me not to worry. If something was wrong with my liver, it wouldn't disappear. If the cancer cells had spread, it would have only grown larger. He said, however, that my liver was a bit smaller than average. Was it a problem that it was a bit smaller? As long as it was functional, the size didn't matter. The public hospital didn't call me to tell me to come see the doctor. My liver was probably fine. Maybe I had too much congee that day, and during the ultrasound, it had obscured the view of my liver. Many days of worrying finally faded away.

I often pride myself that in this world, I'm extremely wealthy, because I have friends who always have my back, gallantly delivering through thick and thin. It's funny, having lived a lifetime, I never knew exactly where the liver and gallbladder were located in the body, only that they were somewhere inside the body cavity, somewhere other than the heart, lungs, and intestines. It wasn't until I went for the ultrasound that I discovered that the liver is located near the right side of the waist and is practically connected to the gallbladder. They're so close that they have each other's backs, true mirror reflections of each other. Of course, the liver is much larger than the gallbladder in terms of physical size, but there are many people who, when evaluated in terms of their spirit, have more gall than liver. Now that I knew where the liver and gallbladder were located, gallantly delivering through thick and thin was no longer a cryptic code that no one else could decipher.[21]

HUNAN LOTUS SEEDS

The setting sun slants   the evening breeze blows
Let's all come sing the lotus-plucking rhyme that we know
Red blooms blaze   white blooms glow
Fragrant wind whips the face, the summer heat goes

You paddle an oar   I punt with a pole
Singing as we pass the small bridge and row
The boat glides fast   our songs in tow
Plucking lotus blooms, our joy clearly shows[22]

IN THE waiting area of the radiation therapy unit, there was a large goldfish tank against the wall, containing around twenty or thirty goldfish. The nursing staff fed them at regular intervals. There were different varieties of goldfish, including Pearlscale, Ranchu, and Black Pearl, but they weren't paired up, and some were just individual fish of their type. Several fish swam upside down, clustering near the water's surface, flipping over to inhale air through their backs. When people approached for a closer look, they flipped over again, as though nothing had happened. I often thought that the upside-down-swimming goldfish would disappear the next day, but after a week, to my surprise, they were still swimming there. Would the radiation affect them? Radiation is light, and light refracts, bouncing from wall to wall, from open doorways and corridors. Did the radiation make the fish swim upside down? Or maybe the radiation affected the building itself. Perhaps the basement was particularly damp, causing the flooring to arch and even curl. The paint on the walls was peeling off, and several large rooms were no longer in use, the machines and appliances draped in white cloth, as the rooms underwent renovation and painting.

Seeing the goldfish tank, for some reason I thought of a trip that a group of us had taken to Hunan Province. The itinerary was meant to include an exhilarating lotus-picking experience, exactly like the one depicted on the cover of the magazine *The Children's Paradise*—people in wooden tubs, rowing to the center of the lake, weaving through lush lotus blossoms, observing water droplets form on the lotus leaves, and reaching out to pluck a lotus seedpod. However, during our trip there was a flood, and we were unable to go lotus picking. This goldfish tank reminded me of the water, flowers, and Hunan lotus seeds. The tour guide had said, Come back again, and next time, you'll definitely be able to go lotus picking. Now, for a cancer patient, that next time felt too far away—maybe indefinitely far, maybe never again.

Beside the goldfish tank there was a small coffee table piled with magazines most commonly found in hair salons: large-format weeklies filled with trivialities and gossip about the lives of celebrities and famous figures, as well as small-format monthlies primarily aimed at women, covering beauty, fashion, cooking, fitness, and a few romantic love stories. These small monthly magazines might also have served as sex education guides for young girls. Each issue always featured a section about sex, with articles like "Why Do Women Tell Lies in Bed?" and topics such as women's fantasies, the difficulties of divorce for women, and so on. Of course, some of them also concerned physical health, for example: how to have a healthy winter; discomfort during pregnancy; and the serious threat of AIDS to women. Cancer was a topic as well, and it was frequently advised that women should perform their own breast exams to detect cancer early on. The articles were accompanied by pictures reproduced from foreign women's magazines, giving people the impression that these were distant foreign matters. I'd also read articles about breast cancer, and thought to myself, This is a foreign women's illness, something distant. However, the images illustrating how to perform a breast exam were imprinted into my mind. I never expected that I'd find a lump while doing a casual self-exam. Hair salon magazines are not without their use to the average woman, and they are often found in medical facilities. In my frequent trips to the doctor, I have noticed that almost every clinic has these publications. And now, here they were in the radiation therapy unit of the hospital, all worn and tattered, their covers and backs missing.

I'd also come to learn quite a lot from chatting with cancer patients every day. Chan Ping, like me, was shocked when she discovered her tumor, and immediately went to a private hospital for surgery, which cost more than 10,000 dollars; as for Wong Fong, she went to a public hospital for her diagnosis and surgery. She didn't have to wait long, and she stayed in the hospital for ten days, paying a total of 300 dollars when she was discharged. The difference was truly staggering. Wong Fong also said she didn't need to have her stitches removed. The doctor used a special kind of thread that naturally dissolved over time. I'm aware there are various types of suture materials. Due to ongoing research and development in the medical community, surgical sutures can be made from materials such as steel wire, silk thread, and nylon thread, as well as catgut and tissue adhesive. The latter two are derived from biological sources and sewn onto the wound. After a period of time, being organic, these threads and adhesives gradually integrate with human tissues and become part of the body. In such cases, the process of removing stitches is eliminated. Tissue adhesive, also known as fibrin glue, is a substance extracted from human blood. Its main component is fibrinogen. When this substance combines with bovine thrombin, it immediately coagulates into a gel-like consistency. Dripped onto wounds, it aids in the healing of sutures.

The stitches on my wound needed to be removed. They were thick, black, and rigid, making a clicking sound when snipped. Clearly, they were very sturdy. I guessed they were made of nylon. Given the length of my wound, maybe stitching it up with thread was for the best so it wouldn't split open; if the tissue adhesive didn't stick, it would have been a disaster. As for Wong Fong, she didn't need her stitches removed—were her stitches made from catgut? Or another kind of thread made from animal intestines, such as sheep gut? Animal intestines merge seamlessly with the human body, humans joining with cats or sheep or other animals. In the global village, everything is interdependent. But would humans ever donate their organs to animals?

In the radiation therapy unit, there were children as well as adults. As I sat on the long bench in the corridor, different people passed in front of me: personnel holding patient files; a staff member wheeling models adorned with plaster heads and glass masks; a female worker pushing a gurney; two male workers pushing a gurney into the radiation therapy room; doctors entering consultation rooms; nurses calling out patients' names in the work area between the two consultation rooms; radiation therapists operating the entry and exit gate; patients entering; patients leaving. There were two children who came every day. They were about seven or eight years old; they had no hair and sat in wheelchairs, wearing face masks. Though they could walk on their own, they were accompanied by their mothers as they chatted about childlike things. They suffered from leukemia and had to receive injections regularly. Receiving those shots must have been painful. Seeing those two little bald heads was heartbreaking.

Several announcements were posted on the window of the basement registration office. QUEUE HERE. SUCH-AND-SUCH DATE IS A PUBLIC HOLIDAY. On the opposite wall, a large poster read: THE SOONER CANCER IS DETECTED, THE MORE TREATABLE IT IS. Well said, but how to detect it? Maybe it was aimed at people who didn't pay attention to their health, brushed off minor ailments, and avoided medical treatment. A small piece of paper stuck to the glass caught my attention on my first visit. I was slightly taken aback. It was an advertisement for wigs, with a number to contact if you needed to purchase one. Who needed wigs? It went without saying that it was patients from the oncology unit, especially those undergoing chemotherapy. Due to the side effects of the medication, their hair was prone to falling out.

Men wearing hats were a common sight in the radiation therapy unit. I noticed them the first time I came to the design department. My initial impression was that of a film set. On film sets, the directors and assistant directors are fond of wearing hats; those young, vainly handsome actors in Qing dynasty period costumes with shaven heads also put on hats when reporters come to interview and photograph them. However, the people wearing hats in the oncology unit were miserable. Some were losing their hair, while others shaved it, forming a peculiar T-shape at the back of their heads that they preferred to cover up. In the radiation therapy unit, hats, except for the nurses' caps, were a symbol of sorrow.

Men don't buy wigs; the people who buy wigs are mainly women. Indeed, I saw a woman whose hair had fallen out, making her look like a defeated bald eagle, but she didn't wear a wig. I don't think hair that short could be styled into a short Jean Seberg hairdo. There were many children suffering from leukemia. They were in the wards in the main building, so I only saw a few of them. There was a seventeen-year-old boy who also came for radiation therapy. He was in the prime of his youth, and should have been at school attending classes and running around the athletic field, but instead he came to the hospital every day. As he himself said, even he didn't know why.

One woman who came every day always caught my attention. She had dark skin, and a penchant for wearing black clothing. Sometimes her clothes had muted, photosynthetic patterns that, from a distance, made her resemble a black panther in a forest. The nurses were rather familiar with her, as she'd been coming in for treatment for quite some time. Later, I found out she had skin cancer and that it was under control. Skin cancer isn't considered one of the more severe types of cancer, and it's often treatable, but the skin can't be washed too much, and it seems that swimming isn't an option. She didn't come for radiation therapy, only for injections. She walked past the rooms with the three large machines in the radiation therapy unit, then entered another treatment room. She was young, only in her twenties I supposed, and she often wore a hat and sunglasses, which made her look like she was on an outing.

Most of the people I talked with were women. Tsou Him was the only man. I suddenly struck up a conversation with him because he happened to be sitting next to me, and he was in a particularly relaxed mood as it was the last day of his six-week radiation therapy treatment. He didn't just talk to me but spoke loudly, essentially addressing everyone. I mentioned I was unsure whether my course of treatment was finished, as it was already the fifteenth day. When calculating the days, should a week be considered seven days, or should it only be based on the days with radiation therapy treatment? I wasn't sure. People undergoing radiation therapy came to the hospital Monday through Friday, taking a break on the weekends; sometimes, however, there might be a session on Saturday.

Tsou Him was just over thirty years old, with a wife and young daughter at home. He suffered from nasopharyngeal cancer. It seemed that people younger and younger were getting cancer. He too had a shaved head, with a T-shaped patch at the back. He carried a pink plastic soap box with him into the radiation therapy treatment room. Did those with nasopharyngeal cancer need soap or a damp towel? I remembered how when I was teaching, for the art and calligraphy classes, children were asked to bring a damp towel in a soap box to wipe their hands. Tsou Him opened the box to show me. It was provided by the hospital, and inside the box was a piece of bone-like plastic that he placed in his mouth during radiation therapy to prevent the rays from penetrating the other side of his mouth. Yes, when I underwent radiation therapy, I also had to place a piece of willow-leaf-shaped plastic, resembling a cuttlefish bone, over the area where I had had surgery on my chest. It perfectly covered my long scar, also serving a protective function, as the radiation was quite intense.

The nurse called my name, telling me to wait for Wu Man-kuen to come out before I was to go in, adding that my fifteen-day course of treatment was over, and if the doctor said everything was fine, I wouldn't have to come back the next day. My joy at that moment was indescribable. Standing at the end of the corridor, waiting for Wu Man-kuen to come out, I loudly shouted to Tsou Him, who was sitting on the bench: It's been fifteen days—I don't have to come tomorrow! He was happy as well, raising his right hand to make a V sign with his fingers. I raised my hand and made one too. How strange that in this strange place, the person with whom I shared a rare, once-in-a-lifetime joy was a stranger, a man I'd just met for the first time. I often heard talk on the radio about sharing: sharing joys, even sharing sorrows. But how are you supposed to take out your sorrows and share them? Sure, a problem shared is a problem halved, but who wants to partake in a slice of that cake? As for joy, is it like candy? Extreme joy is actually a very personal feeling.

After coming out of the radiation therapy treatment room, I saw the doctor. He confirmed that I really didn't have to come back the next day, and neither did Tsou Him. Later, he'd return to participate in a clinical trial. The hospital would select some patients and conduct an experiment, with one group continuing to receive injections and the other not, to gauge the effectiveness of the treatment. In fact, when I entered the hospital, I was aware that there were various treatment methods available. Some people received radiation therapy, some people took medication. Since we were ill, helping the hospital to find the most efficacious treatment was something we could contribute to. When Tsou Him and I parted ways, we said, "See you at the teahouse," and waved goodbye. I didn't see him during follow-up visits because oncology was in the basement and breast cancer was on the second floor, so we didn't run into each other. I believe he's alive and well, because many patients with nasopharyngeal cancer are alive and well.

Radiation therapy isn't itchy or painful. However, there may be side effects—typically, people feel fatigued, and some have difficulty eating; if the treatment is directed at the abdomen, diarrhea may occur. The situation varies, depending on each person's age, physique, and the length of treatment. Tsou Him came to the hospital every afternoon and still went to work every morning. His company was considerate and didn't fire him because he had cancer, and instead even granted him half a day off every day to go to the hospital. Of course, he was fatigued, but he said that he tried to rest as soon as he returned home so that he'd be reenergized for work the following day. Why didn't he take an extended leave of absence? He preferred going to work because there were many people in the workplace and tasks to complete, so he wouldn't concentrate on being sick, whereas staying home all day he'd feel bored and depressed, and would be prone to overthinking. He said his colleagues were kind to him, and no one treated him the way leprosy patients were treated in the past. I found this comforting, indicating that our society seemed more civilized than many places, and it also proved that there was growing awareness about cancer, about the importance of allowing cancer patients to live normally within the community, and to share the same freedoms as everyone else.

The course of treatment for breast cancer is now complete. If you'd like to know what else may help patients, please check out "Math Time" on page 235.

BEARDS AND BROWS

Tumors can develop on every part and organ of the human body, except for hair and nails. Cancer cells do not favor beards and eyebrows, which fall under the category of hair. As for everything else—bones, blood, and muscles—it all is susceptible to disease, even to breast cancer.

Breast cancer in men occurs at a far lower rate than in women, accounting for only 1 percent of total cases of breast cancer. This lower occurrence could be attributed to the fact that men's mammary glands are physiologically underdeveloped; they do not produce milk and cannot be used to nurse infants. Men's breasts only contain a small number of mammary ducts and no acini.

In principle, male breast cancer is a disease that afflicts those who are older. The average age of onset is fifty-seven or fifty-eight. The average duration of the disease before treatment is thirty-one months, longer than it is for women. For most women, the average duration of illness before seeking medical attention is usually around sixteen months. With this longer duration, cancer cells have more time to proliferate and spread. As a result, at the time of the initial diagnosis, the tumor size may already range from two to five centimeters, and in some cases, there may even be skin ulceration.

Compared with women, men's mammary glands are less developed, with only a thin layer of glandular tissue. Once cancer develops, it is more likely to invade the skin, pectoral muscles, and fascia, and to spread faster. Consequently, if a man is afflicted with breast cancer, the treatment outcomes are often less favorable than they are for women.

Breast cancer in men is treated the same way as it is in women, with surgical removal of the tumor, supplemented by radiation therapy and drug therapy. Endocrine therapy is also effective, such as the use of the antiestrogen medication tamoxifen.

Some people in the medical community believe that breast cancer in men is also triggered by estrogen stimulation. However, research results have shown that cancer development relies more on androgens. Thus, endocrine therapy for women may require the surgical removal of the ovaries; for men, the testicles may be surgically excised. The androgen-producing interstitial cells in the testes are not sensitive to radiation, so radiation therapy is ineffective in this regard. Conversely, for women, radiation can be used to target the ovaries.

In Egypt, the incidence of male breast cancer is higher than in other countries, accounting for 5 to 6 percent of all cases. The local population is frequently infected with schistosomiasis. Chronic schistosomiasis damages the liver, reducing the balance of estrogen in the liver and leading to excessive estrogen in the body.

The Ming dynasty scholar-physician Wang Kentang documented a case of male breast cancer in *Standards for Diagnosis and Treatment of Sores and Wounds*. It is said that this individual was depressed because he repeatedly failed the civil service exam, causing him to fall ill.

Between 1980 to 1989, more than two thousand people died of breast cancer in Hong Kong, twenty-four hundred of whom were women and nineteen of whom were men. In 1989, a total of three hundred cases of breast cancer were identified in women, and mine was one of them. At present, there are still men in Hong Kong afflicted with breast cancer, one of whom was recently interviewed on TV. He is seventy-six this year and discovered he had cancer eight years ago. At that time, there was no tumor. He only experienced itching in the chest and bleeding from the nipples.

How to fight cancer? Prevention is better than treatment. Once afflicted, you have to wage a war. Do you still remember "Counterattack" on page 153?

EASTERN DEPOT

ZHOU ZUOREN wrote an essay about death, identifying two distinct ways people depart from this world: either passing away peacefully in old age, or dying a violent and premature death. The first category can be divided further into three types: Some reach old age, and then the lamp runs out of oil; some die suddenly, but because their death is due to internal causes, there are no visible signs of warning; some meet their end due to illness, which may seem benevolent on the surface but in fact is the work of harmful pathogens that employ various sinister means in order to take lives. A swift death, one that occurs within a day or two, is considered a mercy; others are subjected to prolonged torment, comparable to the brutal punishments of the notorious Ming dynasty secret police known as the "Eastern Depot."

Getting cancer is like being captured by the Eastern Depot. Learning of the growth of a malignant tumor is of course shocking, and the details are unknown: Is it in the early stages or late stages? Has it metastasized and spread? Is it possible to live for another three to six months? Everything is unclear, and the mental anguish is extraordinary. Unless the entire mind is anesthetized, there's no way to dispel the uncertainty. After undergoing surgery to remove the tumor, a person's spirits improve, the wound quickly heals, and their mood gradually brightens. They're in no physical pain, just like any healthy person. And so, they go to the movies, listen to music, browse bookstores, and stroll through the arcades. It's truly a golden period.

After undergoing radiation therapy, however, a person becomes weak. No wonder some people believe that the process and aftereffects of radiation therapy are more terrifying than the tumor itself. Some people refuse to return to the hospital after completing only half of their radiation therapy treatment, rendering their previous efforts in vain. I met a patient who'd been taking tamoxifen for two years, then suddenly developed hives from head to toe. The itching was unbearable, so she decided death was preferable to continuing the medication. During her follow-up appointment, she told us she was afraid that the doctor would admonish her, but she didn't care—she was prepared to face the worst outcome, even if it was death. We all worried about her. Surprisingly, there turned out to be a happy ending. The doctor didn't reprimand her at all, but solved the problem by switching her to another medication. Many people are miserable during radiation therapy, often suffering from nausea, vomiting, and a loss of appetite. I was extremely fortunate and didn't experience any of these symptoms. I just felt fatigued and stayed in bed.

After completing radiation therapy, I thought my whole body would gradually become more energetic, just like after my tumor removal surgery, and so, once again I started going with my friends to watch movies and listen to music. The Cultural Centre had its grand opening in November, which was fantastic. It's located in Kowloon, not far from my home. After dinner, I could spend some time there. There were quite a few good programs, such as a rare performance of Beethoven's *Fidelio* staged by a German opera troupe, and a concert by the Boston Symphony Orchestra featuring Anne-Sophie Mutter on violin. Indeed, listening to music can make people forget their sorrows, and it's not particularly strenuous, as you don't have to do anything—you don't need to flip through a book or read words, you simply soar on the music's wings. I usually went to bed at eight o'clock, but when I went out to listen to music, I stayed up until after ten. The concert hall was air-conditioned, so I brought an extra layer of clothing; afraid of getting hungry, I brought a can of milk to drink during intermission. In reality, my body was weak and supported solely by my willpower.

I'd forgotten one of the rules of recuperation: Don't go to public places. Have you heard how much coughing there is during the pause of each movement in the concert hall? They're all people with colds.

I'd just undergone radiation therapy, and the troops in my lymphatic system had suffered heavy casualties. My immunity was low. Immediately after, I caught a cold. As a result, I no longer dared go to the cinema or concert hall, and even my usual afternoon teas were reduced to a minimum; I had to stay at home, listening to records and watching videos. The film festival arrived, with more than a hundred films. Despite having reserved tickets for five or six screenings, I couldn't manage to watch a single one. There was nothing I could do about it. My friend loaned me numerous opera videotapes as compensation. I spent most of my time during this period watching videos of the Peking opera star Mei Lanfang.

My life was simple. I didn't have to go to work, and all my time belonged to me. Every day, I went to the park to practice tai chi and tai chi sword. I ate three regular meals a day, went to bed early and woke up early, and didn't suffer from insomnia. My body should have been able to recover quickly, right? Nope. Radiation therapy really zaps one's vitality. The destructive power of radiation is intense. I felt constantly fatigued. I was most energetic in the morning, and as the day progressed, my energy waned. Come evening, it was as though I was one of those battery-powered toys that slow down as their batteries run low; like a light bulb, I transitioned from bright to dim. During this time, I realized sleep was the best way to combat fatigue. Just one good rest, and I felt revitalized; any slight discomfort I felt in the evening vanished by the time I woke up. Animals have a natural ability to heal themselves. I was pleased to discover I still had this ability.

Gradually, I became aware of my body's condition. I felt good in the morning, and rested early in the evening. I needed to eat at regular intervals and avoid hunger. I could walk for two hours at most; if I walked any more than that, I'd become breathless. Other people got over a cold in a week, but it took me two. Although sleep can alleviate fatigue, too much sleep made me feel groggy, leading to stagnant blood flow. As for reading? I found it impossible to read for hours on end like before—I had to put a book down after ten minutes, at most; sometimes, I couldn't read at all because my body was weak and fluttering black spots appeared before my eyes. I often mistakenly thought I'd fully recovered after feeling good for a few days, but that wasn't the case. I'd do a little more housework, then immediately fall short of breath. There was no cure for being short of breath, no medicine I could take. I could only sit on the bed resting, waiting for it to subside eventually. Of course, there are ways to treat shortness of breath in hospitals. Patients can be put on oxygen, but for general home use, especially if there's no long-term need, where would you find an oxygen tank?

There was a stretch when I was feeling good for an entire week, but I forgot I couldn't overexert myself and eagerly rushed to read a little more. As a result, I became weak again. Health was playing hide-and-seek with me. During the World Cup broadcast, I was delighted, because my body seemed to be doing well, so I watched the soccer games every night for a month, but I paid a steep price: I fell ill for two months after, feeling heavy-headed, turning into a wandering spirit. After my surgery, I couldn't lift heavy objects, and I had to carefully protect my chest when I walked, avoiding bumping into passersby; after radiation therapy, I had to be extra careful not to overwork myself, so as to prevent shortness of breath. The truth was, I couldn't predict when I'd feel energetic or tired. If I woke up in the morning without feeling any pain and without any black spots dancing in my vision, it was like winning the lottery, but how long this state would last, I couldn't predict. Naturally, I couldn't stay out for more than three hours, and chatting with someone face-to-face for half an hour wore me out. Friends would invite me for tea or dinner. I couldn't commit in advance, and could only decide when the time came.

Coming home from the hospital after I'd completed radiation therapy, I was considered "cured," as the tumor had been removed and the course of treatment was over. What else could the doctors do for me? What they could do was remind me to return to the hospital for regular checkups. The first time was two weeks later, then three weeks, four weeks, six weeks. After a year, I only needed to go back to the hospital every eight weeks. Ah Kin called. She'd passed the five-year mark and only needed a follow-up visit every six months. We both found this reassuring. The oncology unit in the public hospital takes very good care of their patients. In fact, even if it's not time for a scheduled checkup, if the patient feels uncomfortable or has any concerns, they can go to the oncology unit at any time, register, and see the specialist on duty. As such, some people undergo chest imaging or multiple bone scans. I'd been fortunate; I hadn't had any particular discomfort. The occasional colds and flu were easily managed with a visit to a general practitioner and some medication.

Each follow-up appointment was scheduled on a Thursday morning. I checked in at nine o'clock, and the doctor came at ten. There were four doctors who took turns examining patients. I probably saw a different one each time. Every patient had their own file, and on the day of the follow-up, more than thirty of these thick paper folders were arranged on the desk in the nurses' office. Except for the initial visit when a urine test was required, subsequent follow-ups only involved checking weight and blood pressure. Upon seeing me, the doctor always asked, How are you feeling? I said, Fine. By fine, I meant my surgical wound was fine, I hadn't found any tumors in my other breast, no lumps under my armpits or in my clavicle area, urination wasn't painful, and my bones didn't hurt. I didn't report my lower back pain or colds. Sometimes I'd say, I'm short of breath. The doctor would ask, Why are you short of breath? I'd say, I get short of breath when I'm tired. He'd say, Then don't tire yourself out. Each time, the doctor examined my chest, armpits, clavicle area, and abdomen, and inspected my surgical wound. Sometimes, I'd lie on the exam table with my clothes off, and sometimes, it was all right if I sat on a chair. Once, a nurse told me, Take off your clothes and lie down on the table. Take off your bra, too. And so, I learned that after my surgery, I could still wear a bra.

For each follow-up appointment, there was usually about a two-hour wait because of the number of patients. What could I do during this time? I no longer had the energy to read books, and if I listened to music, I was afraid that I wouldn't be able to hear the nurse calling my name. So I sat on the bench and rested. But I wasn't lonely because there were always groups of two or three patients chatting about their medical conditions, the circumstances of discovering their tumors, their treatment processes, and numerous insights about food and drink. There were usually three or four newly diagnosed patients sitting at the entrance of the nurses' office, seeming quite spirited and full of enthusiasm. Wasn't I that way in the beginning? After radiation therapy, many people become silent. The elderly are especially frail, and some can barely walk.

I hadn't seen Wu Man-kuen again. How was she? I did see Lee Ping often. As for Zong Suk-man, I bumped into her once when I was having a prescription filled and asked her: How are you? She said, Fine. Because the appointments could take place on any day and followed varying cycles, it was natural for us not to run into each other. I did see Ah Kin during one of my follow-up visits. On the phone, we had realized our follow-up appointments were on the same day, but we had never met in person. I kept my eye on people arriving around ten-thirty. I was sure I saw her: a slender figure in jeans and an off-white sweater, a handbag slung over her shoulder. She'd come with her husband, who later sat on a bench reading a newspaper. I asked: Are you Ah Kin? She said, Yes. Finally, we were meeting! She didn't recognize me because she misheard me on the phone and thought I weighed one hundred and fifty pounds instead of one hundred and fifteen. We didn't talk long, because soon after, I went into the exam room, and it was already past eleven when I came out. I had to rush back home to cook for my mother, so we parted in a hurry. I hope I'll have another opportunity to meet her.

The number of young patients gradually increased. They were in their thirties or forties, married, with young children. Some of them still went to work, and they said that when people at their companies saw them, they looked them up and down to see if their figures had changed. One woman performed a series of gentle exercises outside the exam room, saying it was good for the body; she seemed radiant and in high spirits. Several women chatted and became well-acquainted, exchanging phone numbers and talking cheerfully. One made fun of herself for sleeping all day like a lazy cat; but cats have nine lives, she emphasized. They made the waiting room lively and relaxed. However, there were always people with troubled faces. One person asked a series of questions: How could she still be menstruating after taking tamoxifen? How...? Another stammered that it seemed a lump had appeared in her other breast. Hearing this, everyone suddenly fell silent. Some people took a long time to come out of the exam room; some pressed down on a cotton ball covering the needle puncture site after having blood drawn. They were all trapped in the Eastern Depot.

I didn't make friends with any of the people during these rotating follow-up appointments, largely because I'm relatively quiet and introverted. Once, there was patient who'd found a lump in her breast and seemed to feel discomfort in her neck and armpit area. Just then, the woman who'd been doing gentle exercises loudly exclaimed: Ah, it's too late, you found it too late. I was taken aback. It was as though she'd become a judge sentencing the other person to death. Even doctors wouldn't say such a thing. I'd initially wanted to chat and exchange phone numbers with this group of lively young women, but suddenly a chill came over me. Even in the prison of the Eastern Depot, when faced with imminent disaster, there were still those who wanted to demonstrate their mastery over others.

Several times, I heard the young women discussing bras and where to find them, even custom-made swimsuits. At the word "swimsuit," my eyes lit up, and I decided to search for this store. It was located on the upper floor of a building. From the outside, it didn't look like anything out of the ordinary, just a regular place of business, quite spacious, maybe dealing in prosthetic models or something of the sort, along with selling specialty plastic items and medicinal drinks. I had to buzz the doorbell and state my purpose, and then a woman led me into a small room to look around. Inside pink boxes were prosthetic breasts that had been perfectly molded, resembling put chai ko, a steamed pudding cake that's served in bowls on the street. The peach-colored model was alluring, thick and hard to the touch, yet also soft and lifelike. It was filled with silicone and encased in soft rubber. These were foreign-made products, already molded and available in several sizes. They seemed tailored for foreign body types—even the smallest one seemed like it would only fit a Chinese woman who was five foot two and weighed 121 pounds.

Could it stick to the body? Wouldn't it fall off? The salesperson let me try it, so I stuck it on my chest. It already felt a bit heavy in my hand, and it felt even weirder when stuck to my body. I had to press it tightly to make it stick. It didn't seem very secure because its back and my chest wall were both concave in shape—how could the gap be filled? The salesperson said I could use a bra for support. I usually wore a soft and comfortable bra without padding. For this thing to work, would I need to stuff a bunch of padding on the other side as well? Wearing the prosthetic breast under my clothes, it was as if I had someone else's figure, no longer my own. Aside from the asymmetry, the amazing curves I'd expected were nowhere to be seen. I asked, Can I put it in a swimsuit? My biggest concern was swimming. Could it touch water, would it be hot in summer, what happened if it got wet from sweat, was it safe to wear in saltwater and chlorine, could it be washed? But these were things I could only know after I'd bought and used it. I had sensitive skin, and if my wound became irritated, inflamed, and ulcerated it wouldn't be a trivial matter. The price was also quite high. One fake breast cost 1,800 dollars, so I had to say I'd think it over. On the way home, I kept thinking of that pervert in my neighborhood who kept jars and jars of women's body parts soaked in solution at his home.

I dug out my old swimsuit and tried it on. Hey, it fit, clinging tightly to my body, and it was patterned. If I didn't draw attention to myself, no one would notice. At last, I was able to take a vacation to Pui O on Lantau Island with my younger brother. On a clear summer evening, I swam in the sea with a floating board for half an hour. When I strolled on the beach, the board became my shield. Flipping through the newspaper the next day, I learned that a skilled female swimmer had been bitten in half by a shark during a morning swim in Sai Kung.

One day, Ah Kin suggested I try eating turtle. Let me tell you how to eat turtle, she said. Make soup, of course. You must buy a good turtle. Many turtles are counterfeit. Get a genuine one, a golden coin turtle. The Chinese goods emporium has them, and so does that place in Mong Kok. Now there are fewer shipments coming in. It's not easy to import live animals due to animal protection regulations. So if you come across a good turtle, you should buy it. It wouldn't hurt to buy half a dozen at once and raise them. I still have several at home now. When are you coming over to take a look?

Cooking a turtle isn't hard. First, you bring a pot of water to boil and then you put the turtle in. This is quite important. Unlike fish, turtles shouldn't be gutted first, but blanched instead. Of course, they should be placed into boiling water while they're still alive to allow them to excrete urine, so they'll be clean; otherwise, they'll have a fishy odor from holding on to their urine, plus it's unhygienic. The blanched turtle will slowly come out of its shell, and then you can scrape the black spots off the skin and chop the meat into small pieces. Um, no, I don't dare. Why? If you don't have the guts, don't worry. If you can't do it, come to my place, and I'll teach you. I cook turtle frequently, and eat it about once a week. I often invite my sick friends over to eat with me. When will you join us? Eating turtle is good, it's detoxifying. We're full of toxins.

I couldn't help but make the mental calculations: Eating one turtle a week meant more than fifty a year—in five years, that was more than two hundred. If all cancer patients sought out turtles, wouldn't there be fewer and fewer golden coin turtles, and wouldn't they become more and more expensive? I was a person who didn't even to dare slaughter a duck or a chicken. Asking me to kill a turtle wasn't only against my timid nature but also something I couldn't bear to do. Although golden coin turtles are small, for Chinese people, they are still sacred and auspicious creatures, quiet and unobtrusive, detached from conflict. Taking a life is never good. Having learned to cherish my own life, shouldn't I value other lives? Especially when the process involved such a relentless hunt and brutal death. I translated a short story by the contemporary Mexican writer Amparo Dávila titled "Haute Cuisine," which describes a nameless creature that is both real and imaginary. These creatures grow in the garden, on the grass and leaves, and are especially plentiful during the rainy season. People buy them by the dozens because they are famous delicacies. The labor involved in cooking them is complicated and time-consuming. First, they are fed precious medicinal herbs to purify their bodies, and after a day and night, they are carefully rinsed, then placed into water with aromatics. The focus of the story is the boiling-water scene. As the pot of water gradually heats up, they start screaming, like mice, like newborn babies, like bats, like strangled kittens, like hysterical women. Those cries are forever seared into the female narrator's mind, like leeches attached to her body. Especially on rainy days when water beats against the window, or when a pot of water in the kitchen boils, it's as though she can see their eyes protruding from their sockets. Perhaps because of this short story, I didn't want to cook golden coin turtles.

Placing a living creature into cold water set to boil, so that at first they feel the warmth, and then begin to scald, writhing and struggling, is truly a prolonged and progressively intensifying torture, much like cancer. Isn't it the same cruel torture of the Eastern Depot? One can imagine the golden coin turtle sinking heavily into the water, possibly crying out, but who would hear it? The same goes for crabs, which is why they're now eating humans instead. Many years ago, when we were traveling in Sichuan, a restaurant strongly urged us to try salamander, claiming it was a local delicacy. We went into the kitchen to take a look and decided not to eat it because it was a rare animal, and its cries sounded like a baby's cries. Wouldn't eating it be like eating a person? I decided not to eat turtle, and to eat other foods instead, plants that wouldn't release rivers of blood, such as green vegetables, radishes, and grains. Yesterday, I came across an article saying that soft-shelled turtles, pangolins, and golden coin turtles are actually ineffective in preventing cancer, and furthermore that because turtles are fatty, eating them isn't good for the body. As for pangolins, they're prone to cancer themselves. If even a clay bodhisattva can't protect itself, how can it save others?

A friend of mine was sick. Many years ago, he contracted hepatitis from a blood transfusion. Eventually, he regained his health, and his recovery brought me joy. We were old friends who didn't meet often. We had loved to watch movies, and whenever we got together, we talked about films. Recently, he fell ill again while he was abroad. He didn't sleep for seven days, his lower back hurt, and he had difficulty walking. Upon his return, he was admitted to the hospital. The diagnosis revealed late-stage liver cancer. Everyone was shocked. Within a six-month period, two of my friends with whom I often chatted about everything under the sun were diagnosed with cancer. I underwent surgery and radiation therapy in the hospital, and it seemed that the cancer cells were under control, but as for my friend, the doctor told everyone they were trying their best. At such a promising time, with a solid career and a happy family, was he really going to vanish into thin air in just six months?

My friend stayed in the hospital. When we went to visit him, he got out of bed and walked around a bit, lying down when he got tired. Since the doctor said they were trying their best, how could we give up? My friend also agreed to be treated by a qigong master. Many terminal cancer patients were said to have been cured by qigong masters when Western medicine had no solutions. Some also claimed that practicing qigong led to their recovery. The ward was quite spacious, and he was in a single room. All the windows were tightly shut, and the curtains were drawn, so that not a single ray of sunlight shone through. The room was filled with a strange medicinal scent that came from a special kind of mugwort, and there were yellow flowers everywhere. My friend's complexion was slightly ashen, and though he didn't look thin, he'd already been in the hospital for thirty-three days. His spirits still seemed pretty good.

The qigong master came from the mainland to Hong Kong. Initially, when he began treating our friend, he expressed uncertainty about the first three days. After three days had passed, he said the situation had stabilized, and he continued to treat our friend, stating that there were five stages to pass through. By the third week, he'd passed through four of the stages. I was unaware of the specific details of the treatment, but I heard it involved the channeling of healing energy, or fa gong. The master visited once in the morning and once in the evening, and he taught my friend how to circulate his energy. The master drew meridian points all over my friend's body, and his wife administered moxibustion treatments. On the side table, there was a bowl of medicinal herbs that had been prescribed by the master. His fees were high, and while we had our doubts, we all hoped that he could cure our friend.

The qigong master happened to be present when I was visiting my friend. Knowing that I also had cancer, he inquired about my condition, and told me that the first seven months were a critical period. I did the math—I had just reached the end of that period. Then, the second seven months were a period of potential relapse. If there was no relapse, I could rest easy. By this logic, the riskiest period spanned one year and two months. I thought to myself, there's basically no complete cure for cancer, especially breast cancer. There are many cases of recurrence after two, three, five, seven years, and even after more than a decade. The master's advice was still sound, urging me not to smoke, drink alcohol, or overwork myself, and to sleep six hours every night. Weren't these things easy? I didn't smoke or drink to begin with, and I already slept more than ten hours a night.

The master instructed me to take my temperature three times a day—morning, noon, and evening; as long as I didn't have a low-grade fever, all was well. Of course, I should avoid drafty places so as not to catch a cold, and as Hong Kong's climate is humid, it was imperative to keep warm. He asked my friend's wife to bring over a thermometer and immediately checked my temperature. It was 36.5 degrees Celsius, which is normal. He thought that the hospital's thermometer, which was wrapped in plastic, might be inaccurate. When I took it again at home, the mercury was precisely at the tip of the arrow. The master advised me on my diet: eat Job's tears, that is, coix seed; eat soft-shelled turtle once a week; eat mushrooms. I'd only come to visit my sick friend, but unexpectedly, it felt like I was the one receiving the consultation, so I quickly thanked him and put an end to the conversation.

We had high hopes for the master's abilities. He was alone in Hong Kong and wanted an apprentice by his side to assist him; he hoped his patient's friends or family members could apply to bring one of his apprentices to Hong Kong, so they could combine their efforts to treat the illness. Since the patient was staying in the hospital, the master and his apprentice could live in my friend's home; but over time, it seemed that my friend's condition took a turn for the worse. The master said it was because my friend had fallen while getting up from bed. Not long after, my friend passed away. That last visit to him, that final handshake, became our everlasting farewell.

Another prominent figure in the city had also reached the end stages of cancer. In a last-ditch effort, the family invited a renowned qigong master to manage the treatment. The master, of course, was extraordinary. Legend had it that he could transmit energy through a wall using a red string to guide the qi, much like the mythological matchmaker deity, the Old Man Under the Moon.[23] It was uncertain whether this was true or not, but regardless, the notable figure eventually passed away. In his final two days, presumably because there was nothing more to be done, the qigong master disappeared.

My friends knew I'd studied tai chi but thought I still I didn't get enough physical activity. Moreover, since I spent a lot of time at home, they suggested I should participate in more outdoor and group activities. After considering various options, I chose a form of qigong. Some friends with whom I occasionally drank Chinese tea had also learned qigong, and the results seemed quite good. They practiced standing meditation and even taught me how to do it. And so, I decided to start, one lesson per week, the beginner's course consisting of twelve lessons.

Qigong, much like tai chi, has a myriad of schools and styles.

Naturally, I chose the easiest one, a form that mimics the flight of a white crane, taught by a female instructor. This instructor was in great health, and her appearance was exactly how I expected it to be, her face completely free of makeup, fair and tinged with a rosy glow, as lovely as a lotus flower. There were more than ten students in the class, and we practiced in a large indoor hall. Because we were indoors, there was air-conditioning, and the class wasn't physically demanding at all. However, it happened that I was extremely sensitive to the cold, and I usually had to wear more layers of clothing than the others. Fortunately, I didn't catch a cold during my twelve qigong lessons.

I thought qigong was a profound martial art that involved emitting energy, as you read about in novels where a single palm strike can bring down a tree. My instructor said that required a high level of attainment, and the beginning was just a primer, learning how to circulate energy. Initially, it was a series of gentle exercises, extremely slow. It reminded me of tai chi, with many similar hand movements, but it seemed to lack tai chi's intricate fluidity. Qigong teaches us how to guide our energy, directing the energy from the head down to the feet, then back up to the top of the head, forming a large circle within the body. During qigong class, we often kept silent, without thoughts or distractions, simply following the flow of energy within our bodies, like taking a leisurely stroll guided solely by intention. My classmates claimed they could feel the energy moving, while I was calm and dumbfounded, not feeling anything at all. After attending many classes, I still didn't achieve much in terms of circulating energy. Aside from doing gentle exercises and standing still, I learned the names and locations of a few acupoints, as well as about the Ren and Du meridians on the face, the idea that once the energy flowed from one meridian to another, they were connected. For me, however, all of this remained mysterious and elusive.

Halfway through, we started doing "standing meditation," that is, standing in place without moving. Each class lasted an hour, and we stood in meditation for half of that. Perhaps I wasn't focused enough, but I couldn't conjure up any profound insights by standing there. My classmates, on the other hand, swayed their bodies left and right, back and forth, as though they'd been hypnotized, their entire bodies moving in a trancelike manner. After they'd attended half the classes, many of my classmates came back and reported that their physical conditions had improved—their issues with back pain, knee pain, and joint discomfort had decreased, motivating them to become even more diligent. As for me, perhaps because I regularly practiced tai chi every day before I began learning qigong, I didn't feel any difference. After twelve lessons, the first phase came to an end. The second phase wasn't taught at the same location and would require traveling to a distant place. I had no way of embarking on such a long journey to attend the class. I never managed to learn how to breathe using the Dantian acupoint below my navel or mastered the profound technique of channeling and releasing energy. The instructor told us that after completing the first phase of qigong, we could practice on our own, but we couldn't do the standing meditation alone, because it required guidance from a specialist or someone to look after you—beginners practicing on their own might get carried away, leading to meditation psychosis. And so, I bid farewell to qigong. Since I couldn't do the standing meditation on my own, and I didn't understand how to circulate energy, I'd be better off practicing tai chi and tai chi sword.

Three incidents occurred in the home of my friend who loves cats.

The first incident: A pile of books in my friend's home toppled over. My friend loved reading and had quite a few books at home, and they kept accumulating, so she piled them on the bookcase, and they kept piling up, all the way up to the ceiling. One day, the tower of books tipped over and came crashing down. Fortunately, my friend wasn't sitting beneath the bookcase, and fortunately, her cat wasn't under it, either; otherwise, the cat might have become a cat pancake.

The second incident: Although the cat wasn't squashed by books, it became sick and developed tumors on its body. At first, they were small, numerous button-like bumps on its neck. The owner didn't pay much attention, thinking it was a common rash, but the bumps grew bigger and bigger, and gradually resembled small citrus fruits. She took the cat to the vet immediately. The vet diagnosed them as tumors and recommended surgery to remove them, telling my friend: There's no need for us to run tests. My friend could only nod. Were the cat's tumors benign or malignant? If they were malignant, it would mean cancer. What could we do for a cat with cancer? There was simply no place where a cat could receive radiation therapy. My friend's cat was eighteen years old, and it's said that some cats can live to be twenty-five. Whether one is a person or a cat, many health issues arise with age.

The third incident: My friend's mother fell ill. At the ripe old age of eighty-five, every day she had still been able to go up and down the stairs, read books, and cook, but suddenly she couldn't get out of bed. She had been a healthy, lively, self-reliant elderly person, but now she had to use a wheelchair, and she could no longer do many of the things she loved on a regular basis, so she cried. In the end, she couldn't escape the prison of the Eastern Depot.

Several incidents also happened in my own home. The first was that the oscillating fan stopped working; the blades wouldn't move. I tried to take it apart and fix it, but to no avail—after more than ten years of use, the machine had broken, perhaps due to metal fatigue. It was an excellent fan, stable with a strong airflow, so I went looking for a similar product and found one from the same brand that said it was made in Shenzhen. It looked good, so I bought it and took it home. Who would have thought that in less than a month, it would be broken and belching smoke? Although it came with a one-year warranty, such a lousy fan probably wouldn't last even with the guarantee. And so, I set off again, still looking for the same brand, finding one at the Chinese goods emporium. It looked much prettier, so much so that and I mistook it for a Japanese product. I was delighted to come across another good fan. It was quiet, with gentle colors and a strong airflow—it was nothing like one of those air-conditioning auxiliary fans that are just for show.

Next, the washing machine refused to spin the clothes dry. After the laundry had finished, the clothes inside were still sopping wet. I didn't have the strength to wring out wet, heavy clothes regularly, so I had to replace the washing machine. So many electrical appliances at home needed to be replaced. The iron was acting up—no matter how the dial was adjusted, it remained at the same temperature, even emitting smoke. The refrigerator didn't emit smoke, but it emitted sweat. When I opened the door, the interior was pitch black, and the light wouldn't turn on unless I gave it a good kick. The TV had been snowing for half a year. One of the doors of the kitchen cabinet suddenly tilted and almost fell off. It turned out the screws had rusted and snapped. The steel windows were corroded, paint was peeling off the walls—over the course of about ten years, items made of iron and wood decay and deteriorate. In comparison, human skin seems much more durable. However, you can't help but sigh with emotion, as though you are seeing the retreating figure that Zhu Ziqing wrote about reflected in the domestic sphere.[24]

The most serious incident was that my mother fainted. She simply wanted to walk from the bed to sit on a chair, but she unexpectedly lost consciousness. I don't know how, but I just happened to be standing right next to her. Her body went limp, and she starting falling toward the floor, her whole body devoid of strength. It truly happened in a split second. My instincts kicked in, and I caught her, preventing her from falling. I'd carried this person who weighed seventy-something pounds down the stairs before, but this time, she felt extraordinarily heavy. I summoned all my strength but could only drag her upper body, her legs trailing on the floor. I dragged her to the edge of the bed, pushing her torso up first, then I lifted her legs. At that moment, I collected myself and remembered not to let an unconscious person lie on their back, in case they vomited and choked, obstructing their breathing. I gently turned my mother onto her side. At this point, she began to regain consciousness.

Her loss of consciousness surely indicated something was wrong. I called for an ambulance. Two medical technicians arrived. Since my mother had regained consciousness, they said, The hospital might not admit her for an extended stay. I said, The main concern is her health—if they don't admit her, we can always bring her back home.

There was a foul stench in the room. Everyone understood what had happened. The medical staff said, The nurses will yell if we send her to the hospital like this—it's better to clean her up first. That made sense. I quickly grabbed a few towels, soaked them in hot water, and wrung them out. I spread a plastic tablecloth on the bed and placed a bucket of water by the bedside, cleaning my mother up and changing her into a fresh pair of pants. At that time, so she wouldn't have to get up at night to use the bathroom, we had her wear adult diapers. Because her bowel movement was contained in the diaper, she hadn't soiled the bed. I quickly threw the dirty clothes into the bucket, and the medical staff helped her into a wheelchair, covering her with a blanket. There was no one else at home. I closed the doors and windows, locked up, and rode with my mother in the ambulance to the hospital.

Fortunately, there weren't many patients in the emergency room. My mother's turn came quickly. They rushed to check her heart rate and pulse, and attached electrodes to her chest for an electrocardiogram. They also took a routine chest X-ray. Although she'd been unconscious, now that this elderly woman, whose only ailment was her frailty, was awake and could speak, most hospitals wouldn't admit her but would just prescribe some medication and send her home. I thought this would be the case, because in recent years, my mother sometimes experienced heart palpitations and shortness of breath, and had gone to the emergency room several times, but she was never admitted for an extended stay. She was only kept for observation once and was discharged after three days. So what would happen this time? She ended up being admitted to the hospital for observation and was sent to one of the wards.

How serendipitous it was that I happened to be there to catch my mother just in time. If I'd been standing farther away, she would have fallen to the ground for sure. As a frail eighty-year-old, she might have fractured her spine, elbow, or even suffered head injuries from hitting the furniture. After my surgery, I couldn't lift heavy objects and had to protect my chest wall, yet I managed to lift such a heavy person onto the bed without injuring my shoulder or collarbone. This could only be ascribed to luck. My mother wasn't sick, just old. Her organs were gradually deteriorating, like a lamp running out of oil. Illness can be treated, but aging is something that no one can do anything about. After being hospitalized for three days and undergoing various tests, the hospital transferred her to another facility to recuperate. I visited her every day and noticed there was always an egg on her side table, but she didn't like eggs. The facility rules dictated that patients couldn't stay in bed all the time and must sit up, but whenever she sat in a chair, her feet swelled, so the nurses allowed her go back to bed. Every day, she was administered oxygen from a tank that resembled a water flask; it stood upright like a missile by her bed. When a person grows old, they are subjected to cruel treatment reminiscent of the Eastern Depot.

The incidents occurring in my household and in my personal life kept me so occupied that I almost forgot about the outside world. So many major events had happened in the world. The Berlin Wall had fallen: Rostropovich played the cello at the foot of the wall, girls gave flowers to the soldiers at the fallen wall, people took home bricks as souvenirs, and Bernstein conducted orchestras from East and West Germany that played Beethoven's "Ode to Joy." What an inspiring event this was—the wall dividing Berlin into Eastern and Western Depots had fallen! However, the Gulf War erupted in the Middle East, resembling another Crusade. Was it a war between Christianity and Islam, or was it about dominance in the Middle East? The Israeli-Palestine conflict remained an inextricable knot. Israel had long been a nation reborn, but where was Palestine's land?

Suddenly, the Soviet Union had disappeared. Watching TV every day, one moment I felt joy, the next, sorrow. I didn't know if the many Eastern Depots in the world were dying out, or if they were starting anew.

DAIFU DI

MY PATERNAL aunt's residence was called Daifu Di. The first time I went there, I walked down the main street of the small town, past a long, pale pink wall, and arrived at a wide entrance gate. Stepping back a few paces and looking up, I saw three prominent Chinese characters inscribed on a plaque in the center of the stone-pillared gate: DAIFU DI. I didn't know what Daifu Di meant and assumed it was where a doctor lived, since *daifu* meant "doctor"—I didn't realize it was also a term used to refer to a high-ranking official in imperial times. I'd grown up in a big city, and when I needed medical attention, I saw a doctor trained in Western medicine at a clinic; most of the time, the family doctor came to our home. However, I'd seen old period films where, when someone fell ill, people would say: Please send for the daifu. Thus, in my mind, daifu was equated with doctor. In that case, wouldn't Daifu Di be a doctor's residence? As for the difference between daifu, and the more common word for doctor, *yisheng*, I assumed that those who practiced medicine nowadays were referred to as yisheng, while those who practiced it in ancient times were known as daifu.

Daifu Di was a very large house. Beyond the main hall were the side rooms, and in front of the hall, there was a courtyard. The architectural shape resembled that of the Forbidden City in Beijing, albeit on a smaller scale. It also resembled Lu Xun's former residence that I visited in Shaoxing, but the impression that Lu Xun's residence left on me was that it was only half the size of Daifu Di, as the rooms were situated on the periphery rather than built along a central axis. Daifu Di also had a second floor, where the secluded rooms had been inhabited long ago by the seventh and eighth daughters of the noble mansion. When I went sightseeing at Daifu Di, my aunt was no longer living there because of the Sino-Japanese War—to escape the calamities of war, she'd moved to the countryside, five miles out of town. Our family had also moved to a house in my aunt's hometown to escape the war. It was only by chance that I happened to visit Daifu Di with some employees from my aunt's shop.

A doctor who treated sick people, living in such a huge house? I only knew that in his spare time, my uncle would see townspeople who felt unwell, that he would take their pulse, diagnose their ailment, and sometimes treat them with medicinal herbs. There was a coffin stored in one of the side rooms near the back garden, which further reinforced my belief that of course this had to be a place where a doctor treated patients, and that when patients passed away, they were carried to the backyard. However, I never witnessed any of these things, because the Daifu Di I visited was deserted, except for an elderly caretaker who kept watch over the gate. The only other sign of life was the goldfish swimming in the big water tank in the corridor. The side rooms were once converted into study rooms for children, but I didn't see those, either. It was only many years later that I realized that Daifu Di was not a medical clinic but the residence of a high-ranking official.

My uncle's ancestors had been officials, but according to local word of mouth, the construction of Daifu Di seemed to have been in honor of two women, the Seventh Lady and Eighth Lady. These two wellborn young women lived in their father's home, even after they were married, as was the local custom. Their status soon increased when they became mothers; they were then chosen by the imperial court to serve as wet nurses in the palace. It was unknown which young Manchu princes and princesses they nursed, but they received countless rewards from the court, returning home in glory, residing in Daifu Di instead of their marital homes. Daifu Di was supposedly built because of them, two illustrious women from a prominent family who enjoyed widespread respect and a rare social status even higher than men with beards and brows, all because they had breasts full of milk.

My uncle never treated me for any illness, and in fact, from my childhood on, I had never consulted a traditional Chinese doctor. For minor ailments like a cold or flu, I went to see a Western doctor and brought home the usual liquid or pills, and after a few days, I'd be back in good spirits; perhaps without even taking the medicine, my body's defenses could have recovered on their own. But my mother consulted doctors of traditional Chinese medicine. She'd have her pulse taken and return home with medicinal herbs, which she would carefully study, as though she were counting gold rings, then boil in a pot on the stove, filling the whole house with the aroma of herbs. I've smelled that aroma for many years.

One year, my father complained that he wasn't feeling well and was having lower back pain. He went to the benefits department at his company, and the doctor there diagnosed him with kidney stones, recommending surgery to remove them. My father was deeply anxious. In those days, for most people, undergoing surgery was a serious matter with life-threatening implications. Naturally, he spent all day at home worrying. My mother then suggested, Why not see a traditional Chinese doctor? The one she often consulted was very good, and many people went to him for treatment. My father had never seen a traditional Chinese doctor before, but thought he might as well give it a try. The doctor was elderly, with a head full of white hair. Like other traditional Chinese doctors who sat in the corner of a narrow herbal medicine shop, he had set up a writing desk with brushes, ink, and paper, and a chair beside the desk. This was his clinic. But the old doctor's clinic wasn't even located inside an herbal medicine shop; instead, he'd been invited by the neighborhood welfare association to set up his practice beside the Guanyin temple in a gloomy, dilapidated hut that resembled a thatched cottage. The old doctor examined my father and said that he could treat the kidney stones with medicine instead of surgery. He prescribed some medicine. My father took two doses, passed the stones, and fully recovered.

That elderly doctor would have been over one hundred years old if he were still alive. Where can one find such a doctor? The history of Chinese medicine is a glorious one dating back thousands of years, and includes Cao Cao's headaches and Guan Yu's bone healing during the Three Kingdoms period. There are famous figures, such as Hua Tuo, a master of surgery and acupuncture from the late Eastern Han dynasty; Bian Que, a legendary physician who is said to have lived during the Warring States period; and Li Shizhen, a renowned pharmacologist and physician. There are also the proven curative effects of acupuncture and herbal medicine. However, where can we go to consult a doctor of traditional Chinese medicine? In the city where I live now, traditional Chinese medicine has no official status, and the qualifications of its practitioners are not recognized. They can only exist parasitically in Chinese herbal medicine shops. The signboards displayed in medical clinics all bear the names of doctors educated in Western medicine, black letters on a white background advertising which university they graduated from, their area specialization, where they studied overseas, what titles they received, and which exams they passed. Of course, what's most important is that they've officially obtained a license from the government to practice medicine. As a result, patients feel at ease and seek medical treatment from them.

Chinese medicine, however, is different. Even if a practitioner has extraordinary skills, there are no formal qualifications; just like the wandering doctors in the martial arts realm, with no criteria to distinguish who's a good doctor and who's a quack, it's a matter of luck. These days, I often pass by the Chinese herbal medicine shops and smell the fragrant herbs. I think Western medicine seems a bit domineering, reminiscent of a slaughterhouse, while Chinese medicine appears more benevolent. What Western medicine aims to treat is your illness. They see a tumor and excise it, see a growth and remove it, constantly opening up a person's internal organs—*snip snip, stitch stitch*—and once the illness is treated, their job is done. Chinese medicine isn't like this. They use methods of dissolution, breaking up clumps, clearing blockages, paying attention to the entire body, slowly helping you to recuperate and restore your health.

When I pass by Chinese herbal medicine shops, I always want to go in and have a seat, to ask the old doctor to help me regulate my weak constitution, but each time I stop myself. Which herbal medicine shop should I enter? Which one has a good doctor? The Consumer Council tells us many things, such as which air-conditioner brands perform well, which toys are too loud and unsuitable for children's ears, which cribs don't meet safety standards and may cause the child to fall, which universal plugs are unsafe and may leak electricity. But who can tell me which doctor of traditional Chinese medicine is reliable? How wonderful it would be to establish a hospital dedicated to traditional Chinese medicine, a large facility like the public hospitals but where the diagnosis and treatment are completely based on Chinese medicine, where patients take herbal remedies and receive acupuncture; then, people could freely choose whether to see a doctor of Western or Chinese medicine.

Nowadays, when we talk about the splendid culture of the Tang dynasty, we always say it was the golden age of poetry. The Tang dynasty's advances in medicine were astonishing, no less impressive than that of its poetry; but Chinese people have long valued literature and looked down on science, so poetry is held in higher esteem than medicine. In the seventh century CE, during the reign of Emperor Gaozu of the Tang dynasty, the Imperial Medical Office was established in the capital city of Chang'an as the continuation of an official medical school from the preceding Sui dynasty. The equipment was better developed than that of the Sui dynasty. The Imperial Medical Office was divided into two parts: medicine and pharmacy. The department of medicine had four major branches: medicine, acupuncture, massage, and incantation.

During the Tang dynasty, politics and religion were inseparable. Today, the incantation branch seems rather amusing, but at the time, it was taken seriously. There were both Daoist and Buddhist incantations. Patients had to abstain from eating meat and fish and observe fasting rituals at the altar before they could receive the incantations to exorcise evil spirits. Massage during the Tang dynasty could treat eight kinds of diseases and could also set bones; acupuncture, of course, encompasses both acupuncture and moxibustion. Even now, physicians frequently use acupuncture, moxibustion, and massage to treat illness and strengthen the body.

The most important of the four major branches of the department of medicine was medicine itself, which had the most teachers and students, including master physicians, medical workers, doctors, pharmacists, medical scholars, and medical assistants: 164 people in total. After enrolling in the medicine branch, students were taught basic courses by scholars and teaching assistants; they studied classic works such as *The Book of Plain Questions*, *The Pulse Classic*, and *The Classic ABCs of Acupuncture and Moxibustion*, and then went on to study their chosen specializations. The department of medicine was divided into five disciplines: physical therapy (internal medicine); sores and swellings (surgery); children (pediatrics); ears, eyes, mouth, and teeth (ophthalmology and otorhinolaryngology); and horning (a kind of external remedy). These days, how many years do medical students have to study? In Hong Kong, they study for five years, while in the United States and Germany, it's seven. In the Tang dynasty, students of internal medicine had to study for seven years, those studying pediatrics and surgery had to study for five years, and those studying other subjects for two years. Students constantly took exams, almost every month, every quarter, and every year, and if they didn't pass after nine years, they were eliminated. Instructors of medicine were also required to take exams, and to provide a certain number of patients cured and healed as their assessment, so that those who weren't truly devoted to the profession would be prevented from misleading and misguiding students.

The pharmacy division of the Imperial Medical Office was responsible for planting, harvesting, and storing medicine. In the city of Chang'an, there was a medicinal garden with three hectares of fertile land where commoners under the age of twenty who were smart and capable were selected to become students of the herbal garden. Under the guidance of their teachers, they planted various medicinal herbs, and after graduation, they could be promoted to pickers of medicinal herbs. Places that produced medicinal herbs also employed pickers who collected the medicinal herbs and offered them as tributes to the imperial court in the capital. The scale of this imperial medical school in the Tang dynasty was incredibly grand. Meanwhile, in

Europe, it wasn't until the eleventh century that the earliest medical school, the Schola Medica Salernitana, rose to prominence in Italy. Why is it that China's brilliant medical achievements are overlooked in modern times? I often think that if today there were also large-school institutes of traditional Chinese medicine, instead of affiliated, experimental, or merely nominal ones, they could carry on the tradition of Chinese medicine, and then there would be a group of Chinese medicine graduates who, like doctors of Western medicine, could aid patients.

The neglect of traditional Chinese medicine is a phenomenon that likely started in the early twentieth century. The introduction of foreign scientific and technological knowledge, which emphasized rational arguments, led many people, especially intellectuals and those who had studied Western medicine, to believe that Chinese medicine was unscientific, or to develop biases against it because its efficacy took more time. Take Dr. Sun Yat-sen, for example. He studied medicine at the University of Hong Kong, specializing in surgery and pulmonary diseases. He died of advanced liver cancer, and only consulted a traditional Chinese practitioner eight days before his death. Throughout his life, he received three consultations in traditional Chinese medicine, and only took one dose of Chinese medicine. By that time, he might have come to believe that Chinese medicine also had its merits.

Lu Xun studied medicine in Japan. At first, he didn't believe in the therapeutic effects of traditional Chinese medicine. Later, this person who had studied Western medicine also took Chinese medicine when he fell ill. He recorded in his diary: "Drinking ginger juice to treat stomach problems. Drinking acanthopanax liquor for shoulder pain." China is an exasperating country. It has invented many things, only to see them improved upon and exploited by foreigners, while it struggles to achieve further progress on its own. Take, for example, the compass, the magnetic compass, and the art of printing, to name a few advancements. In the field of medicine, perhaps the most significant achievement is the inoculation against smallpox.

Smallpox inoculations were already practiced in China during the

Ming dynasty. However, what was used for inoculation wasn't cowpox but rather human smallpox, because the source of the inoculation wasn't obtained from cows but from the bodies of infected humans. At that time, doctors stored the diluted smallpox lymph of infected children in small porcelain bottles; the lymph was then smeared onto children's clothing for them to wear. This was known as the "smallpox clothing" method; it was extremely primitive and not very effective. Another method was to dip cotton into the pus of smallpox pustules, then use it to plug the nostrils of the recipient, or to grind dried scabs into a powder that was blown into the nostrils with a silver tube. This final method proved to be effective. It became known as variolation and attracted attention from other countries. Russia even sent doctors to China to study, and the method was passed on from Russia to Turkey and England. It wasn't until 1796 that Edward Jenner, an English doctor from the countryside, invented the cowpox vaccination to prevent smallpox.

During the late Ming and early Qing dynasties, there was a smallpox outbreak, and only some cities and towns had preventative measures in place. At that time, the Kangxi Emperor launched a large-scale mandatory inoculation campaign. He used the outbreaks in Mongolia as an example, requiring the forty-nine banners outside the border and the various Khalkha vassal states to become inoculated against smallpox.[25] The result was that those who were inoculated remained in good health. Unfortunately, this national epidemic prevention campaign was unsuccessful because many people refused to be inoculated. It wasn't until the twentieth century that people realized the benefits of inoculation, but by then, cowpox was used instead. Some people only believed in Chinese medicine and some only in Western medicine. The Kangxi Emperor was an enlightened person in this regard. While he studied Chinese medicine himself, he didn't reject Western medicine. He often prescribed medicine for his subordinates. During that time, he was surrounded by Western missionaries. When he fell ill with malaria, a Frenchman offered him quinine, which quickly cured him. This experience increased his interest in Western medicine. He not only appointed Giovanni Giuseppe da Costa, a missionary who was proficient in surgical medicine, to practice medicine in the imperial court but also appointed Bernard Rhodes and Étienne Rousset as accompanying physicians, and had the French missionary Dominique Parrenin translate Pierre Dionis's *The Anatomy of Man* from French into Manchu. The palace also opened up a special experimental site for the missionaries to develop Western medicine. When the emperor went on tours, he brought many bottles and jars of medicine, which he distributed to the sick.

As an emperor who was also a doctor, Kangxi wasn't half bad. His medical skills were steeped in the essence of traditional Chinese medicine, that is, "strengthening the body's vitality and expelling pathogenic factors." He not only focused on treating ailments but also emphasized taking care of the body, regarding the patient as a whole organism. The doctor's role was to treat the entire person, not just the illness. If prevention is possible, and the body is healthy, then there is no need to go see a doctor. For example, Cao Yin, the renowned Imperial Textile Commissioner of Jiangning and grandfather of the author Cao Xueqin, fell ill with a skin disease and became bedridden, unable to attend court. After two months, he hadn't improved, and his condition became critical. When Kangxi found out, he gave him a prescription for six-ingredient rehmannia, which cured him. On the thank-you note to the emperor for the medicine, Cao Yin wrote that originally he had caught a chill. Because he made the mistake of taking ginseng, his chill subsided, but then he contracted a skin disease. Now, by the immense grace of heaven, the emperor's gift of medicine bestowed the rest of his life upon him. How clever the Emperor Kangxi was! Six-ingredient rehmannia (a type of herbal pill) was a direct treatment of skin disease. What's ingenious is that the emperor not only treated the illness but also understood the patient's lifestyle: Cao Yin was a man of passion and elegance who often lingered in the pleasure quarters, and his body was naturally deficient in yin. The six-ingredient rehmannia was a way to treat the root cause of the problem. Therefore, Kangxi instructed Cao Yin to replace his tea with tufuling, also known as China root, a medicinal herb that can promote diuresis, dispel pathogenic winds, and remove toxins.

He also admonished him: "But you shouldn't take medicine for this skin disease. If poison were to enter the body, I fear later it might turn into leprosy. Apart from salt water, even a thousand remedies wouldn't be able to cure it." The statement "apart from salt water, even a thousand remedies wouldn't be able to cure it" was actually a warning to Cao Yin to be cautious, and that abstaining from lust was paramount, so as not to contract a sexually transmitted disease, which would have been incurable. I hadn't imagined Kangxi to be such a competent doctor. However, in the political realm, his proclamation "In a prosperous era, increase the population, without ever raising taxes" actually harmed China. Because he encouraged childbirth without raising the head tax, the population during Kangxi's reign reached a staggering 400 million, dramatically increasing the pressure on food production, necessitating deforestation and the cultivation of more arable land. Since then, China has steadily accounted for a quarter of the world's population. The severe flooding in eastern China last year can be traced back to the disastrous consequences of that policy.

Postmodern people suffer from postmodern illnesses. What are the symptoms of postmodernity? I'd say AIDS, not cancer. Cancer is a classical illness. In ancient China, cancer was simply referred to as a tumor, and it was recorded more than two thousand years ago. *The Yellow Emperor's Classic of Internal Medicine* mentions muscle tumors and intestinal tumors. During the Zhou dynasty, there were ulcer doctors who specialized in treating swellings and ulcers. These ulcer doctors were surgeons, and their main focus was tumors. The *Treatise on the Origins and Symptoms of Various Diseases* defines a tumor as "a stagnant node that doesn't disperse." As for the earliest appearance of the word "cancer," it was in the *Precious Book of Health Preservation* by the lay Buddhist Dong Xuan of the Song dynasty. However, doctors in the Song and Yuan dynasties generally referred to cancer as a rock, because a tumor is uneven like a rock. And so, the name for breast cancer was just "breast rock." Traditional Chinese medicine attributes the cause of breast cancer to anxiety, depression, liver and kidney deficiencies, and an accumulation of heat and toxins. It's been said that people with breast cancer are often unhappy, and some women even become sick due to their husbands finding new love. Thus, breast cancer has also been called "jealous rock." The most detailed historical account of breast cancer can be found in the *Orthodox Manual of External Medicine* by Chen Shigong of the Ming dynasty, which even includes an illustration of breast cancer. Traditional Chinese medicine also refers to tumors as a "loss of construction" or "loss of glory," because this disease makes people lose their luster and become emaciated. For women with breast cancer, this disease is indeed a loss of glory, as from then on, they've lost the glory of motherhood. Breast removal can be followed by skin reconstruction, but taking the risk of having children afterward benefits neither women themselves or the next generation.

How does traditional Chinese medicine treat tumors? *The Yellow Emperor's Classic of Internal Medicine* mentions the following method of dissipation: "Cut away what is hard, dissipate what is bound, and attack what remains." At that time, Hua Tuo was already surgically removing tumors. Traditional Chinese medicine treatment for breast cancer today actually incorporates methods from Western medicine, such as surgical excision, radiation therapy, chemotherapy, endocrine therapy, and immunotherapy. Some hospitals on the mainland also use traditional Chinese medicine for treatment, starting one week after surgery, and administering one dose daily for three years. This is said to be effective.

Near the ground floor of my building, there is a wet market bustling with people coming and going all day long. All sorts of shops have sprung up like bamboo shoots after the rain. Strangely enough, although there are numerous shops, there's not much diversity, and often the same types of shops are clustered together. For example, there are two variety stores, three bakeries, and, surprisingly, four herbal medicine shops within fewer than thirty steps from one another. The shops on the side streets and alleys have their own local charm, and there are always many goods piled up at their entrances. We pass by every day, and only half the sidewalk is accessible, as the rest is occupied by such foods as American ginseng, dried day lily, red beans and mung beans, dried mushrooms, and dried octopus.

A few herbal medicine shops sell both Chinese and Western medicines. The entire shop is brightly lit, lacking the elegance, tranquility, and fragrance of traditional pharmacies, and there are no ancient drawers covering the walls. There are signs hanging in the shop for the departments of pharmacist-prepared medicine, traditional Chinese medicine, ginseng and antler, and seafood. Such a tiny place, yet it looks like a multistory department store, and it's even divided into sections. Of course, the herbal medicine shops also sell cosmetics, resembling a variety store. However, they still retain the traditions of Chinese medicine shops, with a doctor of Chinese medicine onsite. The writing desk where the doctor sits is squeezed into a corner of the shop. When I pass by the herbal medicine shops, I often look to see what kinds of doctors are there—some are old, some are young. This one has a sign reading TRADITIONAL CHINESE MEDICINE DOCTOR FROM GUANGZHOU ONSITE ALL DAY, that one has a sign that says FREE CONSULTATION, FREE DECOCTION, and another one displays a sign for NEW DOMESTIC METHOD OF TRADITIONAL CHINESE MEDICINE. Whose medical skills are the best? It's really confusing.

It's said that Chinese medicine focuses on tailoring treatments to individualized needs, as though Western medicine treats the human body as something else entirely, because Western medicine talks about bacteria, viruses, nerves, bodily fluids, bioelectricity, tissues, organs, and systems, while Chinese medicine discusses meridians, yin and yang, qi, and internal organs. The truth is, Western medicine and Chinese medicine are similar in many aspects. For example, ancient Greek medicine also regarded the human body as an organic whole. Alcmaeon, the earliest Greek medical scientist who lived in the fifth and sixth centuries BCE, believed that the human body has opposing forces such as dampness and dryness, cold and heat, and bitterness and sweetness. If one side dominates, the person will become sick. Therefore, in order to stay healthy, various capabilities must be kept in balance. Isn't this very similar to the theory of traditional Chinese medicine? After Alcmaeon, three main schools of medicine emerged. The southern Italian school of medicine was represented by the philosopher

Empedocles. Whereas Alcmaeon pointed out dryness and dampness and cold and heat, Empedocles believed in the four elements of water, fire, earth, and air, stressing the need to maintain a balance among them. He opposed treating only the aching head for a headache or the aching foot for a foot ache, advocating for treatment of the whole body instead. The Knidian school of medicine at the southern tip of Asia Minor was influenced by traditional Ionian natural philosophy, as well as by Empedocles, and advocated the theory of balance. The most famous Greek school of medicine is the Kos school represented by Hippocrates, who is called the father of Western medicine. Based on experience and clinical observation, it analyzed the physiological phenomena of the human body in great detail, paid attention to the influence of food and the environment, proposed the idea of four human bodily fluids—blood, yellow bile, black bile, and mucus—and emphasized studying the relationship between human life, disease, and the environment. Hippocrates believed that the causes of people's illnesses were inappropriate natural conditions and abnormal lifestyles, which destroyed the harmony of nature and the physiological balance within the human body.

Due to advancements in science and technology, modern medicine now has tools such as microscopes, scalpels, X-ray machines, ultrasound diagnostic machines, radioisotope detection, and computer scanning, among others. These tools can quickly, accurately, and more effectively analyze pathological sites, in addition to improving our understanding of how medications work in the body, thereby enhancing the brilliance of Western medicine. Chinese and Western medicines have developed under different historical conditions of philosophical thought, social economy, and science and technology. Obviously, they are two different systems, each with its own advantages and disadvantages, offering different interpretations of the human body and even life itself. But isn't the modernization of traditional Chinese medicine, combined with scientific instruments to treat diseases, a breakthrough worth applauding? And likewise, Western medicine now incorporates acupuncture and Chinese herbal medicine, following in the excellent tradition of ancient Greek medicine.

After falling ill, I found myself particularly drawn to traditional Chinese medicine, becoming more attentive to medications and medical treatments, as most other cancer patients probably do. Additionally, because my family doctor had emigrated, I felt as if I had no helping hand to trust in this vast sea of people. However, there are many good doctors of Western medicine, and I eventually found one who is cheerful, converses and jokes with patients, and often answers my questions. Although I only had a cold, he checked my blood pressure and even took my pulse. I said, Wow, doctors of Western medicine also take the pulse. He just smiled. Among all the doctors I've seen, he's the only one who told me, "Don't eat too much meat." Strangely enough, he resembled our previous family doctor. As a result, other members of my family also went to him for treatment when they felt unwell. We seem to have found a family doctor again.

THINGS THAT ARE KNOWN

Can people with breast cancer get married?
Of course. Love transcends the boundaries of race, age, illness, and religion. As long as people love each other, that's what matters.

Can you kiss someone with breast cancer?
Of course. Breast cancer isn't contagious.

Can people with breast cancer have sex?
No problem. Breast cancer isn't AIDS; even with AIDS, appropriate preventative measures can be taken.

Should people with breast cancer use contraception?
It's best to use contraception, because fluctuations in estrogen levels during pregnancy can easily cause a recurrence of the tumor. If pregnancy occurs during a period when cancer is not under controlled treatment, it can lead to rapid spread and metastasis.

Won't women with breast cancer who take medication stop menstruating?
Yes, but some patients don't take medication for an extended period of time. They might stop taking it after one or two years.

What should you do if you discover you have breast cancer while pregnant?
Leave it up to the doctor. Most oncologists would advise an immediate abortion, followed by a mastectomy, and then a course of radiation or chemotherapy. Certainly, there are exceptions, and cases where individuals have successfully given birth.

Are there any counseling agencies?
In some foreign countries, but not in Hong Kong. However, you can call the Anti-Cancer Society Hotline or the Cancer Crusade Angels Service Society or write to a newspaper column such as the Cancer Research Association, and someone will answer your cancer-related questions. Many cities outside of Hong Kong offer services to assist patients.

What does physical therapy entail?
After a mastectomy, some patients may experience edema in the upper limb, affecting the range of motion of the arm. Physical therapy can be done to restore muscle function. Generally speaking, exercising more on your own is fine.

What is occupational therapy?
Helping patients to smoothly navigate the entire treatment process, including preoperative assessment; setting treatment goals and a program; providing postoperative instructions on how to prevent edema; and assisting patients in selecting prosthetic breasts.

When is it appropriate to wear prosthetic breasts?
When the surgical incision has completely healed, and all side effects of radiation have subsided.

What counts as being cured?
If there's no recurrence for several years after treatment, then a person is considered cured.

Why is breast cancer particularly prone to recurrence?
People who are overweight may not change their eating habits and reduce their fat intake after treatment.

Other reasons for recurrence?
The tumor in the breast isn't the original lesion. By the time of the removal surgery, the cancer has already spread or metastasized.

What is the five-year survival rate?
That's the data provided by the medical community to compare cancer treatment methods. A five-year survival rate or ten-year survival rate doesn't mean that cancer patients will only live five or ten years.

Why does the five-year survival rate of 80 percent drop to 65 percent twenty years later?
People who are diagnosed around the age of fifty will be seventy years old after twenty years, and their physical functions will decline. Not all elderly patients die of cancer.

Can frequent X-rays cause breast cancer?
It may increase the risk for people with a genetic predisposition, but typically it would require high levels of radiation exposure.

Which occupations increase a man's chances of developing breast cancer?
There is a higher risk for those employed as an electrician, telephone

line worker, or cable worker, as they are often exposed to electromagnetic fields.

What should you do if there's a lump in your breast?
Not all lumps are cancerous. Most are benign. It's advisable to consult with one or two doctors. Do not apply force or squeeze it, as it may stimulate changes in the tumor.

Are breast cancer exams sexual harassment?
If the breasts aren't exposed, how can an exam be conducted? Palpation is necessary. You can opt for a female doctor for the exam. If the doctor is male, you can request a nurse to be present. In fact, in most cases when a male doctor examines a female patient, a nurse will accompany him. This not only reassures the patient but also safeguards the doctor's own reputation.

Can breast augmentation cause cancer?
Ordinarily not, but if the silicone leaks out, it's harmful to the body. Silicone materials can also block chest X-rays, delaying the detection of breast cancer.

Is late-stage cancer painful?
One-third of patients don't experience any pain, one-third experience moderate pain, and one-third experience severe pain.

Can the pain be alleviated or suppressed?
Yes. Physical pain can be managed with pain relievers, using different medications based on their functions. However, physical pain is only one type of pain.

What other types are there?
Emotional, psychological, and interpersonal. These require the care and attention of family members, doctors, nurses, social workers, and even clergy or volunteers. Some people can effectively manage their psychological pain.

Are there any examples of this?
The psychologist Sigmund Freud refused to take pain relievers and focused on writing to alleviate his pain. The philosopher Ludwig Wittgenstein didn't go to the hospital, relying on meditation and travel to help him during the end stages of cancer. The novelist Aldous Huxley could no longer bear to listen to music, so he turned to visual art and had family members read to him. He even used a recording device to dictate "Shakespeare and Religion."

> *The next chapter describes a foolish person doing arithmetic. The exercise is tedious, echoing what others have already said. If you're not in a good mood, don't bother reading and just skip over it.*

MATH TIME

IN THE past, when it came to eating, I never paid attention to whether the food was good or bad, superior or inferior. I only chose things that were easy to cook and that I enjoyed eating. Often, a meal just consisted of instant noodles. Of course, cooking was all about convenience, which is why frightening dishes such as char siu pork stir-fried with eggs ended up on the table. With the combination of two kinds of animal protein not to mention the barbecued meat and oil-fried eggs, I would have needed four stomachs, like a cow, to digest it properly. I used to consume an inordinate amount of sweets on a regular basis and rarely ate vegetables. As a result of such haphazard eating, I packed on the pounds, weighing in at fifty-three kilograms. I suffered from dizziness, and my blood pressure skyrocketed. The doctor advised me to lose weight, which I assumed entailed eating less starch and more meat. Little did I know that animal protein is high in fat, and I continued to gain weight. After developing a tumor, I had no choice but to change my atrocious eating habits. Of course, I no longer eat sweets, instant noodles, or foods that are high in sodium.

My family belongs to the high blood pressure clan. The family doctor told us long ago that high blood pressure runs in our family. Indeed, my maternal grandfather and my father both died of cerebral hemorrhages; my maternal grandmother suffered a stroke, leaving her half paralyzed and bedridden for more than a year. As a result, the doctor specifically advised us to watch our weight and avoid excessive salt consumption. After undergoing radiation therapy, although I tried hard to get rid of my numerous bad eating habits, my body didn't become healthier. My immune system was extremely weak. Something was either off here or ached there. My whole person was often like a wandering spirit, as though I were only half alive in this world. I always said, This is an aftereffect of radiation therapy, that's an aftereffect of radiation therapy. How could there be so many aftereffects? It seemed that the real reason was an unbalanced diet. I had to do some homework.

My math is poor, and I failed the math portion of my examination for a Certificate of Education. Fortunately, calculating balanced nutrition only requires doing a bit of addition, subtraction, multiplication, and division. Pressing buttons on a calculator is by no means difficult. Balanced nutrition is about absorbing the appropriate amount of nutrients from food to maintain the body's functions. First, you need to calculate how much energy you need in a day. Because age, gender, physique, and activity levels vary, each person's energy needs are completely different, and they differ between summer and winter, and for healthy and sick people. For example, I'm in my fifties, female, 152 centimeters tall, and fall into the category of extremely light physical activity. My standard body weight should be calculated as my height minus 105: 152 − 105 = 47 (kilograms).

I should maintain a weight between 42 and 52 kilograms in order to avoid being considered overweight or underweight. Generally speaking, exceeding 5 kilograms beyond the middle point of the standard body weight is considered overweight; being more than 5 kilograms below the middle point is considered underweight. I haven't exceeded these limits because I've been under 53 kilograms for a long time. Is it ideal? Not at all.

My standard body weight is 47 kilograms. My current body weight is 49 kilograms. My ideal weight, however, is 46 kilograms.

For someone with high blood pressure, it's better to have a slightly lower body weight. If I want to reach my ideal body weight, I must lose 3 kilograms. Three kilograms is 6.6 pounds. I can't lose it all at once—I have to do it gradually, so I've decided to lose 1 kilogram first, reaching a goal of 48 kilograms, and then I'll reevaluate things. How many calories should someone weighing 48 kilograms consume per day? This depends on the intensity of the individual's work. The daily consumption of calories per kilogram of body weight is as follows:

White-collar workers require 25 calories.
Light manual workers require 30 calories.
Moderate manual workers require 35 calories.
Heavy manual workers require 40 calories.

For cancer patients:

Those who are underweight require 40 to 50 calories.
Those maintaining an ideal body weight require 30 to 35 calories.
Those using parenteral nutrition require 35 to 45 calories.

The official name for calorie should be kilocalorie or large calorie, but it's generally just referred to as "calorie," a convention that's become widely accepted. Although I'm a cancer patient, I've been considered "cured" for two years now, so I use the standards for an ordinary person. I don't have to go to work. Each day, I spend more time sitting than walking, and more time sleeping than sitting. Although I also practice tai chi, stroll through the streets, shop for groceries, cook meals, and wash dishes, I still fall under the category of extremely light physical activity. Each kilogram of body weight requires 25 calories, so my daily caloric requirements are 25 × 48 = 1,200 (calories).

This 1,200 calorie amount is the total caloric intake, which is the combined sum of calories from three sources: protein, sugar, and fat. How should they be allocated? Let's start by calculating protein. It's easy. One kilogram of body weight requires one gram of protein. My goal weight is 48 kilograms, so I require 48 grams of protein. One gram of protein provides four calories, so the calorie content of 48 grams of protein is 4 × 48 = 192 (calories).

After surgery and while undergoing radiation therapy and chemotherapy, cancer patients need to adopt a high-calorie, high-protein diet to repair damage to organ tissues during treatment, as well as to promote the growth of immune cells and enzymes that increase the body's resistance to cancer. Thus, it's advisable to consume 1.2 to 1.5 grams of protein per kilogram of body weight. Patients who are long past the date of surgery and radiation therapy should avoid long-term consumption of a high-fat, high-protein diet unless medically necessary.

When it comes to sugars from carbohydrates, I slightly increase the proportion of sugar to 60 percent of my total caloric intake. Why do I do this? Because I need to reduce my fat intake. People with breast cancer must particularly watch out for fat. My daily caloric intake from sugar might be 1,200 × 60% = 720 (calories).

One gram of sugar provides four calories, and the amount of sugar in these 720 calories is 720 ÷ 4 = 180 (grams).

Finally, to calculate fat intake, just subtract the other two items from the total calorie amount: 1,200 − 720 − 192 = 288 (calories). One gram of fat provides 9 calories, so my daily fat requirement is 288 ÷ 9 = 32 (grams).

Based on these calculations, I should consume the following nutrients every day:

Protein	48 grams
Sugar	180 grams
Fat	32 grams

The percentages of each nutrient are:

Protein	16 percent
Fat	24 percent
Sugar	60 percent

Nutritionists traditionally recommend the following calorie ratios:

Protein	10 to 18 percent
Fat	25 to 35 percent
Sugar	50 to 65 percent

In recent years, there's a growing belief that people don't actually need to consume a lot of protein, and fat shouldn't exceed 30 percent, while the guidelines for sugar seem to be more relaxed. In fact, in many regions, people only need 10 percent protein and less than 25 percent fat. In the twenty-first century, the medical community may come up with entirely new standards for balanced nutrition.

People are dynamic, and the calculation for balanced nutrition should also be dynamic, changing along with the person. For example, if a person gains weight, the total caloric intake should be reduced; if they lose weight, it should be increased. When I reach my goal weight, I can create a new calorie table. At that time, my daily caloric intake may increase to 1,300 or 1,450. Maintaining a daily caloric intake of 1,200 calories, the only thing to watch out for is that other vitamins may be insufficient, so this regimen can't be followed long-term. Nutritionists believe that if the total caloric intake is reduced to 1,200 calories long-term, it's necessary to take multiple vitamin supplements.

I made a table listing the total calories, protein, sugar, and fat in the most important foods in my daily diet and followed it accordingly. At first, it felt complicated—how much rice, fruit, fish, and meat I should eat—and I found it tedious. After a week, however, I became familiar with it, and it no longer seemed difficult. It's just that I'm not a computer, and I've always been bad at math. I have no way of knowing some foods' ingredients, so I can't calculate everything. What I eat every day and the calories and quantities recorded on the table aren't too dissimilar, which makes me very happy. After decades of living, it's ridiculous to think that this is the first time I've understood what balanced nutrition is. Spending time doing arithmetic still feels meaningful, and controlling my diet seems to protect me from heart disease and diabetes as well. Cancer patients spend a lot of effort fighting cancer but are often dragged down by other health issues.

The components of protein are carbon, hydrogen, oxygen, nitrogen, sulfur, and phosphorous. Its structure is complex, and it's difficult to break down. Its basic unit is an amino acid, of which there are twenty-two types, but adults only need eight essential amino acids. The body can produce some amino acids, but these necessary eight must be supplied through diet: lysine, threonine, tryptophan, valine, leucine, isoleucine, methionine, and phenylalanine. Absorbing protein actually depends more on quality than quantity. For example, if a bowl of rice contains ten grams of protein, and I need forty-eight grams per day, wouldn't eating five bowls of rice be enough? No. Rice is an incomplete protein, as it lacks two of the eight essential amino acids: lysine and leucine. Foods that contain all eight essential amino acids are called complete proteins. These foods include eggs, meat, and milk. Eggs in particular are the best source of high-quality protein. You don't need a large quantity, but the quality is the highest. It appears that eggs, meat, and milk are the foods to eat. Of course, from a pure protein perspective, that's correct. However, these foods are high in fat and are all animal proteins. The pros and cons of any nutrient have to be weighed before a choice can be made.

Besides animals, plants are also rich in protein. So can't vegetarians just use plant protein? It's not that simple. Plant protein generally lacks several essential amino acids, or has an imbalanced ratio of amino acids, or even too much of a certain type of amino acid that interferes with the utilization of other amino acids. The way to determine what is needed is to use a geometric principal called "complementary adjacent angles." All you have to do is combine animal and plant proteins, or add different plant proteins to supplement the deficient items. For example, rice lacks lysine and leucine, while beans lack tryptophan, so eating rice and beans together provides a complete protein. Similarly, bread lacks lysine but cheese has a lot of it, so eating them together has a complementary effect. Thus, dishes like corn and tofu soup, red bean and brown rice congee, cereal with milk, and cheese sandwiches become protein-rich foods.

I need forty-eight grams of protein a day, but I don't need to be meticulous about whether I get forty-eight grams of complete protein. In fact, half of that is enough, because some essential proteins can be replaced by amino acids synthesized by the body itself. For example, cysteine can replace methionine, and tyrosine can replace phenylalanine. Living in an advanced metropolis in the 1990s, I don't have to worry about a lack of protein. Protein-rich foods are abundant, and consuming too many of them can actually lead to illness. Overly abundant nutrition can make modern people prone to disease. It's easy for me to calculate how much protein I consume each day, because many foods contain precisely seven grams of protein:

1 egg
1 ounce of meat
1 cup of cottage cheese
1 cup of cow milk
1 bowl of noodles
1 cup of breakfast cereal
1 cup of soy milk
half a cup of beans
2 slices of thick-cut whole-grain bread
2 bowls of congee
1 brick of tofu
1 slightly less than full bowl of rice

I need forty-eight grams of protein a day. Choosing seven of the above-mentioned foods is enough for a day's nutrition: just two bowls of rice, one cup of breakfast cereal, one cup of cow milk, and a little bit of meat. I base what I eat off the table, and since calculating calories and percentages is too troublesome, I use the simplest method. A day's balanced diet follows the numbers 1-2-3-4-5-6:

1 cup of milk
2 servings of fruit
3 servings of grains
4 ounces of meat
5 servings of vegetables
6 cups of water

I also use the above allocation method as the basis of my daily diet, and make some adjustments based on it. There are too few vegetables—increasing the amount to around eight to ten ounces is more ideal—

and it's better to add another cup or two of water. Some people may even drink two cups of milk a day, while younger people need to eat around six ounces of meat, and some people are better suited for just one serving of fruit. I'm a rice bucket. I love to eat rice. I eat three servings of grains a day, two of which are almost always rice and occasionally noodles or congee, and the other serving of grain is a breakfast grain, plus a slice of bread with afternoon tea. Plant-based proteins are my primary source of "meat." I hardly eat any beef and very little pork, mainly fish. I keep one meal with animal protein a day, which is equivalent to being a half vegetarian. Why not go fully vegetarian? As I mentioned earlier, I'm not good at math and can't calculate the combination of amino acids. Besides, it's just easier to eat around two ounces of fish, which contains fourteen grams of protein, than two bricks of tofu. The same goes for drinking a cup of cow milk, which is easier than eating half a cup of beans. Besides, it seems that it's not advisable to be a casual vegetarian when the body is weak.

I didn't eat much fish in the past because I didn't like the bones, and I ate pork, beef, and chicken instead. Nowadays, because pork and beef are high in fat, and I don't how many hormones are in chicken, I have switched to eating fish, which has many advantages. Of course, fish also contains fat, and the proportion of fat content varies greatly among different types of fish. Grouper is low-fat, while sardines are high-fat. However, fish fat differs from pork and beef fat. It's an unsaturated fat, and an omega-3 fatty acid, which has a cholesterol-lowering effect. Regardless of which type of meat you eat, fat is not the only factor to consider. Cholesterol is also important, and an advantage of fish is that it is lower in cholesterol. Shrimp is a protein-rich food, and the cholesterol content of shrimp isn't high.

We're "luckier" now than young people of the past, who were forced by their mothers to take cod liver oil every day. During times of economic depression, teenagers are often malnourished. Fish provides us with vitamins A and D, as well as vitamins B6 and B12, and they also contain niacin and biotin. Saltwater fish are more nutritious than freshwater fish, and deep-sea fish are better than shallow-water fish, because they contain high amounts of potassium and iron, as well as precious trace elements such as zinc and selenium. As for iodine, in addition to seaweed and jellyfish, fish is also a good source. Fish that can be eaten with its bones is great, such as sardines, but they shouldn't be so heavily preserved that they're like mummies. In addition to yellow croaker, grouper, red snapper, pomfret, and flounder, I also choose tiny silver noodlefish.

Sugar is a carbohydrate composed of hydrogen, oxygen, and carbon. Its structure is simpler than protein, lacking a nitrogen element, and it breaks down easily. When proteins are broken down, toxic nitrogen-containing substances called ammonia are produced, which must be detoxified by the liver, a chemical factory in the body that converts ammonia into less toxic substances such as urea, uric acid, and creatinine, which are then excreted as urine by the kidneys. Healthy people with good organ function can eliminate ammonia toxins smoothly, but if the body is weak, and the liver and kidneys are damaged, there will be obstacles to excretion, and toxins will accumulate, turning into uric acid and forming crystals. This uric acid naturally circulates throughout the body via the bloodstream and has a particular affinity for lodging in bones and joints, leading to the onset of gout symptoms. Crystals that remain in the kidneys can also form kidney stones. Cancer patients taking anticancer drugs may experience cell death, and the death of a large number of cells can also increase uric acid levels in the body. As such, it is advisable to drink plenty of water when taking medication, thereby increasing urine output, diluting the urine, and reducing the chance of kidney stones. If a person's big toe becomes painful, red, and swollen for no reason, they should pay attention to whether they might have gout and reduce their protein intake, avoiding any kind of beans.

Carbohydrate sugars are much better, just some carbon and water, without nitrogen. Eating too much won't cause poisoning, just weight gain. In this aspect, plants are superior to humans. They can produce their own food using carbon and oxygen in the air and water in the soil to carry out photosynthesis in their leaves, which allows them not only to sustain their own lives but also, surprisingly, to feed many animals. Using the same carbon and water, what humans do is exactly the opposite of plants. Plants constantly synthesize, while animals break things down.

The source of sugar is the seeds, fruit, roots, stems, and leaves of plants. For the human body, there are two types of sugars: good sugars and bad sugars. Those found in fruit and honey are monosaccharides and are natural and harmless to the human body. However, synthetic sugars, such as sucrose, maltose, and glucose, are disaccharides. After undergoing processing and manufacturing, they lose their natural qualities. They taste sweet, but don't provide any health benefits to the human body and can cause weight gain if consumed in excess. Starchy foods, such as rice, wheat, potatoes, and beans, are polysaccharides and are also natural foods. As long as they are not processed or canned, they can provide high-quality sugars.

I need a relatively large amount of sugar, 180 grams every day, so eating more rice is just right for me. Two bowls of rice already exceeds 100 grams, a bowl of oatmeal with a slice of bread can provide 30 grams, two pieces of fruit provides 20 grams, vegetables provide 10 grams, and I can also eat a small sweet potato. If a person needs 200 grams of sugar per day, but their intake is less than 100 grams, that will be a disaster. The body's furnace won't have enough fuel. If you don't give it firewood, it will have to figure out a way to keep the fire lit on its own. Isn't there furniture in the house? Just use the tables, chairs, beds, and even precious furniture like the rosewood and sandalwood Ming-style tables for firewood and burn them all. The body's proteins are like useful, precious pieces of furniture.

Fat, one of the three major nutrients required by the human body, also relies on sugar to help it burn. If there isn't enough sugar, fat can't burn completely and will produce toxic ketone bodies, increasing acidity in the blood. Of course, many people are aware of what happens from eating too much sugar. Too many starches can cause weight gain. Animals, like plants, store excess sugar. The human body stores sugar in the liver and muscles. There's nowhere to place any remainder, so it becomes fat and accumulates under the skin, resulting in a big belly, double chin, and waist circumference of thirty-seven or thirty-eight inches. Fruit is good for the body, but when all is said and done, it contains sugar, so eating too much can cause weight gain and tooth decay. Potatoes and beans, which are rich in starch, can ferment in the intestines, producing gas and bloating in the abdomen. Walking down the street, you might feel like a car constantly emitting exhaust, which is extremely embarrassing. Excessive sugar intake can also interfere with the absorption of B vitamins.

The sugars and starches in food aren't necessarily sweet. You have to chew carefully in order to taste that little bit of surprising sweetness. The sweetest is fructose. For example, when mangoes and bananas growing in the fields start turning sweet, they attract numerous animals. Thus, pineapple fields contain snakes, and bears appear near beehives. For some reason, humans have a sweet tooth, so food manufacturers do their best to add sugar to everything they make—sugar is cheap, allowing for minimum cost and maximum profit. Aside from fructose, the next sweetest is sucrose, and thus we find ourselves buried in a snowstorm of sugar day after day.

Dietary fiber comes from the stems and leaves of vegetables or the outer skins of grains and fruits. It is a plant-based substance that the human body can't digest or absorb. While it was previously overlooked, it is now known to be important. Just because the body doesn't absorb it, doesn't mean it's useless waste. If there's too little of it, the body won't be healthy. There are two types of dietary fiber: soluble and insoluble. Soluble fiber is a type of polysaccharide called pectin that is found in the cell walls of fruits and vegetables. People use pectin from oranges and apples to make jam. In addition to pectin, soluble fiber also includes plant gum, which is a sticky plant secretion found in dried beans and oatmeal. In recent years, the medical community has discovered that wheat bran and potatoes can lower cholesterol and slow the absorption of glucose. Insoluble fibers include cellulose, hemicellulose, and lignin, which are found in whole grain and whole wheat foods, along with many vegetables and fruits. They can increase the volume and weight of feces, promote intestinal peristalsis, and shorten the time it takes for waste to pass through the intestines.

Long-term lack of dietary fiber can cause intestinal disease and arteriosclerosis. For people with breast cancer, it's important not only to reduce fat intake but also to increase fiber intake. Daily fiber intake can be increased to thirty grams because fiber helps to expel waste from the body, along with excess estrogen. Eating more fiber also helps to reduce fat levels in the blood. The average person's daily fiber intake is fifteen grams, but breast cancer patients may wish to increase that amount. Adding red rice or brown rice to steamed rice on a regular basis, eating oatmeal and whole wheat bread for breakfast, and eating more vegetables, fruits, beans, and nuts can all increase fiber intake. Of course, excessive fiber intake can also be harmful, as it may lead to the excretion of minerals such as calcium, iron, zinc, copper, and magnesium.

You'll gain weight if you eat too much fructose and starch, because the excess sugar turns to fat. To control your weight, what you need to pay close attention to isn't sugar but fat. Sources of fat include animal fat, fatty meat, cod liver oil, milk, egg yolks, and oils extracted from plants such as soybeans, corn, peanuts, almonds, coconuts, sesame seeds, and melon seeds. When it comes to fat, it seems that modern people are constantly on guard against a formidable enemy, as though they can't touch any fat at all. In fact, the body can't function properly without fat. In terms of total daily caloric intake, it should account for a higher percentage than protein. Isn't it often said that the body needs vitamins? If you want to get vitamin A, people always tell you to eat more carotene, so you eat a lot of foods containing carotene, which should be enough for your daily intake, but can your body absorb it? Eating it is one thing, but absorbing it is another. Without fat, the body can't absorb vitamin A, because it's a fat-soluble vitamin that only dissolves in fat, not water. In addition to vitamin A, vitamins D, E, and K are also fat-soluble, so although exposure to sunlight can provide you with vitamin D, it's useless without fat.

Humans don't hibernate, so they don't need to rely on body fat as "fuel" during hibernation, like frogs or snakes do. However, humans are warm-blooded animals, and fat can keep them warm, like a soft cushion protecting the body's internal organs. A woman's soft and graceful appearance owes much to the presence of fat. Once that fat is lost, the skin of a beautiful woman will become wrinkled. The components of fat are glycerol and fatty acids, the latter of which can be divided into saturated and unsaturated fats. Put a dish of lard and a dish of peanut oil aside for an afternoon, and you'll see that the peanut oil is still a liquid, while the lard has solidified. The solidified fat is saturated fat, which is harmful to the body, so nowadays butter, lard, and oils containing saturated fat have been demonized. Don't think that only animal oils contain saturated fats. Plants do too. The saturated fat content of coconut oil is almost the same as that of butter; palm oil is equal to butter and lard. Take a look at food labels in the supermarket. Nine out of ten foods contain coconut oil, which is just like butter. I'm afraid that you'll recognize what they call this ingredient—it's goes by "hydrogenated vegetable oil." Coconut oil is certainly cheap, which merchants are happy to take advantage of. This type of oil used to only be for making soap. Let's not turn ourselves into soap bubbles.

Nowadays, everyone chooses oils with unsaturated fats, such as corn oil, soybean oil, vegetable oil, and peanut oil. In recent years, corn oil has become a darling among housewives, which can be attributed to the advancement of information dissemination, as people are now aware that rancid peanut oil can produce carcinogenic aflatoxins. My family used to use peanut oil, but naturally, we switched to corn oil, thinking it was safer. It turned out we were wrong. It's simply not suitable for people afflicted with breast cancer to use corn oil, and the reason for this has to do with unsaturated fats.

Unsaturated fats are divided into two types: monounsaturated fatty acids and polyunsaturated fatty acids. Polyunsaturated fatty acids contain alpha-linolenic acid and linoleic acid, which are essential fatty acids that the body can't produce on its own and must be obtained from food. The problem lies with alpha-linolenic acid. If taken in excess, it can cause breast cancer. Recent medical reports have also pointed out that the excessive intake of unsaturated fatty acids can lead to gallstones and cancer. Recently, a scholar from Hong Kong University of Science and Technology talked about cooking oil on television and suggested that people with breast cancer shouldn't use corn oil.

Regarding cooking oil, let me list the fatty acid content of several oils in a table to make it easier to understand, comparing the amount in each tablespoon of oil:

- • Saturated fatty acids
- ° Monosaturated fatty acids
- ‥ Essential fatty acids
- * Polyunsaturated fatty acids

Coconut oil	•	•	•	•	•	•	•	•	•	•	°
Butter	•	•	•	•	•	•	•	°	°	°	⁑
Lard	•	•	•	•	•	°	°	°	°	°	⁑
Olive oil	•	•	°	°	°	°	°	°	°	°	*
Peanut oil	•	•	°	°	°	°	°	*	*	*	*
Fish oil	•	•	°	°	°	°	°	°	‥	*	*
Corn oil	•	•	°	°	°	‥	*	*	*	*	*
Sunflower oil	•	°	°	°	°	*	*	*	*	*	*
Safflower oil	•	°	°	*	*	*	*	*	*	*	*

As seen from the above table, a lot of solid black circles aren't good, as they're indicative of an excess of saturated fatty acids, and a lot of asterisks aren't good either, as they signify an overabundance of polyunsaturated fatty acids, which can lead to cancer. The more white circles, the better, because they represent monosaturated fatty acids. Peanut oil isn't bad, but it doesn't contain essential fatty acids, and rancid peanuts can produce aflatoxins. Fish oil also isn't bad, but it can't be used for cooking. People with breast cancer seem to have no choice but to opt for olive oil. The medical community has found that countries in the Mediterranean region, such as Greece, have a lower incidence of breast cancer, possibly because they use olive oil.

Why not eat animal oil? Because of cholesterol of course. One tablespoon of animal oil and one tablespoon of vegetable oil provide the same number of calories, but the advantage of vegetable oil is that it doesn't contain cholesterol. In fact, there are two types of fat: true fat, also known as triglycerides, which are composed of glycerol and fatty acids; and lipids, which aren't real fats but are very similar in structure and properties. Lipids are composed of phospholipids and steroids. Steroids are cholesterol. Cholesterol sounds scary, but it's also essential to the body. Without it, even sunbathing won't produce vitamin D, because the ultraviolet rays in sunlight need cholesterol to help convert them into vitamin D. The bile acids used for digestion in the body are also converted by cholesterol. In fact, the body itself produces cholesterol, and there's no way to avoid it. A daily intake under 300 milligrams is harmless. Completely avoiding cholesterol intake is useless, as the body is busy producing it on its own, requiring the teamwork of many departments.

The nutritional content of food includes not only proteins, sugar, and fats, but also minerals, vitamins, and water. In terms of minerals, the biggest headache is probably sodium, as it's so ubiquitous. We need around 300 milligrams of sodium a day, but we often consume more than 1,000 without realizing it. In the past, salt was precious, almost like water in the desert. Coastal areas had plenty of salt, while mountainous regions considered salt as valuable as gold. There used to be a lucrative black market for salt. Does the Bible not say "You are the salt of the earth"? It's also the subject of a poem by Ya Hsien—salt, salt, even the angels wouldn't give her a pinch. Nowadays, however, there's too much salt. Of course, savory foods contain salt, but so do sweet foods such as cake, milk, and sweet breads, which taste sweet, yet contain salt, and the amount isn't insignificant. Half a cup of canned kidney beans contains 600 milligrams of sodium, while canned sardines contain even more. It's enough to turn us into mummies. Salt is sodium, sodium chloride.

The minerals potassium and sodium are like difficult sisters in the human body, with a close relationship that requires maintaining a balance. If there's too much sodium and too little potassium, the body will have problems. When I had high blood pressure, the doctor gave me some medicine and instructed me to eat more oranges, which are rich in potassium and can balance out too much sodium. Generally, processed foods add sodium for its preservative effect, but they don't add potassium. Many foods originally rich in potassium lose this mineral after being processed. The reason why so many people suffer from heart disease nowadays might be that they consume foods high in sodium but low in potassium. How much potassium does a person need a day? It's equal to the caloric intake. As long as the diet is balanced and the daily caloric intake is sufficient, there should be enough potassium. To counterbalance excessive sodium intake, it's best to eat more citrus fruit—one a day is essential. If a food contains 100 milligrams of sodium, it needs to contain 300 to 400 milligrams of potassium to be considered balanced.

Calcium and phosphorus are like twin sisters, and the ideal ratio is one to one. If the ratio is imbalanced and there's too much calcium, it can lead to the formation of urinary stones. We need 600 milligrams of each mineral per day. Phosphorous deficiency is rare, while calcium deficiency is common. The human body has 206 bones and 32 teeth, whose main components are calcium phosphorous and various hormones. Young girls have more hormones in their bones. When they grow old, especially after menopause, the secretion of estrogen stops, and the rate of bone loss also speeds up. As a result, the bones become like wooden pillars hollowed out by termites, and even a slight bump can cause a fracture, especially in the vertebrae.

Because they need to control the hormones in their body, some women with breast cancer have their ovaries removed, and some take tamoxifen, which can lead to menopause. Many women with breast cancer are old and have already gone through menopause. Due to the lack of hormones, their bones are prone to osteoporosis, so special attention should be paid to calcium supplementation. The medical community recommends a dose of 1,000 milligrams or more of calcium, without advising us on what to do about phosphorous. If there's too much calcium and too little phosphorous, stones will form in the body. Milk and cheese are high in calcium, and a cup of milk can provide 300 milligrams of calcium, making it a preferred choice. If you don't drink milk, you can only get calcium from tofu, dark green vegetables, or fish with bones. In fact, the most calcium-rich food isn't milk but sesame. Half a bowl of sesame paste contains 960 milligrams of calcium, which is more than three times that of a cup of milk. Why not sprinkle some sesame seeds in soy milk or on vegetables, and choose sesame whole wheat bread at the bakery?

Small dried fish are rich in calcium and are also sold in supermarkets. Whitebait, which is mild and has no added salt, can be washed and soaked in cold water at home, then mixed with some shredded ginger and an appropriate amount of soy sauce and sesame oil, and steamed on top of rice or noodles for a convenient meal. When eating small dried fish, the whole fish is consumed, including the bones and liver. Small fish don't have much of a liver and have very few bones, but if you eat a large amount at one time, you can absorb calcium and phosphorous from the fish bones, as well as obtain vitamins A and D. Sardines are certainly good, but only canned varieties can be found in the markets, and they are too high in sodium and not ideal.

Iron is a mineral that women need to pay special attention to. Adult men need seven milligrams of iron daily, while women need fifteen milligrams, which of course is due to the monthly loss of iron through menstruation. According to studies, women only lose one milligram of iron per month during menstruation, yet they need to supplement with much more iron, which is strange. Postmenopausal women, like men, only require seven milligrams of iron per day. If someone with breast cancer has stopped menstruating, seven milligrams of iron a day is also enough. Vegetarians are likelier to be deficient in iron because iron is somewhat similar to protein, which has animal- and plant-based varieties, as does iron. Animal-based iron is divalent and easily absorbed by the human body; plant-based iron is trivalent and not as easily absorbed. As such, a combination of animal- and plant-based foods is necessary for proper intake, such as spaghetti with meat sauce, cabbage rolls stuffed with pork, or pork and beans in tomato sauce. Iron from fish is divalent, while iron from eggs is trivalent.

I don't take any vitamins, because medications are essentially poisonous, simply using poison to fight poison, curing one illness but causing other harmful side effects. Taking medication involves mobilizing several organs to deal with it. A typical pill needs many additives: a binder to form the pill and a disintegrator to break it down easily when swallowed; some pills need to absorb moisture from stomach acid to swell and break apart; some, however, can't be dissolved by stomach acid and must function in the intestines, so it's necessary to add anti-cracking and antiacid agents. What if the taste is unpleasant? Add some orange or fruity flavor. The end result is that with a little medication, we ingest many additives, and also face a degree of damage caused by the medicine itself, in addition to requiring the liver to work to detoxify harmful substances.

There are some medications that I have no choice but to take, such as tamoxifen and high blood pressure medication; as for other pills, if I can avoid them, I will. Patients are strange in that they always like to take medication. When people get sick and go to the doctor, the doctor may prescribe medications, among which, some may just be vitamins that don't make a huge difference in a patient's health. Maybe doctors do this because they are well-versed in psychology, and know that patients feel more at ease when they have some medicine to take, like the ancient Roman "placebo."

During the period when I watched the World Cup matches for a whole month, I ended up with red eyes, a heavy-headed feeling, and was unsteady on my feet; worst of all, my ears felt like they were filled with water. I didn't know what had happened. People who've suffered from cancer always have the words "metastasis, metastasis" whirling in their minds, associating everything they feel with pathological changes. I went to see the doctor about my ears, and asked him if there was a tumor in my head. The doctor said, Don't scare me. After a week, I still felt unwell and went to see an ear specialist. The exam lasted only five minutes, and the doctor said there was nothing wrong, but to come back if there was a problem. I asked what he meant by if there was a problem, and he said that if I couldn't hear clearly, that was a problem. I could hear everything, so there wasn't a problem. He also said, I'll give you some medicine—even if you take it, it won't help, but I'll still give it to you. Wasn't the doctor strange, insisting on giving me useless medicine? Perhaps it was because the visit was expensive, 300 dollars for five minutes. Specialists naturally charge higher fees than general practitioners, and 300 dollars was normal, so I didn't complain. But as soon as I left the office, I threw the medicine away.

When I was undergoing radiation therapy, the hospital gave each patient a large package of nutritional milk powder, as well as two types of medicine: vitamin C, three hundred milligrams per capsule, and vitamin B6, sixty milligrams per capsule. After the treatment was over, the hospital stopped the supplements and only prescribed tamoxifen. Did I need to supplement myself with vitamins? There are many books on the market about cancer prevention, stating that a person should consume a lot of vitamin C, as much as 3,000 milligrams per day, ten times higher than the daily standard. Of course, vitamin C is water-soluble, so the excess will be excreted from the body, unlike vitamin A, which can be toxic if left in the body, but what's the benefit of increasing the burden on the kidneys? In fact, too much vitamin C may cause oxaluria, hyperuricemia, hypercalcemia and hyponatremia, and lead to a vitamin B12 deficiency, even kidney stones. It's better to obtain vitamin C by eating oranges, which are sweet and juicy, than by taking pills that are a bunch of dry, grainy, powdery things stuck together, and that include sodium. To increase your resistance and absorb vitamin C, it's best to eat vegetables. Green peppers aren't spicy, and papaya can warm the stomach.

As for vitamin B6, I don't take pills. If I can get it from eating whole wheat bread, red rice, and oatmeal, why would I take pills? When it comes to the huge vitamin B family, including niacin, pantothenic acid, folic acid, and biotin, we don't have to worry at all. Just eat more whole grains and green leafy vegetables, and you won't be deficient.

The term pantothenic acid contains "pan," meaning "all," as it's found in a wide range of foods. The term folic acid contains "folic," which means "leaf," because it's found in green leaves. Only vegetarians need to be concerned, as they may be deficient in vitamin B12.

Vitamin D is the easiest to absorb. Just bask in the sun, take a walk on the street during the day, and even under the shade of trees, there's still enough vitamin D. As for vitamin A, it can also be obtained by eating more vegetables. Carrots contain carotene, and many people eat them excessively. I used to be guilty of this too, eating so many carrots that my whole body nearly turned orange, and even my urine was golden yellow. I thought I had jaundice. Many foods contain carotene. Green leaves contain chlorophyll, and yellow vegetables contain carotene. Eating a variety of vegetables, how could one be deficient in vitamin A? The body can store vitamins A and D. The body can only store vitamins B and C for a short period of time, so they must be replenished every day, which is why people must eat vegetables, fruits, and grains daily.

A balanced diet is something everyone has heard of. It's about evenly distributing grains, fruits and vegetables, meat, and dairy products across three meals a day. I created a table for myself and calculated the nutritional content and calories, but it was merely like creating an ideal realm for myself. Nutritional value doesn't equate to nutritional benefits, and a blueprint doesn't equal a finished product. It's good to eat a lot of nutritious food each day, but is the body absorbing it? Maybe it goes round and round in the digestive tract, and then it's all excreted from the body; perhaps it gets detained in the intestines, creeping like a snail, gradually rotting and deteriorating, acidifying the blood; some foods may interfere with the absorption of other nutrients, so eating them is equivalent to eating nothing. It appears we need to take care of our digestive organs as well.

The easiest food to digest is fruit. An apple takes only half an hour to digest and won't cause any trouble to the stomach. When is the best time to eat fruit? It's not advisable to eat sweet snacks before meals, and the stomach is too busy after meals. It's best to eat fruit between meals. I eat two servings of fruit a day, the first in the morning. After getting up early in the morning, I drink a large glass of water, eat an apple, and have breakfast half an hour later. I have to eat one citrus fruit every day. At three-thirty in the afternoon, I eat an orange.

Nutritionists recommend that it's best to eat foods in groups, as the stomach needs to supply digestive juices each time it digests something. Meat requires acidic digestive juices, while grains require alkaline ones. If these two types of food are consumed in large amounts, the stomach may become overworked with both alkaline and digestive juices, which will neutralize each other and hinder digestion. It's difficult to eat only one type of food for a meal, so we should try instead to avoid eating too much of any one type of food. Generally speaking, vegetables are easy to digest and can be paired with any food. Starch mixed with starch is no problem, and starch can be paired with a little protein without having a big impact on the stomach. Protein is relatively complicated. If a meal contains many kinds of protein, especially animal protein, it may place a greater burden on the stomach. Thus, it's best not to eat beef, pork, eggs, shrimp, and crab in the same meal, unless you want to wage war on your stomach. Milk is the most complex food, so it's best to drink it alone, whether in the morning, afternoon, or evening.

Vegetables contain vitamins. If they're washed too much or too early before use, or overcooked, the vitamins will be lost. It's best to use less water, oil, salt, and cooking time, and to cover the pot. Cooking in an iron wok can give you twenty milligrams of free iron. To absorb iron, you need to pay attention to factors that affect iron absorption, such as phosphorous, phytic acid, stomach acid, tea, and coffee; meanwhile, vitamin D, protein, phosphorus, oxalic acid, and phytic acid can affect calcium absorption. Spinach is rich in iron, but it also contains phytic acid. What to do? Boil it, as the phytic acid will be lost in the water. Aside from spinach, other vegetables such as amaranth and water spinach also contain phytic acid, which can be eliminated by boiling. In recent years, nutritionists have advised us to steam vegetables, which can retain two-thirds of the vitamins, whereas boiling can result in a 50 percent loss. For spinach, however, boiling is better. These days, I rarely steam vegetables, because the vegetables imported from the mainland are covered in strong pesticides, causing many people to go to the hospital after eating them. It seems that boiling them is still the way to go. When cooking vegetables that grow above ground, bring the water to a boil and then cook them. When cooking vegetables that grow below ground, place them in a pot of cold water, then bring it to a boil.

I live on the tenth floor. My tap water is transported from the ground to the rooftop water tank and then distributed to households above the eighth floor. Over time, despite regular cleaning of the water tank, it's become routine that when I turn on the faucet, the water is discolored. After boiling it and pouring it into a bottle to cool overnight, the following day, the bottom of the bottle is full of sediment, and I have to trouble my mother to throw in rice grains and eggshells to clean the bottle. It's a waste to wait until the water is clear before taking a shower or doing laundry. Thus, I bought a high-quality water filter to drink water free of sediment. Everyone should drink six to eight classes of water a day. There's also a lot of water in food, and the water content of vegetables and fruits is better than that of plain water. Food also produces water during digestion. One gram of sugar produces 0.6 grams of water, one gram of protein produces 0.4 grams of water, and one gram of fat produces 1.1 grams of water.

A friend urged me to become a vegetarian, and I'm grateful to him. I'm practically a vegetarian. Another friend advised me to pay attention to the acidity and alkalinity of food and to eat more alkaline foods, and I'm grateful to him as well. I did a little homework, and now I understand a bit more. Oranges are actually alkaline, although they sometimes taste acidic, which is surprising. Fruits, vegetables, and beans are mostly alkaline, as are minerals such as calcium, sodium, potassium, and magnesium; meat and grains are acidic, as are minerals such as sulfur and phosphorous. By eating less meat, I can avoid consuming too much acidic food.

Chinese people seem to research food more carefully than foreigners, classifying foods as warm, hot, cold, and cool. For examples, mung beans are a protein-rich food, which is good, but they're considered "cold" in nature, and may cause stomach pain for people like me whose bodies are weak, so they're not suitable for me. Bananas, persimmons, cantaloupe, asparagus, water chestnuts, and black beans are all considered "cold"; winter melon, daikon, arrowhead, sugarcane, coix seed, and corn are slightly "cool" or slightly "cold." My mother knew this early on, and always said: I don't want to eat persimmons. There are many "warm" foods, including pumpkin, carrots, lentils, sword beans, onions, and garlic; "balanced" foods include papaya, shiitake mushrooms, wood ear fungus, round cabbage, wheat, rice, potatoes, and eggs, among others. Napa cabbage is considered "cool," but how can I give up such a good vegetable? I cook it with a slice of ginger. Chinese people are truly a nation of nutritionists. Tea is also considered "cool," but oolong tea is "warm," so I can drink tieguanyin and narcissus. It seems like I need to flip through Li Shizhen's *Compendium of Materia Medica*.

Zzz . . . Oh, you've dozed off? Sleep is also very important, so I won't bother you anymore.

THRICE STRIKING THE WHITE BONE DEMON

A JOURNEY to the supermarket
Entails borrowing the Monkey King's golden staff
And enacting the scene "Thrice Striking the White Bone Demon"[26]
Strike strike strike, first strike: refined white sugar
A perfectly fine stalk of sugarcane
Washed and melted
Then stripped of its color, crystallized, and loaded with chemicals
Transformed into sparkling white granulated sugar
The minerals in the raw sugar nowhere to be found
Swing the golden staff
Strike down chocolate
Strike down soft drinks
Strike down sweetened breakfast cereals
Strike down sucrose, lactose, maltose
Strike down invert sugar, dextrose, corn syrup
Leaving behind only black sugar, raw cane sugar
And unadulterated honey

Second strike against the White Bone Demon
Strike down refined white flour
Perfectly fine wheat
Ground and ground, bleached and bleached
Wheat germ, malt, and wheat bran nowhere to be found
Nine branches of the gargantuan vitamin B clan
Executed in succession

Nicotinic acid, folic acid, pantothenic acid, linolenic acid
Dismembered dismembered
Manganese, magnesium, iron, potassium, copper, calcium, zinc
Beheaded beheaded
Swing the golden staff
Strike down white bread
Strike down hot-dog buns
Strike down instant noodles
Strike down cookies
Strike down dyed wheat bread
Best to head to a Chinese goods emporium
And buy some buckwheat noodles

Third strike against the White Bone Demon
Strike down refined white rice
Alas, white rice is our staple food
What to do? Check its pulse—
It's still breathing, let's try to rescue it
Buy some brown rice, red rice, and wild rice
Mix them with the white rice, steam everything together
There are more White Bone Demons in the supermarket
Than in *Journey to the West*
There's yet another White Bone Demon
Called refined white salt
The Sodium Chloride Monster
Perfectly fine sea salt
Transformed in a flash
Into inorganic matter
Found in coffee, found in pastries
Found in cough syrup, found in sedatives
Even found in toothpaste
Reminiscent of how ancient Egyptians
Preserved their mummies

Pig of Eight Prohibitions has a great name
First prohibition: preserved meats
Second prohibition: smoked meats
Third prohibition: ham
Fourth prohibition: sausage
Fifth prohibition: pig heads and pig brains
Sixth prohibition: pig hearts, pig lungs, and pig guts
Seventh prohibition: fatty pork
Eighth prohibition: lard
Bean-paste filling is often mixed with lard
Beware of invisible assassins

The Bull Demon King is now overlord of the food world
Even little babies are stuck in its demonic clutches
Swing the golden staff, *strike strike strike*
Strike down cream cakes
Strike down ice cream
Strike down butter
Strike down fruit yogurt
Should milk be struck down?
A wants to strike down powdered whole milk
B wants to strike down powdered skim milk
C wants to strike down powdered infant milk
D wants to strike down all powdered milk
Best to set up a ring to fight it out

Is Princess Iron Fan's fan made of iron?
If not, why isn't she called Princess Banana Leaf Fan?
If it is iron, all the better since it's magnetic
Borrow the princess's fan
And fan away all canned sardines
Canned soybeans, peas, and kidney beans
Canned fruit

While at it, suction away hair spray
Pesticide, perfume, and cleaning supplies
Anything that sprays at the touch of a button
Chemicals with all sorts of idiotic names
This is an iron wok, *leave it leave it*
When it comes to cooking, iron woks are top-notch

*Ah, what should I write about now—scars or
the color green? Oh, you're interested in scars?
Please turn to page 282: "Flipping Through the
Dictionary."*

TREASURE HUNT

IT WAS so strange—suddenly, I realized I couldn't find any high-quality bread. When I went to the supermarket, there was a wide selection of bread, ranging from pale beige to dark brown, some pre-sliced, some individually packaged, with dates on the labels, and names such as LIFE BREAD, and designations like WITH PROTEIN and WITHOUT LARD printed on the cellophane. They seemed to be our bread of life. If you examined the ingredients more closely, however, they included sugar, salt, and hydrogenated vegetable oil. "Wheat" was merely bread the color of wheat. A new bakery had opened in my neighborhood, its name as sweet as its contents. There was also another shop that sold mooncakes and bread. I'd been to all of them. Some breads were stuffed with a slice of cheese or a piece of sausage. Some were filled with bean paste, shredded coconut, or cream. Some were sprinkled with minced garlic and scallions. They were all pillowy soft, as though they could float in the air like hydrogen balloons. Who knew how many emulsifiers, preservatives, and thickeners had been added.

There were originally four or five bakeries near my home, with storefronts selling bread. Inside, they functioned like small factories, producing fresh bread every hour, unlike new-style shops that needed warmers to keep the bread heated. Presumably, these breads didn't need preservatives, but they were still sweet. The finger-shaped bread oozed bean paste from the seams between the fingers, and the pineapple buns were topped with thick icing. The breads in these bakeries had no labels, so I didn't know which ingredients were used or in what quantities. All I knew was whether something tasted sweet or savory. Over time, I'd given up sweets. Of course, I didn't want to gain weight, but there was another reason. For a while, I kept feeling like I had phlegm in my throat. I didn't have a cold, nor was I coughing, and my lungs were fine. Why was there phlegm? Finally, I figured out the culprit: sugar. Eating sweets triggered phlegm, and shortly after eating sweet bread, I would feel it in my throat. Only fruit didn't cause this issue, perhaps because it's a simple sugar.

Buying bread turned out to be a challenging endeavor. It is truly ironic that in a modern, technologically advanced city I had to embark on a treasure hunt when all I was looking for was solid wheat bread for breakfast. Where could I find wheat bread? I had to take a bus to far-off places as though I were on some sort of expedition. Most supermarkets in the city are chain stores, but the goods in the chain stores are not the same. The middle- and lower-class residential areas supply commonplace goods, while the upscale residential areas offer a greater selection. I live in an ordinary neighborhood. There's often a piece of paper attached to the food shelves in the supermarket that reads: SORRY, THIS ITEM IS TEMPORARILY OUT OF STOCK. It could be out of stock for half a year. The upscale residential areas are never out of stock. And so, I set off on an expedition, backpack in tow, heading somewhere a half-hour bus ride away in search of whole wheat bread. In that neighborhood, there were also food boutiques selling all sorts of brown rice, dried beans, nuts, pure honey, and buckwheat noodles.

I decided to try eating cereal instead of bread in the morning, grabbing a box of something that read JUST ADD MILK FOR A BALANCED BREAKFAST. It was really heavy, so heavy I was sure it had to be chockful of sugar. The packaging boasted OATS, WHEAT, HAZELNUTS, RAISINS, CORN, and other names that appealed to me, but never stated the percentage of sugar and salt. The ingredients should have been listed according to the amount of each item. Sugar often ranks among the top three. So much sugar! I gave up. Recently, I've discovered a type of oat bran cereal free of sugar, salt, and preservatives—at long last, I've found my treasure. Now, I regularly eat this oat bran cereal for breakfast.

Around three or four o'clock, I need to have a snack. English afternoon tea used to be my favorite because of the plentiful sweets: freshly baked scones smeared with jam and cream, as well as small cakes and lemon tea—oh, how I truly enjoyed it. Now, I don't dare to imagine it. A slice of wheat bread might make a nice accompaniment for afternoon tea, but I don't embark on expeditions every day. I can't always find sesame buns in the shops near my home and sometimes have to search for them at the wet market. The wet market is a paradise in ordinary neighborhoods. Navigating the slippery aisles, there are always rewards to be found. Green vegetables, radishes, fish swimming to and fro—what don't they have. You can easily fill up a basket. Green peppers, carrots, celery, and tomatoes are best eaten raw; cut them up and arrange them on a plate, sprinkle with sesame seeds, and ta-da, you have a vegetable salad. Sweet potato and lotus root are also fine choices, as are purple heart yams, cooked and split open, their white hearts edged in purple, the spitting image of African violets, and not too sweet. Eating half of a small yam in the afternoon is unexpectedly as delightful as eating a scone. I no longer need to worry about not having the ideal bread.

Traditional Chinese medicine shops actually sell food as well. There are at least five or six such shops in my neighborhood. The entranceways brim with cooking ingredients such as dried day lilies, cloud ear fungus, shiitake, and fat choy. Wouldn't it be great to cook them up with fish or tofu? While the supermarket seems to have upended the old-school general stores, near the wet market, Shanghai shops and variety stores are still standing strong. They have all kinds of dried beans and vermicelli, anything you can think of, even the controversial coarse salt that's like finding a needle in a haystack. Fruit shops, of course, are treasures in ordinary neighborhoods, a valuable addition to the scenery, along with those mobile fruit stands. They offer every fruit imaginable—Hami melons, Peruvian grapes, Taiwanese pineapples, California apples and oranges, Thai papayas... You can pick them one by one with your hands, eating as many different fruits as you like in one day: durian, figs, kiwis, cherries. It's best to live in an ordinary neighborhood.

I didn't grow up drinking cow milk. I tried drinking it, but because I no longer had the lactase enzyme in my body that I had when I was a baby, it always gave me diarrhea. In recent years, however, I tried drinking milk again, partly because of my mother. My mother's body was weak, and the doctor recommended that she drink nutritional milk powder. This milk powder has many advantages: It doesn't contain lactose, so it won't cause diarrhea; the fat is corn oil, which is made up of unsaturated fatty acids and is low in cholesterol; the percentage of sodium and potassium is moderate, so it isn't a burden on the kidneys; the composition ratio of calcium and phosphorous is 1:1, reducing the risk of kidney stones caused by the imbalance of these two minerals; and it's fortified with vitamin C. Milk, of course, supplies the body with amino acids and is rich in calcium. My body isn't strong. As I've grown older, I've likely lost bone density, so I began to drink milk.

I've been drinking nutritional milk powder for several years. When I was undergoing radiation therapy, the hospital gave me the same milk powder; it was as though I'd bumped into an old friend. It's a suitable food for post-op patients, but that particular milk powder is high in fat and made from corn oil, which turned out to be less than ideal for me. It's also sweet and increases phlegm production. After careful consideration, I decided to drink soy milk instead. Compared to cow milk, soy milk has similar amounts of protein, with more iron and less calcium—I had to find another way to supplement the latter. The supermarkets carried tofu, but it came in boxes and was refrigerated. It was a dessert. I didn't know how much white granulated sugar or preservatives had been added. There's a dessert shop downstairs from my home that used to only sell tong sui dessert soups in flavors such as red bean or almond tea. They suddenly started selling soy milk in the morning, a huge pot of steaming hot soy milk to which you could add sugar, deep-fried dough sticks, small shrimp, or pickled mustard strips. Plain soy milk—had I unearthed yet another treasure? An elderly lady in the neighborhood saw me carrying a thermos and asked: Are you buying breakfast? I said, Yes, I'm buying soy milk. Sighing, she lamented: Soy milk nowadays is all made from soybean powder. The Chinese goods emporium sells individual bags of it. I found it bland and tasteless instead of full-bodied, and when I was finished drinking, my mouth felt powdery. No wonder some people decide to make their own soy milk.

My friends joined me on my "treasure hunt." I was never short of food at home because they constantly gave me things: carrots, green peppers, fish, broccoli, tomatoes, and papayas. Some friends who lived far away even brought me stewed bird's nest and large packages of dried beans, nuts, peanuts, lotus seeds, apricot kernels, coix seeds, and gorgon nuts, as well as honey. A friend gave me black sugar and a special bottle of olive oil. The treasure hunt grew more and more exciting.

The film *Indiana Jones and the Last Crusade* is an exciting treasure hunt. Of course, what people are searching for is not bread and vegetables but the Holy Grail. Any wound, no matter how deep or serious, will be healed immediately as long as the water of the Holy Grail is poured on it. The hero is shot in the stomach, but as soon as he is sprinkled with holy water, the wound closes up without even a scar. The more I watched, the more envious I felt. If such a magical medicine existed, no one would be afraid of cancer. Slice open the body, make a cut here, a snip there, splash it with water from the Holy Grail, no need for stitches. When Jesus and his twelve disciples partook in the Last Supper, they shared a cup of wine, passing it around. Jesus said: "This cup is the new covenant in my blood, which is poured out for you." There is no mention of the whereabouts of the goblet in the four Gospels. Some texts claim that the goblet fell into the hands of Joseph of Arimathea who later went into exile, finally ending up in England and, therefore, the Holy Grail might be in England. Some legends suggest that Mary Magdalene got ahold of the Holy Grail and brought it to Marseille, France. More recently, people say that it was the descendants of Jesus, not Mary Magdalene, who took the Holy Grail.

The story of the Holy Grail is complicated. It could be a cup, but it could also be a rock, a small dish, some abnormal phenomena, a womb, or an alchemy symbol. The forms are different, but they have something in common: The Holy Grail is unusually precious, and so it is extremely well-hidden. Ordinary people cannot obtain it; only those who are pure can find it. What did King Arthur's Knights of the Round Table do day in and day out other than search for the Holy Grail? They wiped out bullies, helped the downtrodden, and respected women, which made them model knights. But were these knights really all that righteous? Reading the novel *The Nonexistent Knight* by the Italian author Italo Calvino, you'll encounter a completely different group of knights. They call themselves the Sacred Order of the Knights of the Grail. Living together in the forest, they wear white capes and golden helmets adorned with two swan feathers, and carry long spears and a tiny harp. What do these Knights of the Grail do? Because they don't produce anything but instead rely on their military prowess, they demand that the villagers living near the forest give them cheese, barley, and lamb. Sometimes they use force, riding horses and wielding spears, emptying out the villagers' granaries, torching houses, sheds, and stables, transforming the village into a ball of fire. Where is the knights' spirit of chivalry? They're nothing but a bunch of bandits.

Calvino's novels have long fascinated me. A good novel can really draw you into a colorful, beautiful world, making you forget that you're sick. Reading novels can be therapeutic, but after becoming ill, because I didn't have the physical strength to read, I never finished flipping through that book about Satan—those two characters who fell from the sky are still suspended in midair. Reading takes a lot of energy. My eyes tired easily, so I listened to music. Music is also therapeutic. The ancient Egyptians were probably the first people to incorporate music into medicine. When women went into labor, Egyptians asked shamans to sing to hasten the birth. In *Record of an Embassy to Regions in the West*, written by Liu Yu during the Yuan dynasty, there's a passage about how the caliph of the kingdom of Baoda had a headache that couldn't be cured until a court musician played for him on a new type of seventy-stringed guitar. As soon as he heard the music, his headache subsided. Baoda is present-day Baghdad, and a caliph is now known as an Arab sheikh. In addition to flying carpets, the world of *The Arabian Nights* also had such marvelous music.

Music is actually a kind of undulation. The human body has various kinds of undulations that produce resonance. Music has a beat and rhythm, and the human body has a pulse and breath. No wonder some people practice tai chi and dance tai chi sword to traditional Chinese music from the Jiangnan region. What should I listen to? For a patient, the best kind of music is whatever they like. I often listen to Yue opera selections such as "Meeting in the Pavilion" from *The Butterfly Lovers*, or "Crying Spirit" from *The Dream of the Red Chamber*. I never tire of listening to these songs. My favorite is naamyam, or Cantonese narrative songs, especially "Song of the Exile." Strangely, these are all sad tunes, and yet when I listen to them, I feel calm and detached from earthly affairs, and I think of how life is just a serious game.

Music from the Baroque period is the most soothing kind of Western music, while Mozart tends to be tinged with melancholic joy. When it comes to tales of treasure hunts, listening to Wagner is a must, since everyone in his music is searching for some sort of treasure. In *Das Rheingold*, they are searching for gold. In *Lohengrin*, a knight to guard the duchess. In *Parsifal*, an injured king searches for an innocent and compassionate fool. Eventually, the king is healed by the Holy Spear; in this case, the Holy Grail is a spear with healing powers. The light from radiation therapy is truly like an incandescent spear. Might it be a Holy Grail of salvation? Perhaps the Holy Grail is a painting, a book, a poem, a friend.

MARVELOUS TALES OF FRUITS AND VEGETABLES

SOME THINGS ABOUT CARROTS

Studies say that carotene may fight cancer. Many people misunderstand, thinking it is carrots themselves that can fight cancer. Yes, carrots contain carotene, but not all carotene is found in carrots. Studies say there are "highly reactive particles" derived from oxygen in the human body that can cause changes in the genetic material in cells, which leads to pathological changes. Carotene can neutralize the highly reactive particles, having a "freezing" and delaying effect. Taking six milligrams of carotene a day is said to provide sufficient protection against cancer. Dark green vegetables such as spinach and kale, as well as root vegetables and fruits like pumpkin and papaya, all contain carotene. However, carotene seems to only prevent lung, stomach, esophageal, uterine, and oral cancers. Breast cancer is not specifically mentioned.

SOME THINGS ABOUT CABBAGE

Studies say that Napa cabbage may fight cancer because it contains indole-3-methanol, which can help break down the estrogen linked to breast cancer. How much Napa cabbage should you eat? You'd have to eat a pound of Napa cabbage a day to absorb 500 milligrams of indole-3-methanol. Eating so much Napa cabbage, I'm afraid you might turn into a white rabbit. Cruciferous vegetables, such as cabbage, Brussels sprouts, cauliflower, and gai lan, all contain indole, which may similarly inhibit overactive estrogen, much like the drug tamoxifen.

SOME THINGS ABOUT BROCCOLI

Studies say that broccoli may fight cancer. It turns out that broccoli contains a sulfide that may stimulate enzyme activity in human cells to resist cancer cells. Ordinary vegetables lose many vitamins through cooking, but when it comes to broccoli, whether it's steamed or boiled, the sulfides won't be destroyed. Cauliflower also contains the same sulfide, and the medical community is experimenting with using it to produce anticancer drugs.

SOME THINGS ABOUT SOYBEANS

Studies say that soybeans may fight cancer because they contain phytoestrogens, which appear to inhibit estrogen in animals. Studies say that the incidence of breast cancer among Asian women is lower compared to that of European and American women, possibly due to their higher consumption of soybeans. In an experiment, researchers fed soybeans to a female cheetah. While eating a vegetarian diet may have seemed unlucky to the cheetah, perhaps she was spared from breast cancer as a result. Other legumes, such as peanuts and red beans, contain isoflavones, which studies say may inhibit estrogen receptors, disabling the activity of oncogene enzymes.

SOME THINGS ABOUT MANDARIN ORANGES

Studies say that vitamin C may fight cancer because it's an antioxidant, which may eliminate the damage of oxygen free radicals in the body and increase the anticancer function of immune cells. Mandarin oranges contain vitamin C. Many fruits contain vitamin C, including oranges and lemons, and papayas have even more, but which has the most? Green peppers. Citrus fruits contain limonene, which may inhibit the synthesis of cholesterol in the body and block the activity of carcinogenic enzymes.

SOME THINGS ABOUT ASPARAGUS

Studies say that asparagus may fight cancer and may have a curative effect on breast cancer, perhaps because it contains asparagine. In spite of its name in Chinese, asparagus is not a bamboo shoot. In China, it's also known as "little bai bu" because the roots of the asparagus plant resemble those of bai bu, an herb used in traditional Chinese medicine. According to studies, eating asparagus appears to have an obvious curative effect at the outset, but there's no cumulative benefit from long-term consumption. Cancer cells are like cockroaches: If they're constantly exposed to the same insecticide, they stop fearing it.

SOME THINGS ABOUT JOB'S TEARS

Studies say that Job's tears, also known as coix seed, may fight cancer, and the grain is believed to have an inhibitory effect on cancer cells. Job's tears is rich in protein, calcium, and phosphorous, so it can be cooked and eaten in place of rice. Ancient books don't mention using Job's tears to treat tumors, only to treat skin blemishes. According to the Han dynasty pharmacological compendium *Shen Nong's Classic of Materia Medica*, Job's tears can prevent and cure cramps.

SOME THINGS ABOUT SHIITAKE

Studies say that shiitake mushrooms may fight cancer, and they are believed to boost the body's immune system. Shiitake mushrooms, also known as winter mushrooms, contain ergosterol, which is a precursor to vitamin D. When exposed to sunlight, ergosterol can be converted to vitamin D. To obtain vitamin D from shiitake mushrooms, you have to use dried shiitake. Before consumption, they should first be dried in the sun for two hours. Dried shiitake that have been stored too long won't have any vitamin D. The mushroom family is huge. According to studies, mushrooms may also prevent cancer because they contain interferons and inducers of mushroom RNA, which may inhibit viral growth.

Garlic contains allicin, which has antibacterial properties and may inhibit the development of cancer.

Cilantro contains polyacetylene, which can prevent the synthesis of prostaglandins, inhibit the carcinogen benzopyrene in cigarettes, and reduce the carcinogenic effect.

Licorice root contains triterpenoids, which can suffocate rapidly dividing cancer cells and also inhibit the activity of estrogen.

Peppermint contains quinones, which can interfere with the destruction of DNA by carcinogens.

There's also cloud mushroom, kiwifruit... Suddenly, it seems like everything in the world can cause cancer, and yet countless foods can prevent cancer, leaving people utterly confused. Can so-called cancer-preventing foods really prevent or fight cancer? It sounds like a beautiful legend. Can far-off water really put out a nearby fire? Cancer doesn't form in a day; it accumulates and proliferates over many years. Cancer-fighting foods may not have an immediate effect, either; the benefits accrue bit by bit—how many years does it take for them to become effective? Most cancer-preventing and cancer-fighting foods are fruits and vegetables. Such foods are beneficial to the body, regardless of whether they can fight cancer. Secret remedies are untrustworthy, and witch doctors are unreliable. Eating more fruits and vegetables is still the most practical path to health.

THE BODY'S LANGUAGE

FOR HALF a century, my body and I have depended on each other for survival. Throughout this long period of time, I've barely given any thought to having a body. When I was a child, my mother was naturally the one who took care of it. By the time I could eat and walk, I was still unaware of its existence. Now and then I'd fall, and it was the skin on my knee that was scraped. I'd have a toothache, and it was merely a tooth that was extracted. I didn't truly discover the intimate relationship between my body and me until I hit puberty and began menstruating. How was it that I hadn't tripped and hurt myself, nor was I in pain, yet here I was, dripping blood? My apprehension was accompanied by extreme panic: From then on, as a woman, I was bound to this blood for decades, forever inseparable.

When I first became acquainted with my body, I was full of contempt. This loathing actually had little to do with my body itself but rather with the trouble that it brought. When I was growing up, society wasn't as prosperous and advanced as it is now, and manufactured personal hygiene products were nonexistent. I could only rely on folded straw paper to catch the blood flow. The coarse paper wasn't all that absorbent, and it frequently tore and leaked, but the absolute worst part was the stiffness of the paper—even if I rubbed it in my hands to soften it, it would still chafe the skin between my legs. Every time I had my period, my anguish was beyond words. The older women in my family supplied me with long cloth strips that traditionally were used for menstruation, thin ribbons stitched into each of the four corners. These cloth strips that held the straw paper weren't secure at all, and my underwear didn't have any elastic, so the paper often shifted, and once the entire piece of paper even fell out from under my skirt and onto the ground. The thin ribbons twisted and tangled around my waist, and if I wasn't careful, they'd form tight knots that took half a day to undo, making me so frantic that I ended up running round and round in circles. I kept coming up with alternatives. I tried using the cotton wool we had at home as a substitute for the paper, but it required a considerable amount of this costly item, and after only a few uses, the whole roll was finished. And so, inspired by cloth diapers, I started ripping up worn-out dresses and folding the fabric into small rectangles. These were slightly more comfortable. When I went to school, however, I struggled, constantly worried about staining my clothes. No wonder some people said that when a woman wore all-black clothing, you knew something was up. How times have changed! Nowadays, women can wear white whenever they please, and they can go swimming anytime. Back then, cloth diapers could be washed out in the open, while blood-soaked cloths had to be washed behind closed doors, where no one could see. It was impossible to wash out the bloodstains, and there were always blotches of waxy yellow marks remaining on the fabric, which were disgusting to look at. Thus, my hatred for my body intensified.

Over time, this hatred eventually waned, mostly due to improvements in personal hygiene products, which meant that women no longer had to suffer as much. Several years ago, I toured a factory while traveling in mainland China. There was the customary tea reception at which the factory director recounted various developments over the years, followed by the usual perfunctory applause. During the reception, the director reported that as a token of goodwill toward women workers, every month, the factory gave out extra sheets of straw paper. That's how I learned that the women in this country of one billion people continued to use straw paper. Last year, when my aunt came from the mainland to visit my mother, I made it a point to ask her whether women in China still used straw paper. She said that yes, only young, modern working women had access to sanitary napkins. Upon hearing this, I could merely sigh. Here I was, living in a thriving, world-class metropolis where I now had pristine, soft and smooth, fine-quality rice-white paper at my disposal, wholly unlike grainy gray straw paper, from which you could even pick out the stalks if you tried. Nevertheless, in impoverished and remote backwaters, straw paper undoubtedly must have been a luxury.

Throughout the years, I never fell seriously ill, nothing more than a cold or stomachache. Not that long ago, I had been diagnosed with high blood pressure, but who would have thought I'd end up with a tumor? Undergoing surgery awakened an awareness that I did in fact have a body. For so long, I'd lived as though I had nothing but a mind, oblivious to everything else. I had no idea where the liver and gall-bladder were located. Actually, didn't I study biology in secondary school? How could I have been this ignorant about my own body? Perhaps it was because in secondary school, I only had biology classes and no health education. In biology, they merely taught us about single-celled organisms, gymnosperms, and the like, nothing with any real connection to our own bodies. In primary school, we had one section of health class a week where we were taught to take care of our eyes, ears, spines, skin, and so forth. In secondary school, there was no curriculum instructing us to care for our hearts, lungs, stom-achs, and livers, let alone warning us to be on the lookout for breast disease. Sex education classes have only been implemented in the past couple of years. It's strange: From secondary school on, we cast aside anything having to do with the body and focus exclusively on our minds. Everything is for the sake of the mind. Math, physics, chem-istry, language arts, history, geography, civics, and extracurricular reading are all for mental enrichment. We only get to move around in gym class. Schools used to have lovely morning exercises—now, of course, they've been canceled. Schools no longer value students' bod-ies, or the moral, intellectual, physical, social, and aesthetic aspects of education. They merely force-feed students like ducks so they can obtain diplomas, land good jobs, and become yuppies.

Over more than a decade of formal education, we're molded into people who treasure the mind. Upon leaving school, we tend to seek out spiritual sustenance through reading books, watching films, col-lecting artwork, and buying records, all nourishment for the mind.

Teachers never advise us to buy certain foods. No one says whether we should drink milk or eat less salt and sugar. Everything spiritual is deemed noble and honorable, while everything corporeal is rendered lowly and superficial. Going to a museum to see an art exhibition is a highbrow affair. If an exhibition features a David or a Venus, it signals beauty. However, this kind of beauty seems to be detached from the body, standing on its own as something purely spiritual. Meanwhile, going to the market to buy food is considered a task for uneducated women and children. We have bodies, yet we've grown more and more estranged from them. The Confucian six arts that formed the backbone of education in ancient China were ritual, music, archery, chariot driving, writing, and mathematics. Horseback riding and archery, as well as charioteering, were all compulsory. The Han and Tang dynasties boasted the largest number of people who were masters of both the pen and the sword, and there were also countless knights-errant. Scholars stressed the importance of physical fitness. The statesman Tao Kan, who found himself with extra time on his hands, took to moving bricks as a form of physical activity. Around the time of the Song dynasty, China transformed into a society that placed intellectual pursuits above martial prowess. By the end of the Qing dynasty, the Jurchens, who had once conquered all of China on horseback, could no longer even ride horses.

Ancient Greece was renowned for its love of wisdom, which epitomized the Greek spirit, but the Greeks also cherished their bodies. Being knowledgeable and having strong bodies were of equal importance to them. The Olympic Games are a good example of how the Greeks prized physical exercise. Socrates urged his disciples to grasp the essence of all kinds of knowledge, but he also encouraged them to look after their health. He said, "Through lifelong observation, one should determine which food and drink, and what sort of exercise, best suit one's own body, and one should understand how to live in moderation in order to enjoy good health. By paying attention to yourself, you can determine, better than any doctor, what suits your specific constitution."

The Greeks emphasized physical health and considered health care to be an art of survival. A person could only prevent illness and frailty by successfully managing one's own body. Poor health could lead to forgetfulness, timidity, a bad temperament, madness, and, ultimately, the deterioration of all knowledge acquired by the mind. Socrates's maxim "know thyself" was carved into the ancient Greek temple at Delphi. Today, people interpret this aphorism in a variety of ways, claiming that what the philosopher meant was that if you merely know your own name, you don't know yourself at all—you only know yourself once you realize, as a person, your abilities and usefulness, what is right for you, and what you should and shouldn't do. Over time, to know yourself has come to mean knowing your own mind. Few people suggest that the philosopher's notion also pertains to the physical body. In ancient Greece, wisdom encompassed the knowledge of all arts and sciences, because early Greek philosophy and science were closely intertwined. It wasn't until Aristotle that they were separated, and thereafter, philosophy became known as "the first philosophy" and was considered superior to the rest. In Socrates's "know thyself," the "self" is the union of the mind and body, whereas in Descartes's "I think, therefore I am," the "I" is the mind wholly distinct from the body. His "I" is the thinking I, not the material I. This "I" refers to the mind. For Descartes, the specific property of matter is that it can occupy space but cannot think, whereas the specific property of the spirit or mind is that it can think but cannot occupy space. Therefore, they are two independent entities. Later, Hegel proposed the idea of absolute spirit. He believed that the spirit freely contemplating itself is art; the spirit reverently representing itself is religion; and the spirit conceptualizing the essence of itself and cognizing this essence is philosophy. If absolute spirit is comprised of art, religion, and philosophy, and all else is excluded and disparaged, then why would anyone pay attention to one's own body? Ever since, the mind and body have been separated: form severed from content, a signified without a signifier. Influenced by this line of thinking, intellectuals no longer remember that they have an indispensable body.

I believe Hegel once said that a nation is powerful and prosperous because of its enemies. Citizens consolidate their strength to unite against a foreign enemy, resulting in a common language. While I certainly wouldn't praise diseases, it was a disease that unexpectedly roused my other half from a deep sleep. I rediscovered the body I'd neglected and started learning to listen to its voice.

During childhood, the body's language is a persistent cry. The mother analyzes the various signs and tries to deduce what the body is saying. Is it hungry? Too cold or too hot? Has it been bitten by a mosquito? Where does it hurt? Is it throwing a tantrum? This is the body's golden age: As soon as it speaks, it provokes an immediate response, although the reply may not necessarily correspond to what the body is saying. As the child grows up, the body speaks less and less, uttering only the occasional sound. Diarrhea means you have the chills or have eaten contaminated food. A fever and runny nose indicate you've caught a cold. The body is a well-protected fortress, seemingly impenetrable, the interior guarded by a large army and detoxification chemical plant, strong enough to keep out foreign enemies. Yet in the end, the body inevitably grows old and starts to malfunction, its troops weakening.

Think about it: How many years had those oncogenes been lurking in my body? How many pathological changes had my healthy cells undergone? For the past eight to ten years or so, while I was reading books, watching movies, and listening to records, the macrophages inside me were chasing after cancer cells and gobbling them up. As I frantically punched buttons in front of the TV playing *Pac-Man*, my body's T cells were assaulting clusters of tumor cells, yet I remained oblivious to it all until my immune system couldn't take it anymore, and the tumor grew larger and larger. The tumor was one of my body's more urgent signals, continuously alerting me: Our soldiers are fighting valiantly, but the enemy is relentless. It's impossible to destroy it completely—we can only surround it and keep on attacking. Who's to say, however, that it won't break out of the siege, spread everywhere, and wreak havoc. The body is in immediate danger. Please help! SOS! At long last, I heard the body's language and came to its aid by having the tumor removed at once. As for the few remnants of drifting invaders, I hoped that the macrophages would be strong enough to hunt them down and devour them. Did my body's warning signs appear too late? No—in fact, my body had been speaking to me all along, but I didn't understand what it was saying, nor had I been all that concerned. For example, before the tumor was discovered, why was I always so famished? It could have been that the tumor had depleted my body's supply of carbohydrates, causing my blood sugar to fall. Why was I freezing cold at times, my entire body shivering? Yet, I didn't go to the doctor. I chalked up the weight gain, frequent sweating, and fatigue to menopause. I had no idea that they could be symptoms of other conditions.

After having surgery and undergoing radiation therapy, my previously good-tempered body refused to quiet down and return to its agreeable state. There was always a grumble here, a rumble there. While walking, sometimes my feet would grow weak and begin to ache, and after a mile I would be worn out. When I woke up in the morning, my back muscles felt leaden and lethargic. I was often out of breath and lightheaded. My body was talkative, but I couldn't decode its messages. Did I need to see a doctor? Just about every single day I developed symptoms worthy of medical attention, as my body voiced different complaints on a daily basis. I did go to the doctor several times. At one point, I had trouble walking, sitting was uncomfortable, and I couldn't bend over. The doctor said it was nothing serious—I'd be fine in a few days—and gave me some painkillers. I didn't want to take them and instead followed my mother's traditional remedy of using a pain relief patch for a day. Amazingly, this treatment actually worked.

My body began to speak more and more frequently, protesting a host of injustices, as though a revolution had begun inside me. Was it staging a strike? Requesting some time off? Fighting for special allowances? I had no clue what its demands were. Our past attempts at dialogue hadn't gone all that well, and now I could only be subjected to its lectures. Yet the problem remained: What exactly was it saying? Was my white blood cell count too low? Was I deficient in vitamins or minerals? Communication between people is difficult, but talking to the body is even more challenging. There are so many parts, each with its own grievances, the body's language split into distinct regional dialects. Bones speak the language of bones. Muscles speak the language of muscles. Nerves speak the language of nerves. Ever since humans built the Tower of Babel, we've barely been able to converse with one another anymore.

After my tumor, my body continued to signal SOS. Even my doctor didn't understand the message, and I had no idea how to decipher it. I was body illiterate. In school, we often study a foreign language so that we won't become monolingual illiterates. After leaving school, many of us continue to learn additional languages, for no other reason than a desire to communicate with the larger world and understand what other people mean. Understanding others also helps us to know ourselves. Yet except for doctors, who is fluent in the body's language? I'm an avid reader of fiction. I don't necessarily need to read English-language fiction in translation, but I have to rely on translations when reading fiction from Italy, Germany, and other countries. How much of the spirit of the original work can we glean from the translation? Can a translation properly convey the verb tense in Proust's *In Search of Lost Time*? Does the original Spanish text of Vargas Llosa's *Captain Pantoja and the Special Service* employ an elegant writing style or the spoken vernacular of the streets?

If you open the new Chinese translation of Thomas Mann's *The Magic Mountain*, you'll find the following commentary from the translator: "I have compared the English and Japanese translations of the book and discovered quite a few problems with the translations, especially the English version, where mistranslations and omissions are common." Indeed, in recent years, many people have pointed out that a number of translations are riddled with mistranslations, misinterpretations, omissions, and adaptations. There are unintentional misunderstandings, as well as deliberate simplifications that go so far as to rewrite the text. It seems that if we want to better understand the original work, we need to seek out multiple translations for comparison, or hope that someone else will retranslate the text, or simply learn more foreign languages.

But don't assume that I am searching for the ultimate, perfect translation. I am not. There's never a fixed and eternal "absolute spirit" in books. Translations are interpretations, and the same text holds the possibility of multiple interpretations. Each interpreter can thus proclaim "Madame Bovary is me," and no one will object that there are too many Madame Bovarys. When it comes to translators of the body's language, of course the experts are biologists and doctors, who might seem to be more scientific and objective. From the perspective of the development of humanity as a whole, however, due to disparate experiences, customs, and other factors, there are conflicting interpretations. We've benefited from misreadings and retranslations for a long time. Dare I say that it is impossible to have a single, absolute translation, whether now or in the future?

Besides, doctors these days run the gamut. Personal integrity and ethics vary from person to person—who knows how many mistranslations and adaptations there have been. It's not uncommon for one doctor to recommend surgery and another to say it's nothing at all. Why wouldn't people with ailing bodies find themselves sick with worry? Luckily, good doctors still account for the majority. Those who are eligible to practice must adhere to certain professional standards and continue to learn from direct experience.

The body can speak. Its language includes both sounds and images, and its written words are the signs our bodies reveal. We use EKGs, ultrasounds, and X-ray fluoroscopies to locate evidence of these signs. The body is remarkably adept at expressing itself. Thanks to this skill, people are able to live longer than ever before. Most twentieth-century thinkers have been captivated more by language than any other topic, and unlocking the mystery of language has become the key to turning philosophy into a science. We are born with one mouth and two ears. As we continue to explicate ourselves, we need to listen more attentively, so that our mouths don't become too overactive while our ears atrophy with each passing day. The Earth is an even larger body, and isn't it also giving off sign after sign? If we keep refusing to pay attention, sooner or later we'll lose this ultimate body that we call home.

FLIPPING THROUGH THE DICTIONARY

WHEN THE body loses its healthy state, it is called a malady.
To suffer from a malady means to be afflicted with some sort of mal.
Some maladies cause dermal itching.
Some maladies cause somal soreness.
Malnourishment is a malady of the malfed, also known as malnutrition.
A malady that lasts a long time is a chronic malfunction.
A malady that is severe is malicious.
Common somal soreness is known as normal aches and pains.
Agonizing somal soreness is known as abysmal torment.
The dissatisfaction of many people is called mass malcontent.

If you have a malady, you should treat the prodromal symptoms accordingly.*
A small abnormality is called an anomaly.
World malaise is called mal du siècle.
The softening of muscle tissue is called myomalacia.
One type of dermal lesion is a Malabar ulcer.
Other dermal maladies may include a malar rash, malar flush, Mallorca acne, Malassezia folliculitis, mal de Meleda, and mal morado.
Mistakenly saying an incorrect word or phrase in place of a similar-sounding one is called a malapropism.
A broken ankle is a malleolar fracture.
A dermal lesion on the head may leave a malformed scar.
A poisonous dermal lesion on the thigh may be maldeveloped.

A dermal lesion caused by exposure to the wintry cold is a brumal condition.

A poisonous dermal lesion may be mormal.

A malignant dermal lesion may be cataclysmal.

The amalgamation of multiple boils may be accompanied by an erythemal response.

A festering dermal lesion may be malodorous.

Being overworked is to be malrested.

Developing a workplace malady may be a result of malmanagement.

A malady caused by excessive work may be due to workplace malfeasance, also known as malconduct.

One should not allow oneself to be maltreated.

A basketball injury may result in mallet finger.

A broken bone that heals abnormally is a malunion fracture.

Stagnation of the blood is hemal stasis.

A misalignment of the teeth is malocclusion.

A spasmodic action of the hands is malleation.

Arthritis of the hip is malum coxae.

Cholera may lead to malabsorption and maldigestion.

Both cholera and malaria were once thought to be miasmal diseases.

Mental malaise is a characteristic of a maladjusted psyche.

Excessive indulgence is a maliferous infatuation.

A habit that cannot be cast off is a malevolent addiction.

A love that one cannot free oneself from is a maladaptive obsession.

An irrational fear of physical intimacy is malaxophobia.

In *The Dream of the Red Chamber*, Miaoyu, with her maladaptive obsession with cleanliness, and Daiyu, with her maliferous infatuation with flowers, both suffered from maladies.

A chronic, nonhealing ulcer that affects the weight-bearing areas of the foot and may trigger an inflammatory response is called a mal perforant.

A medical condition characterized by insufficient or abnormal blood

flow to an organ or tissue that may cause inflammation of the
heart, brain, liver, or kidneys is called malperfusion.

A rare inflammatory condition mainly affecting the urinary tract is
called malakoplakia.

A bacterial infection that may cause inflammation of the liver, spleen,
and lymph nodes is called Malta fever, also known as brucellosis.

A surgical incision of soft areas of the body, especially the abdominal
wall, is called a malacotomy.

An abnormal new growth in the body is neoplasmal.

A malignant neoplasmal growth may be a symptom of terminal
cancer.

Neoplasmal growths may feel like a malediction because they are the
most difficult tumors to treat.

A person suffering from a malady requires formal medical treatment
for optimal healing. The effectiveness of the formal medical treatment
depends on changes in the condition of the malady, which can be
divided roughly into four situations:

1. Maximal recovery
2. Improvement
3. No change
4. Deterioration

There is no such thing as maximal recovery, or a complete cure, for
cancer. After formal treatment, the gradual recovery of one's health
indicates an improvement. Maintaining a stable state in this way
should be considered the optimal "cure."

Treating a malady can also be divided into periods of therapeutic
effect according to time:

1. Immediate therapeutic effect: During the formal course of
treatment, the condition of the malady improves to the point
of disappearance.

2. Short-term therapeutic effect: Within weeks to months after
the formal course of treatment ends, the symptoms of the
malady improve or disappear.

3. Long-term therapeutic effect: More than a year after the formal course of treatment ends, the symptoms of the malady improve or disappear.

Cancer requires a much longer period of therapeutic effect than the above; it is a special, lifelong period of therapeutic effect. It can continue for ten or twenty years, because it is never known whether cancer cells have disappeared completely.

The normal stimulation intensity of human pain perception, called the pain threshold, is divided into two types:

1. Pain perception threshold: The sensation of pain felt by the body. When nerve endings in the skin are stimulated, they transmit messages to the brain, causing pain, starting with the minimum stimulation intensity.

2. Pain tolerance threshold: The maximum stimulation intensity of pain that a person can tolerate. Different parts of the human body have different perceptions of pain. The cerebral cortex can regulate pain perception, and when the stimulation reaches a certain intensity, facial muscle contractions, accelerated or paused breathing, sweating, and other reactions will occur. Some people believe that the pain experienced during childbirth is the most intense.

The pain experienced by patients in the terminal stages of cancer is also said to be among the most intense stimulation. However, most hospitals can administer painkillers to patients, reducing their suffering. The truth is, every cancer patient has experienced the maximum intensity of the pain tolerance threshold, which occurs when the doctor announces you have cancer. This pain is extremely intense, constantly gnawing at your mind, and there are no painkillers to alleviate it.

Dermal wounds heal by filling with granulation tissue, and the result is called a scar. Scars are composed of mature fibrous connective tissue, which is white in color. The older the scar, the firmer its texture.

This is because the collagen fibers in old scars undergo hyaline degeneration. Excessive scar hyperplasia can form solid elongated nodules that protrude from the skin's surface, becoming keloids. Thus, some people believe that after surgery, one should refrain from eating raw fish to avoid the excessive proliferation of scar granulation tissue.

A malamute is a large dog breed. It is not a malady that renders one unable to speak.

Malacostraca is a class of segmented crustaceans, which includes lobsters, crabs, crayfish, and shrimp. They are not crustaceans that need to see the doctor.

Malacology is a branch of zoology that studies mollusks, not maladies.

A malduck is a seabird, not a duck with a malady.

A malakatoone is a large peach.

A malanga is a root vegetable.

Malachite is a green mineral used for making ornamental objects.

The improvement of a malady is called normal convalescence.

The significant improvement of a malady is called optimal recuperation.

The complete improvement of a malady is called maximal recovery.

The word "recovery" is entirely unrelated to any malady.

LOOKING GOOD

A COUPLET from a Du Fu poem reads: "Is there no green essence food, to keep my complexion looking good?" Recently, whenever my friends see me, they all remark, Your complexion looks good. Of course, they're trying to comfort me. However, I myself know whether my complexion looks good or not, and likewise, I have the best understanding of my body's condition. Strangely, ever since the Lunar New Year, my health has been surprisingly good. In March and April, there was a severe type A flu outbreak. Many people fell ill, but I was completely unscathed, unexpectedly possessing a strong resistance to the virus. Thinking it over, maybe I've been using the most ancient methods to keep my complexion looking good: moderate exercise, adequate sleep, balanced nutrition, and a cheerful mind-set. A friend taught me meditation. On rainy days, I no longer need to go to the small park to practice tai chi. I can simply meditate at home, using diaphragmatic breathing, which is very easy. Meditating once or twice a day feels great. Because tai chi is an aerobic exercise, my instructor had only taught us the forms and not the breathing techniques, so perhaps I hadn't taken in much oxygen during my previous exercises. Balanced nutrition is beneficial indeed. Consuming more fruits and vegetables makes me feel refreshed, and I sleep soundly all night until dawn. Of course, maintaining a relaxed and cheerful state of mind is the most important thing. If you spend all day wondering whether you'll survive or how long you'll live, your complexion will only worsen. Who in the world can know for sure how long they'll live? What's there to worry about? It's better to cherish each day one is alive, and to live joyfully. Someone asked Saint Francis of Assisi, who was watering the flowers, If you were going to die tomorrow, what would you do? He replied, I'd continue watering the flowers.

On days when I'm in good spirits, I stroll down the streets with my camera in tow, taking pictures of interesting and simple things along the way. Today, I'll wander down Shanghai Street, a long and unpretentious street running parallel to Nathan Road, with more than seven hundred shops. I can take my time. The Gascoigne Road Flyover threads through a multistoried parking garage, extending out from the building. It's truly a bizarre sight. This small classical red-brick house. Is it a museum? No, it's a homeless shelter. It's a beautiful building, but the homeless people don't care for it, because a house isn't necessarily a home. That old bookshop has been around for decades. We often passed by it in our youth. The entire shop is filled with old books, heaped from the floor all the way up to the ceiling by the entrance; they look like they could topple over at the slightest touch. The owner spent many years standing and even sleeping outside the door, but now there's a half-lowered metal shutter, and a small book stall has been set up outside. *Click, click*, I snap a few photos. These are charcoal portrait drawings done in imitation of photographs. The displayed artworks include portraits of Sun Yat-sen, movie stars, and unidentified elderly people. Here's a small stall for mending clothes. A wooden box holds all the tools to make a living. Evidently, business isn't good, as the master mender sits on the small wooden box, smoking. This is a stall selling wood-shavings oil and bone brushes. Are there still women who use wood-shavings oil to comb their hair into long braids? *Click, click*, here's a tiny park. Homeless people sleep on folding canvas beds, and homeless dogs sleep on park benches.

As I reach Argyle Street, I'm already feeling a bit worn out. The name of this street evokes diamond-patterned socks which, according to *Esquire*, look best paired with casual shoes and corduroy pants. But there are no argyle socks on this street. A long-standing shop sells wooden clogs. In our younger days, we all used to clatter down the streets wearing wooden clogs—*click-clock-click*. The clog shop also has cutting boards and wooden pastry molds. In a few years, will the street be renamed? A couple of letters dropped, the name changed to "Age Street"? Growing into old age alongside a street.

I try venturing to farther-off places and staying out longer, to see if my physical strength can hold up. First, I go to Ocean Park to watch the dolphins perform, to see the sea lions and walruses swimming, and to look at penguins in an icy glass enclosure, standing on rocks and stretching their flippers, deep in thought. After four hours, I'm beat. While riding the escalator down the mountain, I have to sit on the steps. Of course, the person in charge notices and says over the loudspeaker, "You can't sit on the escalator steps." I ignore him. Fortunately, I soon reach the ground and sit down on a rock, resting for a long while. I also take a trip to Guangzhou, the farthest place I've been since my illness. The reason is the book fair. Ten of us go together—it's so lively. It's been a long time since we've traveled in a group. The book fair is packed to the brim, practically suffocating, but I still quickly make a round before heading back to the hotel to rest. My friends go again in the evening, and once more the following day, everyone buying some books; there aren't many good ones, but I'm happy. Later on, maybe I can travel to even farther-off places, such as Kyoto, India, Barcelona, or Bolivia. Life is worth celebrating; being alive means there are always possibilities left.

Breast cancer is an illness of the mammary glands. Only mammals have mammary glands, thus, breast cancer is an illness specific to mammals. The Earth has existed for 4.5 billion years, and mammals have been around for 180 million years, since the heyday of the dinosaurs, when giant reptiles ruled the Earth. Primitive mammals were probably lizard-like pelycosaurs—humans can really be called descendants of the dragon. The great era for mammals, however, was 70 million years ago; by that time, dinosaurs had already gone extinct. With changes in climate and shifts in geology, the Earth produced new habitats, and mammals that were able to adapt to these conditions rapidly proliferated.

Scholars who study the history of the Earth refer to the Age of

Mammals as the Cenozoic era, dividing it into seven epochs: Holo-cene, Pleistocene, Pliocene, Miocene, Oligocene, Eocene, and Paleo-cene. The Miocene was a golden age for mammals; between the Holocene and Pleistocene, beginning about two million years ago, there were four major ice ages, causing all life on Earth to freeze or starve to death multiple times. Strangely, many mammals survived the severe cold due to their thick coats and layers of body fat. The Ice Age led to the extinction of several animal species, including the early ancestors of mammals, such as the Aepycamelus, Ceratogaulus, Bal-uchitherium, and Syndyoceras, all of which have disappeared. This is the cruel reality of nature. However, the extinction of mammals such as the South African quagga and Steller's sea cow was not due to natural selection or disaster, but rather to death at the hands of fellow mammals: humans. As humans wiped out other animals, they also slaughtered each other, whether intentionally or unintentionally. Cancer is the loudest alarm bell of the twentieth century.

The English word "mammal" is derived from the Latin word for breast, which mammals use to feed their young. Most uniparous animals only have one pair of breasts. For multiparous animals, the number of breasts is proportionate to the number of offspring per pregnancy. Wolves have eight breasts, and the opossum, which is a marsupial, has thirteen. Many animals' breasts are just nipples that secrete milk, and one nipple can determine whether a new life will survive or perish. Take, for example, the opossum. Thirteen nipples can breastfeed thirteen joeys. If there are more than thirteen in a litter, the joeys who can't latch on to a nipple will starve to death. Newborn joeys are underdeveloped and must nurse in the mother's pouch. Female mammals have breasts and nipples, but the platypus lacks a similar milk-producing organ. Milk simply oozes out of pore-like holes in the abdomen. Having no nipples to suckle on, the young just lap up the milk with their tongues. The platypus is a strange mammal that both licks milk and is born from an egg. Australia's red kangaroo has two nipples, each of which secretes a different kind of milk. One nipple secretes milk to feed the joeys in the pouch; the other secretes milk containing one-third more protein and four times more fat to feed the joeys that have left the pouch. By extension, should humans feed babies high-protein powdered milk as well?

The whale also has no exposed breasts. Milk seeps out of small holes into the mouth of the baby whale, also known as a calf, which consumes the most breast milk of all animals, drinking 600 liters a day, of which 50 percent is fat, thus doubling in weight within a week. The cow milk that adult humans drink every day has a fat content of about 30 percent, or 250 milliliters per cup, while the fat content of skim milk is as low as 1 percent. Whales and dolphins are born tailfirst. Because they have no gills, they have to breathe air through their lungs. When a baby whale is born, the tail leaves the mother's body first to prevent it from drowning. After the head emerges, the mother whale lifts the calf above the surface of the water to take its first breath of air.

Breasts are the secondary sexual characteristics of mammals. In fact, among mammals, the majority of prominent secondary sexual characteristics are found in males, such as the manes of baboons and lions, the antlers of deer, the long noses of seals, the beards of human men, and the colorful faces of mandrills. Only human females have developed prominent secondary sexual characteristics: breasts, which have played various roles as times have changed.

Over many years, humanity has progressed rapidly from our establishment as a new species, far surpassing other animals on Earth. What will be the extent of our development? Perhaps the extinction of mammals won't be brought about by another great Ice Age but rather by humans themselves.

What do the pyramids of Giza in Egypt remind you of? I am reminded of Günter Grass's *The Flounder*, in which he imagines that Stone Age women had three breasts, a golden age for matriarchal society. Breasts are the source of life. Egyptians believed that a person's passing was not the end of existence but the beginning of a new life. These Egyptian houses of milk, of varying sizes, standing guard in the boundless

desert for a long time, are the most profound images of early human civilization. They are undoubtedly humanity's ode to motherhood.

India is a country that loves cows. One art historian's discussion of Indian art began with the following: On a map, India looks like a cow's udder hanging down into the Indian Ocean, the udder so fat, the inside seemingly swollen with endless milk; the teardrop-shaped Ceylon, at its southern tip, is just like a drop of cow milk. The Indus and Ganges rivers, like two mammary glands, flow through the great plains of India. Such fertile land birthed the splendid culture and art of ancient times... Indian Mother Goddess

statues are graceful and elegant, with ample breasts, representing Mother Earth, as well as humanity's pursuit of immortality.

In his epic poem *The Iliad*, Homer praises Artemis, the goddess of fertility. This is a statue of her. Count her breasts: She has more than twenty of them, symbolizing an abundance of milk and numerous offspring. She stretches her hands before her and appears to be concentrating solemnly, praying for the blessings of future descendants. During the 1980s, the Goddess Temple from the Neolithic Hongshan culture was excavated from the Niuheliang archaeological site in Liaoning, China. There were six nude female statues, in addition to the group of female statues unearthed earlier from the nearby site of

Dongshanzui. They are relics of a matriarchal society, dating back more than five thousand years. These statues all have ample buttocks and breasts, as though they are pregnant. Humans worshipped them, praying for fertility and bountiful harvests.

Rome wasn't built in a day. Yes, the mother of Rome was an eight-breasted wolf who nursed two abandoned babies, who grew up to

establish the Eternal City of Rome. This statue is a Roman memorial
for the she-wolf. Even a wild wolf would feel compassion at the sight
of these abandoned, hungry babies, and would give them her milk.
Breast milk can feed people and build nations.

Angels are genderless, and they aren't nude. They have their own
attractive features: strong, beautiful large wings. In this age, there
are also women who are smart and capable, neither humble nor

haughty, who are able to stand on their own feet; they are, in fact, also angels.

It is said that Jesus only suckled at Mary's right breast because the left breast is closer to the heart. While Jesus suckled milk, he listened attentively to his mother's rhythmic pulse of life.

Goddesses of the past were always naked, yet chaste. But why does this Iranian goddess need to cover her chest with her hands? Many women in Islamic countries have to wear headscarves and face veils, and even their deities appear in a half-concealed man-

ner. When did a woman's here and there, and this and that, become taboo? During the Middle Ages, the Crusaders spread the practice of covering women's heads from the East to the West. The Middle Ages was a time of many prohibitions.

From this sixteenth-century painting, it appears that upper-class women, shown bathing and dressing, transferred the responsibility of breast-feeding to their maidservants. As breasts became symbols of sex, their function of feeding babies gradually declined. In the nineteenth century,

the French painter Pierre-Auguste Renoir said, "If women in this world didn't have breasts and hips, perhaps I wouldn't paint anymore." Breasts have attracted all sorts of gazes—aesthetic appreciation, salaciousness, envy, jealousy—losing sight of one thing: breastfeeding.

Han Chinese people have long prided themselves on their proper attire and decorum, considering it the distinction between civilization and barbarism. Of course, sitting so prim and proper all the time, how could someone end up baring any skin? Under such repression, some peculiar books, bold in both text and images, became popular among the general population, but we won't go into that now. Published in 1617 during the Wanli reign of the Ming dynasty, Chen

Shigong's *Orthodox Manual of External Medicine* contains an illustration of a woman's diseased breast; its inclusion was permissible because the book was a medical text. This picture is probably the earliest depiction of breast cancer. Thus, during the Ming dynasty the disease entered the people's field of vision.

After the Industrial Revolution, twentieth-century women fled the domestic sphere in droves and went to work outside the home. Prioritizing their careers, they switched to feeding their babies cow milk. Add to that societal change the pressures of overpopulation, and it's no wonder that the women depicted in Fernand Léger's painting seem to have an elevated status, despite the fact that the central figure only has one breast. It's reminiscent of the Amazon women warriors in Greek mythology, who, for ease in battle—such as commandeering an army and shooting arrows—cut off their left breasts.

When a breast collapses into a hole, that's breast cancer. Henry Moore's prophecy: If all the women in the world were afflicted with breast cancer, would humanity become extinct? Would it then be the era of test-tube babies and cow milk?

An advertisement for remedying breast defects reads: BREAST CANCER IS MORE HEARTBREAKING THAN LOSING AN ARM. Do you think it means that losing an arm is only a personal misfortune, while breast cancer cuts off the continuation of life? No. It's actually promoting prosthetic breasts. When what is fake is considered a "pro," many women become emboldened to risk their lives in order to enhance their breasts, no longer satisfied with their natural form. Humans have long assumed they can subvert nature.

Women today hope their breasts look as good as the glass pyramid in front of the Louvre. Does the transition from the three great pyramids in the Giza Desert to the single pyramid in front of the French royal palace reflect the evolution of the human milk house? The former are sturdy and enclosed, in harmony with the natural environment, as vast and boundless as Heaven and Earth; the latter is light, transparent, open, and full of seductive allure, its interior space capable of bearing witness to the passage of time. O breasts, our source of life, I mourn your waning.

NOTES

1. The monetary amounts referenced throughout the book are given in Hong Kong dollars. When the book was originally written, the exchange rate would have been approximately 7.7 to 7.8 Hong Kong dollars to 1 US dollar.

2. *Strange Tales from the Liaozhai Studio* is a collection of classical Chinese short stories by Pu Songling (1640–1715). Written over a forty-year period from the late 1600s to the early 1700s, it includes nearly five hundred tales in sixteen volumes, typically involving ghosts, shape-shifters, demons, and other supernatural beings.

3. *The Legend of the Swordsmen of the Mountains of Shu*, written by Huanzhulouzhu (pen name of Li Shoumin, 1902–1961) and published in serialized form between 1932 and 1948, is considered one of the most influential martial arts novels and has been adapted into numerous films and television shows. Set in ancient China, the story revolves around the adventures of various swordsmen and swordswomen in the mythical Shu Mountains.

4. According to traditional Chinese medicine, a full-term pregnancy lasts for ten lunar months.

5. *The Dream of the Red Chamber*, also known as *The Story of the Stone*, is an eighteenth-century novel by Cao Xueqin (1710–1765). Considered one of the four great classic novels of China, it is renowned for its intricate depiction of the rise and fall of a noble family during the Qing dynasty and is celebrated for its detailed observations and exploration of daily life, social structures, fate, and spirituality.

6. *The Five Books of the Lives and Deeds of Gargantua and Pantagruel*, often shortened to *The Lives of Gargantua and Pantagruel*, or just *Gargantua and Pantagruel*, is a series of five novels written in French by François Rabelais (born c. 1494–1553) in the sixteenth century. The books follow the lives of two giants, Gargantua and his son Pantagruel, and are

known for their hilarious, satirical, and often bawdy tales, with a mix of adventure, comedy, and philosophical ideas.

7. *Children's Games* is a famous 1560 painting by Pieter Bruegel the Elder (born c. 1525–1569), one of the most important artists of Dutch and Flemish Renaissance painting. This oil-on-panel painting is renowned for its depiction of more than two hundred children engaged in roughly eighty different games and activities and serves as a visual encyclopedia of the games played by children in the sixteenth century.

8. *The Classic of Mountains and Seas* is an ancient Chinese text featuring imaginary creatures and plants alongside a few real ones. Sometimes described as a "Chinese bestiary," it also references medicinal remedies, folklore, mythological figures, and lands with strange inhabitants. The date of its compilation is uncertain, but it was assembled over several centuries, with most of its content likely finalized by the Han dynasty. *Investiture of the Gods* is a sixteenth-century Chinese novel that blends history, mythology, and fantasy, narrating the fall of the Shang dynasty and the rise of the Zhou dynasty. Attributed to Xu Zhonglin (1567–c. 1620), it interweaves real historical figures and events with deities, immortals, and demons. Published in the sixteenth century and attributed to Wu Cheng'en (c. 1500–c. 1582), *Journey to the West* is regarded as one of the four great classic novels of China, chronicling the adventures of the monk Xuanzang and his three supernatural disciples as they journey to India to obtain Buddhist scriptures.

9. The *Book of Songs*, also known as the *Book of Odes* or *Classic of Poetry*, is the earliest extant Chinese collection of poetry. It was compiled sometime in the first millennium before the common era, and the poems it contains are traditionally said to have been collected by none other than Confucius.

10. This passage is from a poem by the famed Tang dynasty poet Du Fu (712–770) called "On Seeing a Student of Lady Gongsun Dance the 'Sword Dance.'"

11. Wang Sishi (1566–1648) was an important late Ming and early Qing commentator of Du Fu's poetry. His annotated work *My Subjective Interpretation of Du Fu's Poetry* is considered the first independent analysis of Du Fu's poetics and was completed in 1645.

12. Zhang Liang (c. 251 BCE–189 BCE) was a prominent political strategist and statesman revered as one of the "three heroes of the early Han dynasty" for his pivotal role in helping to overthrow the Qin dynasty and establish the Han.

13. The eponymous *Zhuangzi* is an ancient text containing stories and philosophical ideas attributed to Zhuang Zhou, also known as Zhuangzi (fl. fourth century BCE). Its core is ascribed to Zhuangzi and was written during the Warring States period, with subsequent portions added later. While very little is known about his actual life, Zhuangzi came to be a pivotal figure in Daoist thought, and the *Zhuangzi* is a foundational Daoist text. Zhuangzi's "Essentials of Nourishing Life" tells the story of Butcher Ding (or Cook Ding), who uses his deep understanding of Daoist principles to carve oxen with effortless precision.

14. This saying is based on the belief that female crabs taste best in the ninth lunar month, while male crabs taste best in the tenth lunar month.

15. Until the mid-1990s, Sha Tin Public Hospital, also known as Prince of Wales Hospital, provided medical services for the nearly 25,000 Vietnamese refugees held at a neighboring detention center. The influx of Vietnamese refugees into Hong Kong peaked in 1989.

16. Daoji (c. 1130–1209), more commonly known as Ji Gong or Mad Monk Ji Gong, was a Zen Buddhist monk from the Southern Song dynasty. Transformed into a popular figure in Chinese folklore and Buddhist culture, he is revered for his eccentric behavior, disregard for monastic rules, and supernatural powers, which he used to help the poor and weak.

17. "Wandering Free and Far" in *Zhuangzi* uses allegorical tales and paradoxical anecdotes to expound on the Daoist ideal of achieving a state of mental freedom and spiritual wandering by transcending human-made constraints.

18. Tsang Tsou-choi (1921–2007), also known as the King of Kowloon, was a Hong Kong artist famous for his distinctive calligraphy, which he painted on public walls and pillars throughout the city, claiming the area of Kowloon as his family's ancestral land. Initially viewed as graffiti, his work eventually gained recognition as an important part of Hong Kong's cultural heritage.

19. The *Zuo Tradition* is an ancient Chinese narrative history that covers the period from 722 to 468 BCE and serves as a commentary on the *Spring and Autumn Annals*, an annals text associated with the ancient Chinese state of Lu.

20. Sha Tin Public Hospital is also known as Prince of Wales Hospital. See also note 15.

21. The title of this chapter is an idiom that literally means "the liver and gallbladder reflect each other." As the liver and gallbladder are closely

connected organs, this expression is used to describe relationships in which there is an exceptional level of mutual understanding and support. In order to re-create Xi Xi's pun on "gallbladder" and "liver" while also conveying the meaning of this idiom, I have translated it as "gallantly delivering through thick and thin."

22. These lyrics by Wei Hanzhang (1906–1993) are from the art song "The Ballad of Picking Lotus Flowers."

23. The Old Man Under the Moon is a mythological figure in Chinese folklore, often depicted as the god of marriage and love. He is traditionally believed to tie an invisible red thread between those who are destined to meet and marry, symbolizing a predestined and unbreakable bond.

24. This is a reference to the famous essay "Retreating Figure" by the prominent modern Chinese author Zhu Ziqing (1898–1948), published in 1925. In the essay, Zhu vividly describes his memory of his father's receding figure.

25. The banner system was a military and administrative structure established by the Manchu leader Nurhaci, the founding emperor of the Qing dynasty. Initially exclusive to Manchu households, as the Qing extended its rule, it later expanded to include Mongols and other ethnic groups, creating separate banners to incorporate these diverse populations. The Qing dynasty ruled over Mongolia through a combination of direct administration and indirect control via the banners, which were granted a degree of autonomy in internal affairs but were required to follow the directives of the Qing government.

26. This chapter alludes to a famous tale from the novel *Journey to the West* in which the Monkey King thrice battles the White Bone Demon, a shape-shifting malevolent spirit who transforms into various innocent forms. It also mentions other characters from the novel, including one of the monk's disciples, Pigsy, whose name literally means Pig of Eight Prohibitions; the Bull Demon King, a powerful, shape-shifting demon; and the Bull Demon King's wife, Princess Iron Fan, who wields a fan made of banana leaves that possesses magical properties, such as the ability to create powerful gusts of wind and extinguish fires.

AFTERWORD

XI XI (西西, also known as Sai Sai) was one of the most beloved and celebrated authors in the Sinosphere. Though she published nearly forty books in her lifetime, spanning a wide range of genres, until recently she has been largely underserved in translation. Officially named Cheung Yin, she began publishing under the pen name Xi Xi in 1960, inspired not by the name's sound or meaning but by the visual appearance of the Chinese characters: The character 西 evokes the image of a girl in a skirt with her legs akimbo in a hopscotch square, and the character's doubling suggests the movement of skipping from one square to another, just as frames in a film create an illusion of motion. This rationale for Xi Xi's pen name is characteristic of the joy and whimsy that her writing exudes.

Born in Shanghai in 1937 to parents of Cantonese ancestry, Xi Xi was the second oldest of five children. She grew up in a close-knit community in Shanghai, where her schoolmates nicknamed her "Wonton Noodles," a Cantonese specialty. In 1941, after Japanese troops entered and occupied Shanghai, Xi Xi's family fled to her aunt's village in Zhejiang Province (an experience she relates in the chapter "Daifu Di"). When the war ended, Xi Xi's family returned to Shanghai, where her father worked as a clerk at a British shipping company, Butterfield & Swire. She lived with her extended family in a single-story home, one which notably had rare modern conveniences like a showerhead and a flushing toilet. The Communist victory in China in 1949 shuttered the shipping company, and Xi Xi's father, unable to find work, left for the British Crown Colony of Hong Kong, eventually landing a job there as a ticket inspector for the Kowloon

Motor Bus Company. In the fall of 1950, twelve-year-old Xi Xi, accompanied by her mother, older brother, two younger sisters, and maternal grandparents, traveled by train to Hong Kong, where they reunited with her father. Her youngest brother was born shortly thereafter.

In Hong Kong, Xi Xi attended the Heep Yunn School, a prestigious Anglican girls' secondary school, where she was educated in both Chinese (Cantonese) and English. Though her family had lived comfortably in the mainland, in Hong Kong they struggled financially. Xi Xi's tuition fees were often late, and she lacked adequately warm clothing in the winter. In spite of these challenges, she thrived as a student, particularly excelling in writing and publishing her poems and essays in the school magazine. She attended the Grantham College of Education (now the Education University of Hong Kong), and went on to teach Chinese, English, and math at a government primary school for twenty years. Given the surplus of teachers in Hong Kong, she took an early retirement in 1978 in order to focus on her writing, and she supplemented her income by writing newspaper columns and occasionally filling in as a substitute teacher.

Xi Xi began her literary career as a poet, publishing her first poem when she was fifteen. After writing mostly poetry and essays throughout her teenage years, one of her earliest short stories, "Singing With Children," inspired by teaching students from impoverished backgrounds, won first place in a literary competition in 1958. She continued to gain attention as a fiction writer, publishing the critically acclaimed story "Maria" in 1965, and a novella *East Side Story* (adapted from *West Side Story*) in 1966, using the cinematic technique of montage to tell the story from multiple perspectives. The 1960s was Xi Xi's cinematic decade (as she recalls in the chapter "The Bathroom"). She participated in the film club Studio One, directed the experimental film *Milky Way Galaxy*, and wrote scripts for the Shaw Brothers Studio, and movie reviews. The work for which she is perhaps best known, the novel *My City*, was first serialized in 1975, and published in book form in 1979, breaking new ground as one of the first literary works to depict Hong Kong through the eyes of its everyday young people. During this time Xi Xi also cofounded two important periodicals, *Thumb Weekly* and *Su Yeh Literature*, the latter of which evolved to include the nonprofit publishing house Su Yeh Press.

By the 1980s, Xi Xi had become a renowned literary figure in Hong Kong. In 1983, her literary fame soared beyond the colony when her short story "A Woman Like Me" won the esteemed *United Daily* fiction prize in Taiwan, an accolade that earned her an avid readership in Taiwan, where she became so popular that she was sometimes mistaken for a Taiwanese writer. Her longtime publisher was the Taipei-based Hung-Fan Bookstore, and she introduced the work of several important mainland authors, including Mo Yan, Yu Hua, and Wang Anyi, to readers in Taiwan as part of a series for Hung-Fan.

In 1989, Xi Xi was diagnosed with breast cancer, and she began to write *Mourning a Breast* intermittently during her treatment and recovery. Published in 1992 in Taiwan, the book was received as the first literary work to chronicle a Sinophone woman writer's journey with breast cancer. It was a success with both critics and readers: The *China Times* in Taiwan named it one of the best ten books of 1992, and it won *United Daily*'s Readers Best Book of the Year Award. It was loosely adapted as a film in 2006 (*2 Become 1*, directed by Law Wing Cheong), and a simplified Chinese edition was published in mainland China in 2010 by Guangxi Normal University Press.

Although Xi Xi's cancer never returned, the damage she had sustained in her right hand from one of the treatment procedures led to a gradual loss of mobility; by 2000, her right hand was fully nonfunctional, and she trained herself to write and work with her left hand. As a form of physical therapy, Xi Xi began to sew and soon developed an interest in handicrafts, building dollhouses and making cloth dolls and stuffed animals. She exhibited many of these works publicly, and under the name of Ellen Cheung she was named the Designer's Collection Champion at the second Hong Kong Teddy Bear Awards. She also transformed these hobbies into books, such as *The Teddy Bear Chronicles*, a playful photographic showcase of handmade teddy bears modeled after figures from Chinese history and Western culture, and *The Monkey Chronicles*, a unique cultural history of monkeys, featuring photos of hand-sewn puppets with accompanying text, designed to heighten public awareness about conservation.

Xi Xi earned numerous accolades from around the world, including the 2019 Newman Prize for Chinese Literature (Poetry) and the 2019 Swedish Cikada Prize for East Asian Poetry. In 2022, the Hong Kong Arts Development Council presented her with a Lifetime Achievement Award. Despite a physical decline in her health in the last years of her life, she remained active as a writer, publishing, among more works of fiction, her third volume of poetry, *Carnival of Animals*, which was presented in bilingual format with my accompanying English translations and illustrations by twenty-seven Hong Kong artists. Her last literary work was a poem, "Weary," which she wrote in November 2020 and which concluded with these lines:

> I'll miss my friends
> The places we've lived together
> Our days of youth and health

On December 15, 2022, Xi Xi was admitted to the hospital and diagnosed with heart failure. She passed away peacefully three days later on the morning of December 18 at the age of eighty-five, surrounded by family and close friends.

Like Xi Xi herself, *Mourning a Breast* is nonconventional and inventive. It defies categorization, blending multiple genres, including fiction, nonfiction, and poetry, but also conversations, dictionary entries, lists, calculations, and images. Xi Xi's original publisher classified it as a novel, but as Xi Xi herself notes in the preface, some readers may prefer to regard it as a collection of essays. While the narrator shares many commonalities with Xi Xi, numerous fictions are woven into *Mourning a Breast*, including several invented characters. In this regard, the book is similar to her semi-autobiographical novels *Birds of Passage* (1991) and *Weaving Nests* (2018), which intertwine reality and fiction to record her experiences as a child of migration.

One of the first Chinese-language works about breast cancer, *Mourning a Breast* was considered groundbreaking for its time, delving into both the physical and psychological responses to the disease, exposing common myths about breast cancer and confronting the shame often associated with it. Likewise, Xi Xi's exploration of the gendered aspects of the disease, especially what it means to lose a part of the body so traditionally tied to one's gender and sexual identity, could also be viewed as radical. And yet, certain elements of the book may seem dated to the contemporary reader. In this regard, it is important to view the text as a cultural product of the early 1990s, specifically pre-handover, colonial Hong Kong, acknowledging that there have been huge advances in medicine and science and changing understandings of sex and gender. Though one of Xi Xi's aims in writing this book was to encourage people to look after their health, one should not turn to this book for specific medical advice. Still, more than three decades after its initial publication, *Mourning a Breast* continues to be a source of encouragement and companionship to readers, with insights about illness and body literacy that remain not only relevant but profound.

I first encountered Xi Xi's writing in graduate school when I read *My City* and "A Woman Like Me." A decade later, I began translating her poetry, followed by several of her short stories, and I was soon drawn to *Mourning a Breast* for its innovative form and important subject matter. Moreover, it is arguably one of Xi Xi's most significant and personal works, and yet, it had not been translated in full into any language. Translating *Mourning a Breast* poses many of the same challenges and delights I found in translating other works by Xi Xi, namely, her fondness for wordplay. In her prose as well as her poetry, Xi Xi gleefully pushes the boundaries of language and demands of her translator an inventiveness equal to her own. For example, in the chapter "Flipping Through the Dictionary," she presents a list of dictionary entries, each one of which is derived from the graphical component for illness, including unexpected words that seemingly have nothing to do with illness, but describe a kind of vegetable or insect. How could such a text that so firmly hinges on the graphic qualities of written Chinese be rendered in English in a way that captures both meaning and playfulness? After weeks of flipping through several dictionaries of my own, studying the most common prefixes and suffixes for medical terms, and a lot of trial and error, I came up with the root "mal" and compiled a list of illness-related words containing some variation of "mal," along with other terms and phrases unrelated to illness, discovering delightful new words such as malakatoone (a large peach), tatterdemalion (a ragamuffin), and skinny-malinky (an extremely thin person); the latter two sadly did not make the final cut. Of course, in this process, attempts at semantic equivalents gave way to near approximations at best, and at times, even words with completely different meanings, but in this case, playing Xi Xi's language game was necessary to bring the pulse of the chapter into English, and there was also the occasional seren-dipitous gem of a near-perfect match. This was by far the most dif-ficult and time-consuming chapter to translate, but also the most satisfying and enjoyable.

While other chapters do not take wordplay to this extreme, the title of the chapter I have translated as "Gallantly Delivering Through Thick and Thin" presented a formidable challenge, as it is a pun on an idiom that literally means "the liver and gallbladder reflect each other" and is used to metaphorically illustrate an intimate and neces-sary relationship. Then there are instances where Xi Xi combines her love of language play with her predilection for intertextuality, as in "The Dream Factory," where the narrator ponders a passage in the *Zhuangzi* in a way that riffs on its title, prompting me to render it "Wandering Free and Far," instead of following one of the more common translations, in order to convey her reading of the passage. This brings me to another characteristic of her work that can be dif-ficult to translate: Xi Xi's breadth of knowledge, especially as exem-plified in *Mourning a Breast*, which is replete with allusions. There are no formal citations in the Chinese text, which at times has entailed embarking on scavenger hunts of varying levels of complexity, leading me to scrutinize the typeface and punctuation of certain sections of *Madame Bovary* in the original French, or to study the same scene from Kurosawa's *Ikiru* over and over, or to comb through Xenophon's writings in search of Socrates's advice to his disciples. Ultimately, I decided to use my own English translations for the texts Xi Xi quotes so I could render them according to how she understands them in the book. Meanwhile, informed by the narrator's strong feelings about how to denote dialogue in translations of *Madame Bovary*, my translation follows Xi Xi's own method for marking dialogue in the book, which is to say, it's largely unmarked, other than a few conversations indicated by em dashes.

Finally, I have taken a mixed approach to transliterating names and terms. For proper names and terms associated with Hong Kong and/or Cantonese culture, I have used a form of Cantonese romanization. For proper names and terms from imperial China or related to the mainland, including terms from traditional Chinese medicine, I have used pinyin romanization, which is based on Mandarin. Of course, many of these choices are intuitive and not clear-cut. I wrestled with how to transliterate the name of the official residence described in "Daifu Di" (and at one point, even considered trying to translate it into English); my initial impulse was to render it based on Cantonese, but since this particular residence is located in Zhejiang Province, following the Mandarin pronunciation felt more appropriate. Similarly, I transliterate the words for *doctor* in this chapter according to Mandarin pinyin. In "Counterattack," when the narrator discusses how one of the Chinese words for *hormone* is based on sound, instead of choosing between Mandarin and Cantonese, I opted to use both transliterations. As Xi Xi herself spoke three Chinese languages—Cantonese, Mandarin, and Shanghainese—and Hong Kong is a multilingual city, such a mix feels appropriate.

In many ways, bringing *Mourning a Breast* into English has been a collaborative endeavor, one punctuated by the humility, grace, humor, and friendship that permeate the text itself. Without the support of the National Endowment for the Arts, I am uncertain whether I would have embarked on this project in the first place. Without the tireless advocacy of Li Kangqin and her colleagues at New River Literary, I am unsure whether this book would have ever found a home. I am grateful to Susan Barba and the editorial team at NYRB for providing *Mourning a Breast* with a supportive home where it can thrive, and for meticulously reading multiple drafts of my translation and offering perceptive feedback that has strengthened the book. Ho Fuk-yan has selflessly shared his expertise on all things Xi Xi with me, tracking down invaluable resources, answering my never-ending questions, and keeping my Xi Xi collection stocked with books, journals, and other Xi Xi–related materials—even when I am halfway around the world, Mr. Ho ensures I stay connected to my extended Xi Xi family. Eva Wong Yi has enthusiastically joined me on count-less treasure hunts, helping me to decode Xi Xi's clues and solve many of the book's puzzles; additionally, her master's thesis on breast can-cer autopathographies and poems, which includes an analysis of *Mourning a Breast*, inspired me to think about the text in new ways. Wei Yang Menkus continues to be one of my biggest cheerleaders in translating Xi Xi, encouraging me and aiding me in deciphering particularly tricky passages. Fellow Xi Xi aficionado Dorothy Tse has championed this project from its inception. Newell Ann Van Auken generously shared her expertise on early Chinese literature and culture, especially regarding monsters and other strange creatures. Qiaomei Tang and He Bian offered in-depth replies to my queries on Qing medical history. Members of the Translation Across the Humanities group and the Chinese Humanities and Arts Workshop at the Ober-mann Center for Advanced Studies at the University of Iowa read and provided feedback on a draft of "The Doctor Says." My translation has been enriched from reading writings on *Mourning a Breast* by Howard Y. F. Choi, Ho Fuk-yan, Esther M. K. Cheung, and Jessica Tsui-yan Li, and from excerpts of the novel previously translated into English by Caroline Mason, Esther M. K. Cheung, and Michelle L. Y. Kwok; I am particularly appreciative of the pioneering and impassioned efforts of Dr. Cheung, who passed away in 2015, far too soon.

Of course, the guiding light behind my translation has been Xi Xi herself. I had very much hoped that she would have seen this book come to fruition with her own eyes. I am honored that she trusted me with her words, allowing me to transport her extremely personal story into English. Even more than that, however, I cherish her friendship, and I am heartened that her gentleness and warmth live on through her writing. Xi Xi was unfailingly compassionate, generous, observant, unassuming, and funny, and her love for her city, especially its young people, never wavered. When I returned to Hong Kong in July 2023 for the first time since the Covid-19 pandemic, I visited Xi Xi's final resting place at the Diamond Hill Garden of Remembrance, joined by friends and writers Ho Fuk-yan, Stuart Lau, Louise Law Lok-Man, Lawrence Pun, and Eva Wong Yi. As we paid our respects to the modest memorial plaque displaying her legal name and black-and-white photo, we agreed that she needed some miniature toys to accompany her. Afterward, we ate lunch at a dim sum restaurant overlooking Victoria Harbour in the Cultural Centre that *Mourning a Breast* describes as resembling a bathroom.

As Xi Xi contemplates in the preface, "The term 'mourning' actually suggests that while we can't undo the past, we can focus on the future and hope for rebirth." This book is not only about mourning a breast, but also mourning an ever-changing Hong Kong.

—JENNIFER FEELEY

OTHER NEW YORK REVIEW CLASSICS

For a complete list of titles, visit www.nyrb.com.